For Felix, Olivia and Sidney with love

before
we
say
goodbye

Madeleine
Reiss

ZAFFRE

First published in Great Britain in 2018 by
ZAFFRE PUBLISHING
80-81 Wimpole St, London W1G 9RE
www.zaffrebooks.co.uk

A CIP catalogue record for this book is
available from the British Library.

ISBN: 978-1-78576-419-6

also available as an ebook

1 3 5 7 9 10 8 6 4 2

Typeset by IDSUK (Data Connection) Ltd
Printed and bound by Clays Ltd, St Ives Plc

MIX
Paper from
responsible sources
FSC® C018072

Zaffre Publishing is an imprint of Bonnier Zaffre,
a Bonnier Publishing company
www.bonnierzaffre.co.uk
www.bonnierpublishing.co.uk

Part One
Winter

Chapter 1

SCOTT OPENED HIS BEDROOM DOOR AND A BLUE FOAM BULLET hit him between the eyes.

'Yesss! Bang on target!'

Danny's delighted face gleamed at him in the dim hallway and, despite being barely awake, Scott couldn't help smiling back. Even this early in the morning, his housemate's glee was hard to resist.

'Don't you ever sleep?' Scott asked, edging round him and going into the kitchen. He hoped there would be enough milk to at least soften his cereal but he wasn't optimistic. Three months of living in a dank student house in King's Cross with one of the least-domesticated individuals on earth had made Scott realise just what stamina was required to keep it stocked up with even the most basic necessities of life.

'I've a theory that we all sleep too much,' Danny said, pulling out the stool from under what the estate agent details had fondly described as a breakfast bar but which was, in fact, a length of chipboard propped up on a couple of spindly legs. 'Don't you want to know how I did it?' Danny asked, and then, without waiting for an answer, he plunged into his explanation.

'I set up a program on my laptop. The webcam detected movement and prompted the mechanism I made with part of an old food mixer and a battery pack to release the trigger. The challenging bit was finding the exact right spot to place the gun. I had to factor in your height and the speed at which you were likely to open the door,' Danny said and Scott shook his head in what he hoped was an appropriately awestruck fashion. Like any creative person, Danny relied heavily on an appreciative audience.

'One day you'll rule the world,' Scott said, pouring a meagre trickle of milk onto his cornflakes. Danny smiled so widely that his small grey eyes disappeared completely into a series of complicated folds. He seemed to possess more skin than other people. Danny's speciality, other than setting up elaborate surprises, was to pull the loose flesh on either side of his face and stretch it out a good two inches from his jaw line, giving him the look of a collared reptile.

'There's another of those gross slugs,' said Danny with a shudder, pointing to the giant black beast lying draped, like a desiccated tongue, over a dish on the draining board. 'I don't even know where they come from.' He looked around him fearfully as if he was expecting an army of the creatures to rise up from the floorboards and devour him. 'I think we should sprinkle it with salt. In fact, we should put salt all over the floor and they'll fizzle to death in the night.'

'I'll get rid of it,' Scott said and he scooped the creature up in a piece of kitchen paper and escorted it out of the back door, taking care to place it somewhere where it would be safe. The scrubby garden was in the grip of a frost and the lawn and pathway had a hard lustre. The sycamore tree by the fence stretched its slender arms into the white sky. Scott liked winter for the way it seemed to freeze time – the days merging more easily into the nights so that they were harder to count.

'Are you going to the SU tonight?' Danny asked when Scott came back in. 'It's two pounds fifty a pint between half five and half seven and a silent disco. It's a cheap night out and I could do with one of those.'

'I'll be there, although I don't really get dancing on your own,' said Scott. It seemed to him that the whole point of music was that it should blast out and fill the room all the way to the roof and everyone should be able to share it.

'I think MAR-SI-A might be going,' Danny said, giving Scott a side-eye look.

'Is she?' Scott said, trying what he thought might pass for an off-hand tone of voice, but Danny's knowing, origami-like expression revealed that he wasn't in the slightest bit deceived.

'She made a particular point of saying she was going to be there. Almost as if she thought I would pass the information on to someone who might just, possibly, be interested.'

Marsia (spelled with an 's', not a 'c', as she had made clear the first time Scott had met her, as if demonstrating just how unique she was) was studying English Literature. She wore almost transparent blouses and touched her hair frequently as if she needed to check its – admittedly – lustrous fall. He had noticed her from day one when she had been leaning against a wall outside the lecture theatre, her arms crossed, looking as if she would prefer to be elsewhere. He had been intrigued by the contrast between her disdainful face and her softly curved body, although he felt just a little ashamed of himself for noticing the latter. He didn't want to be one of those men who talked to women's breasts or who dismissed people just because of the way they looked and he worried that he was shallower than he wanted to be. When he had been about seven and briefly left to his own devices with some magazines and a pair of plastic scissors he had cut out the pictures that he had found particularly appealing. His mother had walked into his room to the sight of thirty or forty chests, Blu-Tacked to his walls.

'Oh God,' she had said. 'They are all someone's mother or sister or daughter. Women are not just made up of separate bits.'

In the end she had allowed him to keep the two images of his choice and he had settled for Marilyn Monroe and Miss Piggy, both ladies who seemed to him to embody the feminine charms he admired and which he sensed his mother would find acceptable in the way the models in balcony bras were not. Now, at the age of nineteen, he thought his attraction to women with confidence (and ample cleavages) was born of his lack of experience. He liked women who seemed to know their own value because they would allow him a more comfortable reticence.

'Are you not going in this morning?' Scott asked Danny who was dressed in a Snoopy T-shirt and some alarmingly droopy boxers.

'Got an essay to write. I'll go in later,' Danny replied.

Scott knew his housemate was already struggling with his uni work. He had met Danny's father when he had first moved in and seen the way Danny's body had sagged slightly under the weight of his father's arm across his shoulders.

'He's going to be a lawyer,' his father had said in a voice that hovered somewhere between pride and command. Scott was studying Biological Sciences, which was so absolutely what he wanted to do that he felt sorry for Danny's predicament. He had never known his own father and his mother was not the sort of person to impose her unsatisfied ambitions on him. Her hopes for him were not about academic excellence or career success, but they brought with them a burden of a different kind. Despite his mother's watchfulness, which had always made him feel like he was her only real aspiration, he had been free to make his own choices. He couldn't remember a time when he hadn't cared passionately about the environment in general and the sea in particular. This impulse seemed to him as innate as his inability to lie successfully, his tendency to heat rash and the way his hair stuck up in a weird fashion, whatever he did with it.

'Don't worry,' he said to Danny. 'You know you can always decide to do something else if this doesn't work out. There are a million things you're good at. You don't have to be good at this.'

Danny smiled wearily. 'Try telling that to my dad,' he said and he sloped off to his room.

Scott had been lucky to secure a flat so close to the university. Plenty of his peers had much further to travel. When his mother had dropped him off at the beginning of term she had been dubious about the tidemarks that rose up the outside walls and the smell of rotting vegetables that clung to the place, but he had loved it instantly. His bedroom was sparsely furnished with a desk and a bed that sagged in the middle but it had a window that looked out onto the garden and a fireplace with a massive marble surround and floorboards that one of his predecessors had painted in black and white squares like a giant chessboard.

After a hasty shower – the spored cubicle was not a place you wanted to linger in – Scott decided to walk to college. By the time he had got himself on the Tube or waited for the bus it was almost quicker to go on foot, and, in any case, London was still new enough to be a novelty. Scott loved the way the city caught him up in it and carried him along heedlessly, as if he was a bottle floating along the Thames. Sometime during his first week in London he had gone to Waterloo Bridge and looked down into the grimy, sheeny mass of water and had felt overwhelmed by the sense that he had a part share in it. The river and the city along its banks seemed to be waiting for him to discover it. He had spent his childhood in a small town and although he felt disloyal, now that he had left, he realised how much he had longed to get away. He relished the fact that he could walk down the intricate, still unfathomable streets and nobody would know him. Back at home, if he picked his nose in a public place someone would make a note of it.

After his lecture Scott spotted Marsia in the canteen. He debated whether to go and join her, wondering if perhaps she had chosen to sit alone for a reason. He didn't want to force his company on her. While he hovered with his tray she looked up and caught his eye and waved at him, so he took a deep breath and weaved between the tables and chairs towards her, hoping that he wouldn't trip. Now would not be the moment, he thought, to spill tomato soup and coffee all over the place. He suspected that Marsia, with her green eyes and sulky mouth, had a low tolerance for fools.

'Is it OK to join you?' Scott said and then immediately cursed himself for asking the question. He probably sounded apologetic, unsure. Women like Marsia – although he knew she was his age, she seemed so much older – surely liked men who were assertive. What would Hugh Jackman do? He often resorted to thinking of how the actor might behave in any given situation. It seemed to him that Hugh Jackman, with his sure jaw and wide chest, would never feel a moment's doubt. He would probably act as if it was Marsia's lucky day that he happened to be there when she was all on her own, with no one to talk to.

'Have you just had a lecture?' she asked. Her hair was pulled back from her face and her fingers on the table were tipped with a strident pink. She seemed so dauntingly formed that it made him feel fuzzy around the edges as if, by comparison, he hadn't yet quite come into focus.

'Yes,' he said sitting down opposite her. 'It was about the reason why there are two sexes,' he added and then felt himself flush. Out loud, his words sounded like a chat-up line. He hadn't needed to sit through Professor Langley's informative but over-long lecture on the evolution of sexual reproduction to see nature's startling efficiency in his own reactions to Marsia.

'And what *is* the reason?' she asked, resting her chin on her hand and looking at him. She was poised. That was the exact word for her. When animals were poised, he thought, it was generally because they were about to launch themselves for the kill. 'Surely we'd survive much better as a species if we had more choice about who we were able to reproduce with.'

She was poised *and* clever. He didn't have a hope.

'Well, it's still open for debate. There are lots of theories but it seems to boil down to the fact that if we reproduced like fungi, who apparently have about thirty-six thousand mating types, then mutations would occur very rapidly. A mushroom doesn't have to go far to create another mushroom. It's harder for humans because they have less choice but it's a better way of ensuring the strength of the species.'

He thought briefly about making a joke about how he was a fun guy, but thought better of it.

'I see,' Marsia said. 'I thought the reason there are two sexes was something to do with how genetically superior eggs are to sperm. If men were able to reproduce without any help, the human race would probably be very feeble.' She had a way of half closing her eyes when she smiled and this gave her a slightly condescending look that Scott found inexplicably attractive. *I should find her annoying,* he thought, *and yet all I want is for her to smile at me again.*

'Well, yes. There's that,' Scott said, and he took a scalding gulp of his soup.

'Are you going to the party tonight?' she asked.

'I thought I would,' he said, trying to make it sound as if he had a hundred other places he could be.

'I'll see you there, then.' She got up and hitched her bag onto her shoulder. He watched the easy way she walked through the tables and chairs that he had found such obstacles and then returned to his soup, now made tasteless by his burnt mouth.

In the SU where, despite the cheapness of the beer, he stuck, as was his ingrained custom, to a single pint, Marsia danced – all swaying hips and expressive arms – to her own private tune. She offered him her other headphone so that he could share Calvin Harris and 'How Deep is Your Love?' He wasn't sure about love, but he thought he was feeling some version of it.

They sat at a table by the wall and he kissed her. Her mouth was cool, then warm. They went outside and kissed some more. He thought she would be more restrained but she seemed urgent. Her tongue pushed into his mouth. He touched her breasts through her shirt and felt her hand go between his legs. He thought perhaps that they were moving too fast, then not fast enough. He thought of her long, pink-tipped fingers and the way she had of standing with her hands at her waist as if she was showing herself off and he felt dizzy.

Sometime later they went back inside, holding hands. He wondered if they would go home together and whether suggesting it was too pushy, too eager. He thought she was probably the sort of girl who lived in a room with cushions and a vase of peacock feathers and a family watercolour propped up against the wall. He pictured his shower facilities ripe with reproducing mushrooms and his clothes spread out in an insalubrious mass on the floor and had just decided he would suggest going back to her place when Danny, who had unhappily made the most of the two happy hours and was profoundly and mournfully drunk, dragged him away.

'I need to shhpeak to you,' his housemate said. 'I can't cope anymore with being here.'

By the time Scott had talked Danny out of his idea to run away to Cuba and suggested that his housemate sat down and had an honest talk with his father, the party was over. He looked around for Marsia and saw her walking towards the exit and rushed to get his coat. In the cloakroom a girl was on her hands and knees on the floor.

'I've lost an earring,' she said, looking up at him. 'I dropped it somewhere here.'

She had dark hair, cut close like a cap, and pale skin.

'My mother gave them to me,' she said desperately and although the thought of Marsia waiting outside tugged at him, Scott got down on the floor and started searching. The girl really seemed upset and the sooner he found the dratted earring, the quicker he would be able to get away.

'It's a gold hoop,' she said, running her hands across the floor and then reaching beneath the cupboard that ran the length of the wall.

'You take this section. I'll do the bit between the coats,' Scott said, thinking that a methodical approach was likely to be more successful.

After about five minutes of fruitless searching, he asked, 'Are you sure you dropped it here?'

'I'm absolutely sure,' the girl said, getting up and showing him the single earring in her ear. Her tights had holes in both knees. She was small and neat, like a bird. He thought her rather plain. He tried not to feel irritated. How long would Marsia wait? He thought she probably wouldn't linger very long at all.

'They were an eighteenth-birthday present.' Scott noticed her mouth tremble, and so he renewed his efforts, pushing aside the selection of trainers and boots that had accumulated on the floor. After another five minutes he saw a glint on the floor in front of him.

'I've found it!' he said, holding it out to her on the palm of his hand and she gave an exclamation of pleasure.

'Oh thank you so much. I'd almost given up hope.' She took it and placed it carefully in her pocket. Scott got to his feet. If he was quick Marsia might still be outside.

'I'm Emily by the way,' she said holding out her hand, almost as if they were at a conference or something.

'Scott,' he replied, shaking her hand before hastily making for the door. Outside, there was no sign of Marsia and Danny was being sick on the pavement. On the night bus home, Scott propped his housemate up against his shoulder and scanned his phone.

We have your test results. Please can you come in to see the doctor at your earliest convenience.

Chapter 2

JOSIE STARED OUT OF THE WINDOW. SHE HAD THE FEELING that there was something she had to do, but she couldn't quite catch what was hovering at the edge of her mind. Mondays were always quiet at the bed shop. Buying a new bed was seldom a decision that people made alone, unless they were just looking for a standard single for a child's bedroom or for a rented house. Saturday was when people's minds turned to springs and ticking. They would come into Sweet Dreams in pairs and solemnly test each of the beds in turn. Still in their coats and shoes, they lay side by side, looking up at the ceiling, their hands crossed at their waists like effigies on tombs. Some of the couples became quite skittish in the presence of a memory foam divan or a deep-filled orthopaedic mattress and would throw themselves about, giggling foreplay for what they would be doing later to christen their new acquisition.

In the years Josie had been running the shop, she had become adept at reading people. There were the couples that had just moved in together who were looking for a new mattress to cement their relationship and exorcise the bed ghosts of previous lovers. There were others, maybe married for a few years, who were hoping that the bounce of Yorkshire wool and pocket springs would inject some buoyancy into bedtime. Elderly people often wanted an upgrade from double to king-size because their days of lying spooned were over and they thought that by some magic a larger bed and new mattress would counteract the night sweats and aches. Then there were the recently single who were searching for I-can-do-what-I-want-now beds to accommodate their defiant crumbs.

Josie still found it strange that she had ended up there. It wasn't the sort of job you dreamt of having when you were young. It had started as part-time work when Scott had still been a baby. She had seen a sign in the window advertising the position and gone in on impulse, and within a couple of years she had become the manager. There were times when she thought she should perhaps find work that was more challenging. She had had a vague ambition to be a palaeontologist but after doing geography at university, she had delayed the post-graduate degree that was required. She had thought that she might go back into education after a break, but the years had slipped by and then Scott had fallen ill and everything else had become irrelevant.

He had been seven years old when it had become apparent that there was something wrong with him. Until then he had always been a child who found sitting still difficult. At six months he had wriggled his way off a beach blanket like a crab making for the sea. At a year he had careered around the house with destructive enthusiasm and at three he had climbed up the garden wall and sat at the top swinging chunky legs. When he was five years old, he had run ahead on walks, stopping only to unearth creatures from the cracks in logs or to cup the sandy water from rock pools, as if he was prospecting for gold. During a winter which was beset by storms that saw the sea lashing the cliffs and trees toppling from root to tip across the roads, he developed flu-like symptoms – a high fever and deliriums which left him hollowed out and weak. He never quite seemed to recover. He stopped eating anything but the cheese biscuits she fed him in small segments through his dry lips. His breathing became more laboured.

'It's like I've been hoovered out,' he said one day, and then on the way to the toilet he fainted.

'My heart is beating so hard,' he said when he came to and she laid her hand on his chest and felt the crazy pulse of him under her fingers. It was as if his heart was trying to get out of his body.

A queasy round of hospital visits had followed. A period of time in which she had sat, clenched, in a series of small rooms while her boy's body was examined. Chest X-rays, electrocardiograms and echocardiograms – words she had never even heard before became the everyday currency of their lives. Tubes were forced through blood vessels into his heart. The internal map of him was suffused with dye to trace its passageways and dead ends.

'Heart failure,' someone said, eventually, and her own heart had stilled as if it too was suffering a malfunction.

'It doesn't mean his heart has stopped. It just means it's not working very well.'

'How?' she had said, feeling for the word inside what felt like the suck and swell of dark oil.

'To put it in its most basic terms, it's pump failure, probably caused by a virus. Scott's heart muscles have become inflamed.'

What virus? When? She tried to remember what she might have missed. Some food not properly washed? Someone laying infected hands on him? A cut not adequately plastered? She assumed it must have happened when he had fallen ill earlier in the year but she wasn't sure.

'You may not even have noticed him being particularly unwell,' someone said, recognising her anxiety, but it didn't soothe the guilt Josie immediately felt.

In that single, dizzying moment Josie's world had tilted and never quite righted itself again. Sometimes she thought back to the oblivious person she had been before and she no longer recognised herself in the terrified, pinched, pleading person she had become. There followed weeks and months of operations to repair valves, a complicated regimen of medication, liquid diets to boost his growth, a frantic rush to the hospital in the middle of the night when she couldn't rouse him from a sleep that felt like death. More tests and then an operation to fit a pacemaker that gave them hope for two months before it stopped functioning. More tests and more tubes. More days spent lying together on Scott's narrow hospital bed while she held on to him as if it was nothing but her vigilance that was keeping him alive.

'I'm afraid his only option at this stage is a heart transplant,' the doctor had said some time afterwards. 'I can't tell you when. It may take a week to find a donor. It may take a year.'

'Has he got a year?' she had asked. It seemed to her a ludicrous question. He was seven years old. He still believed in the tooth fairy and thought that a dragon lived inside the walls of Bamburgh Castle.

'He might not have,' the doctor had said, moving his pen under his palm, rolling it back and forth across his desk as if he was trying to smooth something out.

She took Scott home and waited, knowing that what she wished for above all other things was going to mean the greatest possible sorrow to someone else. As the weeks went by, she lost even this passing compunction. She began to long fervently for the right accident at the right place. She lay awake at night willing the disaster. Waiting so avidly for a death made her feel ashamed but not so much that she didn't still pray for it. She became fierce and frantic. Every day was an ugly fight.

She was never quite sure exactly what Scott understood about what was happening. He cried sometimes when hospital interventions hurt and once, she found him sobbing in the garden because he didn't have the strength to walk all the way to the shed, which housed his collection of bottled insects and lobster claws and dried starfish. But mostly he was strangely accepting of his new, constricted life. She took comfort from his patience, grateful for what she thought must be a childish inability to recognise or fear the things that adults knew. Even the stretch of a year was incomprehensible to most young children, let alone the possibility that, one day, they too would be adults. She thought perhaps he could not mourn what he didn't know he might have.

'Today was a good day,' he had said once when they had managed to walk together along the beach and he had sat watching her as she chipped away at the cliff face, hunting for fossils.

'If tomorrow isn't, I will remember today.' He smiled at her, his blue eyes bright in his pale face, as if it was enough to be there with the clouds chasing the watery sun and the waves curling around the base of the rocks. It had made her almost angry, the way he had sat raking through the sand as though the feel of it was a pleasure. She was greedy for all his days to come. She couldn't settle for now.

The shop bell sounded and Picasso came in with his customary bang of the door. Picasso, a school friend of Scott's, was actually called David, but he'd been given his nickname by George the warehouse manager, a person prone to finding weakness and pursuing it to the death. George had seen Picasso doodling cartoons in his lunch break and had mocked him for it ever since. Much to Picasso's annoyance the nickname had stuck and now pretty much everyone used it in preference to his given name. It was Picasso's job to do the deliveries, which more often than not also involved taking the old beds away.

'It's not lugging them down the stairs I mind,' he had told Josie once. 'It's the fact that you get TMI from people's mattresses; they are as good as maps. Stains clustered across the same degree in longitude . . . Friday-night missionary position. Extensive ground covered with a degree of overlap . . . adventurous, multi-partner shagging. Central saturation . . . single guy with bad skin.'

Josie had told him that he was the one giving out too much information, but she thought the boy was wasted at Sweet Dreams. He had the sharp, derisive eye of a satirist.

'Morning, Josie.' Picasso still had the half-awake look he always wore until at least midday.

'Hello,' Josie said, going into the little office off the showroom floor and checking her computer. 'There are six deliveries today. Spread out all over the place. One in Seahouses, one in Ashington, so you'd better get your skates on. Do the ones in town first.'

Picasso nodded his head absently. He seemed preoccupied.

'Is everything OK?' Josie asked. Picasso had a girlfriend, a fragile-looking beauty about whom he was in a continual state of anxiety.

'Lois had a dream where I was an ant and she was riding on my back. She said ants in dreams represent an annoyance. Do you think she was trying to tell me something?' Picasso gnawed at his fingernails and looked at Josie.

'Ants are hard workers. Maybe her dream was about how much she relies on you,' said Josie, consolingly. She thought Lois spent far too much time dwelling on her unconscious and not nearly enough time out of bed.

'Hmm,' said Picasso. 'Maybe.' But he looked a little more cheerful and went into the office to check with his nemesis that the van was loaded and ready to go.

With no customers to attend to and the shop arranged and rearranged to her satisfaction, Josie had no distraction from the nagging sensation that something wasn't quite right. She wondered if it was normal to feel so bereft when your children left home or whether Scott's illness had made her less able to cope with it than other parents. It was what she had longed for and thought at one time that she would never see – Scott becoming an adult, moving on like all of his peers, and yet now that it had happened she felt as if her connection with life had been severed. She wasn't sure who she was anymore.

Three months ago she had driven him to a house in King's Cross and had helped him unpack his boxes. She hadn't known in advance what he had chosen to take with him and had been moved almost to tears by the strange collection of objects she pulled out – a little china cat she had given him years ago, a lumpy vase he had made at school, a photo of the two of them that he had cut to fit a picture frame he had bought at a charity shop. She had felt then, even more keenly than she had through all the desperate days of his illness, how much sorrow there was in love. You felt it in all sorts of ways you never expected. She had heard someone describe being a parent as having to accommodate a slow, pulling away, and it was true, even for those parents who hadn't had to cope with almost losing their children. The process started as soon as they drew their first breath through their bluish, beaked mouths and continued all the years you had them.

Josie remembered a trip to Prague Scott had taken when he was sixteen. She hadn't wanted him to go. She had never wanted him to be anywhere other than where she could reach out for him, but she had known, or at least forced herself to accept, that she had to let him do the things that other children took for granted as part of their coming of age. He had been away for a few days when her phone had rung in the night. Instantly awake, she had answered it in a blind panic. She had never lost the habit of vigilance. All she had been able to hear was the sound of a train like the beat of a heart. She had spoken, said his name, but there had been no answer and she realised after a while that he must have rolled over onto his phone and called her by accident. She had lain for several minutes with her mobile pressed to her ear, travelling alongside him, imagining the rail track snaking its way across the side of a mountain, through clusters of pine trees, past villages with unfamiliar roofs. Then, after a while, the phone had cut off and the train had taken him away from her.

At lunchtime, Josie left George in charge of the shop and walked down the high street to get a sandwich. It was a bright, sharp-edged day and after being in the muted light of the shop, which was designed to create the atmosphere of calm desirable in bedrooms, Josie found herself almost blinded by the sunlight, which bounced off roofs and pavements and gave everything a painful golden edge. Inside the café she ordered her food and sat down at a table in the window. She usually made some lunch at home and brought it to work with her, but this morning she had opened her fridge to a nub end of elderly cheese and a soft tomato and closed the door again quickly. Since Scott had left she had been less assiduous about stocking up on food. There seemed little point now that she no longer had his wolfish appetite to cater for and she couldn't be bothered to cook for herself. There was something so lonely about single pork chops and lasagne for one and a loaf of bread was stale long before she managed to get even halfway through. She felt nostalgic for the times when she used to go to the bread bin and find it annoyingly empty. She shouldn't have been cross. She would have been glad to find it so now.

She took a nibble of her sandwich and then tried phoning him. His mobile rang unanswered and Josie felt another small stab of disquiet. This was the second time she had tried calling without success. He was usually very good about getting in touch at least once a week, but she hadn't heard from him for a fortnight now, not since he had gone back to university after the Christmas break. He had turned nineteen over the holiday, a day he had celebrated with his customary glee. He saw each birthday as a milestone won. He was the only person she had ever met who rejoiced in the fact that he was a year older.

He was probably busy, she told herself. All those lectures and essays to write, not to mention getting to know the city and the clubs and pubs and his fellow students. When he was a boy, there had been a gang of local children who ran wild through gaps in fences and hedges, treating all the gardens as their shared kingdom. Scott had always stayed out after all the other children had been called in, lured back to their homes by their mothers' voices and the smell of food. *It's still early*, he would say when she finally found him by knocking on all her neighbours' doors. *It's still light.* He was probably caught up in his new life the way he had been in his old one, staying up late, making the most of every day. She had an image of him walking over a London bridge. It was from bridges that you really saw the girth and span of the city and felt its rush and beauty. Perhaps he couldn't hear his phone. Perhaps he was on his way to meet someone, or deep in the underground, standing on the edge of a platform feeling that tarry surge of warm air that signalled that a train was coming.

Later, as Josie wandered around the house, pulling curtains together and turning out lights, getting ready for an early night and a book she was halfway through, she resisted the temptation to ring Scott again. She didn't want him to think that she was hounding him. She didn't want him to know that she was missing him so much that she no longer knew how to shape her days. He would surely ring tomorrow and when he did, she wouldn't demand to know why he hadn't rung before. She wouldn't ask any of the questions she knew made him impatient about how he was feeling or what the doctor had said about his annual angiograph. She would keep her voice light, neutral, interested, but not too much, and he would tell her which bridges he had crossed and how London was wide and wonderful and full of new adventures.

Chapter 3

SCOTT WAS AN EXPERT IN MATTERS OF THE HEART. HIS HAD been flown in a helicopter from a hospital in Birmingham all the way to Newcastle where it had arrived in a cool box, coated in saline and covered with ice. Although he hadn't seen it at the time, he knew what it would have looked like. It would have been the size of a small fist, not valentine red, but rather a muscular yellow, not visibly beating but still functioning under its own electrical system.

His mother had taken the phone call. She had come into his room and stood by the bed, holding the bag they always kept by the door. The fact that she had carried it upstairs when it was already packed, showed what a panic she was in. Her eyes had been wide and scared, as if she had seen a ghost, which, in a way, she had, because Scott's second chance to live was given to him by the parents of a child called Aadash who had drowned in a pond when he was trying to feed the ducks. Scott and Josie knew this because a year after his transplant they had been to visit the family. Josie had taken flowers and a letter, which spelled out what she would never have been able to say directly to them.

'I hope I've found the right words,' she had said, tucking the letter into the side pocket of her handbag.

Aadash's mother Ashish Kohli had touched Scott's face and given him a photograph of a boy and a plate of sticky spirals she had called sweets. Scott had been nine at the time and had been disappointed not to be given chocolate. On the way home his mother had cried silently, thinking that Scott, who was sitting on the back seat of the car, wouldn't be able to see, but he had charted the progress of her tears in the wing mirror. He had diverted her with 'Meals on Wheels', a game Josie had invented which involved creating a credible meal from the pictures of food on the side of passing lorries. He even let her claim a Waitrose truck he had already seen which acted like a wild card and meant she could choose any ingredient. This was a big sacrifice because Scott liked winning.

His heart had turned out to be a keeper, despite a blurry period when he was rushed back into hospital because it seemed as if his body was rejecting the gifted organ. He had also suffered several aggressive infections when his life had hung in the balance, although he hadn't known at the time that there was so much at stake. There was a lot he couldn't remember clearly, but he could still recall the responsibility he had felt that his heart should carry on beating, not only for himself and for his mother, but also for his donor's parents who wrote to him every year on his birthday. They always ended their letters with the words *from our hearts to yours* and enclosed a ten-pound note, which made Scott feel a bit uneasy, as if he was getting a dead boy's pocket money.

His mother had told him before his operation that people didn't feel with their hearts but with their brains and that he would still be the same person afterwards, just stronger and less tired, but even now that he was grown-up and there was very little about the heart and its functions he wasn't drearily familiar with, the notion that he had taken on someone else's hopes and desires lingered. He still wondered if somewhere inside him there was a shadow of another boy with a round, puzzled face and dark eyes.

The thud of his transplanted heart didn't fluctuate after a long run or when he kissed a girl, but had an unchanging rhythm that seldom deviated from its almost mechanical pulse. He felt such things only in the deepness of his breath or in the rise of his blood. Left unconnected by the transplant surgery to the nerves that regulated its beat, his heart felt separate from himself. He worried sometimes, although he knew it was irrational, that this inability to show evidence of fatigue or desire in his core, the place that had generated a million love songs, meant his feelings were not quite to be trusted.

Now Scott was sitting in a hospital room, which seemed to have darkened around him, so that only the desk and the doctor sitting opposite him were properly lit. He was aware of a kind of buzzing sound in his ears, as if his body was trying to block out the doctor's words and of a feeling of panic that started in his hands and then seemed to take possession of the whole of him.

'There's been a significant thickening in the epicardial and intramyocardial arteries,' the doctor said, assuming, rightly, that she didn't need to worry about using layman's terms. Being a transplant patient had very few perks, but having doctors talking to you as if you understood what they were saying was a definite bonus. The other, not so great thing was their tendency to swing their computers round to show you your X-rays, as if they assumed you were inured to the sight of the inner workings of your body. Scott had never quite got over the small horror he felt to see the vessels of his heart laid out for inspection. The doctor pored over the sinuous spread of veins and arteries as if she was contemplating one route over another on a road map.

'The angiography reveals narrowing, here, here and here,' she said, jabbing at his heart with the sharp end of her pencil.

'I am sorry to say it looks very much like cardiac allograft vasculopathy, CAV,' she said, looking at him at last. She had pale skin and almost colourless eyes and a tracing of blue veins in her neck. She looked like an X-ray of herself, Scott thought and then tried to focus on what was being said. He had always expected this, or some version of it – thickening, infection, blockages, ruptures, aneurisms and tumours – the words that would signify that his heart, for all its valiant pumping, had begun to degenerate and his life was once more in danger.

'How've you been feeling?' she asked.

'Pretty good,' Scott replied, but his response was more habitual than truthful, for he had been aware for as long as a couple of months of a fatigue that came and went that he had told himself was due to the upheaval of leaving home and getting to know a new place.

'No swelling in your legs? No breathlessness after climbing stairs?' the doctor continued, as if, as well as being familiar with the movement of the blood passing through his arteries, she could also trace his thoughts. He shook his head.

'I've been a bit tired,' he admitted.

Scott looked out of the window. The sky was the dull silver of a tarnished coin and the plane trees seemed all the starker for their spiky baubles. For a moment he felt a regret so deep it threatened to overwhelm him. He knew transplanted hearts did not last forever but recently he had allowed himself to believe that Aadash's heart was special. Now that his life, his proper life, was spreading out in front of him, he had tricked himself into thinking that his heart would continue its necessary beating through all that was to come. He thought of his mother standing at the end of his bed with her fists tight, ready for battle and his throat closed as if his body was trying to hold on to his inherited heart. What would she do when he told her this? How could he prepare her?

Outside, the air had the static fizz of coming snow and people hurried past, heading for comfort and company. He wanted to make a noise. Nothing as loud as a scream – he wasn't so lost to himself that he didn't still hang on to his sense of what people should and shouldn't do in public. He had been in London long enough to see the way people's eyes moved around the crumbled men who shouted, caught up in their own vehement story, the ones that wore heavy coats when the sun was shining, or who gathered their possessions to them as if they were the last defence. He just wanted to check that he still sounded like himself.

He found he was chanting under his breath – the sound he used to make when he was a boy and had a particularly arduous or scary task in prospect. He could remember resorting to this comfort on walks to school when a day of tests lay in wait, or once when he went caving, forced into it so as not to lose face amongst his peers, and found, as he lay on his stomach in the rank squeeze of the tunnel, that he couldn't move at all.

He started running – slowly at first and then faster and faster, past a restaurant where a child had his face pressed to the window, his tongue squashed flat like the belly of a snail, past the rhythmic railings of a park, past a house where two men sat tightly wedged together on the doorstep, the open door behind them emitting the smell of food, something savoury and rich, and Bowie singing 'Wild is the Wind' – on and on until his breath came in little ragged gasps that sounded as if he might be crying.

He stopped at last. He wasn't sure how long he had been running. There was a small enclosure just off the pavement with a bench, a tree, some shrubs, and he sat down, breathing heavily. Spots floated in front of his eyes like a 3D movie. As he sat hidden from the street his first feeling wasn't fear but rather loneliness. He knew that the terror would come. He could feel it waiting in his mouth like the juice that gathers before you vomit. He had felt lonely before, but only the kind that was mixed with boredom and was more about waiting for something or someone and not wanting to. This was different. This was a sense of being the only one. Of being chosen for a particular sort of isolation that he could never share. He waited for the pain to pass. He knew it would. Nothing, after all, had really changed. He still didn't know when he was going to die.

Chapter 4

AFTER THE USUAL DELAY, FREYA, JOSIE'S NEIGHBOUR, answered the door. Josie was relieved to see that she was fully dressed. There had been times when Freya had appeared on her doorstep wearing only a jumper and slippers. She had trouble remembering skirts and Josie had witnessed many a postman retreating hastily from the sight of her.

Freya was slowly slipping away. Over the last year or so, her dementia had escalated, and now her fragments of lucidity were getting further and further apart. If she had any relatives, Josie had never seen them and if it wasn't for Josie and another neighbour who lived three doors down, Freya would never have any visitors, apart from the desultory carers who parked their cars at hasty angles, made a cling-filmed sandwich and left as quickly as they could. Josie didn't blame them exactly, looking after Freya was a thankless task and they were paid by the visit rather than by the time they spent there, but it made Josie angry that this was all that Freya was entitled to. She had worked for forty-four years in the shoe section of the department store in town and had done the cricket teas doggedly every Sunday after she had retired and now all she had to look forward to was these fleeting, unwilling visits. A series of strangers, often a different one every day, who were not unkind, but who never looked at her, didn't know that she had once saved a child from drowning or that she could tell what shoes you needed to the half size with one glance.

'It's you,' Freya said, smiling. Everyone was 'you' to Freya since she couldn't remember anyone's name.

'You're the one with the lovely face,' she had said to Josie once. 'That's how I know it's you', and Josie had thought it was one of the nicest things anyone had ever said to her.

Inside, the house had the same smell it always did – Cumberland pie and dust and tobacco. Freya opened the pies, which were one of the only things she would consent to eat, along with chocolate-covered raisins and Kit Kats, and then became distracted between the opening of the cellophane and the cooking and so the pies lay around the house in various stages of decomposition. She spent almost all her time, night and day, sitting in a chair lined with newspaper, grinding out her fags on the edge of the dining table. Josie had tried several times to clear some of the debris that accumulated around her, the way that sand collects at the bottom of a windbreak, but Freya always objected to these endeavours.

'I know where everything is,' she said, waving her arm across the room as if it contained all she could possibly want. Her legs were white and as slender as a girl's but her face was grooved with lines like the ones she scored with a fork across the tub of 'Utterly Buttery' when she had forgotten what a knife was for.

Her house was still. The only things that moved were the motes of dust that rose from the carpet when you stepped on it and a small toy penguin that sat on the table and swayed in gloopy blue liquid when Freya knocked against it. Freya took a daily newspaper, which she looked at carefully before placing it on the chair to sit on. She particularly enjoyed pictures of semi-clad girls and photographs of the Queen, who was ten years older than she was which just went to show, Josie thought, what good food and walks with corgis did for you. She wondered what the Queen would look like if she subsisted on Cumberland pies and chocolate raisins and TV shows about storage facilities.

'I'm just checking if you need any shopping,' said Josie, making space on a debris-covered chair and sitting down.

'Yes, I do,' Freya said, getting a biro and a scrap of paper from her desk. Josie was alarmed to see that the desk too had now become a repository of cigarette ends. One of these days Freya was going to set the house on fire, she was sure of it.

'I'd like two Cumberland pies, four chunky Kit Kats, four AA batteries, a large packet of TENA Ladies, Twenty Silk Cut,' said Freya, writing laboriously, 'and some drops for dry eyes.' Josie didn't know why Freya bothered to write the list out; she always wanted exactly the same things.

'I'll be able to get everything, but maybe not the eye drops today. It's Sunday and the chemist is shut,' Josie said.

'Is it Sunday?' Freya asked looking surprised.

'Scott's not answering my phone messages,' Josie said, unsure of why she was telling her neighbour this. Maybe it was because she knew Freya would be a safe repository for her confidences. Even if she would be able to recall what she had been told she had no one to share the information with. Freya's face lit up. Scott was one of the few people she could reliably remember, although Josie wasn't sure that Freya actually knew he was no longer living next door.

'I've a soft spot for that boy,' Freya said, and she hugged her arms round herself as if she was remembering something lovely. 'He brings me things he finds on the beach,' and Josie knew that Scott as a little boy, and the day Freya had married her late husband Chuck and the time she broke her arm trying to scale a lamp post were all happening at once, as if she had screwed time up into a ball and placed it in her pale lap.

'I'm worried in case he's not happy,' Josie said.

'Well, I've never been a student but I imagine no news is probably good news,' said Freya, her awareness that Scott had left home surprising Josie.

'Perhaps he's found himself a girl?' Freya gave Josie a look that was almost lascivious. Josie always found the alacrity with which Freya immersed herself in details of the sex lives of others rather disconcerting. Her knowledge of the on-and-off relationships of celebrities was encyclopaedic.

'If she makes her booty any bigger it's going to burst,' she had said once while examining a picture of Kim Kardashian. 'And then she'll be in no fit state for any more sex tapes.'

'I just wish I knew he was all right,' Josie said.

'Isn't it more that you wish *you* were all right?'

'What do you mean?' Josie asked. 'I'm fine. I miss him, of course, all parents go through that, but I've got my own life.'

'It seems to me, and don't take this the wrong way,' said Freya, sounding as if she wasn't worried at all about which way her companion would take her words, 'but your life until now has just been him. Just him. Yup.'

She often ended her sentences with this jaunty little affirmative, as if using the word to anchor herself to what was left of her memory.

'I wouldn't have had it any other way. It had to be like that,' Josie said.

'When I was looking after my mum in her last illness, there were days I hated her almost as much as I loved her,' Freya said. 'Just when I thought I couldn't bear it anymore, when I didn't even want to touch her, she would do something that brought me back to her. She would say something that made me remember how she'd been before.'

'I've never felt like that about Scott, even when he was ill,' Josie said.

These days she couldn't quite recall the exact sequence of things, but rather remembered her life with her son as a series of snapshots – Scott as a baby lying on the carpet giving the same, great, intake of shivering breath each time she passed a muslin cloth over his face and chest. Sitting with him on the sofa, his hand resting against her face as she was feeding him, as if to reassure himself she was still there. A toddler Scott running into the sea dropping his clothes behind him as he went. A bunch of flowers picked from the garden and tied up with string he had given her one Mother's Day. The time she had woken after a bad bout of flu to find him sitting by her.

'I'm guarding you,' he had said. His wooden sword laid across his lap.

'I feel better, already,' she had replied, reaching for the soft squeak of his skin.

'I couldn't have a better mother, even if I'd made you up,' he had said, looking at her with earnest, devoted, eyes.

She could still feel in the very depths of her the almost savage love she had felt for him as a small child. She had worshipped the creases under his knees, the dimples at the base of his fingers, the fresh sourness of his smell when she pressed her face to his stomach. She was getting like Freya, she thought. The past was becoming more vivid to her than the present. The old woman sat in her living room with memories swirling round her head like dusty silk scarves. Every now and again she would pluck one from the air, examine it briefly and then relinquish it again.

'You did a very good job of looking after him,' Freya said, 'but now's your chance to do something for yourself. You're still young. Still young. Yup!'

'It's like I'm having to re-think who I am now that Scott isn't around. I don't know what to fill my head with anymore.'

'Who you are now is a gorgeous, kind woman, who does more for other people than she does for herself, and who could do with having a bit of fun,' said Freya firmly. 'If you wore something other than those endless saggy sweaters, you might even get yourself a man.'

'You are a meddlesome old bag,' said Josie getting up and putting on her coat.

'But you love me, right?' Freya said.

'Hmm, I'm not sure about that,' Josie said. 'Try and eat something other than chocolate raisins.'

'Buy something form fitting. A nice top that shows off your curves,' Freya shouted after her as she shut the door.

Chapter 5

SCOTT WAS AWARE THAT HE WAS SPENDING TOO MUCH TIME lying on his bed but he felt lethargic. His room was chaotic and he knew by the slightly fetid smell of his own body that he should probably brave the shower enclosure. He couldn't bring himself to ring his mother, even though she had left a series of increasingly anxious messages. He knew she would be able to tell from his voice that something was wrong. He had often been irritated by her ability to detect changes in his mood, an inconvenient characteristic in a mother, particularly as he had got older. *I've always been her specialist subject*, he thought, and then wondered what their relationship would have been like if his heart hadn't failed him. His illness had made him both cleave to her and chafe against her. He thought perhaps he hadn't always been kind.

'Stop watching me,' he had said once, when as a drooping, self-obsessed teenager he had caught her looking at him in that fearfully loving way she had. He had probably been a bit under the weather, or perhaps it was just that he had been beset by the uncomfortable, scratchy yearnings of being the age he was.

'I want to get away from you. I can't breathe,' he had said, and he could remember the way she had ducked her head as if he had hit her.

'Go and get a fucking life,' he had continued, shamefully feeling his power over her and unable to stop the desire to express it. He loved her, he knew he did in the waves of contrition and exasperated affection that frequently overwhelmed him, but he wanted the beam of her regard to be not so relentlessly pointed in his direction. Her love bound him up and made him more secretive, less able to tell her things than he might have been if she hadn't so desperately wanted to know.

In the three weeks since his hospital appointment he had tried to carry on as normal. Getting up, going to uni and participating in the routines that had already been established of lectures and drinking and sleeping until midday served to stop him thinking about what was going on inside him. A few days ago he had been walking over a footbridge and he had briefly allowed his fear to surface. He had let himself imagine what might happen next and the horror of it had stopped him dead in his tracks. He had stood frozen, unable to move forward or to go back until, eventually, someone had brushed past him and set him once more in motion. He heard the doctor's words and saw her face. He had been in the business of illness for long enough to know what her cautious, almost embarrassed expression had signified. It was what doctors looked like just before they told you there was not a lot else they could do – a kind of awareness of coming shame.

Ever since the night in the union bar, Marsia had been by turn flirtatious and then bewilderingly elusive. She had come up behind him one day and kissed him on the back of his neck and then laughingly pulled him into the library, where he had leaned into her against the shelves of critical theory until he thought their combined weight and combined ardour would cause books and shelves to topple, but then avoided his repeated texts asking her to go out for a drink.

'She's damaged,' Danny had concluded with one of his wise, folded-up expressions. 'I'd give her a swerve, mate.'

Scott wasn't altogether sure of the level of his housemate's relationship expertise. Danny had a girlfriend from home, a chirpy individual with bushy hair who brought him food in casserole dishes, whom he treated with the sort of careless regard that you might extend to a pet.

'In any case, I hear via the jungle drums,' Danny had continued, 'that she's having a thing with her tutor', and although Scott hadn't believed him at the time, a few days later he had seen Marsia with the man in question, laughing up at him in that sexy, derisory way that Scott had fondly imagined was her response solely to him. The tutor's face had done that thing of softening that Scott recognised was what men's faces generally did when something else was hardening.

There was a knock and Danny poked his head through the door.

'There's a party,' he said. 'Fancy coming?'

'Why not?' Scott said. Being alone in his room had started to drive him mad.

It was freezing. The sky had a purplish tint and there was a breathless, waiting quality to the air. The party was in a house in Plumstead – a big, tatty villa on a main road with what looked like towels covering the windows. When they arrived, there were already a couple of slumped bodies in the front garden and someone had dropped a whole bottle of wine on the path.

'Dancers,' Danny said reverently as they went in. 'Hundreds of them. Central School of Ballet, no less.' It was clear to Scott that Danny's beef stew-toting girlfriend was in danger of being confined to the past.

The place was so full it was hard to find even a corner to stand in. There were a high proportion of bulky men and delicate-looking girls. It seemed that Danny hadn't realised that the party was fancy dress, because the two of them were the only ones not in outlandish costumes. A man dressed in chain mail lurched against him, almost knocking Scott over. He smelt authentically rank, as if he had recently been around a fire eating meat with his hands.

'Here's something to cheer you up,' Danny said, appearing suddenly beside him and pressing a tablet into Scott's hand. 'This is our kind donor,' he said pulling a young woman by the hand. 'Scott, this is Ophelia.'

Ophelia had pale hair and dry skin and beautiful bony shoulders emerging out of her pre-Raphaelite-inspired dress. Danny looked at her as if he was thinking of eating her.

'Go on, live dangerously,' he said, and Scott thought there was little point in demurring. What difference could it make after all? Taking ecstasy was something he could tick off the long list of things he wasn't supposed to do. He had always had to be so careful about what he put into his body. He had had years of taking pills – immunosuppressants, antibiotics, anti-inflammatories, statins, steroids and vitamins. His mother had drummed into him the dangers lurking in soft cheese, raw meat, unwashed vegetables, grapefruit juice, passive smoking, alcohol, bacteria, sunburn, saliva and foreign water. Living had always seemed like a perilous business to her.

Danny produced a bottle of vodka and Scott took a mouthful and swallowed his bile-green pill. People were dancing so close that he could stand still and be caught up in the motion of it. The floor buckled beneath the weight of the fifty or so bodies crammed side by side. Ophelia was plastered against Danny and they were kissing. Scott felt the heat and rush around him as a kind of ease. His body, and the secret he carried within it, was shared, somehow, in the thick of arms and lights and movement. His fear was softened and smeared. *Nothing matters*, he thought and gave himself to the collective dance.

'It's snowing!' someone said, some indefinite time later, and there was a rush to the door. Outside, the promised snow had come thick and fast, covering everything it touched – turning the mundane shapes of the street into things of mystery. Someone opened a window and put the speakers on the sill, covered with bin bags, and the party continued outside. The snow on Scott's face felt warm. He tilted his head up and watched its dancing, relentless tumble. The man in chain mail was scooping up the snow into his helmet. Two girls were doing a duet on the pavement, their feet hidden in the fresh fall. Scott felt a sudden, crippling sadness. The air outside was dense with the weight of what was falling from the sky. *I'm falling too*, he thought. *We all are, even those spinning girls with their silky arms held above their heads, and although we know this about each other and ourselves, we don't really believe it.*

'We meet again!' a voice behind him said, and he turned to see the girl whose earring he had found in the cloakroom. She was shivering in a thin, draped dress covered all over with what looked like blue swirls and yellow blotches.

'Hello, Scott, I'm Emily,' she reminded him. 'How come you're not dressed up?'

'I didn't know I was supposed to,' he said. 'What've you come as?'

'The theme is famous paintings and I'm Van Gogh's *Starry Night*.' She raised her arms and then he could see the stretch of a star-studded sky hanging down from her body. 'I made it myself.'

'Still got your earring?' Scott asked, feeling suddenly bad that he hadn't remembered her name. There was something transparently eager about her that made him want to be kind. Her hand went up to her ear to check and then she nodded.

'I try really hard not to, but I'm always losing things,' she said.

'You look really cold,' he said. 'Would you like to go back in?'

She turned and led him back down the pathway to the house and produced a bottle of wine and two glasses, which was nothing short of a miracle, given the crashing muddle of the kitchen. He thought wine on top of the vodka he had already drunk was probably tempting fate, but he felt reckless. *Perhaps they have got it wrong*, he thought. Perhaps his blood was flowing as freely as that of a normal person of his age. Perhaps being cautious would make no difference at all. Besides, he was sick of being careful. He wanted to be part of this white, swirling, night, not someone who was waiting for it all to be taken from him.

They sat on the stairs and she told him that she was one of four children, that the family home was in a village just outside Cambridge, that her father was a businessman and her mother a yoga teacher, that she made all her own clothes, that she had once been stung by a scorpion and that she loved Nutella and hated Marmite. In his turn, he talked about his hometown of Alnwick, the castles along the Northumberland coast that he had felt belonged to him when he had been growing up, Archie his Labrador with his baggy, old eyes, why he had chosen Biological Sciences to study (I'm going to be a conservationist) and why he loved whales and dolphins.

He didn't tell her about his heart. He had made that mistake before and discovered that people were either a little freaked out by the notion or overly interested in the mechanics of it all. Since he had been at college he had enjoyed the anonymity of seeming like someone with a standard set of organs that were not the subject of scrutiny and curiosity. He knew he might not be able to keep up the illusion for much longer but he wanted to try and do so for as long as possible. He found it easy to talk to her because he didn't fancy her. She wasn't his type at all.

'Aren't you a little too old to like dolphins?' she teased. Scott noticed that when she smiled her lips pulled right back, revealing small, white teeth, perfectly even, except for a slightly twisted one on the top right-hand side. It served to make the rest of her mouth seem more perfect in contrast.

'Most people grow out of *Free Willy* and *Flipper Swims Again*, or whatever the film was called. The only adults that like dolphins are those New Age types who hang mobiles of them in their windows.'

'You never grow out of dolphins,' he said. 'When you see them, you don't know whether to clap or cry. They are so improbable, somehow, that, after they've gone, you think that perhaps they were never really there – that you had conjured them up like a dream. They are perfectly, magnificently, untouchable whatever man throws at them – chemicals, fishermen's nets, underwater drilling and explosives, plastic bags and the tiny beads found in cosmetics that never break down but which end up in their stomachs. Not to mention the people who want to eat them and put their penises in glass jars. They have a special kind of power. It's a bit like magic. Knowing they are there makes my life better,' he said and then stopped. He thought perhaps he was being too weird and earnest. She was staring at him intently.

'I've never seen one in the flesh,' she said.

'You see them quite often on the Northumberland coast.'

'I'll have to visit sometime,' she said and then coloured and looked away from him.

'I think it's time I was getting back,' he said.

'Yes,' she said, jumping to her feet as if she thought she had been keeping him there against his will.

'I expect I'll see you around.'

She nodded and smiled at him as if she thought he was just being polite, which, in fact, he was.

On the way to the bus stop, under the still-falling snow, he decided he would go back home the next day. He didn't know how he was going to be able to tell his mother but he couldn't delay it any longer.

43

Chapter 6

JOSIE SAW SCOTT AS SOON AS HE CAME OUT OF ALNMOUTH station. She was standing by the car, watching everyone as they emerged, to be sure that she didn't miss him. There had been a time when he was little when she had found it hard to distinguish him in a crowd. She used to scan the stage during Nativity plays and search for him across the school fields on sports days. It was almost always another parent who pointed him out to her and then she would see him; of course, she would think, there he is. It was as if while they had been apart she had imagined him differently and was surprised by the way he looked in real life. She always felt a small roil in her stomach of love and pride and disbelief that he was hers.

Scott had finally rung her after a three-week silence and announced that he was coming home. She hadn't been expecting a visit from him so soon and she was worried about the work he was supposed to be doing, but she thought perhaps he would manage it better in the peace and quiet of his bedroom.

He was used to taking care of what he ate and drank but she suspected his standards might have slipped a little. It had been hard for her to relinquish responsibility for him. Caring for him, monitoring what went into his body, how much sleep he got, the regular administration of the medicines he had to take for the rest of his life, had become a full-time job for her and since his absence she felt she had been made redundant.

He wore a long, dark coat she had not seen before and one of his odd, Dickensian-looking hats. He had always had an eccentric taste in clothes. A favourite outfit of his was a pair of leopard-print trousers and a jumper that looked like it was made from underarm hair. He tended to pick up garments and mix them together in odd combinations – a tweed jacket with shorts or, once, a stripped poncho over a pair of what looked very like jodhpurs. He had gone through a whole period in his early teens when he had insisted on carrying a black umbrella with a bamboo handle everywhere he went. Even at this distance she thought he looked rather pale, although he was still moving fast, the way he always did – as if he was late for something. *I must buy him vitamins*, she thought, and then waved to attract his attention.

He saw her straightaway. She looked nice. She was wearing a new red jumper and her hair had grown a little and was soft around her face. She jumped up and down and clapped her hands. She had an unselfconscious way of showing her pleasure. He had always liked the fact that she didn't really seem to care what other people thought of her.

He waved back, giving his familiar, beaming smile, and walked towards her.

He's lost weight too, she thought. 'Hello, my darling,' she said and put her arms around him. He smelt different – a kind of metallic odour she associated with trains and buses and big cities. Just for a moment she felt a kind of resistance in him, a slight holding of himself apart, but then he returned her embrace.

He felt weak with unexpected love. He knew that after half an hour or so this feeling would inevitably transform to a more irritated affection, but at that moment, standing at the station, it was as if he remembered her all over again. Her hair scratched his face as it had always done. She smelt of oranges and salt and home. How could he say what needed to be said? He thought perhaps it would break her.

'Hello, Mum,' he said and kissed her.

'Are you OK?' she asked him, pushing him away from her slightly so that she could see him better, but he avoided her scrutiny by going round to the back of the car and depositing his rucksack in the boot.

'I'm fine. Just a bit knackered,' he said as he got into the car.

He looks older, Josie thought. I've only not seen him for a few weeks and he has changed such a lot. This was just another stage of the pulling away. Suddenly she remembered the funny, uncoordinated, elbows-out style of dancing he used to do as a child whenever he heard even the shortest burst of music from a car window or a shop door. But she hadn't seen him dance for years; it felt strange to her that his odd, unselfconscious perambulations had once been so familiar to her. She experienced a surge of love so intense that she felt like crying. *Remember you promised that you wouldn't get all heavy*, she told herself. She was going to be relaxed and carefree and they were going to have a good time together. She had always wanted him to think well of her, to find her convivial company; someone he was glad to spend time with. It horrified her to think that he might come and see her out of duty. She was going to feed him up for a start, and maybe take that coat to the dry cleaner's. Above all, she was going to make sure he didn't know how much she was missing him. She was wearing a new sweater and she had done her best with her hair this morning, even though she had made the mistake of going to bed with it wet and now it stuck out slightly on one side.

The route into Alnwick – dark trees, pale walls and then trees again – seemed different to him now, as if he had been away a long time. They drove past the statue of the lion on a column, with its absurdly rigid tail and the old railway station that was now a bookshop and then continued on as far as the Playhouse. They turned off Broadgate and passed houses drenched and darkened to slate-grey by a recent downpour, and on up to King Street with its rows of terraces – identical on both sides of the street – with flat, bay-less frontages that looked slightly unreal, like a stage set. His mother's house was the last one on the right-hand side and Scott remembered the feeling of insecurity it had given him as a child not to live slotted into the neat row but rather on the edge, where instead of a safe wall there were trees and bushes that had been allowed to grow as they wanted and were matted and impenetrable.

He wasn't sure how he was going to bring up the subject of his recent diagnosis. It wasn't something you could just blurt out. He needed to lead up to it in some way. He thought it was probably best if they went out somewhere and then he could explain it all when they were walking, so that he didn't have to look directly into her face as he said the words. He was surprised she hadn't already asked him what had happened at his check-up. He thought maybe she was deliberately holding her questions back so as not to appear too concerned.

'I'd like to go fossil hunting,' he said when they got inside the house, and his mother turned to him and smiled, her face full of pleasure.

'Oh yes. We haven't done that together for ages,' she said. 'I expect you'll also want to see your friends. Don't feel you have to be with me all the time,' she added hastily, which made him smile a little because he knew that she would prefer it if he stayed in.

'I'm not sure who's around, to be honest. There's Picasso, of course,' he said, thinking that he would do his best to avoid people. Each person he didn't tell made him feel his separateness more. It added a layer to the crust he was building up around himself. His mother had made his previously chaotic den look more grown-up. Most of his stuff was still there but all the surfaces shone and she had put a vase of flowers on his desk and placed a towel and a bar of soap on the end of the bed. She had decided that he had made the transition to guest, and the thought touched him, as did the cling-filmed batch of brownies on the kitchen table. The childhood treat had always been protected in this way, as had every other piece of his food. The very air had been a hazard to his mother. The taste now conjured up the same consolation he had felt in the days when any sadness could be put right simply by biting into the soft chocolate.

Bowick Beach was a fifteen-mile drive away and they arrived to find the place deserted. His mother was carrying her rucksack which contained her fossil-hunting tools – a couple of hickory hammers, chisels, specimen boxes, goggles, gloves and, of course, the camera with which she took her photographs of the finds that couldn't be brought home, those that were too large or precious to take away. She was bright with happiness, pointing things out to him as they walked along the beach, stopping to examine stones, asking him if he wanted a drink from the flask of tea she also carried. The sea was puddle-brown and had frisked itself into lumps of thick spume, which blew up off the beach as the wind caught them.

They made for a stepped area of limestone south of the town, which was covered twice a day when the tide was high. The carboniferous rock was thick with crinoids, or sea lilies, fossils of ancient, basic creatures with backbones and feeding arms that looked more like plants than animals. They had bowls of them at home – cross sections of the stem that looked like crude beads, but they had never found a complete one. The feathery arms were so delicate that it was very rare to find one intact. Josie passed Scott a hammer and chisel and he set to work, chipping away carefully at the sides of the rocks, hoping as he always did that one day he would find the perfect specimen – arms all present and attached to the ridged central bone. Bending down made him feel unsteady, as if the rocks under his feet were shifting slightly.

They found the usual selection of coral-covered rocks looking, with their wormy twists, like bleached-white brains, and a shell fossil which Josie said was called a spirifer, but for all their efforts, the flawless sea lily remained as elusive as ever. They sat on the beach and drank musty tea from his mother's ancient flask.

'There've been reports of another bottlenose dolphin making this bay his regular visiting place,' said Josie. 'I wasn't sure whether to tell you, not after last time.'

Scott looked out to sea in alarm.

'There've been regular sightings?' he asked scanning the waves.

'Yes. It was only occasionally at first, but it's becoming a more regular occurrence.'

'Have people been behaving like dicks?' he asked.

'Well, I read in the paper the other day that one bloke has been attempting to hitch a ride. Holding on to its tail. The dolphin seems to have been given a name – probably by the tourist board, keen to get more punters to the area. They are calling him Leonardo on account of the fact that he has been spotted nudging driftwood along with his nose.'

Scott snorted. 'He's got his own bloody name,' he said. 'Every dolphin makes itself known by its own particular series of clicking and whistling sounds.'

Josie looked at Scott's indignant face and smiled. He had loved dolphins and whales ever since the day they had come across three beached sperm whales at Beadnell. It was shortly after he had been finally allowed out of the hospital after his transplant. He had been very weak, still unsure of his footing.

'It feels so soft under my feet,' he had said as he had walked barefoot in the sand. She remembered she had wanted him to keep his shoes on, anxious that he might get a cut from a sharp stone. Any small fissure in his skin provided the potential for an infection. Despite her entreaties he had kicked his trainers off.

'There's no point in a beach unless you can feel it,' he had said.

The three whales were lying side by side. Scott had stopped dead and then suddenly run towards them. She remembered telling him not to touch, already reaching for the antiseptic gel she always had to hand. The doctor had said that even the soil had the potential to make him ill and she had been sure that dead whales must be top of the list of things not to handle. She could smell the beginnings of their decomposition, thick and fetid in the air. Scott went under the taped barrier, which had been erected to keep the public at bay, and moved from whale to whale, touching each of them gently on their massive sides and Josie had had to duck hastily beneath the tape and pull him away. The eyes he had turned to her had been wide and astonished.

'They are so very much,' he had said inexplicably as she had scrubbed fretfully at his upturned palms.

It had been the beginning of what amounted to an obsession. Throughout his recuperation he had read everything he could get his hands on about cetaceans and then the summer Scott turned eleven, a dolphin which was given the name Harry had turned up at Bowick Beach. He was a young bull, who had some-how become separated from his pod, or had perhaps decided to go it alone. He seemed to be recklessly courting attention – swimming up close to boats and trying to interact with startled swimmers. Scott used to go down to the beach and try and shoo him away, casting furious looks at the tourists who waded in to have their picture taken with him or who hired boats so that they could hang over the side and stroke him.

'They are going to make him lose his wildness,' Scott said. 'It says on this website that you shouldn't encourage dolphins which come too close to humans. It makes them forget who they are.'

That summer Scott took up almost permanent residence on the beach. With the help of the local Marine Conservation Soci-ety, which had accepted him as a volunteer despite his young age, he had written and printed out a leaflet warning of the dangers of interacting with dolphins both to them and to the public, which he handed out to anyone nearby. He even got a slot on the local radio in which he pleaded for people to keep away from the dolphin.

'He's not a toy,' he had said in earnest tones. 'He has a brain much bigger and more complicated than ours. He gets scared just like we do. He has a family somewhere. He's already losing his colour and turning white because of the pollution in the water near the sewage pipe. He's not ours, you see, even if it seems as if he is.'

The summer turned to autumn and still Harry was the focus of attention. Groups of young men egged each other on to swim with the dolphin and even try and mount his slippery back. One particularly cretinous bunch attempted to pour beer into his open mouth. One morning a boat went too close and clipped the dolphin's side with its propeller. Harry disappeared for a week or so and Scott alternated between hope that the accident had at last driven him away back to the other dolphins and fear that the wound had been too severe to recover from. Three weeks later, Harry was washed up on the beach, the gash on his side much too deep for him to survive. Scott barely spoke for a week. Josie could still remember his body, tight with misery and fury.

'They killed him,' he said when at last he was able to articulate his misery. 'They may as well have clubbed him to death.'

'I never get tired of the sea and sky,' his mother said now. She smiled at him. *She's getting older*, Scott thought with surprise.

He hadn't noticed it before. Her jaw line was softening and her eyes, watering in the wind, were traced around with fine lines.

'I've missed you,' she said, and then, as if she wanted to take the words back, she said, 'although I haven't missed the smell of your shoes or the way you used to wake me at two in the morning coming in from God knows where.'

'I've missed you too,' he said and found that he meant it. She drove him mad sometimes but she was his whole family.

I'll tell her now, he thought. There would never be a better place than this beach. It was big enough and empty enough to absorb the shock.

'What are you thinking about?' she said. 'You look just like you used to do when you were hatching a plan.'

She screwed the lid back onto the flask and restored it to its pocket on the side of her rucksack. The gesture was intensely solitary. He knew she had stowed it away in exactly the same fashion after a hundred solo excursions, a hundred hours spent chipping away at rocks or looking for fool's gold in the cliff face. She was so often on her own.

He couldn't tell her yet. Even as a child he had known that his illness was far harder for her to bear than it was for him to endure. He knew she had settled on having him forever.

'Are you lonely, Mum?' he asked, not knowing that was what he was going to say.

She looked at him. Her eyes were the same ridiculous turquoise-blue they had always been despite the fact that they were less open now and shadowed by slightly heavier brows.

'No, I'm not,' she said firmly. 'I have work and friends and more to do than I can fit into the day.'

'Why have you never had a boyfriend? A proper, lasting one, I mean.'

'It just hasn't happened. I've never found anyone to suit me.'

For some reason her words made Scott think of Emily. She had said something similar to him at the party about the fact that she never seemed to be able to find the right person. 'I'm very picky,' she had said in that slightly prim way she had and then she'd laughed and tugged at her tufted hair. As she had lifted her arm he had seen the side of her breast through her draped costume and he had looked away. He wondered what had made him think of her just at that moment; perhaps it was simply because her obvious regard for him felt comforting and made him feel he wasn't quite as alone as he thought he was. The drive to couple up, to find affection and satisfy lust seemed to him to be a governing force. He couldn't conceive of living for years without having it, as his mother had done.

He found it hard to imagine how other men would see Josie. He felt a bit embarrassed even thinking about it. One of Scott's peers, a skinny boy called Travis who wrote the words of gloomy poems on the back of his hand, had once made a comment about her being 'quite hot' and earned himself a thump in the stomach from Scott. It just wasn't appropriate for your friends to say that sort of thing, although when he had told his mother, looking slyly at her to see her reaction, she had turned a bit pink and looked really pleased and she was always especially smiley with Travis when he came to the house.

'I don't meet so many people,' she said lightly, looking away from him. 'Not many single men wander into the bed shop and I don't fancy George.'

They both laughed at the thought of George as a prospective suitor. It wasn't just his truculent personality that stood in the way of romance, it was the way he ran his fleshy hands across his stomach at the prospect of food, and his collection of beer cans that apparently filled up the entire living room of his house and his tiny feet that made him look like an upside down triangle.

There had never really been anyone else since his father had disappeared. Scott had heard the story of what had happened many times. She had tried to keep her words measured, only telling him what she thought he would understand, but he had seen the damage. She had been six months pregnant when Peter had gone out one night and never returned.

'He didn't take anything with him,' his mother had said, as if that proved that he hadn't abandoned her.

'If he had been planning to leave me, he would have taken stuff. He only had his wallet and the clothes he was wearing,' she said, as if she could still see the picture of it clear in her mind.

'He said he was going to get a bottle of wine and some lemonade for me. I couldn't drink enough lemonade when I was pregnant with you. That night Peter was exactly how he always was. We hadn't rowed or anything. It was a normal Friday night.'

Scott had learned to dread the times she spoke of his father. It always seemed to have the effect of damping her down, making her quiet and unreachable. Her desolation sometimes used to make him feel abandoned too, as if the loss was a shared one, but at other times it had made him angry. He could remember as a child thinking that if his father ever came back, the first thing he would do was stab him with the wooden sword his mother had bought him to punish him for the hurt he had caused her.

'Your father used to do that,' she would say when Scott sucked his spaghetti up all in one go, or sat on the toilet reading and he would feel as if his similarity to his father was a kind of haunting for her. He had speculated over the years about what might have happened to Peter; if perhaps he had been burdened by a terrible secret and had walked into the sea or become entangled in a shady deal that had ended in disaster. At other times, he thought his father was almost certainly alive and had simply decided he wanted another life and was currently holed up in a villa in Spain with an infinity pool and a leathery complexion. He only thought of him as an idea, something that had never been real, but he had been a living, breathing person to his mother, and that sometimes made Scott feel peculiar, as if he hadn't been party to his own beginning. He had once found a picture of his parents in a drawer, in a silver frame, which already looked as if it belonged to another era. His mother was standing smiling in a flowered dress, her hair piled up on top of her head, her arm around a man with shoulders too broad for his jacket who was looking away from the camera. *A picture from before she was mine*, was how he always thought of it when he looked at it.

He never asked Josie what he suspected was true – that Peter had left because he didn't want to have a child – but the feeling that he had been the cause of his mother's unhappiness had been with him for as long as he could remember and had only been reinforced by his illness. He thought that between them – his father and himself – they had taken everything from her and yet she had never shown any resentment. He had loved her then and loved her now for acting as if he was a blessing. She had always looked at him as if he was all she needed.

'Do you wish you'd never met Peter?' Scott asked and she turned to him with sudden indignation, as if what he had said had been hurtful.

'How could I?' she said, touching the side of his face gently. Scott felt like crying so he got up quickly, picked up her rucksack and put it over his shoulder.

'Let's go back, it's getting cold,' he said.

At some point on the drive home, with the rain beating against the windscreen and the trees looking as if they had no memory of leaves past and leaves to come, feeling weakened by what he hadn't been able to say, he made a resolution. He would find her someone to love so that she wouldn't be alone when he wasn't there anymore.

Chapter 7

A S SCOTT WALKED DOWN GOWER STREET TOWARDS COLLEGE, past groups of tourists with their heads up like meerkats, sniffing the culture on the air, he pondered the question of how people found partners when they were older. Since his return from Alnwick, it was a subject that had preoccupied him a lot. It wasn't as if people his mother's age went anywhere much – at least not to the parties and gigs that had been the scene of his few conquests. He couldn't imagine his mother kissing someone she had just met, not even quite sure what they looked like in daylight. He supposed it must happen for them when they were introduced to other single people in the pub or at dinner parties or at one of the classes and groups his mother went to. His mind shied away from the thought of plumbers and gardeners setting aside their tools for some afternoon pleasure or of people who fell in love with other married people.

What was the procedure? At what point between the starters and main course was the deal struck? He had trouble imagining romance for anyone over, say, twenty-five. He didn't really like to dwell on it – unable to contemplate the notion that people, and his mother in particular, felt as he did. Surely it all smoothed out as you got older – that rough feeling of wanting and the desire to be wanted. It must get more manageable, he reasoned, duller, like old vinyl records.

He conjured up the ideal man – thirty-eight to fifty years old (although fifty seemed ancient to him, he had to allow for a wide margin); a good job, so that his mother wouldn't have to sell beds for the rest of her life; active in a likes-long-walks kind of a way, he wasn't looking for someone who risked his life climbing mountains. He would have to have a passing interest in fossils or the ability to pretend that he had. Someone who would treat her with kindness – praise the wonky pots and the misshapen knitting. This imaginary man would ask her to gather up her hair so that he could stand behind her and fasten the clasp of the necklace he had just given her. He would whisk her out of cars and into restaurants and send her off for weekends of pampering, although Scott only had a vague grasp of exactly what pampering involved. The perfect candidate would know the lie of the land; which direction the sun was coming from and what makes rain, and wouldn't pretend to like dubstep or drive a metallic-coloured car with his arm out of the window. He absolutely had to be someone who acted his age, rather than tried cringingly to stay young – so no random sportswear, no baseball caps or fedora hats, no skate shoes, no beaded jewellery or festering festival bracelets, no quiffs and most definitely no shorts with cargo pockets. What was needed was someone who knew a good thing when he saw it and who had the tenacity to hang on.

When it came to the ideal man's looks he had less of a clue. It was hard to tell from one photograph what Peter had actually looked like and the people his mother had fleetingly dated since had been a mixed bag. Dark, well-built, confident-looking he thought. He knew nobody who remotely fitted his prototype man, nor did he have any mates with widowed fathers or eligible uncles. Signing her up to some sort of dating agency would require her participation right from the beginning and would be too time-consuming and about three people in the country looked at newspaper classified ads. He couldn't imagine her going on Tinder or some other dating app since she had trouble even remembering to charge her phone. It struck him that she was, in fact, a very private person. She hated reality TV shows, saying it was disgusting that people got off on watching other people making fools of themselves. She didn't even use social media; something that had been an advantage when he was younger since she hadn't been able to see the escapades his friends posted on Facebook, but which now seemed to him like a wilful shutting off from the world.

'I've got nothing to sell and nothing to say,' she had said once, with that tone of voice she sometimes employed that brooked no argument. It had seemed to him then that his mother might as well live on an island or up the turret of one of her beloved castles, her wild hair pinned to her head, not even contemplating the possibility of letting it down so that a prince might attempt to climb its tangled mass. It wasn't going to be easy to find her someone to love but he couldn't allow himself to fail. He couldn't see any other way of blunting the coming hurt.

As he went through the front entrance he bumped into Emily. It seemed as if the girl was everywhere. She was dressed in a blue skirt made out of some satiny stuff and a blouse with a lace collar and close up he saw that her eyes were a strange yellowy green and fringed with long, dark lashes.

'Oops! Hello again!' she said, promptly dropping her bag. It landed upside down on the floor and disgorged its contents. He knelt down to help her retrieve her notebooks and a pen with a jester's head and a lipstick without a lid that had accrued a dusty crust.

'It seems I'm always on my knees in front of you,' he said and she gave him a snaggle-toothed smile.

'It's where you belong,' she said, suddenly haughty and he saw that despite her girlish clothes and her shyness she had a seam of something strong running through her – a layer of iron ore that bisected the quartz.

'My lecture has been cancelled. I'm just going to get some breakfast. Would you like to come?' she said. She didn't quite meet his eyes as she spoke. He had no real inclination to go, he had already had breakfast and had some work to finish and he thought that perhaps if he said yes she might take it as a sign that he was interested in her. He was still holding out increasingly despairing hopes that Marsia might discover that her tutor was a predatory knob and turn to him instead, although he knew getting together with a girl, any girl, was tantamount to letting them form an alliance with a phantom.

At his bleakest moments he thought it was very possible that his life would end without him ever being properly loved, or perhaps, more importantly, without him having used his ailing heart to its fullest extent. The year he had turned sixteen, Travis's family's au pair, a melancholy Greek girl, had tenderly and silently rid him of his virginity. He had thought perhaps he loved her, but when she had gone home, driven back to Crete from Alnwick by the weather and the poor quality of the tomatoes, he had barely missed her and he had realised that it had just been the idea of her waiting for him in Travis's attic in her dressing gown, her flesh goosebumpy, that he had been in love with. Since then he had dated a couple of girls, but nothing he could call a proper relationship. It made him wonder if perhaps he wasn't really equipped to find a partner for his mother. How could he possibly identify something that he had never known himself?

'It's my treat,' Emily said and it was perhaps a desire not to be alone with the thought of what he might not have engulfing him, rather than wanting to be with this particular person, that made him accept.

It seemed that Emily was something of a regular at the little Italian café, three left turns from Grafton Street, because the proprietor lit up at the sight of her.

'Emeeely!' he said. 'My favourite customer.' He made a great show of wiping the table in the corner and settling her down and then kissed her hand with what Scott considered was unnecessary Italianism, although Emily seemed to enjoy the attention.

'Are you breaking my heart with this young man?' he said, making sad eyes and clutching at the front of his apron, and Emily laughed. Scott ordered a coffee and some toast but Emily was brought an enormous plate of egg and chips and a blueberry muffin without her having to ask for anything. She ate methodically and with focus, as if engaged in some sort of competition.

'Did you have a good time when you went home?' she asked, looking at him over the top of her coffee cup, and he realised she must have checked with his friends where he was. He didn't remember telling her he was going to Alnwick.

'It's not that I'm stalking you or anything,' Emily said hastily. 'Danny just mentioned you had been away.'

'Yes. It was fine. My mum got my coat dry cleaned and bought me a tub of multivitamins and Archie my dog ate one of my socks and my essay notes.'

'What does your mum do?' Emily asked, wiping up the last of her egg from her plate with a piece of bread.

'She works in a bed shop. She's really good at selling beds but I think she would have liked to have done something else,' he said.

'Why didn't she?' Emily asked putting her cutlery down straight on her plate like a good child. Scott found he liked the economy of her – the careful way she held her cup, her small, considered movements. She made everyone around her look too present, too flamboyant.

'I don't think she ever got round to it,' he said, knowing he couldn't explain the way he had become his mother's life. Everything she might have done, everyone she might have met had been lost in the all-encompassing task of looking after him.

'I'm going to make sure I do everything I want to do,' Emily said, pushing her plate away from her with a satisfied sigh. 'I'm not going to let anything hold me back.'

'Sometimes things happen to stop you in your tracks,' Scott said, 'and there's not much you can do about it.'

'It won't happen to me,' she said, her mouth set in a firm line.

'What do you want to do?'

'I'm going to be a travel journalist. I like the idea of being on the move. Only having with me what I absolutely need and no more. I want to discover stories no one else has told.'

Emily had a tiny smear of egg on her chin and without thinking, he reached out and wiped it away. She jumped at his touch as if it had stung her and wiped frantically at her face with a napkin, so that all he could see were her cat-yellow eyes and her precise brows.

'You'll rub your face away,' Scott said, 'which would be a real shame.' And then, when she lowered her head, looking pleased, he wished he hadn't said something so obviously flirty. He hadn't known her for very long but he already knew she was not someone to toy with. He could read her pride in the set of her shoulders and the way she stuck her chin out when she suspected someone was taking the piss.

'What does your father do?' Emily asked, clearly trying to regain her equilibrium.

'He left before I was born. At least, we think he left, we've never been sure exactly what happened to him.'

'How awful!' Emily said, opening her eyes wide.

'You don't miss what you have never known,' Scott said, although he knew he was being flippant. He had spent a large part of his childhood wanting a father, even at times believing that he might not have become ill if Peter had stayed. He had thought when he was small that men were imbued with extra strength, the sort that could bend metal and hold disaster at bay. Even now when the wanting had faded and having a father had stopped being the urgent thing it had seemed when he was younger, he was still aware of a gap. It was as if there was a part of himself he had never fully known.

'Does your mother have a boyfriend?' Emily asked.

'No,' he said. 'I'm actually thinking of trying to find her one.'

'Isn't it usually best if people find their own partners?' She was frowning at him as if she was puzzled about something. There was a tiny crease on her forehead like the disturbed skin on cooling custard.

'It's hard to explain, but I don't think she will find anyone for herself,' Scott said. He thought for a moment that he might tell Emily why finding someone for his mother had become so important to him. *She will need all the help that she can get. I've taken so much from her and am going to take still more,* he wanted to say, but he didn't. Sitting with Emily in this café was the most restful he had felt in days and he couldn't resist the way she looked at him as if everything he said was fascinating.

'She's very lonely,' he said. 'Lonely and a bit stubborn and living and working in Alnwick doesn't really present her with a lot of opportunities to meet new people.'

'So how are you going to do it?' she asked. 'Walk around London with a sandwich board?'

'Well, that might work, although it would probably attract the wrong type.'

'You could stand under Eros on Piccadilly Circus with a megaphone,' she suggested and laughed loudly. The proprietor put his head up at the sound, like a dog hearing the scrape of his food bowl, and came over to their table. He rested one hand on Emily's shoulder.

'Can I get you another coffee, Emeeely?' he said. He had taken off his apron and was aggressively slim hipped and tight trousered. *I wish he would keep his hands to himself,* Scott thought furiously and then felt surprised by his own reaction.

65

'You could just sign her up to a dating agency,' Emily said when Casanova had slithered off again.

'The problem is that she will never agree to anything like that. Whatever I do has to be something she doesn't know about and doesn't have to be involved with.'

'I don't see how you are going to be able to pull that off,' Emily said. 'How will you set up the dates?'

They parted company when they got back to college. Emily turned to look at him as she was walking down the corridor and gave him a funny little wave. Halfway through his afternoon lecture he felt his phone go and saw a message from her: *I think I've got an idea for Project Boyfriend . . .*

Chapter 8

IT WAS A BIG DAY AT SWEET DREAMS. IT WAS THE TWENTIETH anniversary of the shop and to celebrate Josie had decided to put on a display of famous beds. She had spent hours in the evenings at home planning it all, knowing as she compulsively filled out spreadsheets that this was a displacement activity designed to stop her dwelling on how empty the house was and how odd and distant Scott had seemed on the phone when she did manage to make contact with him. She couldn't help wondering if there was something the matter with him that he wasn't telling her. She had always known that his heart was unlikely to last forever, but he had been so well over the last few years that she had begun to believe that he was the exception to the rule. Only the other day she had read about a man who had lived for over thirty years with a transplanted heart and medical advances were happening all the time – new drugs, new interventions.

She had sometimes thought that her grip on his life was stronger than his own. It wasn't so much that he didn't immerse himself in living; indeed, she had often wished when he was a child that he wasn't quite as interested in the world around him as he had been. He was always up to his elbows in water and mud and he had stood on that beach guarding Harry through all weathers while she had hovered beside him with blankets and hot drinks, but she could never quite understand the easy way he seemed to take his life and its constrictions. She never saw in him the terror she herself felt at the thought that his life might not be endless. Instead, he seemed only to move from day to day with a kind of light, accepting joy that she found inexplicable. It was only in the way he accumulated facts that she detected what might be interpreted as unease. While other children might have spent the long periods of recuperation after operations watching TV or playing video games, he had used the time to suck up knowledge greedily, as if he knew that he had to make a running start to absorb all there was to know. He had a phenomenal memory and retained everything he heard or read. She used to tease him a little when he came to her and put his hand confidingly on her knee and shared some newly gleaned piece of information about animals or climate change or the fact that water spiralled down the plughole in different directions depending on your position in relation to the equator. He gave out facts as if they were the treats he had to offer. She thought that as he grew older and knew more about his condition he might start to fret about what might happen to him, but he never demonstrated the slightest fear.

'Don't worry,' he had said to her once, when his narrow body was wracked with yet another infection. She had been sitting by him trying not to hear the struggling breath of the little girl in the next bed.

'I'm here,' he said and fell asleep holding her hand.

The showroom was almost ready for its big reveal. Josie had tacked black paper up over the windows to create an air of mystery. The cottage-style single with pine headboard and blue ticking mattress had become Red Riding Hood's Grandmother's bed, complete with a vintage quilt and a life-sized stuffed wolf in a bonnet and glasses. A pile of luxurious, alpaca wool and damask mattresses teetered on a divan base. Josie had sprayed an old football green and inserted it between two of the mattresses to represent the 'Princess and the Pea' story. A dishevelled double littered all around with detritus and swathed in Egyptian cotton sheets was Tracey Emin's bed. A low, white futon with the signs 'Peace Bed' and 'Head Bed' and a duvet patterned with doves passed for John and Yoko's protest love nest and the antique-style four-poster had been draped in red and yellow silk and trimmed with tassels to make a Bed of Ware. Josie hoped the effort she had put in would be worth it. Sales had been sluggish since the autumn and Josie thought her bed tableaux in addition to a 20 per cent price slash would perhaps attract new custom. Initially, George had been all for the idea until Josie had turned down his suggestion of creating a bed with a real-life reclining nude.

'If you want to get noticed, that'll do the trick,' he had said. 'Lie her out in the window, and give her some grapes to eat. Sex sells beds.'

Josie had been firm on the matter despite the fact that it was a nice change to see George so animated; his default position was determinedly morose. She had briefly thought of putting Picasso's Lois in a body stocking – the gig would have been second nature to her, but dismissed the idea quickly. She would have to raise sales without resorting to underhand tactics. With only one delivery that day, Picasso himself had been helping out, adding details and fiddling with covers and sheets.

'I'm pretty certain the Emin bed had a couple of pairs of dirty pants hanging off it,' he said now, standing back to appraise it.

'We are going for an approximate look, rather than an exact replica,' said Josie hastily. 'I don't think used underwear will appeal to our customers.'

'I could mock a pair up with a bit of paint.'

'No it's fine. Let's open the doors,' said Josie to discourage him from further creative in-put.

Waiting outside were a few promising-looking couples, a family with two young children, a middle-aged man in a waxed jacket and Mrs Glenn who worked at the charity shop in the next street and always turned up for openings and sales, even if she never bought anything. It wasn't exactly a rush, Josie thought, but it was a good start.

The children made straight for the piled-up mattresses and started to scale the sides making the whole edifice rock alarmingly. One of the couples lay down on the John and Yoko bed and looked solemnly up at the ceiling as if they were thinking about the impossibility of world peace.

'I wonder if you could help me,' the middle-aged man said. 'I'm looking for a single bed, something comfortable. It's for my mother.'

Josie took him over to the catalogue to show him various options.

'It needs to be one with an adjustable end. She can't sit up by herself, you see.'

Josie noticed the bluish shadows under the man's eyes and the fact that he had missed a patch of hair when he had shaved.

'Is your mother ill?' she asked.

The man nodded and his mouth went small and firm, as if he was trying to keep from saying too much.

'I have to get her something that will fit into her living room. She can't get up the stairs anymore.'

His face moved, as if he had felt a sudden chill, and Josie knew he was on the verge of tears.

'Let's find her something really nice,' she said gently. 'How about this one?' She pointed to a picture.

'It will be her last bed, won't it?' the man said, turning to her as if he thought working in the shop gave her some sort of insight into how long the bed would be needed.

'You never know,' Josie said.

'When we were small, my brothers and me, we used to get into her bed in the morning. There would be a great heap of us, crawling all over her and she would laugh as if she thought it was a great thing to be woken up at the crack of dawn.'

Bed chosen and paid for, Josie watched him leave the shop and walk away down the pavement, his head down, his hands in his pockets, thinking about his long-ago, just-woken mother – the way she had smilingly pulled back the blankets and let them all in to share her musty warmth.

By the end of the day they had sold twenty-three beds, which was a record, even for a Saturday. Although it was dark and there was a chill wind blowing, Josie didn't want to go straight home. She felt a kind of restless, buzzing energy that she knew would be hard to contain once she was in her four walls. She walked past the cinema, but she had seen one of the films and the other didn't start for another hour. It was hard to find company at the spur of the moment. Everything had to be planned in advance. Josie had a lot of friends. You couldn't live in a town the size of Alnwick almost all your life and not know people. But she didn't know anyone she could call now for a drink. They would be moving through their rituals with their evenings all accounted for.

The clothes shop on the high street was still open, and although she had vowed never to grace its doors again as much because of the way the clothes fell apart as its dubious manufacturing practices, she thought going in would delay her return. The opened door released the smell of rubber and cheap cotton and almost as soon as she started walking down the shop's cluttered aisles she regretted coming in. The place made her feel instantly gloomy. She fingered a scarf, a handbag, toyed with the idea that a floridly decorated skirt would do well in the summer, but she didn't really want any of it. She had the sensation, which she had experienced more and more lately, that she was simply eking out time. Children arrived like bomb blasts destroying the life you had before and you spent so much of their childhood wishing they were a year older, one stage further along, thinking that it might be easier then, but it never really was and then they grew old enough to leave and you realised you hadn't made the most of any of it. That you wanted back what had, in so many ways, been so difficult to endure. Parenthood played with your head. It was a twisty, terrible, wonderful thing.

She thought of the man in the bed shop and found that she was perilously close to tears. A young couple, she with black hair to her waist, he thin and undernourished-looking, were holding scrappy dresses up against the woman and looking in the mirror. She was beautiful enough to wear even these unpromising garments and look lovely.

'I think the red one,' the young man said, and his face blazed with love, making him suddenly handsome.

'I think the red one too,' Josie said and then thought: *I am becoming one of those people who start up conversations in shops.* The couple smiled at her shyly, and Josie thought then she might really begin to weep. There on the glaring shop floor, in full view of the line of people behind the till, counting down to seven o'clock.

She stumbled her way out and made for home. There was no putting it off any longer, and, after all, it wasn't so bad. There were some nice duck eggs and peppers and she would make an omelette. She would light a fire, taking time to build a good solid foundation so that the reluctant chimney would draw well, then she would persevere with the tricky cardigan she had started knitting the day before – more of a coatigan, really, which would be useful when the weather turned warmer. Archie would be waiting with his foolish, blind love. It was enough. It was more than many people had.

Chapter 9

'I'M TRYING OUT THE CAMERA ON MY NEW PHONE,' SCOTT told his mother, in what he hoped was a casual voice as they drove to Embleton. He knew she had been surprised when he had turned up in Alnwick the day before without any warning.

'Why are you back again so soon?' she had asked him. 'Is everything all right?' And she had scrutinised his face as if she might find the answer written there.

'I just have a difficult essay and I can't get it done with Danny distracting me,' he had replied and he thought he had reassured her. He knew that she had a tendency to fasten onto what she wanted to hear as a way of allaying her own fears.

'Well, don't try your camera out on me,' his mother said predictably.

'I might or I might not,' he teased her.

She drove at her usual breakneck speed down the narrow roads they both knew so well, tapping impatiently on the steering wheel when the cars ahead slowed at bends or hesitated at junctions. The tangled hedges, the intricate, exposed branches of the trees, the hard grooves of earth and the petrified grass gave the countryside the look of something veined that had been stopped in its tracks. The pulse and sap, which surely must be waiting somewhere, blocked and held back by the cold. An image of Emily blowing on her fingers to warm them up came into Scott's mind; her lips pouted, her breath making white puffs, her eyes wide and glistening.

On the beach the wind was brutal and Archie hampered their progress. Furious at being wrenched from his place in front of the stove, he lagged behind looking peeved and they had to stop every few minutes and call out to him to keep up. The last of the snow lay in stripes between the ridges of sand, looking as if a giant, clawed creature had drawn its paw across the beach, leaving white marks where his talons had penetrated. The sea had taken on a dense, sluggish swell as if it too was in the grip of the cold.

A last-minute gathering of the mad swimmers, as he thought of them, had been convened and he had agreed to go along with his mother. When they arrived at the usual bathing spot, the clan was already gathering, getting ready to attempt the dash into the water. Scott recognised some of the regulars – Eloise, a stringy older lady who wore a black swimming hat and faded coral wetsuit, an ensemble that made her resemble a matchstick, was limbering up with some vigorous jumping exercises that looked as if they had come out of an ancient health manual. Sonia was wriggling around inside her changing tent as if she was fighting something beneath its towelling folds. Roger was smearing his softening pecs with lumps of what looked like beef dripping and rallying the troops with encouraging words. There were a couple of other people whom Scott didn't recognise and he thought they must be more recent conscripts.

'Why do you do this?' asked Scott with genuine bafflement as he trained his phone on his mother.

'It makes me feel alive,' she said smiling, trying to dodge out of sight of the camera.

'Don't you dare film me going in,' she said and she took off her coat to reveal the wetsuit beneath. One of the things he liked most about his mother was the way she was always prepared. A Swiss army knife to slice through picnic cheese, a little first-aid kit in a plastic bag in case of fossil hunting-related accidents, pound coins in a panda-shaped purse for car parks and super-market trolleys and the *Big Issue* seller who could spot her as a soft touch at a hundred yards.

'I don't read it, of course,' she would say, tucking the maga-zine under her arm as if it was a copy of the *Financial Times*, 'but I don't want to discourage the effort put in and Ralph has such speaking eyes.'

Scott thought Ralph should be up for a BAFTA.

He watched his mother and her fellow swimmers cross the beach towards the sea, his camera trained on their tentative, wobbling steps.

'In we go!' Roger shouted as if he was going over the top of a trench. His mother gave a kind of gasp and threw herself in and started swimming frantically, as if she had a finishing line in sight. Scott got up and approached the edge of the water, still filming, and his mother turned over, her neo-preened feet bob-bing in front of her.

'It's wonderful!' she shouted. 'Come on in!' But Scott shook his head and she laughed. Her face was as guileless as a child's.

There's something the matter with him, Josie thought as they sat by the fire. She still felt cold from her swim, despite a mustard footbath and two pairs of socks. He seemed tired and he was behaving oddly. All his usual enthusiasm, his fervent aim to get every second out of every day, seemed to have deserted him and he had barely talked about London and what he had been doing there. She didn't know what all this filming was about either. That was new. He had followed her into the garden when she put the rubbish out, taking pictures of the pebble path she had made, or rather was making, because it was an ongoing project. She had started it years ago – collecting stones when a day had been particularly memorable and marking them with the name of a place or a date with a Sharpie. She kept the stones until there was enough to do another short stretch and placed them in wet concrete in a haphazard path that snaked across the lawn, halfway to the garden gate. Some of the earliest pebbles she had placed there had faded, the writing no longer legible, but she liked the feeling of their bumpiness – a foot memory of high days and holidays. *It's been a while since I've added any new stones*, she thought. He had filmed her making supper – a not particularly successful attempt at a goat's cheese and onion tart that had emerged from the oven blackened around the edges. And then there were all the questions. Up till now, Scott had manifested a healthy disinterest in her thoughts on most subjects, but now he seemed to have developed a mania for quizzing her.

'What's your favourite colour?'

'Tell me a joke.'

'Give me an account of a typical day in the shop.'

'What makes you happy?'

'What do you want from life?' This last question was the hardest to answer, since she had been brooding on the matter herself for the last few weeks.

'What's with all the questions?' she asked at last, exhausted by the interrogation.

'We are looking at how people interact with their environment this term,' Scott answered, but there was something about the quickness of his reply and the way he lowered his head that made her suspicious. When you have a baby, you imagine that you are going to produce a version of yourself, someone you will completely understand because they share the shape of your chin or learn your name before they learn any other, but it wasn't true. It wasn't reproduction, but rather the creation of a whole separate being. Someone who had secrets you would never know and who could sometimes feel like a stranger.

'You *are* all right, aren't you, my darling?' she asked. 'Did the angiogram show any changes?'

'I'm fine, Mum,' he said, and she got up and put her arms around him, expecting him to bat her off as he usually did after the couple of seconds he normally allowed for such an indulgence, but this time he let her hold him. He felt tight, like the skin of a drum, she thought, stroking the back of his neck.

'I think you should find someone to be with,' he said after she had moved into the kitchen and begun washing up. She came back into the room.

'Why do you say that?' she asked, surprised. He looked resolute, almost stern, and her anxiety deepened. There was something about his mouth and eyes that she didn't recognise.

'I think it would be good for you. You're getting very insular.'

She took the word as the condemnation he had surely intended it to be and was suddenly angry. From the perspective of leaving home and living in London Scott now clearly found her wanting. The new, non-insular, out-in-the-world people he had met had caused him to think less of her. He was trying out new words for old ways. *I've given everything to you*, she thought. *I've been glad to. I would do it all again, but it hasn't left space for anything else.*

'I don't mean insular, exactly,' he said, perhaps seeing that he had wounded her, 'just a bit cut off. Wouldn't you like to have someone to share your life with?'

For some reason, perhaps prompted by the feeling of hurt that her son's words had engendered in her, she thought of Peter. From the moment he had pulled her into the alleyway by her parents' house and cupped her chin like he had a palm full of coins, she had loved him. It had all been so long ago and yet she could still feel the sensation of his finger travelling just under the material of her sweater from one side of her throat to the other. She had felt herself curve and become pliable, like plastic left too near a flame.

She remembered the morning she had told him she was pregnant. They had never talked about having children. When she thought back, she couldn't really remember the two of them talking about anything important at all. His easy, desultory manner, the way he always acted as if he was still finding his way, entranced her. He was so different from everything she had known before. Her parents, who had been almost middle-aged when she had been born, had always seemed so firmly shaped, so solidly them, that she had been drawn to his fluidity.

'Don't angst so much,' he used to say whenever she talked about the future and she had accepted this as a kind of rule of their relationship. She chose to celebrate what she told herself was his gift of being able to live in the moment. What a child she had been! She couldn't believe now that she had left something so fundamental to chance. She had known that her news would change everything, but she had hoped that her love for him would make the difference. It's the *idea* of children he hates, she had told herself as she had waited, perched on the sofa in the tiny flat they rented, holding a cushion against her stomach, ready for the big reveal. But he will love this one in particular, because we made it. How could he not? It wasn't until he turned towards her and she saw the blankness in his face that she understood that nothing she could give him would be enough.

For months she refused to believe that he had left her of his own volition and when Scott grew old enough to tell, she had always stuck to that early version of events – that Peter had not left them but rather had come to some sort of harm – something that had prevented his return. She had been so scared and lonely during her pregnancy, charting her baby's progress with fear-filled wonder. She thought now of the way the pain of Scott's birth had consumed her, allowing for no other sensation, the way her feelings for his father had. She had said Peter's name aloud as Scott had finally slipped into the world, caked in vernix, feet marked so deeply with lines that they looked as if they had been scored with a butcher's knife. She thought maybe it had been the very last time she had asked for Peter before a new duty and a new love had replaced the previous pain. She had been exhausted but filled with tenderness that seemed to turn her blood molten. *I know you*, she had thought. *I would know you anywhere.*

'No, I don't feel cut off,' she said now, although only the other day she had felt her new separateness as a kind of marooning. People said that you were always a mother and the worry and the love and the joy continued forever, but she had lost what she had come to rely on. She was no longer needed as she had once been.

'I've always managed very well on my own.' She said the words with a kind of pride and a kind of grief.

'But you don't have to,' he said, exasperated. 'Won't you at least consider the idea?'

'You don't go looking for love,' she said. 'It comes and finds you.'

Scott gave a despairing sigh and poked a finger through the yellow, loose-knitted jumper he was wearing.

'You'll wait forever,' he said and her anger suddenly evaporated. He looked so disconsolate, so like he had as a child when things were not going quite his way. Maybe leaving home had made him worry for her, she thought. She remembered the pity she had often felt for her own mother who had seemed to be so easily satisfied by what Josie had thought of as a meagre, trammelled life. When she had visited her parents and seen the same chicken casserole cooked the same way, the same outings to the same places picked over as if they were something still to wonder at, she had thought it a thin way of living.

'One of my mates at uni has an uncle who's single,' Scott said, all in a rush as if it was something he had been keeping to himself but could no longer contain. 'He sounds really nice and I think he'd be up for meeting you.'

She was astonished. This clearly mattered to him more than she had realised. 'Oh Scott,' she said, 'you can't just set me up with random people.'

'Think about it at least,' he said.

Later, lying in bed listening to the way the branches of the tree scrapped and skittered against the window, she thought of what it might be like to be touched again and to feel the singing spark of something new.

Chapter 10

'WHAT MUSIC ARE YOU GOING TO USE?' EMILY ASKED. SHE had kicked off her slightly worn velvet shoes and was sitting curled up on the malodorous sofa in Scott's living room.

'I'm not sure,' Scott said. 'She likes The Beatles. I thought maybe "Golden Slumbers" and "Carry that Weight", the last tracks on *Abbey Road*. You know that famous bit – *and in the end, the love you take is equal to the love you make.*'

'You can't just use any music you want,' Emily said. 'I don't think The Beatles are going to be that thrilled with you putting it out there without paying, and there's no way you can afford what they would want, even if they agreed to it.'

'So, let them sue me,' Scott said. The chances were that he wouldn't be around to face the repercussions. Some days what was happening to him filled him with a dreadful, obliterating terror, but on other days he managed to push the fear aside, the way you hum against words you don't want to hear. It wasn't as if any of it was really a surprise. He had always understood, the way you understand the dip of the sun in the evening or the absolute redness of blood that he was probably going to die earlier than other people, although lately he had come to realise that there was a big difference between thinking you know something and really feeling it in your bones.

He and Emily had spent all their spare time over the last few days putting the video of his mother together. When she had rung to tell him about her idea to post a film on social media as an advert for a boyfriend for his mother, his first instinct had been to reject the plan. He knew Josie would never agree to such a thing. She wouldn't even bank online because she was worried that there might be a man hunched over his computer somewhere with grasping fingers poised, just waiting for her to allow him access to her overdraft. She most certainly wouldn't contemplate allowing even a part of her life to be made available for anyone who might stumble upon it. And indeed, he did feel a little guilty about exposing her in this way, but he put aside his doubts because he could see that it was a potentially efficient method of getting her dates. In the end it might only attract a few candidates of the hunched-over-a-computer kind who would not be at all suitable as a life partner for his mother, but at least it was worth a shot. After all, he only needed one perfect man to come forward and the job would be done.

The video was almost ready. It wasn't the slickest thing he had ever seen, but it showed Josie as she was, despite the some-what wobbly images that went out of focus more often than not.

'I'm looking for someone for my mother,' the video began. 'Not just anyone, and this is the vitally important part – it has to be someone who is good enough for her, because, although she doesn't know it, she deserves the very best.'

In the film Josie walked down the pebbled path that didn't quite lead as far as the gate, but ended up a few feet short. It showed her lying on her bed in her swimming costume wriggling madly into her wetsuit, clouds of talcum powder in the air. It traced her mad dash into the sea and the distant glow of her face as she bobbed over the waves. There was a section of her giving a detailed and rather excitable description of the fossils she kept in a box under the sofa. He had filmed her cooking her disastrous tart ('No foodies need apply'), sucking the ends of her hair as she watched TV ('Some unappealing habits are inevitable'), an account of her job in the bed shop ('She makes quite dull things, really interesting') and a snatch of Josie singing along to 'The Wind Beneath My Wings' on the radio and getting the words wrong ('It might be better if you are not too much of a muso').

The film ended with Scott's voice, off screen, asking her: 'What do you want from life?' and focusing on her crazily blue eyes and her hair, dark and messy and still tied up on the top of her head as she had worn it during her swim. She thought for a minute, pulling the goofy face she put on when she was a little embarrassed.

'I don't really know,' she said, her eyes swivelling upwards as if she was seeking divine inspiration. 'What does anyone want? To be useful . . . to not let anyone down . . . to be loved and remembered kindly, or, failing all of that, to find a completely perfect fossil of a sea lily.'

'Are you sure she won't see it?' Emily asked, stretching her arms out over her head and yawning. He had grown quickly accustomed to the way she settled herself down in the house as if she belonged there. He found himself looking forward to seeing her and prepared for her arrival by changing his T-shirt and trying to damp down his wild hair. Danny had come in the previous day and found them working together and had raised an eyebrow; a slow, measured lift of one sandy arch, which was an expression Scott knew he had worked long and hard to cultivate.

'Glad to see you've finally pulled,' he had said to Scott later, and although it had been on Scott's lips to deny it, he found to his surprise that he quite liked the thought of her being mistaken for his girlfriend.

'No, she never looks at Facebook or anything like that,' he said now in response to Emily's question.

'How are you going to explain the dates without telling her what you've done?' Emily asked. She had approached the project with a great deal of focus and now that it was almost finished it seemed she was having some last-minute doubts.

'That's going to be the difficult part,' said Scott. 'How can I explain finding a load of available men? It'll be fine if she falls for the first bloke, but that's a bit unlikely and I can't keep saying that they are friends of friends.'

Emily thought for a moment. He noticed that her dark brows exactly matched the colour of her hair. He thought that she looked artful, like a girl in a painting.

'I suppose you can make up a story about how you are doing some research project about single men as part of your course and keep interviewing people she might like. My mum only seems to have the dimmest grasp of what it is I actually do at uni.'

'I'm not sure she'll buy that and, besides, what college student would be in a position to interview people from all over the country? It just doesn't ring true.'

'Then you'll just have to convince her that you have registered her at some sort of dating organisation. If she's as unwilling as you say to find a boyfriend, she might be relieved you are doing all the organisation for her.'

'I don't even know if she will agree to seeing anyone at all,' said Scott, thinking of his mother's set, furious face when he had suggested it. He thought in retrospect he probably hadn't been as diplomatic as he could have been. If he had the luxury of time, he would have been able to approach it all in a more measured fashion, but then, if he had time, he wouldn't ever have thought of it. He was doing it for her. He was sure that she wouldn't be able to bear the burden of what was to come unless she had someone to help her.

'I'll just have to make it up as I go along,' he said. 'The other important thing is to make sure that each of her dates is sworn to secrecy about the video. They'll all have to be told to be very vague about how the date was set up.'

'It's exciting,' said Emily, smiling. 'Can I go through them all with you? I might even find someone *I* like,' she said, looking at him from under her eyelashes.

'Maybe nobody will respond. It might disappear without a trace,' he said and for the next hour or so they fiddled with the soundtrack until the video was as good as it was ever going to be.

'Shall I upload it?' said Scott, hesitating at the last minute and she stretched past him and pressed the key on his computer and the thing was done. He set up a new page on Facebook to link to the video and then invited his friends to like it. He also put the link on Twitter and Instagram.

'We should have champagne,' she said. 'The way you do when you launch a boat.'

*

In the pub, where he bought two glasses of flat champagne for what seemed to him to be an eye-watering amount of money, she sang a karaoke 'Wonder Wall' in a sweet, sarcastic voice. He noticed, without being aware of consciously looking, that her legs were slender and that her bottom lip was redder and fuller than the top one, as if she had been biting it.

'What's happening between you and Marsia?' she asked when she came back to the table, with a slight over-emphasis on the 's' that made him laugh.

'Nothing much,' he answered ruefully. 'I think she likes older men and tutors in particular.'

'She's a fucking idiot, then,' Emily said, looking at his mouth, and for a moment he thought he might kiss her. Her jumper had fallen off her shoulder and her skin was creamy and curved like polished stone. The sudden impulse caught him by surprise. He hadn't been aware of wanting her. It was as if she had curled up alongside him while he had been sleeping. Her eyes were wide and waiting and colour had suffused her face so that she looked suddenly lovely. There was that stillness between them that he recognised as the pause before movement, the static lull that marked the point of a decision. He made what he thought was the right one.

'I think it's time I was getting home,' he said, and she moved back from him sharply as if she had been caught in a misunder-standing.

He walked away from the pub feeling the hard pull of desire. The need for closeness, the drive to hide in someone else, the sheer obliterating pulse of wanting seemed to transcend every-thing, even the failure of his body. The urgency was maybe even stronger than before, like something he grasped for because he knew it was passing. He couldn't tell her what was wrong with him because afterwards she would look at him differently, and then it would be as if he really were dead.

When he got home, Scott was expecting a few random messages, but when he switched on his computer, he was shocked to see that his video had had 120, 056 views and 750 likes.

Chapter 11

DESPITE THE NEW COURSE OF DRUGS HE HAD BEEN GIVEN at his last visit to the hospital, Scott was beginning to find that the energy he woke with most mornings was gone by the afternoon and when he walked fast he was now sometimes aware of a new breathlessness, deeper than he had ever experienced before. There were times when he had to stop and lean against something and gasp for air, as if he had been underwater for too long.

After their drink in the pub, Scott hadn't seen Emily for a couple of days and he thought perhaps she was avoiding him because she had been hurt by his abrupt withdrawal from her, but then she had texted him, the ping of his phone in the lecture hall drawing the gimlet eye of Professor Langley. Scott was carrying on as usual with his course, turning up dutifully for all his seminars and handing his essays in on time. He didn't know what else he could or should do. Although there were desperate days when he thought it was unlikely that he would be able to carry on much longer, he wasn't ready, yet, to relinquish the hope that he would have enough time to graduate and maybe even to work. Danny, who was making his way drearily and unwillingly through the stuff of proof and precedent, teased him about his ambitions to save the world.

'Get real, man,' he had said only the other day when Scott had mentioned something about global warming. 'The genie is out of the very big, industrial-sized bottle.'

Scott only knew that he wanted to make some sort of a difference, although he himself winced at the unrigorous, shapeless nature of his ambition. He had seen pictures of the emptied bellies of whales; their organs twisted round with entrails of plastic and footage of hermit crabs which, failing to find new shells to inhabit, had crawled instead into discarded bottle tops and aerosol canisters, and he had condemned the carelessness of the human race. And yet he wasn't free of the impulse to open a window and throw out what he no longer needed although he restrained himself from doing so and he desired the next new gadget with as much greed as anyone else. He also thought there was something mind numbingly wearisome about people who held forth about all the ways that human beings were failing, but nevertheless he felt that if he could save just one thing, it would mean that his life had mattered. There was so much still to learn. There were places in the ocean so deep that they hadn't ever been properly explored. It was possible that the organisms that populated this unmeasured, lightless domain might provide solutions to many of the world's ills. With a fervour that he found difficult to articulate, he wanted his small part in making something safe – a hand in ensuring that dolphins would keep breaching and the air would always be worth breathing and that summer would forever hold its special character, distinct from winter.

Your video is trending! Emily's text had said. *Any likely candidates? Need any help going through them? I'm thinking you might need a woman's opinion.*

He had never expected the video to be so popular, but it appeared to have touched a collective nerve. He felt a sense of pride that his mother had attracted so much attention, and then, just as quickly, was anxious that he was doing it all behind her back. The numbers were overwhelming. Little did she know that thousands of people had seen her wriggling into a wetsuit and baking a scorched tart and sucking the ends of her hair. The film had had more views than Emma Thompson being sprayed with manure in a fracking field and a toddler in a hat with pig's ears singing, 'Show me the way to go home'.

He had logged onto the Facebook page and discovered hundreds of messages waiting for him. The first few names were familiar:

Hello Scott. What you doing? Does your mum know about this? Seems a bit desperate, mate, if I'm honest. Hope you're well otherwise. Matt

Scotty Boy, Somewhat weird, but I'll share. Let's have a drink next time you're back? P. H.

If I were twenty years older, I'd be in there. Always did fancy your mum. Consider it disseminated. BTW did I leave a leather jacket at your house? Travis

But there were many others from strangers. There were messages from the inevitable nutters who claimed they had met his mother in a previous life or who said they would be praying for her soul. One respondent who had posted five messages seemed absolutely fixated on the quality of his mother's stools, asking that a photograph of a sample be sent to him for 'visual analysis'. There were a number of sad stories about love found and lost or never found at all. There were people who said they were lonely and some who pretended they were not. There were men who laid themselves bare (some literally) and others who were all bluster. Some talked about their hearts and others talked in numbers – their bank balances, the girth of their muscles, the number of times they had won medals or been promoted or climbed Mount Kilimanjaro.

Many of the respondents had ignored his age stipulation – there were several from boys not much older than he was, which made Scott feel nauseous, and an even greater number from men who were clearly looking for someone to nurse them through their last days. There were also a lot of messages from women, even though Scott had made it clear it was a man he was looking for. There were messages offering companionship, cooking classes, tips on where to find the best fossils, mortgage advice, stair lifts and funeral arrangements (she wouldn't like those!) and at least ten outright marriage proposals. One individual with protuberant ears had taken a selfie on what appeared to be the edge of a cliff, holding out an engagement ring and another had sent a picture of himself, dressed in a sheet fastened on one shoulder like a toga, playing the harp with the caption: *Marry me and let's make sweet music together.*

Thanks, I could do with some help, Scott texted Emily back, knowing that what he should really do was ignore her message or reply saying something polite but discouraging, but he found that he wanted to share the reaction to the video with her and see what she made of some of the stranger respondents. He had grown accustomed to her sly sense of humour and the way she always said what she thought. He told himself that there was no reason why they shouldn't see each other as long as he didn't dwell on the sheen of her skin or the way she had of tracing the outline of her top lip with her finger when she was thinking. He would be clear with her that all he wanted was friendship and then he couldn't be accused of encouraging her. It wouldn't be fair to let her love him.

His doorbell went and when he opened it, Emily was standing there dressed in a brown coat and a red scarf, her eyes bright. She held up a bottle of rum.

'Thinking juice!' she announced.

'You look just like a robin,' he said, feeling an almost ungovernable desire to touch her. He put his hands in his pockets.

'Let's have a look at all the loons,' Emily said, sitting down cross-legged on the floor and pulling his computer towards her.

'I think the best approach is to make a spreadsheet. You'll never keep track of them all otherwise,' she said, pouring hefty slugs of rum into two mugs. Emily took great pride in her efficiency. She approached every task with a meticulous eye. In her immaculate room there was just her computer and a sewing machine and a tightly made-up bed. Only in the rack of clothes was there a hint of her exuberance – lace and sequins vied for space amongst the mannish suits and velvet robes.

'I like to keep track of everything,' she said. 'Otherwise things get lost.'

They scrolled through the replies with Emily letting out the occasional outraged snort when they came upon a particularly choice message.

'This one says he plays table tennis in the nude!' she said. 'Agh, he looks as if he's never seen the light of day.'

They laughed unkindly at the man's head which was as round as a ping-pong bat and the way he stood with his arms tightly held to his body as if he was about to start marching.

They eliminated the aged, the infirm and the pre-pubescent, the fourteen men who were wearing cargo shorts and the twenty-three with band T-shirts on. Then they narrowed the search down to those who appeared sane, had spelled everything correctly and were not too weird-looking.

'That still leaves us with three hundred and fifteen possibles,' said Emily, who was flushed with rum and the thrill of the chase. 'And they're still coming.'

'Who knew there were so many lonely people out there,' he said.

Emily stopped her perusal of the computer and turned to look at him. 'I sometimes think you seem a bit lonely.'

'Do I?' Scott said, uneasy that the conversation had suddenly taken a personal turn.

'That night at the fancy-dress party when you were standing outside, I was watching you a bit before I spoke to you. You looked as if you thought you were the only person left in the world.'

'I didn't realise you had been spying on me,' he said, trying to avoid her gaze.

'I wasn't spying, just looking.' Her shoulders went high and she gave him that slightly imperious look he remembered from before.

'It feels to me as if you are holding something back,' she said.

'I'm just a typical, uncommunicative bloke.' He tried to speak lightly, although he felt as if something was catching in his throat.

'I don't live with my parents in the house I told you about,' she said in a rush. 'I was lying about it all. The vegetable patch and the swing and the three other siblings and all the rest of it.' She looked at him as if she was waiting for his condemnation.

'Where do you live, then?' he asked.

'I lived with my grandmother until I left for college,' she said. 'Three streets down from where my mum lives. I don't even have a dad. That was all crap about me gardening with him.'

'Why don't you live with your mother?' Scott asked, wondering about her absent father but not wanting to push more information out of her than she was willing to give. He knew what it was like to have to explain a parent away.

'I was told when I was eight that I couldn't live with her anymore,' Emily said. 'She collects things. Lots of things. It was fine at first. I mean, she has always had a lot of stuff, but you could still move around when I was little, but then it became impossible. She filled each room up until only my room was left and a little corridor down the stairs and one side of the hallway. She can't help it. When she started putting things in my room too, they said it wasn't safe for me. It was a fire risk and that, anyway, it wasn't healthy trying to live in such cramped quarters. She filled the bath with magazines. My grandmother said I could live with her.'

'That must have been awful,' Scott said, seeing the pain and love in Emily's face. He wanted to put his arms around her.

'I could never have anyone back for tea. I felt so ashamed. That was the worst of it; feeling ashamed of her. She's lovely. Really she is, but no one seems to be able to stop her.'

'What does she collect?' he asked.

'Multiples of everything,' said Emily. 'She never buys one of anything. That's the root of the problem. It makes her feel safer if she has spares.'

'Do you see her?' Scott asked.

'Yes. When I'm back, I spend time with her, although I still sleep at my grandmother's house. My old bed is covered with shoes, almost as high as the ceiling. Heels and trainers and sandals, all brand new. She never wears any of them because she doesn't really go out anymore. Gran brings the shopping in for her and she orders other stuff online.'

'How old's your grandmother?' Scott asked.

'That's the thing. She's nearly seventy-nine now and she finds it a struggle. I don't know what will happen to my mother when she dies.'

'I don't know how you turned out so perfect,' he said and then immediately wished he hadn't said the words out loud. He thought he had only been thinking them. She smiled at him and he could see the colour climbing up her neck like the spread of an opening flower.

'I knew my mother loved me,' she said. 'It was a difficult, funny-shaped love, but it was love all the same.'

This is when I should tell her, Scott thought. *I've only been in her life for a couple of months. She will get over it.*

But he couldn't find the words. He didn't know how to begin.

He felt a keening sense of loss. *My heart might stop now, this minute*, he thought. There would be no sign, no acute pain of the sort depicted in films and on TV when middle-aged men clutched at their chests and sank sweating to the floor. His enervated heart had no early warning system. When it came it would be all of a sudden like a light being extinguished. He took a reckless mouthful of rum.

'I think we should get on with this,' he said, and obediently she turned back to the job.

A couple of hours later, after selecting from the possibles those who said they were solvent and had a vague resemblance to Hugh Jackman, or at least had some dark hair and a chin, they had five names. They had had a few disagreements about who to include in the shortlist – Emily seemed to have a weakness for men with sideburns and a poetic bent and she hated a couple of his more outdoorsy choices ('I can't stand men who look like they take a disproportionate amount of pride in how much ground they have covered,' she said inexplicably). Five candidates didn't seem a lot, considering how many replies there had been, but Scott reasoned that they would do as an initial batch of dates. He was unlikely to strike gold immediately.

'Go on, make the call,' Emily said.

He took a deep breath and contacted the first person on his shortlist, a man called Clive Berriman who looked quite athletic in his picture and was wearing a standard-issue fleece and jeans and an open smile. Scott had hesitated a while at his pose – one foot up on a rock, which looked a bit unnecessary and made him seem like a show-off, but he had to allow for some weaknesses or he would have nobody at all for his mother to meet. Clive was forty-three and worked as an architect. He said he had never been married, although there had been a couple of 'near misses'. He said he thought Josie was 'his type' and that he was a 'legs man', which made Scott shudder a little but he told himself to get over it. Nobody, after all, was perfect and wasn't he himself, a self-confessed bosom fan? Although he thought it unlikely that he would lead with this disclosure if he was applying to be considered for a date. On the plus side, Clive lived in Newcastle, which wasn't far away.

After their brief conversation Scott messaged him telling him about the stipulation that he should on no account mention the video and suggesting a Sunday afternoon a week away. He also said he would let him know more details nearer the time. The reply came almost straightaway – *Great! I'm chuffed you chose me. Looking forward to spending time with your beautiful mother*, which Scott reckoned to be on just about the right side of effusive.

'Now all I've got to do is persuade Mum that meeting up with him is a good idea,' Scott said.

Later, after Emily had gone, Scott rang his mother. She answered her phone almost instantly.

'Hello, what's up?' she asked as if she was expecting bad news.

'Nothing much, everything's fine,' he answered. 'What are you doing?'

'Just sold a Victorian-style bed with bolster cushions to an assertive American lady who said she wanted it for her dogs. Other than that, I'm trying not to watch George eating a Pukka Pie with his fingers,' Josie replied.

Scott laughed. 'Exciting times,' he said. 'How's Picasso?'

He knew he was prevaricating but he couldn't yet work out exactly how to explain to his mother that he had set up a date for her with a stranger, even if that stranger could be Hugh Jackman's second cousin, if you squinted a bit.

'Lois is claiming to have ME, which is terrible if it's true, but I suspect she has confused the condition with terminal laziness,' Josie said.

'Picasso is now working two jobs to keep her in watermelon juice and flax seed.'

'He should find someone better,' Scott said, and then he took a deep breath. 'Which brings me on to the reason I phoned you,' he said. He was nervous and so he spoke quickly so that she wouldn't have the chance to interrupt.

'I don't want you to over react, but do you remember that conversation we had about you perhaps dating someone? Well, I've really been thinking about it. It seems to me that you could start out low key. Not expect anything much. On either side, I mean. Just a sort of friendly thing. So . . . I've set you up on a blind date with that man I mentioned to you before.'

There was a silence at the other end of the phone.

'Hello, Mum, are you still there?' Scott asked.

'Say what you just said again,' Josie replied.

Scott panicked at the ominous tone of his mother's voice and rushed to explain.

'I really want you to be happy. I know you say you don't want or need anyone, but it seems to me that you are pretty lonely. I'll only pick people that I think are really, really nice. You don't ever have to see them again if you don't want to.'

'I'm so angry with you I can hardly speak,' Josie said.

'I hope you don't mind but I've set up the first date for next Sunday.'

'Well, you can bloody well unset it,' Josie said, and rang off. Scott stared at his phone. His mother had never cut short a conversation before, even when he had been at the height of his teenage rebellion. He would phone her back when she had cooled down. Perhaps he hadn't explained it to her properly. There must be some way to make her understand that what he was proposing was a good idea. She was never going to meet anyone in Alnwick.

Chapter 12

Hello Scott

Great video! Your mother is beautiful (I'm a legs man) and I would like a date with her. I'm unattached, solvent and have many interests. My friends are always trying to pair me off with people but I have never met anyone perfect. I've had a couple of near misses but after the first bloom has worn off, I usually find that there is something about them to dislike – the way they laugh or the fact they drink cider or talk too much when I'm driving. Maybe Josie will be different.

Clive Berriman

Josie had taken Freya's latest bit of unsolicited advice to 'do something with your dreadful hair' and was lying in the salon with her neck jammed up against the rinsing sink. It had been a while since she had done anything other than trim her fringe with the scissors on her Swiss army knife and the stylist had picked through her ragged tresses with a faint air of astonishment.

'We'll take care of those stray greys and give you a few layers. Get rid of some of the thickness at the top,' she had said in a tone of voice usually reserved for the very old, which both annoyed

Josie and made her want to laugh. If she was really as confident as she pretended to be she would go on her blind date – scheduled to take place that afternoon at Alnwick Gardens – with thick, greying hair intact, but she had bowed to convention. She only hoped she would not end up looking like the stylist whose own hair was so rigid it was as if she had dunked her head into a fast-chill cabinet. Freya had also been to blame for Josie's change of heart about Scott's plan to set her up with this friend of a friend of his. She hadn't been able to establish exactly how or when the arrangement had been made.

'You should listen to him,' Freya had said between mouthfuls of chunky Kit Kat. 'I'm not saying that you can't live without a man, God knows, I loved my Chuck very much but, between the two of us, he couldn't find his way out of a paper bag; it's just that having someone to love makes you better than you might have been. You become someone special through their eyes. Special. Yup.'

Josie had been astonished by the old woman's words. It was by far the most emphatic speech she had ever made and, still taken up by the surprise of it, she had phoned Scott back.

'I'll do it if I must,' she had said. He had been pleased. She had heard it in his voice. She still couldn't fathom why it meant so much to him.

As Josie gazed up at the ceiling trying to ignore the cramp in her neck and look as if she was enjoying the rather weird and perfunctory way the stylist was now massaging her temples with sharp fingers, she thought of Scott's first visit to the barber, made when he had been about six years old. Until then, he too had been a victim of her penknife and she had occasionally trimmed his almost white curls just to keep them in check. She had loved the abundance of his hair and the way it flew around his face when he was running. It had been he who had instigated the haircut, perhaps because someone had said he looked girlish, she couldn't remember now, and so she had taken him and sat and watched as his hair had fallen in pale half-circles all over the linoleum floor. From behind she had seen his new shape emerging – the transformation from baby to boy and his face in the mirror solemnly assessing this change for himself. He looked cleaner, sharper edged, as if his puppy fat had been sheared away along with his curls. When the barber had finished, he showed Scott the back of his head with a hand-held mirror and Scott had nodded and made a strangely adult movement, smoothing down the hair over his ears with his fingers. It was this gesture that Josie had found heartbreaking at the time because it implied a self-awareness he had never demonstrated before.

At home, she changed into the dark green shirtdress and boots that she had purchased hastily after her session in the salon, catching sight of her highlighted hair in department store mirrors as she passed from stand to stand, worrying that perhaps the artfully tousled look she had emerged with was just a shade too bright, too young. She wondered what the man she was to meet would be like. She had been furnished with just the barest details – his name, age, profession and the fact that he lived in Newcastle. She supposed all children wanted their parents to be happy; it lessened the burden to feel that they were not the only repositories of affection. She had been glad that her own parents, now dead, had had each other. Theirs had been a fortuitous marriage because it was unlikely that anyone else would have taken either of them on. Their relationship was forged in rings of steel by a mutual dislike of almost everything but car-boot sales, canasta and Jamie Oliver, who they had worshipped with a fervour that was akin to religious faith.

Her date was sitting reading the paper when she walked in. Even if she hadn't arranged to meet him at a particular spot in the Alnwick Gardens café she would have recognised him straightaway. His perusal of the paper was a little too intent. He raised his head when she approached and she was pleasantly surprised by his handsomeness. It was of the conventional, firm-chinned variety and his eyes were a puppyish, conker brown.

'You've had your hair done!' he said and then stopped, embarrassed, as if he had caught himself saying something wrong. 'I can tell it's fresh from the salon.'

He got to his feet and held out his hand. 'It's perhaps a bit early for kisses,' he said. 'I'm Clive Berriman.'

His grip was firm, and Josie took a surreptitious look at his feet. She had a tendency to use men's footwear as an indicator of character. She was relieved to see neither cowboy boots nor the pointed shoes she so disliked. He was wearing reassuring brogue-style boots with a bit of wear to them. It was one thing her buying new boots for the date, but there would have been something a little desperate if he had done the same. *I'm sexist in all sorts of ways I never imagined*, she thought.

'Shall we have a walk around?' she asked.

At this time of year the garden was a pared-back version of itself, with arches and pathways only just beginning to soften into spring. They walked up the steps alongside the elaborate, snaking fountain, which was still until they reached the halfway point and then sprang suddenly into splashing life, causing her companion to jump slightly. Josie laughed at his expression.

'I didn't expect it to be working,' he said, seeming slightly put out by her laughter.

'It always takes people who haven't been here before by surprise,' Josie said to make up for laughing at him.

'I hear there's a poison garden here. Can we go and see it?' he said in response and she got the impression that he was keen to seem back in charge after his momentary lapse in confidence.

They went through the scull-and-cross-boned gate into the enclosed garden where a woman was already showing round a small group of chilly-looking people.

'This is, of course, not the best time of year to see the garden as so many of the plants are still dormant,' the guide said. She was tiny and wore an oversized anorak and had a red-tipped nose that she rubbed repeatedly with a tissue.

'This is the Strychnine tree,' she said. 'Its Latin name is *Strychnos nux-vomica*, which gives you a bit of a clue about the poisonous effects of the seeds inside its fruit. It attacks the nervous system and can be fatal, but in small quantities it is used to treat heart disorders, depression, migraine and symptoms of the menopause.'

'Convenient substance for men to use to bump off their middle-aged wives, then. Tell them it will cure their hot flushes,' Clive remarked in a voice loud enough to cut through the guide's narrative. Josie laughed a little because she felt the situation demanded it but she didn't find the comment particularly funny. The guide looked at Clive and smiled politely and then soldiered on.

'If I pull back this protective sheeting, you can see a *Ricinus communis* shrub, which you might know as the castor-oil plant. When it flowers it produces seeds that are very toxic. Four seeds can kill an adult, although it appears ducks are relatively immune, needing to ingest at least eighty seeds in order to feel an affect!' The woman dabbed at her nose again.

'Our guide looks as if she could do with being put out of her misery. I suggest hemlock,' Clive said in a carrying undertone and this time Josie felt embarrassed and couldn't even summon up the smile she knew he was expecting from her.

By the time they had inspected the laburnum tree and had heard about the damage it was possible to inflict with foxgloves, belladonna and aquilegia, a narrative that was punctuated by Clive's witticisms, Josie had had enough and steered him out of the enclosure. She thought perhaps his loquacity was due to a lack of confidence. It was easy to forget when you were nervous yourself, that the other person could feel the same.

'Well, that was interesting,' Clive said. 'I like to learn something new every day. I'm a very curious person.'

They walked along the upper portion of the garden, which was littered with water sculptures, which gushed against steel and marble. It was refreshing in the summer months to feel the spray and watch the children standing squealing underneath the water, but now their icy spurts made Josie shiver.

'Are you cold?' Clive said, noticing the shudder that had gone through her. 'I'm wearing an exact replica of the jumper

Shackleton wore on his expeditions. I could roll in snow and not feel a thing.'

'Shall we go to the Treehouse Restaurant and get something to eat? It's just over there,' Josie said. She thought that its quirky wooden structure and wobbling pathways would appeal and, indeed, Clive was enraptured by it; so much so that he insisted in taking several photographs of joists and edging, while she stood shivering outside. *There's nothing wrong with him*, she thought as she watched him crouch outside the building examining the cladding; he was certainly handsome – just the physical type she was attracted to – long legged and sturdy-looking and his conversation was lively and interesting. Perhaps her inability to warm to him was due to the fact that she was out of practice. Once they got inside and sat down by the fire, it would surely be easier.

Josie had been to the restaurant before but it always made her smile – with its twinkling lights and higgledy-piggledy windows, it was like an illustration from a children's storybook; you could almost imagine that you might be served your food by an outsized woodland creature in a felt waistcoat.

'Mmm. Swedish sauna meets Squirrel Nutkin,' Clive remarked, as they were led to their roughly hewn table. 'Be careful not to get a splinter,' he said, looking roguishly at the waitress.

Oh my God, Josie thought, *it wasn't just that I was chilly or that it's been years since I last went on a date, I'm trapped in a tree house with an idiot.*

Good manners and the thought that Scott would think she hadn't given the date her best shot got Josie through her stuffed chicken breast and half a bottle of red wine.

'What do you want from life? Are there things you still want to do?' she asked him as they drank their coffees. He looked at her. *He really does have the most beautiful eyes*, Josie thought. *Perhaps I should just sleep with him.*

'I want to build something I'm proud of,' he said, which Josie considered a fair enough answer from an architect.

'You can't argue with a really fine building. It's the people cluttering them up that are the problem.'

And there it was – the final nail in the tree-house wall. It didn't matter about his brown eyes and the fact that his arms, exposed now that he had shucked off the Shackleton, were muscled in just the right way; she just didn't like him. Despite the warmth of the room and the effects of the wine, the man was as cold as ice.

'Shall we get the bill?' he asked. 'This is on me.' And without waiting for her answer, he summoned their waitress.

'I find you very attractive,' he said, leaning towards her after he had dispatched the waitress with a wink and his credit card.

'I'd very much like to see you again,' he said, and she could tell that he thought it was a foregone conclusion that she would want the same.

'I don't think we are suited,' Josie said. There wasn't any point prolonging the agony. 'I've had a lovely time and thank you for lunch, but I don't think I'm what you're looking for.'

'How do you know what I'm looking for?' he asked and she could tell he was shocked, although he hid it by getting up hastily, leaving an ostentatiously large tip and signalling for his coat.

'I think you want someone more self-sufficient than I am,' Josie said as they left, feeling suddenly sorry for him. He seemed diminished somehow, despite his explorer jumper and all his talk, and she wanted to give him an out. He'd come all the way from Newcastle and bought her lunch; it was the least she could do.

'I like independent women,' he said. 'I think you might prove to be a little needy.' He said the words with a look of distaste.

'Perhaps you're right,' she said, and they parted company at the entrance to the gardens. She watched him walk quickly down the street as if he was hastening away from the scene of a crime.

Chapter 13

Hello Scott
   #Iwantadate #crazythingspeopledoforlove #turquoiseeyes
#amwriting.

'I'd love to come with you,' Scott said, thinking how much he liked Emily's voice on the phone – it was as precise and neat as the rest of her. He didn't know why he had ever thought her plain. She was perfectly and completely herself.

'Oh I'm so glad!' said Emily sounding surprised, as if she hadn't really expected him to accept her invitation to come home with her to see her mother. 'It'll be a bit boring, mind,' she added, clearly anxious that he wouldn't have any great expectations of the visit.

'We'll have to stay the night with my nan. She talks a bit and she'll make you eat fairly gross stuff. And I've told you about my mum . . . well, it is a bit . . . disconcerting at her house.' For the first time, Emily sounded a bit unsure, as if she was regretting the idea.

'Are you trying to put me off?' Scott asked, finding that he really hoped she wasn't. The thought of being able to be near her for a whole day made him feel suddenly happy.

'No,' Emily said. 'I'm just emphasising to you that it might not be the most glamorous night away ever.'

'It's all right, Emily. I'll come.'

'OK then,' said Emily, turning brisk. 'I'll see you at King's Cross Station.'

She was standing outside the Harry Potter shop where a long queue of Chinese people were waiting to have their picture taken with half a trolley. She had a tiny rucksack at her feet and was wearing a dark hat with a narrow brim. She smiled widely when she caught sight of him and waved.

'I wasn't sure you would turn up,' she said. 'Let's get tickets quickly. There's a train in fifteen minutes.'

'Why did you invite me to come with you?' Scott asked when they were settled on the train. He could feel her thigh against his own, and could smell whatever it was that she wore as perfume – something sweet, like jasmine. She took off her hat and ran her fingers through her hair.

'I wanted you to know about me,' she said simply, and then she looked out of the window as if she was a little embarrassed by her words. Scott felt a constriction in his throat. She was so lovely he barely knew what to do with himself. *I want to kiss her. I want to kiss her. I can't kiss her.* He wondered that he could feel such terrible pain and still remain sitting upright. *I can't go on. I can't go on. I'll go on.* The train passed through the outskirts of the city and then the landscape opened out into fields that had just begun to green. The colour was so slight and tentative that it seemed to hang like a mist over the ground. *It all carries on regardless*, Scott thought. The earth turns, the plants begin their blind, oblivious pushing out, but he was no longer part of the cycle. He had been shunted off the track.

'I've brought food,' Emily said, unzipping her suitcase and pulling out two foil-wrapped parcels.

'And what meal is this exactly?' Scott asked in a teasing voice.

'I always eat on trains. It doesn't matter what time of day it is,' Emily said and passed him a thickly sliced beef and horseradish sandwich.

'I thought we should see my mum first and then go to my grandmother's house afterwards,' she said.

'I'm happy to do whatever you want.'

'I might just take you up on that,' she said smiling. She balled up her foil and threw it gently at him.

Cambridge station was in the process of being renovated and the pewter-coloured sky was lanced with red cranes. Weary taxi drivers and parents in Land Rovers picking up school children from the station sounded their horns and gesticulated at each other. Scott had the sense, as he often did when he was with Emily, of being in a foreign country. Her presence made things seem exotic and interesting and even a dusty building site seemed to take on a special allure. The bus to Stapleford came almost immediately.

'It's twenty-two stops,' Emily informed him, putting her rucksack on her lap and pointing out various landmarks as the bus lurched on.

'That's the botanical gardens. People queued there for three days to see a rank, flesh-eating plant produce its only flower in ten years.'

'Not that much happens in this town, then,' Scott commented, which made her laugh.

The bus passed terraced houses with well-painted front doors and bucket bikes stationed on gravel forecourts and then went onwards through Great Shelford and through some almost-countryside into Stapleford. They disembarked by a flinty church.

Scott could sense that she was becoming nervous because she kept up a steady stream of chat as they walked through the village. They stopped outside a nondescript, thirties terrace and Emily took a deep breath before she knocked on the door and then, after hesitating a moment, put her key into the lock.

'It's difficult for her to get to the door,' Emily explained, and when they had inserted themselves into the house, Scott could see why. The hallway consisted of a narrow passageway through towering piles of books and games and newspapers that were stacked up against both walls as high as the ceiling. Emily pushed against another door that seemed resistant to being opened.

'Hello, Mum, we're here,' Emily announced and Scott heard her mother's voice greeting them before he actually saw her. He was so distracted by the scale of the pile of stuff in the centre of the front room that at first he couldn't even make out where she was sitting. The curtains were drawn and the only light came from a standard lamp that was teetering on top of a pile of books.

'This is my mother Brenda. Mum, this is Scott,' Emily said.

Brenda got to her feet from the sofa and Scott followed Emily's nimble dance across the floor, which navigated the piles of clothes, cushions and boxes via a slender stretch of carpet. Scott's first impression was not at all what he had been expecting. He had imagined Emily's mother as someone stooped beneath the burden of her possessions, but she was dressed in a vibrant red dress and she had an animated expression. He could see Emily in her pointed chin and slight build and the way she moved her hands. She hugged Emily tightly and extended her hand to Scott.

'I'm very glad to meet you,' she said. 'I hope that Emily has warned you sufficiently about the state of my house.'

Scott didn't quite know how to respond. Saying that he had been told what to expect seemed a bit rude, and Brenda laughed at his visible confusion.

'It's OK. I can imagine what she told you,' Brenda said. 'I've prepared drinks,' she added, conjuring up from behind the sofa a tray on which there was a jug of some sort of juice and three glasses.

'So Emily, my darling, is this handsome young man a boy-friend or just a friend?' She laughed again when they both said 'friend' at exactly the same time.

'How are you getting on in London, Em? Is it wonderful? Are you learning a lot?'

Emily talked about her course and her tutors and some paintings she had seen at the National Gallery and Brenda listened with keen attention. Emily had squeezed herself onto the sofa next to her mother, leaving Scott the only other seat, which was a piano footstool crammed into the corner of the room. He was struck by how different Emily was with her mother. All her crisp briskness was gone and in its place was a gentleness that he had never seen before. At one point she took her mother's hand and held on to it. He wondered what it must have been like to be a child in this muffled house with its piles of never used spares; things one on top of the other, marking the layers of passing time.

'It was as if I couldn't ever quite reach her,' Emily had said on the bus. 'There was always too much in the way.'

Brenda must have noticed Scott looking around the room, because suddenly she announced: 'I'm going to have a clear-out soon. I've been going through my things and have decided I am going to be ruthless. I'm going to hire a skip.'

Emily smiled at her mother and said, 'That sounds like a plan.' But Scott could tell that she had heard these words or similar ones many times before.

'It would be wonderful if you would come and visit me in London,' Emily said. 'I can take you to the museums or perhaps a West End show.' But her voice lacked conviction.

'I'd love that,' Brenda said. 'Perhaps I will one day.' But she said it as if a train ride to London was like a journey to a distant land and then, glancing down, she noticed that Emily's ballet pumps were a little worn and she got to her feet.

'I've got a pair exactly like that. Brand new. Now if I could just remember where they are . . .'

'I've got loads of shoes,' said Emily trying to forestall her, but Brenda had embarked on a mission. They could hear her upstairs, dragging things across the floor, the sound of hard objects falling.

'She won't be able to find them and she'll get upset,' said Emily in a despairing tone of voice.

They waited for fifteen minutes, and then Emily said: 'I think we'd better go.'

They went upstairs to say goodbye. Scott could hear her telling her mother to stop looking and then the sound of Brenda wailing for her to stay for just a little while longer until she found the shoes.

'They are red; just like the ones you are wearing. I bought them years ago. I thought you might need them one day. No, don't touch that pile. You'll muddle everything up.'

Then he heard Emily's voice sounding as if she was talking to a child: 'It doesn't matter, Mum. It really doesn't matter.'

Emily's grandmother Lorna's house was like a skeleton version of her daughter's; it contained only the absolute basics. A plump and breathless woman, she greeted Scott with enthusiasm and then she and Emily went almost immediately into what Scott recognised as an often-repeated routine.

'She seems worse than ever,' Emily said.

'I've tried. Believe me, I've tried. There's no help for it,' Lorna said. 'She's burying herself alive.'

As predicted, supper at Lorna's was an endurance test. Scott waded with resolution through a mountain of cabbage and grey mince but was relieved when Emily said they would skip dessert and go to the pub instead.

'It's not like you to be off your food,' Lorna said, waving at them from the door and looking up into the darkening sky as if she was expecting an alien landing rather than the rain that was forecast.

As they stepped outside it began to drizzle, lightly at first or they might have been tempted to retreat back to the house, but only a short way further down the road it began to come down in earnest. Scott and Emily were almost instantly soaked to the skin. Emily grabbed hold of Scott's hand as they ran and pulled him through the gate and into the church portico.

'I'm freezing,' Emily said, shivering in her thin coat.

Scott put his arms around her and held her. She felt hot, almost feverish, and he could see the parting in her hair, white and clean like the central marking on a road. She raised her head and looked at him.

He kissed her.

He couldn't help himself. She fitted against him as if she was supposed to be there. Her lips were soft and open. She made a sound deep in the back of her throat. *I would be safe if I stayed here forever*, he thought. *Nobody could die while they were kissing like this, feeling the heat and rush, lost to everything else.* He unbuttoned her coat and then the front of her dress and put his hand on her skin, feeling her tremble under his touch.

Chapter 14

Dear Scott
  I'm not anyone's idea of love's young dream, but I know I have a lot to give someone who is prepared to let me love them. I don't suppose I'll make the shortlist but nothing ventured, nothing gained.
  Christopher

This time, she wasn't going to bother too much about her hair or her clothes, Josie decided. If this latest man didn't like what he saw, then he could just lump it and, after all, in the unlikely event that he was going to turn out to be the love of her life, he would have to get used to her low-maintenance status. After her date with Clive she had rung Scott to tell him she didn't want to meet anyone else, but he had sounded so crushed that she had capitulated. Her second date had been selected from some sort of an agency. Scott had been evasive when she had asked him for details.

'I'm handling it all,' he had said, 'there's nothing for you to worry about,' which did nothing to settle her anxiety. 'He's called Christopher Darkling. He sounds fun. He flies kites and has a boat moored on the Thames. I'm not sure exactly what he does for work. He said something about pest control. But I expect he's pretty high up . . . I don't think he's an actual rat catcher,' Scott had added, but he didn't sound very confident.

'Nothing wrong with rat catchers,' Josie had said stoutly, not wanting him to think her a snob. 'It's an absolutely essential service.' Although she did briefly hope that her date had washed his hands well before they broke bread together.

Remember what you were telling yourself about wasting your life, she thought as she locked up the shop and set out for the restaurant where she was to meet him. Scott was right. She owed it to herself to make an effort.

By the time she got to the bistro, Josie's resolve had faltered. There was something demeaning about it. Here she was on Friday night, feeling tired after a busy day in the shop, with a ladder in her tights and a yellow stain of curry sauce that had dripped onto her jumper from her lunch-time wrap, about to walk into a room and meet a stranger. Would he be there already? Would he be sitting feeling anxious, or bored? Did he have an exit line prepared? Perhaps some prearranged signal he would send furtively on his mobile phone that would trigger a fake emergency call and allow him to escape – maybe a pest-related incident involving a plague of rats or a storm of locusts that required his immediate attendance. Josie almost turned and walked away, but the thought of Scott's disappointment prevented her. *You're over-thinking this*, she told herself. What was the worst that could happen? She would spend an hour in the company of a man who wasn't her soulmate. Or he could, of course, turn out to be an axe murderer.

She felt her face flush as she pushed open the door and was greeted by a young woman in a neat black dress.

'I'm meeting someone,' she said, suddenly panicked that she didn't know which name the table had been booked under.

'My son arranged it,' she said feeling even more foolish. 'Scott Hudson.'

'Ah, yes,' the woman said, and for a moment Josie thought there was a slightly amused tone in her voice, but then she told herself she was imagining it. People had blind dates all the time.

'Your companion has not yet arrived,' the young woman said, taking Josie's coat and showing her to a corner table. Josie was glad of the candlelight that would hopefully disguise her hastily applied make-up.

Fifteen minutes and one glass of wine later, he still hadn't turned up. Josie began to allow herself to be relieved. *I'll stay and order the best steak and eat it in comfortable isolation*, she thought. *There is nothing I can do about it if he decides not to come.* She picked up the menu and was choosing between a pepper and a garlic sauce when the door swung open. She looked up and her heart sank. It was definitely him – she could tell by the surreptitious way he was scanning the occupants of the tables.

'I'm so sorry I'm late,' he said. 'The train just stopped. No explanation, nothing.'

He had a lovely voice – low and rather melodic – the sort of voice that would have made Josie want to meet the speaker if she had heard him on the phone. It didn't match the man's appearance at all. It was as if a Shakespearean actor had got caught inside a faded cherub. He had a head of tousled curls and a round, pink-cheeked face. He looked as if someone had smudged his features by rubbing them with their fingers.

'You look lovely,' Christopher said. He had a charming, dimpling smile that seemed to stretch across the whole circumference of his face. 'I'm delighted to meet you.'

'Me too,' said Josie, trying to sound enthusiastic, but Christopher gave her a keen look and laughed.

'I get the impression you are here under duress,' he said.

'My dear son thinks I am a lost cause,' she said, thinking again of the word he had used – *insular*. Perhaps Scott was right. Perhaps she was crumbling away like a fossil left too long exposed to the briny air.

'That can't be true,' Christopher said. 'Someone like you could have their pick.' He twinkled at her over the menu. *He looks a bit like a Victorian dowager peeping over the top of her fan*, thought Josie, and then chastised herself for her lack of charity.

'I fancy a great, big, stonking steak,' he announced and she laughed and found herself telling him that she had been about to order one for herself when she thought he wasn't going to show up.

'This dating business is an ordeal,' he said. 'But you just have to crack on. Faint heart never won fair maid, and all that.'

It seemed that Christopher had been cracking on for some time since he had been looking for a partner for the last five years.

'I've been on 142 dates,' he said.

'All of them first dates?'

'A good proportion of them,' he said ruefully, tugging at his errant curls in comical dismay. 'What's the common parlance? They keep putting me in the friend zone. The trouble is, I've got lots of friends already. I want someone to adore.'

The steak arrived and they talked about his boat ('fully fitted with a wood stove and all the mod cons'), kite flying, which made Christopher almost incoherent with enthusiasm ('it's like you're up there dancing with it'), the pros and cons of various different sorts of beds, the persistence of the household flea ('It's my company. I don't actually do the exterminating anymore'), children in general and teenagers in particular ('I've got three. They treat me like I'm some sort of imbecile').

'Where's their mother?' Josie asked.

'She's very much around. We parted on good terms. We loved each other for a number of years, but it faded. A bit like a photograph you leave exposed to sun and then one day you realise that almost all the colour has been leached out of it without you really noticing. We tried a few things, for the sake of the kids – therapy, weekends away, massage oil, that kind of thing, but in the end we gave up. She's married again. Nice bloke. Works in the city and cooks Michelin star-level dinner parties.' He gave her a wry look and she laughed.

When he mentioned that he had to be careful about not missing the last train back, she realised with surprise that an hour and a half had passed without her noticing.

'I think you are wonderful,' Christopher said with admirable candour.

Josie looked at him. 'I think you're wonderful too,' she replied.

There was a pause and he looked at her, his pale blue eyes shrewd and resigned.

'I hear a "but" coming,' he said.

'I don't want to waste your time,' Josie said. 'I like you immensely, but there's no . . . ' She faltered, trying to find something clear but kind to say.

'No attraction,' he finished for her.

'I'm sorry,' Josie said, feeling terrible.

'It's the story of my life,' he said sadly.

They parted outside the restaurant with a comradely embrace.

'I want you to know', Christopher said, 'that date number a hundred and forty-three was one of the very best.'

'You never know, date a hundred and forty-four might be the one when all the stars align,' Josie said and he smiled.

'You've got to keep the faith,' he said and he waved his hand in farewell.

Part Two
Spring

Chapter 15

Dear Scott

I hope your lovely mother finds happiness. My wife is terminally ill. I know it and she knows it, but we don't talk about it. I met her thirty years ago and we have barely been apart since. Now I read to her and try and cook things she might eat and take her to the toilet, which makes her cry. She is gathering herself, making ready to leave me. How can someone be here, sitting on the sofa mending a jumper, watching TV, her head in the silk scarf she ties so carefully every day and then be gone?

Richard

It's hard to see the point of anything, he thought as he lay looking out of the window at the sycamore, which was just beginning to swell and thicken. There was a sycamore in his garden at home. He had watched it throughout his childhood – seen its seasonal manifestations from stout twig to bulb, from acid-green flower to emerald canopy, then its final, golden blaze before it succumbed to months of dulled stillness. He used to try and catch the swirling seeds in his cupped hands. He remembered the way he would wait for them, convinced he was in the right place and then, at the last minute, they would drift away, beyond the reach of his fingers. It had been pollarded several times over the years but nothing held it back for long – the leaves emerging defiantly from the wounds in its trunk. When he was in his fact-finding stage, or at least at its peak, he had never quite stopped marshalling life into lists and categories; he had been able to identify all the trees in his neighbourhood. The sycamore: The wood is used to make the necks and backs of violins and eating bowls. The bark is dappled and prone to scaling. It is easily confused with maple. The Ancient Egyptians thought the tree connected the world between the dead and the living. It can survive for five hundred years.

It will still be there, hundreds of years after I have had my own short passing through, Scott thought now and he hated its longevity and the relentless way it carried on its endless, mindless cycle. Emily had told him that she had read somewhere that trees could communicate with each other. 'Not actual language as we know it,' she had said in answer to his scepticism. 'They talk to each other through the threads of fungus that link each tree to another.'

'That's not a conversation, that's a biological imperative,' he had said pompously, keen to transmit an air of someone who was not easily fooled. Trees might be able to communicate their need for water, or share the news that sap was rising, but they couldn't tell each other they were dying; that they were terrified of the bulging rot, deep within their circled trunks, that was eating them from the inside out.

Some days were better than others but Scott could feel himself slowing down. Just walking up the steps to his front door made him feel tired and there had been a couple of times recently in lectures when he thought he might be going to faint. The pale-skinned doctor had said that the next thing to try was coronary stenting.

'At best it will be a stop-gap,' she had said.

'How long have I got if I don't have any more treatment?' Scott asked with an attempt at what he thought might be an insouciant smile. He wasn't actually sure what an insouciant smile was, but he imagined it would be the sort of smile a man of the world might give if he was in the same situation. He was thinking of the slow, wolfish smile perfected by Hugh Jackman. The question made him feel humiliated but he was dammed if he was going to let it show. The doctor had fixed him with an unsmiling, watery gaze. He wondered what she did for fun. He thought maybe she was the sort that went for long runs in the rain and came back saying she felt invigorated. There was something implacable about her.

'You know I can't give you a definite answer to that question,' she said and Scott had nodded, hoping he seemed like someone who could take such a statement on the chin rather than feel it in his dodgy heart.

'I think the time may have come for you to take a break from college and go home and have your treatment at the hospital in Newcastle. It'll be better if you are nearer to where you can be looked after.'

Scott nodded again as if what she was saying was perfectly reasonable. She wasn't to know that he had not yet told his mother about what was happening to him. On his last trip home during the Easter break he had spent the time monitoring a series of dates he had arranged for her. She had been so caught up in preparing for and then enduring a string of disastrous meetings that she had barely had time to look at him, let alone ask him any leading questions. He had masked his growing fatigue by spending a lot of time in his room pretending to labour over an essay that was due in at the beginning of term. On days when he felt stronger he had driven to Bowick Beach where he had spotted Leonardo on three separate occasions, his powerful tail flukes propelling him forward, much too close to the shore. The dolphin had already become a tourist attraction and groups of people with binoculars and cameras had taken to gathering on the beach in the hope of witnessing him performing sleek, showy jumps. Every time Leonardo obliged with a rubbery rise out of the water there would be a collective clamour from the crowd – a kind of rising shout. He wished the animal would stay further out at sea where he couldn't be corrupted by human admiration and, more disastrously, human intervention. The bottlenose dolphins' undoing was their curved faces that gave the illusion of a human smile. He was seduced by the riddle of dolphins. Despite years of research no one really knew exactly what went on in the intricate folds of their brains, which were much larger than the human version and packed with the cells and neurons responsible for the best of human characteristics – things such as empathy and intuition and compassion. They learned fast, they could recognise themselves in mirrors, they knew by using the most sophisticated echolocation whether one of them was pregnant or diseased. They protected their families. They could heal their own wounds. They touched each other with what looked like gestures of love. They were comically horny. They whistled and clicked out the names of the dolphins in their pod. They could rest with one half of their brains while the other half stayed alert for fifteen hours straight. What else might they know? What secrets would they disclose if they could speak to us? Scott thought that the yearning for dolphins was a yearning to believe that they were wiser and more advanced than human beings and were simply biding their time, waiting to show us all a better way to live.

Scott had begun to feel panicky about his ability to find anyone his mother could tolerate, let alone fall in love with. Time was running out. He had taken to asking potential suitors what their three favourite things were. He thought that it would help him to make better and more informed choices, but it hadn't worked very well so far. He had recently read an article about the Optimal Stopping Theory which was something to do with selecting a hundred men and going out with 37 per cent of them and then settling on the next person who was better than all the rest. He thought maybe Josie had reached that point in the process or perhaps it was he who had. Maybe he should just tell her to try and work on a relationship with the next person she could bear to be in a room with. So far she had met with, and rejected, a man who, she said, kept leaning forward and smelling her hair; a gym instructor who apparently told her that her legs could do with a bit more toning; a frail librarian with a spitting lisp who had claimed he was forty-four but who Josie said wasn't a day younger than ninety-eight; a biology teacher who had dissected a prawn on his napkin to show her its sex organs; an unfortunate chap who had made the mistake of wearing orange suede shoes; and a man in a very tight jacket who kept asking her if she would like to see the hunting rifle he had in the boot of his car.

'Don't you think you might be being just a bit too fussy?' he had said to her in exasperation. 'Are you sure you are giving them all a proper chance?'

Josie had turned on him with uncharacteristic fury. 'I'd rather live alone for the rest of my life,' she had said through gritted teeth, 'than spend it with a spitting Tory in tangoed shoes and with fishy fingers.'

In her rage she seemed to have made an amalgam of all of her unfortunate dates. They had now become one single, impossible man.

After his appointment at the hospital Scott had rung the university to tell them that he was going to be away indefinitely.

'I'm not sure when I'm coming back. I have to have an operation,' he had said. Although he knew he probably would never return, he wanted to avoid having to admit out loud that his time at university was over, and to spare his tutor having to find the right words of consolation.

'I'll send you work. You are so able, I'm sure you'll catch up,' his tutor had said and Scott was grateful that at least he had this to hang on to.

Danny had helped him pack up his belongings, which mostly involved him getting in Scott's way and taking things out of boxes that Scott had put in. Scott had filled him in on the barest details, not wanting to incur the other boy's pity.

'It's a real shame,' Danny kept saying, as he flitted around the room or went into the kitchen, returning with pans and plates that didn't belong to Scott.

'Why didn't you say something, mate? I'd have kept the noise down a bit if I'd known. I'll keep your room free for you.'

Scott appreciated the gesture, but thought that his housemate would soon have to find someone to replace him. Danny had looked stricken but in a few weeks' time it would be as if Scott had never been there. The space he had created for himself would be filled the same way that undergrowth quickly sealed over the site of a bonfire.

'Just keep my stuff for me until I can arrange for someone to pick it up,' he had said and given the other boy an awkward hug.

As Scott walked to his meeting with Emily he tried to imagine the words he would say to her to explain why he was going home. They hadn't slept together yet. She hadn't seen the scar that bisected his chest and puckered his skin like the edging on one of Josie's wonky flans. They had come close to it on the trip they had taken to meet her mother, but he had held back because he didn't want her to be tied to him any more than she was already. He thought of what it had been like to kiss her under the shelter of the church portico and the way they had lain together giggling in the single bed in the spare bedroom that was supposed to be where Scott was sleeping alone. Lorna had been quite firm on the matter.

'Only people who pay the rent can have sex in this house,' she had said, which had provoked Emily into teasing her about her own romantic entanglements.

'Those are mine to know and you to never find out,' Lorna had said surprisingly and Emily made a scandalised face and then tried to hide it.

'You don't imagine that it all stops down there when you reach a certain age, do you?' Lorna had said, indicating her ample nether regions and making Emily splutter into the cup of thin hot chocolate they had been forced to drink before going to bed.

It had been Emily who had come to him when Lorna had finally finished her endless perambulations around the house, beautiful in a white nightie that her grandmother still kept ready for her under the pillow in her old bedroom.

'I was wondering whether you wanted to investigate "down there",' Emily had whispered, laughing. Standing at the doorway, her face flushed, she had looked defiant and vulnerable all at the same time and Scott's body had suffused with heat.

'I think we'd better abide by your grandmother's rules,' he had said and, unable to sleep, he had held her all night.

As he left the Tube and began to walk towards Greenwich Park, he could feel the warm breeze that silvered the chestnut trees as they revealed the paler undersides of their newly minted leaves. London tugged at him as if a length of twine attached him to the city. He had been so keen when he first arrived to claim it as his own, but now it felt as if all he had been able to do was to borrow it for a while. This afternoon it looked beautiful in all its tatty glory – the way things always did when you knew you did not have them for long.

He arrived fifteen minutes early and waited for her in the courtyard of the Observatory next to the metal orb representing the Eastern and Western hemispheres of the earth. The place was full of the usual sightseers taking pictures of each other with their feet straddling the meridian line that ran across the courtyard floor, marked out with the names of countries and their degree of longitude from point zero. There had been times recently when he had felt burdened by a newly sharp awareness of what was around him. It was as if the world had come suddenly into focus so that he was forced to look at things minutely – the arched pattern of the bricked floor under his feet, the way the sun caught the top of the railings, burnishing them, the glossy plait down a girl's back that looked like it was threaded with a hundred different shades of gold.

In the end he had given up watching for Emily so that she arrived in front of him without any warning. For a moment it felt as though he had never seen her properly before. Her face glowed as if she had just been running. She was wearing mismatched earrings – a pink feather in one ear, a tiny diamond in the other. There was a little speck of sleep in the corner of one eye. Her mouth with its distractingly voluptuous bottom lip was a little dry and rough-looking.

'I've never been here before!' she said. 'Is this really where the earth divides?'

'I don't think it divides as such,' Scott said. 'It's just a way of measuring time.'

He watched while she did what everyone did when they came here for the first time; she walked solemnly along the silver-trimmed line – one small foot in front of the other as if she was on a tightrope.

'I'm in no-man's land,' she said laughing. 'Neither in the East nor the West, but in the tiny sliver in between.'

'That's where time stops,' Scott said, and kissed her.

135

They walked around the Observatory for a while and then went back down the hill and through the park. The sun had dropped suddenly behind the trees and without its warmth the afternoon revealed itself as still in the clutch of winter.

'I think I love you,' she said with that assumed bravado that always made him feel tenderly towards her. When he didn't reply immediately, she looked embarrassed.

'Oh God. I've blown it, haven't I?' she said. 'I knew I shouldn't have said it. I'm so stupid.' And she put her mittened hands to her face.

'There's something I have to tell you,' Scott said. He didn't know how to explain it. The words skittered away from him like dice across a polished table.

She listened intently to him. At some point in his narrative, he saw her stagger and an expression that looked like protest or anger crossed her face. He came to the end of what he had to say and stopped. For a moment they stood looking at each other. In the late afternoon light her skin glowed like a pearl.

'So you see,' he said at last, to fill the silence that stretched tightly between them like a length of pulled elastic, 'I can't love you back, although I want to. I'm so, so sorry.'

She cried silently; her face completely still, so that the tears ran undisturbed down her cheeks.

'There's always hope,' he said, echoing the doctor's words, 'but maybe not a lot of it.' He couldn't bear that he couldn't have what he so much wanted. He wanted to be able to be with her. He wanted his chance to love her. It was what every other person in the world took for granted. His chest and throat filled with the unfairness of it. For the very first time in his life he wanted passionately to be someone else – a regular person with regular prospects. Other people could wander hand in hand in parks, or laze in rowing boats or dance with their faces pressed close together. They could say they loved each other with the expectation that the love would last, if not for a hundred years, at least through an indefinite number of glorious summers.

Emily rubbed at her face with her gloved hands and turned away from him.

'I'll completely understand if you never want to see me again. *I* don't want to see me again,' he added, making an effort to speak lightly and to appear as if all of this was something he had come to terms with. He knew she saw him as someone with reserves who didn't need other people to prop him up, and so he tried to maintain the illusion of solidity, although what he really wanted to do was to throw himself screaming on the ground. He needed to feel the comfort of her arms around him. She would surely be able to take the loneliness of it away. He was relying on her to know what to say and do.

She turned back towards him and he could see that she was making an effort to master herself.

'I can't . . . I just . . .' she said and this time she turned and started walking away.

Scott stayed where he was long after her departure. He was stuck to the slope of the grass as if he was pinned there. It was with surprise that when he next looked around him, he discovered that it was almost dark. The crowds of people had dispersed and the trees had begun to assume their looming night shapes. At that moment, the laser that stretched from the meridian line at the Observatory and across the sky was illuminated. He followed the acid beam with his eyes. He remembered Emily's earlier walk along the earth-bound version and imagined her now, passing along the shard of light, her feet carefully balancing on its taut, green thread, following its path until it dissolved, somewhere out there, over London, further than he could see.

When Scott had first come to London, he had loved the Underground, imagining travelling under tower blocks and roads and monuments and houses where people were making love or arguing or having breakfast, but now he felt a kind of breathless dread as he descended the escalator. Posters advertising things he probably would never see moved past his head. *I've done nothing, contributed nothing*, he thought. *I will slide out of the world as if I have never been here.* He liked rum and raisin ice cream, parcels from Amazon, video games, vinyl records, finishing an essay, Kendrick Lamar and Lily Allen, the sweet spot at the base of a girl's back – that little dip, made for licking – but these were not things that fixed him, the way older people seemed sure and formed, certain of what they had to offer. He would not now have time to become who he was meant to be. As he moved downwards he felt the heaviness of the earth above him.

Sitting opposite him on the train a woman with her scalp shining through thin hair was reading her Kindle and next to her there was an elderly man with blue eyelids and hands with swollen knuckles. Further along the compartment a couple sat next to each other in sulky silence. The girl had been crying recently, her face had a bitten look as if she had been out in the wind and the man, his face flushed, sat with his legs wide apart, his arms crossed, bristling with fury. Scott hated his shoes, which were shiny and pointed. They were the shoes of a twat, Scott thought savagely. *How come he gets to sit there in his shoes with his ugly, meaty hands and bullet-shaped head? How come he gets to breathe?* Fast on this anger came the realisation that he would swap places with any of his fellow travellers. *Given the chance, right now I would have stringy hair and swollen knuckles and wear crap shoes and live with someone I couldn't talk to properly.*

'What you looking at?' the young man asked, eager to pass on the blame for why he was feeling as he was.

Scott shrugged. He felt reckless, untouchable. The man was loathsome. Scott felt him to be an affront. 'You,' he said, and found that he was smiling.

'Well, fucking well stop,' the man said and his face firmed and became intent as if in relief for something else to focus on other than himself, sitting on the Tube, not knowing how the hell he was going to ever feel anything but angry.

The young woman put her hand on her companion's arm.

'Never mind, Paul,' she said. 'Leave it.' Her voice was low, conciliatory. The man shook her arm off and she recoiled as if she thought he might hit her.

The Kindle woman looked up in alarm, pulled by a new vibration in the air from whatever world her book was holding her in, then dipped her eyes again.

Scott held the man's gaze. He couldn't seem to look away. The man thrust his head forward.

'Fucking. Well. Stop looking at me. Wanker.'

'*You* are looking at *me*,' Scott said, and he smiled again. Knowing himself to be unbearable. Wanting the other man to rise to it. He could feel the fist against his face already and the welcome, obliterating pain.

The man got to his feet, and his companion curled herself away from him. She put her hands to her face. Her nails were ragged, as if she had been scratching something rough.

'Now hold on, lads.' The old chap had risen from his seat. The newspaper on his lap fell on the floor. He made a kind of distressed movement with his hands as if he was looking for the pole to keep him upright.

Scott got up too so that he was standing face to face with his adversary.

He saw a look almost of astonishment cross the other man's face, and for a moment Scott wondered if, after all, the moment would pass and they would sit back on their seats, assiduously avoiding each other's eyes as decorum decreed. But then it became clear that the man didn't know any other way out but the one he was obliged to take. Scott had set in motion an inevitable sequence of events. The blow, when it came, was much harder than he had been expecting. His head snapped back and the light in the carriage temporarily dimmed, but he managed to stay standing.

'Do you feel better now?' he asked. He could taste blood in his mouth.

'No. I bloody well don't,' the man roared, and he gathered his fist again. This time the punch knocked Scott off his feet. He slid onto the floor. Above him the handles swung slightly as the train went round a corner. *I'm lying on the floor of a Tube train*, Scott thought, and the notion seemed ridiculous to him. He started laughing.

'You mad fuck,' the man said.

The train stopped and the doors opened. The man pulled his girlfriend to her feet. Before they left, he aimed a spiteful kick to Scott's side with his pointed shoe.

The train took off again. Scott could feel the sucking pull of it beneath his back and the little shudder as it picked up speed. The old man bent over him. Scott could see the broken thread veins on his nose and the ragged age spot that spread over one cheek. *It looks like an island*, Scott thought. His face and side hurt, but he felt a kind of calm. He knew it would be temporary and so he held on to it tightly like a shield.

'Are you all right?' the old man asked and touched Scott's chest. 'Shall I get someone?'

'No, I'm fine thanks,' Scott said, letting himself be helped up. He sat back on his seat. The Kindle woman had moved away further down the compartment.

'What on earth possessed you?' the old man asked, his faded eyes watering. He passed his swollen hands across his brow. Scott could see he was trembling and felt suddenly contrite.

'I'm sorry. I'm really sorry,' he said.

The train stopped again and this time Scott got out. He stood on the platform until the Tube pulled away and caught the eye of the Kindle woman who looked blankly at him, as if he wasn't really there.

Chapter 16

Hi Scott

I've never stayed in one place long enough to fall in love.
I've hooked up with a lot of people, but no one has made me
want to settle down. There are times these days when I find
myself in some new place and it doesn't seem as exciting or
as beautiful as I expected. I think perhaps I need someone
to help me see things properly again. Does your mother like
to travel?

Garth x

Scott spent all of the next day wandering around London with
his rucksack on his back, knowing he should begin his journey
to Northumberland but unable to get himself to the station. It
was partly that, once he was on the train, he'd know his time in
London was really over and he wanted to take a last look at the
things that he had so recently discovered, but it was also that he
was dreading having to tell his mother the truth. He remembered a time, years ago when he had broken one of her favourite
vases. It had stood on the mantelpiece and he had wanted to
know what the swirling blue glass would look like if he held it
up to the light. It had been heavier than he had expected and
had slipped from his fingers and shattered on the floor. He had

stood in the room, hearing his mother's rushing steps, dreading her expression when she discovered what he had done, and he felt the same fear now. He didn't want to have to see her as he said the words that he knew would undo her.

He went to Waterloo Bridge and stood for a while, remembering the first time he had been there and how happy and heedless he had been. The thought of Emily's face, shuttered and pale, kept coming back to him. *I don't need anyone if I am to die*, he thought as he walked along the river. Animals sense the end and find a place to lie down where they can be alone. It was a dignified way to die. *I'll do the same*, he thought.

The first pub he came to was relatively empty with only a scattering of what looked like tourists and a young man sitting reading *Shantaram* with his book propped up against the cruets, as if he was hoping to draw attention to his good taste. Scott felt a wave of irritation that he seemed prey to these days. He ordered a whisky, which was something that he had never done before. The bartender was a shiny-skinned chap with excessively groomed facial hair.

'Make it a double,' Scott said, and the cocky bartender delivered it with a sardonic flourish. He sat at a table in a corner of the room. The whisky was warm in his mouth and throat and had a smooth, oily texture. The *Shantaram* boy looked at him curiously for a moment and then went back to pretending to read. *He's probably waiting for a girl*, Scott thought, and sure enough, moments later, she appeared with thick plaits emerging from under a purple beret, clutching *Shantaram* to her chest. At the sight of the reading boy who had been flinching every time the door opened, she held it aloft with a heroic air, as if going into battle. Scott tried to imagine their earlier conversation. Had it been she who had suggested the book as a visual aid to romance because she had been reading it at the time? Had the boy then expressed astonishment at the coincidence of their literary preferences and then hastily gone out to buy the book? He looked the dissembling type – something about the way his shirt was buttoned to the chin spoke of secrecy and the copy of the book looked suspiciously new. He supposed meeting up in a pub with a stranger was as good a way as any to find someone. The boy might fall in love with the girl, despite her dubious taste in hats and the pair of them might go to India and discover something or other.

He went over to the bar and ordered another drink. This time the bartender was positively derisive.

'Another double?' he asked, and then actually twiddled the end of his ridiculous moustache. *I must add that to my list of undesirables*, Scott thought. He didn't want his mother to spend her life with someone who looked like a diminutive Poirot.

'Yes,' he said as firmly as he was able, and the man placed the refilled tumbler with exaggerated care onto a coaster.

'What you drinking?' The girl appeared by his side as if by magic. He hadn't noticed the door opening.

'Whisky,' he said.

'Do you want to buy me one?' she asked. Her hair was rolled into little spirals and fastened up in a haphazard way. He thought she was maybe already a little drunk from the way she leaned against the bar. She was wearing a low-necked jumper that displayed the top half of her breasts and some brightly coloured trousers that looked a little too thin for the weather.

'Why not?' he said, and the bartender sighed heavily.

'Thanks! You've saved my life, it's freezing out there,' the girl said, following him back to the table and settling down opposite him.

'I'm Brigid, by the way. Nice to meet you.'

'Hi, I'm Peter,' Scott said. He took a great gulp of his drink and for a moment the room split apart and he saw two of everything – the multi-bulbed light fitting, the too-long stretch of the bar. He moved his head feeling a nauseous roil and then her face came back into focus.

'Are you all right? You look a bit strange,' Brigid said.

'It's been a hard day,' Scott replied.

'I can see that,' she said, looking at his face. The punches he had sustained on the Tube had left him with a swollen lip and darkening bruises. 'What happened to the other bloke?'

Her accent was what he had come to think of as fake London – a kind of verbal swagger that sounded inauthentic. She was clearly posher then she wanted to appear.

'You don't want to know,' he said.

She was in between trips away. Just come back from Malaysia and planning to go back as soon as she could get the money together.

'I'm always on the move,' she said with a little laugh and bent towards him so that he could see all the way down her jumper.

They talked about where she had been and where he hadn't. She touched him twice on the arm. He bought some more drinks. The room divided again and, this time, took longer to come back into focus, but he welcomed the way his thoughts had become muffled and indistinct. *It's like being covered with snow*, he thought.

'I think you're fit,' she said, and although he knew she had said it out of habit, he kissed her. Her mouth slid under his. He put his hand on one of her breasts.

'Whooa,' she said. 'You're in a hurry.'

'Yes I am,' Scott said, and so she drank the inch or so still left in his glass, and got up.

'I'm staying in a house round the corner. Friends of my parents. I'm house sitting and feeding their disgusting cat. Do you want to come back with me?'

They walked down the street arm in arm, as if they knew each other. *This is how I am going to spend what's left of my life*, Scott thought. *Getting off my face and sleeping with people who don't care enough about me to feel any damage. Or people who are already too damaged to notice the difference.*

The house was tall and groomed and inside Scott was blinded by light gleaming on white and steel. He could see the evidence of Brigid's stay – the glasses on the polished coffee table had left marks and there were clothes on the floor and the smell of cat shit in the air.

'The beast has an arse like the Channel Tunnel,' Brigid said, and took off her jumper. She wasn't wearing a bra and her breasts were caramel coloured from the Malaysian sun. She led him into a bedroom and onto a bed covered in a pale throw. There was a moment of hesitation between getting her clothes off and his, when he felt suddenly frightened, as if he had forgotten exactly where he was, but then he let himself take in the shape of her arms and the way she arched up from the bed towards him and he forgot for a while that he was dying.

Scott woke on Saturday morning and didn't recognise the room he was lying in but then Brigid walked in with a tray of breakfast things and he remembered what had happened the night before.

'I took some money from your wallet,' she said. 'I didn't think you would mind. I've been out to get us croissants.'

She settled herself on the bed and poured coffee from a cafetière. She looked different to how he remembered her. Her face was scrubbed clear of make-up and she had let her hair loose from their clips so that it fell in stumpy ringlets around her face. He thought she looked plainer and more vulnerable or maybe it was simply that he hadn't really looked at her properly before. Why had he stayed? He hadn't intended to. Now he was stuck there with someone he didn't know who appeared to have appropriated his shirt. He could smell cat shit and his head throbbed.

'I've really got to go,' he said, wrapping a sheet around him and getting up carefully. The room buckled and rippled and he swayed.

'How come you've got that massive scar?' Brigid asked, pointing at his chest.

'I had an encounter with a shark' he replied, and she laughed as if she didn't really believe him but wasn't interested enough to find out the truth.

'I thought we could spend the day together,' Brigid said, beginning to stuff a sliced croissant with great lumps of red jam. *I'm going to be sick*, Scott thought. He only just made it to the bathroom. He knelt on the floor holding on to the toilet pedestal while he vomited. He subsided at last, wiping his face with the edge of the sheet. He thought at first his eyes were watering from the effort of retching, but he discovered he was crying. He couldn't seem to stop.

'What's wrong with you?'

He looked up to see Brigid leaning against the bathroom door. 'I'm dying,' he said.

'Well, we did rather go for it last night,' she said. 'You'll feel better now you've been sick.'

'Can I have my shirt?' he said.

She took it off slowly. In the morning light her skin looked more yellow than caramel.

'Let's go and have a drink. Hair of the dog. What does that mean anyway? I've never known what that means,' she said and made a sad, snorting sound that might have been a laugh. All her brash swagger of the night before had disappeared and suddenly she looked very young. He could see a dark red mark on her neck. He hoped he hadn't given it to her.

'It's from a time when they treated bites from rabid dogs by taking hair from them and putting it on the wounds,' he said.

'You're very well informed.' Something of her confidence from the night before seemed to return. She put her arm on her waist in what looked to Scott like a gesture she had been told was seductive.

'I can't. I'm sorry,' he said.

For a moment she looked as if she might cry. Her face trembled a little and her pale lips tightened and then, as if pulling back from the edge, her expression hardened.

'Piss off, then,' she said, turning away from him.

He gathered up his clothes and dressed hastily while she got back into bed and lay watching him.

'I thought you were a good person,' she said as he went out of the room.

He closed the front door behind him and walked away. Feeling the clean chill of the air on his face, his first impulse was relief at his escape, but this feeling was quickly replaced by a sense of guilt. He thought of the way she had posed against the door, the morning sun leeching the colour from her hard-won tan, and of her counterfeit defiance. It seemed possible to cause harm even if neither of you really cared, even if all you were looking for was a way to escape pain. He felt less stricken when he arrived at the Tube and saw that she had taken all of the money from his wallet.

Chapter 17

Hello Scott

I would very much like to be considered as a candidate.
I'm forty-four and an accountant. I have all my teeth and
quite a lot of my hair, although I find I need to spread it
around more than I used to. I like to think of myself as fairly
fit. I train by running up and down the railway bridge every
evening.

Yours in hope

Julian

Josie saw Scott's rucksack as soon as she walked in the door.
Her first impulse was delight, but this was swiftly replaced by
a feeling of anxiety. Why had he come back again so soon?
She called out his name and heard his answering shout from
the front room. He was sitting in the armchair by the unlit
stove.

'Hello, Mum,' he said, getting to his feet and coming across
the room to embrace her.

'What've you done to your face?' she asked.

'I fell over,' he said and she could tell he was lying.

'Why didn't you tell me you were coming home?' she asked.
'I've not got your bed ready.'

He looked at her for a moment without speaking. His heavy-lidded blue eyes were as beautiful as ever but in addition to the angry bruises, the skin around his mouth was paler than the rest of his face and his cheeks were slightly mottled. She had trained herself to notice the slightest differences in him. His fluctuations over the years had been her barometer of happiness. *He's ill again*, she thought and at the same time she wondered about the vase of tulips on the mantelpiece. *I should really put them in new water before they begin to smell*, she thought, but she couldn't move. An early wasp was banging against the glass of the window.

'There have been changes in the walls of the arteries,' he told her. His voice was resolute but she heard the wobble in it.

'How bad?' she asked. Her arms were shaking. It must be colder in the room than she realised. She moved towards the stove and reached for the matches and began to break the kindling twigs in half. The snapping noise sounded loud,

'Let me do that,' he said, coming towards her. She put her hand up to stop him and the matches spilled onto the floor. She knelt down and began gathering them up but there seemed so many of them. They couldn't possibly all have come out of the box, she thought. She hadn't known she was crying until she saw that her hands were wet.

'Please come and sit down,' Scott said, but she couldn't. She thought that if she sat down she would never get up again.

'What have they said?' she asked, not wanting to hear the answer.

'CAV. It seems to be progressing quickly.'

She had known that this was what would probably happen. This or some kind of cancer caused by the drugs he had to take.

She knew the statistics and likely outcomes and she had seen the graphs – those measured lines that only moved one way – falling quietly off the edge of the paper, and yet it wasn't until this moment, standing with the matches still scattered around her feet and the wasp banging again and again at the window, that she really understood that loving him, watching him, giving him every minute of her time and all her energy hadn't, after all, been enough. She had a sudden image of the way Aadash's mother had sat, all those short years ago, her hands crossed in her lap as if she was holding herself in.

'There're things they can do, right?' she said. 'Angioplasty or bypass surgery?' It helped her, as it always had, to think about what could be done. What could be done had always filled the space left by terror.

'They are going to try stenting,' Scott said. The pale-faced doctor had described the metal-mesh tubes that would be left in his body to widen his arteries as 'scaffolding'. The word had made him think of his arteries as the hallways to his heart, their ceilings propped up like a subsiding building.

'There are some drugs they can put on the stent that will help to reduce further blockages.'

'Yes,' Josie said. 'And there's always another transplant. I'll talk to the doctor and they must put you on the list straightaway.'

She could do this again. They could do this again and he would survive. He would need a bigger heart this time. She felt feverish now that the first clasp of shock had begun to leave her. This time it would have to be a young man's heart, not a boy's. Young men died more often than children. They took risks. They drove too fast and experimented with drugs. They rushed through life as if they were immortal. She thought she might be panting. She recognised this shameful greed from the first time round. *Love makes me heartless*, she thought.

'It'll be all right,' she said, and she held him close to her. She held on tight to stop him slipping away.

He felt her hot face against his own. He was relieved that he had told her at last. Her body seemed to thrum against him. He thought of how quickly her mouth had changed from the slackness of shock to a familiar, tightened curve. She had felt the earth shift but it hadn't taken her long to find her feet again. This was terrain she knew and she stood braced on it, getting ready to fight. He loved her readiness for battle, but he was also wearied by it. He had wanted her to mourn longer. He had wanted to feel her alongside him just for a short while, but it wasn't in her nature to allow herself to be disarmed. He thought of the way she used to line up savings tins on the windowsill labelled with the words – '*holiday fund*', '*school shoes*', '*Christmas*' and '*emergencies*'. Those makeshift banks had been an indomitable metal army marshalled by her against whatever skirmishes the passing year would bring. She had always been determined that nothing would catch her by surprise.

'There are sometimes problems with re-transplantation,' the thin-skinned doctor had said, leaving her words hanging in the air as if she hadn't really intended them to arrive anywhere. Scott hadn't needed to ask her what she meant. He already knew how difficult it was likely to be the second time around. It wasn't just that he could become too ill to tolerate another transplant, or indeed that a suitable heart might not become available in time, it was also that Scott must now surely be pretty low down the list of priority cases. Such things were decided purely on expediency and cold, hard facts and he knew that in weighing up who was more likely to benefit from a new heart in the longer term, someone who hadn't already had a transplant would be more likely to be chosen. Getting one heart was lucky. Getting a second felt as if he was taking more than his share of good fortune – if good fortune was how it could be described, when the gift was the result of loss. There would come a time at some point in the future when hearts would be grown almost as easily as cabbages, but that was a long way off when no doubt the world would be full of other, wonderful, inconceivable things and terrible, heartbreaking things too. It would just be another version of the one he was living in now. He wondered if, at a time when hearts bloomed in laboratories, there would still be tigers and wetland grasses and baobab trees.

'I'll make your bed,' Josie said.

By the time Scott got up in the morning, Josie had arranged an appointment for the next day at Newcastle Hospital at the cardiac unit that dealt with adult cases. His treatment before he went to London had been managed by the paediatric team there and Scott knew he would now have to get used to a whole new set of doctors, who would be familiar with his hefty file, but not him. He felt tired at the thought of going through all of the getting-to-know you conversations that inevitably would ensue.

'I'll come in with you,' Josie said. She had clearly been up for hours because the house looked windswept, as if she had set a series of jobs in motion; moving through each room in a flurry of brooms and dusters, rearranging and then abandoning each task before she could set it right again. Books were pulled from shelves and piled up on the floor, ornaments had been taken down and left in odd places, and she had rolled up the rug in the living room and had left it out in the garden.

'I've been spring-cleaning,' she said when she saw him looking around for somewhere to sit and shelter from the storm.

'I think it would be better if I went in for my hospital appointment by myself,' Scott said, knocking into the flapping lid of the pedal bin as he reached for the cereal.

'You won't ask about everything you need to know.' Josie stopped her whirl around the kitchen and looked at him in dismay. 'I need to be there to get all the facts.'

'I'll tell you what they say,' Scott said, clearing a space at the table.

'That's not the same thing.' She paused and then looked at him accusingly. 'How long has it been since you found out that things . . . things were not going so well?'

'Only a few weeks,' said Scott, avoiding looking at her.

'When, *exactly*?' she asked.

'When I got back to college after Christmas.'

'That's a few months, not a few weeks!' Josie exclaimed, sitting down opposite him at the strewn table.

'It doesn't make any difference.' He could feel himself becoming irritated. This was why he had delayed talking to her. He'd known she would react like this.

'What do you mean, make no difference?' Josie said. She was all flushed and she had managed to get a lump of Blu-Tack stuck to her hair and she was wearing a huge shirt that was buttoned up all wrong. She seemed to have had a go at her fringe because it was a little too short, giving her face a surprised look. If he hadn't been feeling so annoyed with her he would have laughed.

'We would have been able to set things in motion much earlier. You could have come home and I could have looked after you and we would be much further along with your treatment by now.'

'I just wanted to pretend for a while that it wasn't happening,' he said.

She looked at him and for a moment he thought maybe she would say she understood. Her determined, frantic face went vague, as if she was feeling a sensation deep in her body that she couldn't quite identify. *I'll tell her about Emily,* he thought, *and the way that the whole of London is there for the taking and how it feels to stay up until five in the morning so that it seems you are cheating time.* But then her odd, irresolute expression hardened into its old battle lines.

'You're going to get better,' she said and the moment to confide in her passed.

I should never have let him go to London, Josie thought as she sat, exhausted, amid the wreck of her house. Scott hadn't said anything more; he'd just taken his coat and gone out of the door. She heard the car pull away outside. Should he even be driving? She ought to have known that he couldn't look after himself properly. God knew how much time they had wasted while he had carried on pretending that everything was fine. He had been back home three times, *three times*, and failed to say a word. Instead he had insisted that she went out on the series of hopeless dates he had arranged for her. He had even furnished her with a list of the next batch. It was sitting in front of her amongst the debris on the table:

Mark: *1. White-water rafting; 2. Travel; 3. Quiz shows.*
Steven: *1. Sunsets; 2. Dogs; 3. The Gower Peninsula.*
Terry: *1. My man cave; 2. Lego; 3. Lemon drizzle cake.*
Matt: *1. The smell of new leather; 2. Traction engines;*
           3. Game of Thrones.

She crumpled up the piece of paper and threw it across the room. She didn't understand what had got into him. It was almost as if he had given up. It seemed to her that he was rejecting her care, all her years of careful ministrations. She knew that sorrow was waiting for her to falter. It sat inside her with its mouth gaping like a hungry bird. She loved him so. He didn't understand how much she loved him. After a while she got up and began putting all the things she had pulled out back into their places. The house slowly restored itself under her hands.

Scott parked the car at the golf club at Embleton and started walking along the beach towards Dunstanburgh Castle with Archie. The waves moved softly across the sand leaving a ghost mark as they pulled out – a sheeny shadow that made a double tide-line. He could see the castle ahead with its crumbling turrets and ruined fortress, which rose from the slope of the green hill like a set of knucklebones. He crossed the orange-tinged sand to the dunes and took the narrow path through ferns and marram grass. He already felt out of breath and his arms prickled as if he had been sweeping them through nettles. Although he had walked for over half an hour, the castle seemed no nearer than it had before. It shifted and blurred like a mirage. He stopped for a while to rest. Archie was slowing down too and seemed grateful for the reprieve. The sea was still and flat and had borrowed a shimmer from the hazy sun. He could remember the stretch of his legs and the pull of a kite behind him as he ran along this beach as a child; the tug of the line between his fingers, the feeling of power it conferred as he controlled its fall and rise. He couldn't run anymore. His body was letting him down. Just then he saw a white crest a few yards out at sea and then the unmistakable sickle-shaped dorsal fin of a bottlenose dolphin. The creature seemed to be swimming towards the shore and Scott found himself rising instinctively on the balls of his feet and shouting out, his hands cupped around his mouth. He doubted it could hear his thin voice over the wide stretch of sea and sand but he could not help his warning cry. The dolphin breached twice, landing with an explosion of white and then disappeared from view.

Scott walked a little further to the layered outcrop of rock that looked like a giant's arm with its bent, stony hand dipped in the water and sat on it. The castle had at last materialised and stood above him, more solid and defiant than it had looked from a distance. Something about the way the walls of the castle loomed over him reminded him of the sperm whales that had been washed up on Beadnell Beach when he was eight years old. Both castle and whales shared the same, massy, indomitable shape. Even though the whales had been dead – indeed, already degenerating, you could smell the hot meat of them in the air – they had remained miraculously intact. They had lain in the shallows, side by side as if they had found the edge of life together and their ancient-looking bodies had been scored in a hundred places by the rocks that had pierced them while they had fought the diminishing air. The desire to be near them had been irresistible and even though his mother had not wanted him to, he had pushed his way through the flimsy barricade. He had felt dazed in the hard, bright sun after weeks of being indoors and yet he had been propelled forward. What he wanted, above everything at that moment, was to make some acknowledgement of their presence. To show that he recognised their splendour and knew the way they had once swum through the sea, mysterious and imperishable. Touching their half-buried heads, even briefly, had felt like a mark of respect, the way pilgrims touch the site of miracles.

Chapter 18

Hello Scott

I don't think I have ever truly been in love with anyone.
Perhaps I'm just not capable of it. There is a bit in the brain
that lights up when you are in love. It's called the ventral
tegmental area, which is where people feel pleasure and
reward. It's possible that bit of me never developed. Or per-
haps I was born without it. In any case, I am willing to give
love a try. Your mother has a lovely neck. I attach a photo.
I am sorry it is rather dark.

Stephen

Josie had unwillingly agreed to wait in a nearby coffee shop
while Scott went in to his first appointment at the hospital.

'I'm on my mobile, if you change your mind,' she had said
and he had pretended that this might be a possibility.

He was ushered through to see Dr Moulton without having
to wait. The cardiologist was standing at the window when he
entered the room, peering out at a couple of roosting pigeons,
and Scott gave a little cough to announce his arrival. The doctor
turned with a start.

'Ah, hello. It's Scott, isn't it?' Dr Moulton said and shook
Scott's hand over the desk.

With antennae honed from years of exposure to doctors, Scott's heart sank a little at the sight of this new one. He looked like the kind that strutted around the ward with adoring acolytes in his slipstream, never stopping long enough to actually listen to what anyone had to say. He was handsome in a TV doc kind of a way – clean shaven and firm chinned and he was wearing a tapestry-effect waistcoat covered in tiny parrots. *I bet he wears a beaded necklace at the weekend*, Scott thought gloomily.

'I'm up to date with what's been happening with you,' Dr Moulton said, sitting down on his chair and looking at Scott intently. *Oh God, he's trying to establish a 'relationship'*, Scott thought, hoping the consultation wouldn't last long.

'What do you feel about it all?' Dr Moulton asked, looking steadily at Scott. He had curious eyes – dark blue, almost navy – which had a downward slant to them. They made him look slightly troubled which, no doubt, went down a storm with the nurses.

'I'm feeling great,' Scott said sarcastically.

The doctor gave him another of his sad-eyed stares.

'We'll do the operation next week. It's a fairly straightforward procedure, although you might have to stay in overnight, depending on how you feel.'

Scott nodded his head.

'I gather you have come back from university so that your mother can take care of you.'

'I don't really need anyone to look after me,' Scott said.

'Well, maybe not just now, but in the coming months the situation might well change,' Dr Moulton said.

'How much time is this going to buy me?' Scott asked, expecting to be fobbed off as he always was. He had come to realise that doctors were unable to put a time to anything. When asked a straight question they acted like builders who have been asked for a quote and who shake their heads and suck their breath in and tap on calculators.

'It's hard to say ...' the doctor began, but Scott interrupted him.

'It's harder to hear, so force yourself,' Scott said.

'I'm sorry. I'm forgetting you probably know as much about this as I do, more, probably. It's not going to cure you, but it will give you a few months and then we can think again. We might be able to consider another transplant but you know how that goes.'

'I do,' Scott said.

'Why don't you bring your mother in next time and we can talk about it all properly,' Dr Moulton said.

'I'm nineteen and a half.'

'I know. It's just good to have someone else with you when it comes to the difficult conversations,' Dr Moulton said.

'I'm better than my mum when it comes to difficult conversations,' Scott replied.

'Why's that?' Dr Moulton asked.

'She gets ... over ... over involved.' He wondered why he was telling the man this. He must be falling for his soulful gaze. He thought the poor nurses probably didn't stand a chance.

'Well, she's your mother, she's as involved as it's possible to be and I'm guessing she will have been to hell and back over the years.'

'She's sure I'm going to get better,' Scott said.

'She wants you to get better and that sometimes feels like certainty.'

Scott nodded again, overcome with a feeling of sadness that he had not been expecting. He thought of the way Josie had tried to put the matches back into their box, as if something was escaping from her.

'She's on her own, you see,' he said, and then thought damn, he's good at this, despite his silly waistcoat.

'That must be hard for her,' the doctor said in a gentle voice.

'I've been trying to find her someone to be with when . . . you know . . .' Scott trailed off wondering again why he was being such a sap. The TV doc was no doubt going to start shooting his cuff to get a glimpse of his over-elaborate diver's watch.

'You want her to have someone to help her get over losing you,' Dr Moulton said in a tone of voice that suggested that nothing could be more reasonable. Scott was furious with himself for being perilously close to tears. *He'll bring out the dreaded box of tissues in a minute*, Scott thought. It was what all doctors did when they hadn't a clue about what to do next.

'It's pretty tricky finding someone for someone else. It's even harder than trying to find someone for yourself,' Dr Moulton said. 'It's almost impossible to second guess what someone might find attractive.'

'She's very, very fussy,' Scott said. 'I mean she shot one bloke down because he was wearing the wrong *shoes*!'

'Well, I guess you two have quite a lot in common, then,' Dr Moulton said, smiling for the first time, and his face creased up in a disarming way so that the curves in his cheeks almost met his slanting eyes.

'I saw you checking out my waistcoat,' he said and Scott found himself flushing.

'And how exactly are you going about your impossible task of trying to find your mother a boyfriend?'

'I put a video of her on YouTube.'

Dr Moulton, did a double take that was almost comical. 'Well, that's a very practical approach, I suppose,' he said gravely.

'She doesn't know anything about it. I've had literally thousands of messages,' Scott said. 'The problem is that a good proportion of them are a bit weird.'

'I would imagine that that might be the case,' the doctor said, ducking his head. Scott suspected he might be trying not to laugh.

'There's a man in Panama who's convinced Mum's his soulmate. He messages me almost every day. I haven't the heart to tell him that my mother is unlikely to want to hook up with a tour guide with bulging eyes who uses exclamation marks as full stops.'

'Do you really know what your mother wants?' asked Dr Moulton. 'It's difficult to know what creates that special spark. You often don't recognise it until you see it.'

'I'm playing the numbers game,' Scott said. 'I reckon if I set her up with enough of them, there will surely be someone she will fall in love with.'

'Hmm, love, like hope, is a bit of a slippery thing.'

'Are you married?' Scott asked. Something about the tone in the doctor's voice made him think that he might have been talking about his own experience.

Dr Moulton hesitated.

'My wife died three years ago.'

'I'm sorry,' Scott said, feeling his response was inadequate. There should be better words to say when someone tells you that they have lost someone.

'We met at the park. My dog fell in love with hers almost at the same time as I fell in love with her.' The doctor looked as if he might be about to say something else, but he changed his mind.

'Anyway, I'll see you next week, Scott,' he said and he stood up and presented his hand again.

'How did it go?' Josie asked as soon as she saw Scott. 'I've had so much coffee, I feel as if I've lost control of my lips. You were in there for ages.'

'It was fine,' Scott said, picking up the menu and scrutinising it.

'But what did they say? Did anyone say anything about another transplant?'

'Dr Moulton said it might be possible. I think I'll have a cheese melt.'

'Never mind the sandwich,' Josie said impatiently. 'Tell me exactly what the doctor said.'

'We mostly talked about other things.'

'What do you mean "other things"?'

'Just ... stuff,' said Scott. 'He said he wanted to see you next time.'

'I *knew* I should have come with you,' Josie said in exasperation.

Scott had decided to spend the afternoon with Picasso and Josie had taken the opportunity to visit her neighbour, whom she hadn't seen for a couple of weeks. Freya seemed particularly distracted today. She jumped back and forth in the accounts of her life in such a startling way that it was impossible to keep track.

'What's happened to your glasses?' Josie asked.

Freya was holding what looked like an outsized monocle to her eye.

'I'm not sure. They could be anywhere,' Freya said waving at the piles of stuff around her. 'I'm making do with this. The lens fell out of my magnifying glass which was lucky.'

'I'll take you to the optician next week,' Josie said. 'I've got Tuesday off.'

'There's no need,' Freya said in a placid tone. 'I'm making do and mending, like Mum says we must. Yup.'

She looked up at Josie through her makeshift eyepiece. Her one magnified eye looked huge, the pale grey iris encroached upon by a dark, greenish band like a ring around a planet.

'It's Saturday evening. What are you doing here with me? Why are you not getting yourself glammed up to go out with a nice man?' Freya asked.

Josie ducked her head to escape the other woman's beady scrutiny and started to unpack the contents of her shopping bag.

'What do you need all these batteries for, anyway?'

'In case of power cuts,' said Freya vaguely, 'and don't think I'm so doolally dip yet that I won't notice that you never answered my question.'

'Scott's ill again,' Josie said.

'Is he?' Freya said.

'His heart is failing.'

'He's got a good heart,' Freya said.

'He'll have another transplant,' Josie said. 'He'll be fine.'

Her words curled around her in the dusty room and when Freya didn't fill the ensuing silence with the comfort she was seeking, she felt a rising panic. He would graduate. He would marry. She would hold new flesh in her arms. He would have time to look back and assess the triumphs and the sorrows of his life. She had repeated this mantra ever since she had discovered that he was ill again as a way of calming herself. *I will be strong*, she thought. *He needs me to be strong. I have to be strong enough for the both of us.*

'I had a boy,' said Freya suddenly tapping her cigarette against the edge of the table. The penguin moved lazily in its silky blue water.

'What do you mean you had a boy?' asked Josie.

'Who would buy that bit of tat?' Freya said. She was looking with distaste at the television screen where a person in a red fleece was holding up a chipped teapot to the camera.

'What were you saying about having a child?' She had always understood that Freya and Chuck had been unable to have a family. Freya seemed to lose her thread and started to talk about a holiday in Norfolk she had taken with her sister when they were both eighteen. They had met a couple of boys at the campsite, soldiers on leave.

'My one was a peach,' she said. 'He had wide shoulders and he laughed at everything. The whole world was funny to him. I kissed him, just the once. The night before we left.'

'What happened then?' Josie asked, but she knew the story had already slipped away and become tangled up in the skeins of another memory, this time of watching her mother make Yorkshire pudding.

'They were as high as a book and as thick and golden all over,' she said. 'I think I'll make some now.' But even as she was getting up to go to the kitchen the thought was pulled from her again and wound around another time and place. It seemed to Josie that Freya's haunches had taken on the shape of her chair the way meat fat gathered and hardened in the roasting dish.

'Yes. I had a boy when I was sixteen,' Freya said. She turned away from the TV and looked squarely at Josie. Her eyes were such a pale grey that they looked unfocused, as if she was looking inwards.

'Did you?' said Josie, unsure how reliable this particular memory was.

'He was perfect. Fists like shells and a suck on him to rival a hoover. Yup,' said Freya.

'What happened to him?'

'My mum and dad made me give him away,' Freya said and a shadow passed over her face as if the light outside had darkened. 'I wasn't married.'

'Who was the father?' Josie asked, keen to catch at this thread while it still hung clear.

'He had a deceiving sweetness, like raspberries,' said Freya.

'Ran away as soon as it all came out. Scared of my father and his shadow.'

'That's very sad,' said Josie.

'I still wonder what my boy is doing. What I would have made of him and he of me if we'd had each other.'

The two women fell into silence. Josie found it soothing being with the old woman. Her shuttered house felt like an escape from the real world.

'I would like to go to the sea today,' Freya announced as if Josie had asked her where she wanted to go, which she most definitely hadn't. The thought of driving Freya anywhere was alarming.

'Let's have a cup of tea first,' Josie said, hoping that the impulse for an excursion would fade away and be replaced for a request for some shopping or that perhaps Freya would embark on one of her tangled tales of falling in love with her husband in the Lake District and be diverted.

'I was in two minds about him at the start of the holiday,' she had said once of her late husband. 'He wasn't a talker and I thought he left it too much to me to make things happen. I thought him a little dozy. But on the third day we went on a walk round Coniston Water. It had been windy and then the wind suddenly dropped and the lake was like a silver penny. "If I can make this stone skip four times," he said, "then you'll marry me." He threw the stone and it only bounced three times and it made me laugh. He looked so disappointed. I found myself saying I would give him one more chance. It was just something to say really. It took nine tries before he managed it, but when he did he looked so happy that something turned in me. I thought him bold to risk something so important on the throw of a stone. I knew he would have stood there for a hundred years until he got his four skips. In the end it was as quick as that. Yup.'

Josie binned two half-eaten cottage pies and made tea. It was hard to find a cup without a cigarette butt floating in it, so she took the opportunity to scrub them all in hot water.

'Let's go now while the sun is out,' Freya said, and Josie came back into the room to find her neighbour already in her coat, a woollen hat rammed down over her sparse curls.

In the car, Freya looked out of the window, exclaiming at the changes she could see – buildings where none had been before, lost shops, an old friend's house turned into an apartment block. Josie wondered when her neighbour had last been out and felt a wave of guilt that she hadn't thought to take her somewhere before.

'Chuck used to say I was like a mountain goat,' she said, when they arrived at Beadnell Beach. 'The way I used to scramble over the rocks.'

Today, scrambling was out, but the two of them managed to walk a slow half a mile or so along the beach. *She is going to go any minute now*, Josie thought. *She'll turn her head and not know me, or herself, and then she'll be frightened and I'll have to get her back into the car.* But whether it was the sun on their faces, or the way the sea and sky were endless so that there was no need to try and remember anything because it was all there, laid out for them, Freya stayed in the present, glistening day.

Just before they left the beach, when they were almost at the car, Freya suddenly stopped. Josie thought that perhaps she had tripped but the old woman crouched down and then slowly and creakily laid herself out on the sand.

'You'll get wet,' Josie said, envisaging not being able to get Freya up and having to leave her there until she could fetch help.

'I used to do this all the time,' Freya said and she stretched her arms wide, making marks in the sand. 'I'm a sand angel,' she said and smiled gappily.

She fell asleep in the car on the way back, her head wedged against the window, and when Josie parked the car outside her house and woke her, she had slipped into another slice of time.

'I've been somewhere nice, I think,' she said. 'Have we been to the Lake District?'

Once Freya had been settled in her chair and the sand shaken from her coat and hat, Josie made her escape. She wondered if the hours that they had spent together that afternoon would be lost forever to Freya, or whether somewhere, deep in the fibre of what made her what she was, they would exist, unreachable, but intact, like something buried in the earth.

Chapter 19

Dear Scott

You know that feeling you get when you see someone for the first time and it is as if you know them already? That is what it was like for me when I saw the film of your mother. It was weird. I recognised her even though I have never seen her before. It would make me so happy to have a date with her.

Ted

'You're kidding, right?' Josie said.

'No. I've set you up with two more dates this weekend,' Scott said.

Josie walked into the living room from the kitchen. Scott was lying on the sofa tapping away on his computer. Apart from a couple of outings with Picasso, he had hardly left the house. All his old vigour and restlessness had slipped away from him and had been replaced with a weary air of resignation that broke her heart. The night before he had said that he didn't think there was any point in having the angioplasty procedure that was booked for the following week.

'What good will it do?' he had said.

His question had made her feel so furious and despairing that she could hardly speak.

'How can you just give in?' she had said at last and when he didn't reply she had caught hold of one of his arms and shaken it.

'I won't let you give in,' she had said.

'Don't you mean you won't let yourself give in?' Scott had said, his face set and pale. His answer had made her feel suddenly off balance, as if the ground under her feet had shifted.

'Scott, I can't be meeting new people,' Josie said now, standing over him, still holding the dripping plate she had been washing. 'Not when we have this to cope with.'

'This will help us cope,' he said, looking at her with some of his old determination.

'How can you think that sitting in pubs and restaurants and wandering around parks and gardens with complete strangers is going to help the situation?'

Did he not see how important it was for them both to focus on getting him better? Nothing else mattered. In any case, she was hardly in the right frame of mind to be making small talk with men who in the normal way of things she would be crossing the street to avoid.

'You're being ridiculous,' she said, shaking the plate in agitation so that drops of water fell on his face. Scott wiped his forehead with the sleeve of his jumper. He closed the lid of his computer and placed it on the floor beside him and lay staring up at the ceiling. She thought perhaps she had hurt him. She shouldn't have called him ridiculous. Young people hated to feel as if they were not being taken seriously. They disliked it almost as much as being accused of inauthenticity. Being 'fake' was the ultimate sin; one that could get you ostracised by your peers and yet it seemed to Josie that teenagers were continually trying out different personas; attempting to find one that fit.

'I'm sorry,' she said, putting down the plate and coming to kneel beside him. 'I shouldn't have said that. I know you've been trying to help.'

'I want you to have someone when I'm not here,' he said and she saw that this had been his plan all along. He had already accepted that he was going to die. He had reconciled himself to it months ago. That was why he had started this ridiculous quest to find her a man. Did he seriously imagine it would make any difference to her at all? Her heart felt like ice inside her, as if it had frozen itself to her ribs. She thought maybe she was dying too. Scott's hair had grown long again and today he had gathered it up in a wonky topknot to keep it out of his eyes. Despite his paleness and the way his blue eyes looked cloudy, as if a caul had been pulled over them, he was beautiful to her. She couldn't give up on him the way he seemed to have given up on himself.

'Why did Peter leave?' he asked suddenly turning his face to hers.

'I've never been absolutely sure,' Josie said.

'He left because he didn't want a baby, didn't he?' Scott asked, sitting up. His fists were curled up under the too-long sleeves of his floppy jumper. 'If it wasn't for me you would still be together.'

'That's not true,' Josie said. 'It would have been something else a little further down the line. I didn't know at the time, but he wasn't a keeper.'

'I want to find you a keeper.'

'My darling boy, I can't seem to do it for myself. How could you possibly manage it?'

'It's the law of averages,' Scott said. 'There has to be someone absolutely perfect out there.'

'I'll go on the wretched dates, if you will have the operation on Monday.' It was her only bargaining chip and she was cashing it in.

He looked at her and gave one of his wide smiles. It made his face look childish again. For a moment he looked as if there was nothing wrong with him.

'It's a deal!' he said.

On Saturday morning Scott volunteered to go with Josie to meet Ted, a man who had sounded almost poetic in his conviction that Josie was his ideal woman. 'I feel as if I have been waiting all my life to meet your mother,' he had said on the phone. 'Looking at her, hearing her speak, makes me feel happy.'

'His three favourite things are fresh bread, collecting mushrooms and wild bears,' Scott said.

'Hmm, sounds cute,' Josie replied, but Scott thought she was unconvinced.

They walked along Broadgate, past St Michael's Pant, a fountain topped with a statue of the winged saint with a slain dragon. Scott remembered standing in its shallow basin as a child, feeling the cold water on his feet. The streets had embraced the turn to summer with tautened awnings and newly painted furniture already optimistically placed outside restaurants and coffee shops.

'You go in after me,' Josie instructed as they neared their destination – Josie's favourite place to have lunch.

'Sit several tables away and don't try and catch my attention.'

'Shall we have a sign?' Scott asked. 'I mean, if you want me to stage an intervention or something.'

Josie laughed.

'I'll touch my nose in a lingering way,' she said.

Ted turned out to be a tiny man with a face that looked as if it had been squashed in a vice. Josie and Scott looked at him through the window.

'Maybe it's not him,' Josie said hopefully.

'I think it is,' Scott said. 'He said he would be wearing brown. I didn't think he was going to be dressed from head to toe in it as if he is auditioning to be a goblin.'

'Maybe you could call him and tell him I've been suddenly taken unwell,' said Josie.

'You can't do that!' said Scott. 'Go in and I'll wait a couple of minutes and follow you in.'

Josie gave a theatrical sigh.

'The things I do for you!' she said.

Scott watched as she approached the table and saw Ted rise to his feet almost knocking his chair over in his eagerness. Looking at his mother you would imagine that she was delighted too. She was smiling at him as if he really was Hugh Jackman. *I will have to insist on better photographs in the future, or at least pictures of the men standing up, in full light*, he thought. I know Josie doesn't set much store by appearances, but this man really did look like an extra in a Star Wars movie. Ted turned his head and Scott was horrified to see that he was sporting a ponytail. He kept blooming quiet about that, Scott thought furiously. There is no way I would have given him the time of day if I'd known about his scrawny head appendage.

He pushed open the door and went inside and found a table tucked away around a corner so that he could observe the couple. If it had been him he would have been rubbing franti-cally at his nose by now but he knew she would sit it out and try and make the wood elf feel as good as possible. It was what she did, making people feel better about themselves. Looking at her laughing with Ted, he thought how beautiful she looked with her fall of hair and that way she had of talking with her hands. He had always found it a struggle to say nice things to her. He had wanted to say how glad he was that she was his mother but it was as if he couldn't quite bring himself to say what he knew would make her happy. I wonder why that is, he asked himself. It wouldn't be as if I was being fake, it was perhaps more that he was scared of appearing so. You couldn't just say such things out of the blue. You had to choose your moments and none of the moments had seemed quite right. He thought of Emily whom he hadn't heard from since the day at Greenwich Park, with her pearly face turning away from him. Words had failed her too. He wondered what she was doing at this moment. He imagined her in a vivid-coloured dress standing in a party room full of men replete with endless life. They would be trying to catch her eye. Perhaps someone would succeed and she would listen to him with her head to one side, the way she used to listen to him and maybe, after a while, she would let one of the vigorous, profli-gate men hold her and she would sway in his arms, feeing the beat of his steady heart.

Ted got up to buy another couple of coffees and he caught his mother's eye.

'*HE'S GOT A COIN PURSE*,' she mouthed at him and pointed at Ted's back. Scott could see that he was paying for the coffees by making painstaking piles of copper on the counter. The girl behind it was twiddling the ends of her hair and looking at Ted as if he was a beetle that had appeared from behind a slice of carrot cake. Scott made a scandalised face at Josie and she began to laugh so hard, she dribbled a bit of coffee down her chin and had to flail around on the floor to recover her dropped napkin.

'Well, I don't think Ted Roper is the man for me,' Josie said after he had been politely dispatched and she and Scott were walking back to the house.

'What exactly was it about him that didn't attract you?' Scott asked.

'Was it the way he paid for your coffee with twopence pieces or the fact that he has three rabbits that hop about his living room shitting pellets?' Scott asked and his mother laughed and then stopped abruptly and it was as if the sound had been plucked from the air.

Chapter 20

Hi Scott
    I can't believe I'm doing this. I don't want to appear arrogant but I've never been short of dates. I like the fact that your mother doesn't know just how pretty she is and I would like to be able to convince her.
    Grant

Looking out of the window the next day as she did the washing-up, Josie was cast down to see that it was still raining. Her second date of the weekend, with a dentist called Grant, was at eleven o'clock at the café in Barter Books. He was the first person she had been out with who actually lived in Alnwick. Apparently Picasso's family had known him for years and had suggested him as a potential candidate to Scott. She hoped this date would turn out to be better than her last. She thought of Ted's small, white hands and shuddered slightly. She went upstairs and pulled on a T-shirt, followed by a shirt, which made the navy jumper she put on top look rather lumpy. *I am rather lumpy, so there is no use in pretending I'm anything else*, Josie thought as she gathered up her hair into a loose bun. *How come I don't seem to be able to manage the artless updos I see in magazines?* Josie wondered. It was more of a case of 'updon't' when she tried anything similar.

It had only been a couple of months, but already the ministrations of the hatchet-headed stylist were a distant memory. In any case, five minutes outside would turn her hair into a frizzy mess. Peter said it had been her complete disregard for anything remotely feminine which had first attracted him, which she had taken as a compliment at the time, but which made her speculate after he had disappeared whether he had gone in search of someone with more womanly attributes – someone who put perfume on her pulse points and knew the leg-lengthening value of a nude court shoe. She wondered, not for the first time, why it was that women seldom saw themselves in their entirety but rather as a series of failings, linked together to form an unsatisfactory whole. She never split people down in this way when she met them, getting rather an entire sense of them as beautiful or funny or kind, and yet when thinking about how she presented to other people she thought that they would notice only those things she would prefer to be hidden.

The bookshop was crowded and, looking around her, Josie couldn't see her date. She wandered down the aisles of shelves for a while, picking up a volume of Northumberland folk tales and a recipe book for one-pot suppers. There were a couple of places that would fit the description of a café in the building and she walked from one end of the shop to the other but couldn't see any bemused-looking men. Scott should have implemented some sort of system – perhaps the carrying of a flag, a method adopted by tour guides in tourist spots. In the end, Josie bought herself a cup of coffee and settled down in an armchair with her books.

'You're not Josie, are you?' someone said. She was deep into a story about the Laidly Worm, a Northumberland tale of transformation – another slain serpent; this time one whose destruction had brought a dead sister to life, and his voice startled her. She looked up into a face that wouldn't have looked out of place on a coin – aesthetic cheekbones and an aquiline nose and dark, almond-shaped eyes. He was unambiguously handsome. She thought there should be a statue of him somewhere, dressed in skimpy animal fur, holding a spear.

'I am,' she said, getting to her feet and extending her hand. He held on for slightly longer than was necessary and looked intently at her. She had an impulse to laugh at the obviousness of this move. *Someone should tell him*, she thought, *that women are not so easily fooled*, and yet she found herself blushing under his scrutiny. She pulled her hand away, annoyed both at his lack of subtlety and at herself for responding so predictably.

'I'm Grant. I'm sorry I'm late,' he said, taking off his jacket and sitting down in the chair opposite hers. 'One of my regulars cracked a tooth on a pistachio nut and was in agony.'

He smiled, revealing a row of perfect teeth, not Hollywood-white but some judiciously chosen shade more appropriate to the dank climate and often grey skies of Northumberland. She could tell by his clothes, the crisp, button-collared shirt, the well-laundered jeans, that he was someone who cared about his appearance. He was tall and beyond that seemed to take up more than his allotted amount of space – his arms resting widely on the arms of his chair, his legs stretched out. She found his apparent ease and confidence alluring and yet it also goaded her. She recognised this sensation of irritation or resistance, she couldn't exactly define it, as the beginning of attraction.

'You are far too beautiful to be on your own,' he said and she resisted the impulse his words provoked in her to duck her head.

'And you have far too perfect a smile not to be able to pull as easily as, no doubt, you pulled out your afflicted patients' tooth this morning,' she said looking at him squarely, knowing she was sounding a little stiff, but unable for the moment to think of another way to respond to his overt and, she suspected, knee-jerk admiration. This was clearly the way he spoke to all women. She thought his patients probably loved him even when he was poised over them with his drill; the women, at least; the men (unless male dentists with faces like Roman emperors was their thing) would probably think he was a bit of a jerk.

'It's not getting women that's my problem,' Grant said. 'It's keeping them.'

'I am beginning to see why,' she said and he laughed.

'You have a way of showing your disapproval that is very attractive.'

'I don't disapprove of you. I barely know you,' she said.

'What do you look for in a man?' he asked, taking a sip of her water and looking at her over the rim of the glass.

'I don't think I have a particular type,' she said. 'As my son has no doubt informed you, it's been a while since I've had a proper relationship. If it wasn't for him I probably wouldn't be looking for anyone at all.'

'He seems to be very determined,' Grant said and she thought briefly about telling him the reason Scott had embarked on the search, but then changed her mind. She was unlikely to see this man again and she didn't want to tell a stranger what she had only recently discovered herself. There was hardly a moment when she didn't think about what was going to happen to Scott and what she could do, but she found there was a brief consolation in not having to talk about it now.

'What do *you* look for in a woman?' she asked him.

'Madly blue eyes, dark hair, rough hands from the excavation of fossils (*Scott had clearly told him a lot about her*), and a slightly prickly personality,' he said with a counterfeit gallantry that should have made her wince but instead made her smile. What could it be like to feel as if you were duty bound to seduce everyone you met? The man must get exhausted.

'When was your last long-term relationship?' she asked.

'Depends what you mean by long-term,' he said evasively, suddenly looking so shifty that it made her laugh out loud.

'You know, a committed relationship that lasts longer than the first dazzling weeks. Someone that you imagine you might be able to be with for ever, even if that doesn't prove to be the case.'

'I've been married twice, if that's what you mean.' She thought his face moved with some particular feeling – perhaps regret, although he spoke lightly and the impression was almost immediately dispelled by the cocky grin he flashed at her.

'Why didn't your marriages last? If you don't mind me asking. It's fine if you don't want to talk about it.'

'There is no one to blame but myself. The failure of both of them was due to my own inability to decide what it was I really wanted. I mean, I thought it was what I wanted at the time, but I couldn't seem to sustain it somehow. It's too easy to say, I fell out of love, but that is what it felt like. I think I fall in love and out of love more frequently than other people.'

'Perhaps it was simply that you shouldn't have got married in the first place,' she said and he shrugged.

'Maybe I'm not the marrying kind,' Grant said.

'Well, at least I know not to hold out any great hopes, then,' she said.

'Although, of course, I may at last strike lucky,' he said, his eyes moving over her face and resting somewhere at the base of her throat and she felt a sudden pulse of desire. It came out of nowhere, almost as if he had charmed it out of her.

'Shall we get some fresh air?' she said, wanting to move away from his scrutiny and her own unreliable response to it.

It had stopped raining and the air smelt sweetly of wet stone and wood. They left the bookshop and walked back through town, talking about the ordinary things of first dates – their respective jobs, their family backgrounds – he had wanted to be a dentist since the day he fell off his bike and smashed his front tooth. She also learned that he hadn't seen his mother for six years. She lived in France and they had become estranged over an argument about money.

'She's always wanting money for some hopeless scheme or other or, more usually, some hopeless man or other – she has a taste for younger men,' he said.

They walked to his house, which was a pretty cottage next to a side entrance to Alnwick Gardens – a wrought-iron gate made up of glossy black flowers and birds.

'I'm guessing it's probably too soon to invite you in,' he said.

'I've a feeling it might not be such a good idea,' she said, although part of her wanted to.

'I would very much like to see you again,' he said and she was taken aback by how earnest he seemed, although, of course, this was what he did best – making women feel they were indispensable to him. She hesitated. He was definitely not what Scott would refer to as a keeper. She knew she would just be a distraction for him but, after all, wasn't that what she wanted too, someone who could help her forget for a while what really mattered? It might also keep Scott quiet if she was able to say she was seeing someone for a second time.

'Give me your phone,' she said. She punched her number in and he had the grace to look surprised.

Chapter 21

Scott

I think I am in love with your mother. Do you believe in love at first sight? I do. It's happened to me a few times. Once I fell in love with a woman on the train and although I didn't need to get the train again – my journey had been a one-off, I was visiting a relative in Birmingham – I kept getting the same train every day just so I could see her. For ages all I did was look at her. It took me four weeks to pluck up the courage to speak to her. When it came to it, she wasn't at all what I expected. She was very rude, unnecessarily foul-mouthed, and when I got closer to her, I realised that her eyebrows were tattooed on.

Yours in hope

Tristan

'He's nicer than he looks,' Scott said as Josie and he waited for Dr Moulton, who was doing his rounds. Scott had undergone his surgery the day before and had wanted to leave the hospital immediately, but Dr Moulton, who had brought him a copy of *National Geographic* and *GQ* and a bar of fruit and nut, had insisted he stay overnight.

'Chocolate, a story about storm chasers and pictures of Margot Robbie,' Dr Moulton had said. 'I think that covers pretty much all your hospital needs.'

'I hope he says I can go home. I'm desperate to get out of this place,' Scott said now, his body itchy from the hospital sheets and inertia. His chest was tender and his groin felt sore where the catheter had been inserted, but he didn't see the point of lying in bed. Every minute he spent there was making him feel worse. The man lying opposite him on the ward was breathing laboriously, making a rattling sound at the back of his throat and he could hear the ominous advance of the trolley, which heralded the dispersal of limp biscuits and pale tea. Dr Moulton put his head around the curtain.

'Can I come in?' he asked.

Today his waistcoat of choice was a flamboyant, swirling affair in sunset colours. Scott tried to avert his eyes, but found himself irresistibly drawn to it as if he was rubber necking an accident.

'I chose this waistcoat especially for you, Scott,' he said, smiling. 'I thought you would admire its subtle sophistication.'

'It's . . . it's remarkable,' Scott said.

'It's very nice to meet you at last,' Dr Moulton said to Josie, who reacted in exactly the way Scott could have predicted. He didn't know why she always took everything anyone said that related to his health as a criticism.

'I would have come before but he wouldn't let me,' Josie said, bristling.

'Can I go home?' Scott asked.

'Has the nurse been in to check you out?' the doctor asked.

Scott nodded.

'We don't want you rushing around.'

'I won't let him rush,' Josie said.

'In actual fact, Scott might find he feels a bit better than he has recently,' Dr Moulton said. 'His breathing will be easier.'

'How long will the stenting continue to have a positive effect?' Josie asked.

Dr Moulton sat down on the end of Scott's bed. *Uh oh, serious talk alert*, Scott thought.

'Transplant patients have a much higher rate of restenosis than people who haven't had a transplant,' Dr Moulton said. 'Are you familiar with the condition?'

'That's when the arteries become blocked again, isn't it?' Josie said in the same repressive tone of voice she had used the whole time the doctor had been with them. It was as if she thought the entire medical profession was trying to pull the wool over her eyes. Scott wished she would just chill a little and not act as if the whole world was out to get her.

'Yes. We are not absolutely sure why it happens. It might have something to do with the scarring that occurs during stenting. It might be caused by the body's prolonged attack on the immune system.'

The doctor was talking far more formally to his mother than he had to Scott. He thought the man was showing off a bit. Dr Moulton might be very good at extracting information from a person but Scott still suspected he was a little arrogant. You surely had to have an over-inflated sense of your own importance in order to imagine that you could get away with wearing a garment that looked like someone had voided their stomach post-pepperoni pizza on it.

'What will you do if that happens?' Josie asked, her eyes fixed firmly on the doctor, as if she was in charge of an unsteady toddler.

'It becomes increasingly hard to do any more surgery. The blockages can sometimes become more diffuse.'

'Then we would do another transplant, right?'

'It's certainly a possibility,' the doctor said carefully. Scott knew the tone of voice. It meant I am not shutting you down, but you have to be realistic. His mother showed no sign of picking up the unspoken cue.

'Is he on the list now?' she asked, 'because if he isn't, I'm selling my house and taking him to America. They are trying all sorts of new things there. I've read about it.'

'Let's see how we go and we will reassess the situation in a few weeks,' Dr Moulton said. He put out his hand to touch Josie on the arm, but she pulled away. Scott knew his mother was inured to the medical toolkit of comforting gestures and platitudes.

Dr Moulton disappeared again and then returned shortly with the news that Scott could go home as long as he promised to go straight back to bed.

'I know how to look after my son, Dr Moulton,' Josie said grandly, spoiling her sweeping exit by forgetting her handbag and having to go back to the ward to retrieve it. Scott waited for her by the car.

'Do you know he was standing in the middle of the floor holding it,' Josie said indignantly as she got into the car. 'I wouldn't be surprised if he had been rifling through it!'

'I'm sure Dr Moulton has no desire to dip his hand into the fluff and sand and bits of fossil that usually accumulate in your bags,' Scott said. His mother had a worrying hectic flush on her face and her hands were gripping the steering wheel even more tightly than they usually did.

'He was trying to fob me off,' Josie said, her mouth set in a furious, tight line. 'And did you see that waistcoat! The man's a fool. I'm going to ask if you can see another consultant.'

'I quite like Dr Moulton. He's a straight talker.'

'I don't care how straight his talk is. I want someone who is going to commit to doing something.'

'What I fancy right now is an enormous ice cream,' Scott said.

'Well, you can't have one,' Josie said, putting her hand up to one of her flushed cheeks.

'I know it's on the list of banned substances,' Scott said. 'But I've always wanted one of those swirly ones in tall glasses with cherries and nuts and shit on the top.'

'Cherries and nuts and shit it'll be, then,' said Josie, almost smiling. He suspected that her long-held policy about ice cream had only been overturned because she thought Dr Moulton would take a dim view of her decision.

They parked in the street by an ice cream and coffee shop tricked out like a fifties diner and Scott ordered the tallest knickerbocker glory money could buy, and worked his way through it as though he had never eaten before. He thought it was probably the most delicious thing he had ever tasted.

'I've had a deprived childhood,' he said.

Josie made a humphing sound and sipped her coffee.

'So you quite liked Grant, then?' Scott said, looking at her slyly.

'He wasn't as terrible as some of my other dates have been. Not that the bar has been set very high.'

'Does that mean you are going to see him again?'

'I don't know, Scott,' Josie said. 'I haven't really made up my mind.'

Her evasive tone of voice made him think that she was prevaricating and that she liked Grant more than she was willing to admit.

'I think you should,' he said and Josie stuck out her tongue at him.

'Mind, if he could see you now, I don't think he'd be that keen,' Scott said.

'You do know it's unusual for a boy your age to be so preoccupied with his mother's love life, don't you?'

'These are unusual times,' he said. 'And they call for unusual measures.'

'You are a fool.' Her face softened when she looked at him in a way that always made him panic because it usually indicated that she was going to get all heavy.

'Talking of fools,' he said in a neutral voice designed to distract her from what he thought she might be about to say, 'what was all that about selling the house?' he asked, scraping the last of the jam and cream off the inside of the glass.

'I'll do it if that's what it takes,' she said.

'Where exactly are you planning to live after you have blown your money on my medical expenses?' he asked.

'I'll rent,' Josie said. Her eyes were strained and the skin underneath looked thin and grey. He saw she had attempted to tame her hair by sticking an incongruous butterfly-shaped clip into the side of her fringe. He felt a great lurch of tenderness for her. She was so heartbreakingly transparent and yet so oblivious to what she showed, like one of those tiny, gossamer fish, which seem as insubstantial as the air but have extraordinary resilience. He had owned a fish tank when he was a child. It had been one of his mother's attempts to provide a pet without exposing Scott to the dangers of claws and teeth. The tank had started out full of colourful tropical fish in a variety of sizes but one by one they had died until only a miniscule, glassy fish was left. It swam round and round, eating the food Scott provided, unaware of its dominion over its small world. Every day Scott would come down expecting the fish to have died and every day it was still there, riding the thin bubbles, threading its way through the plastic seaweed as if it was on a mission. Scott had named it 'Legend' because he had been convinced that it would live forever. He had become so accustomed to the notion of the fish's immortality that he couldn't remember exactly when he last checked it was there, but one morning he found that the tank was empty. Scott turned over the blue glass pebbles and threaded his fingers through the weed, but there was no sign the fish had ever been there. There were no tiny bones, no cloudy piece of skin. It was as if it had just worn itself away

Chapter 22

Dear Scott
   *Your Mum is ☺. I feel a distinct flutter in my 🐟 when
I saw her in her wetsuit 🐺.*

While Scott was out with Picasso, Josie went to the hospital to
see Dr Moulton. She wanted to talk to him without Scott being
there so that she could speak freely. Her son had a tendency to
think she was making too much of a fuss, as if that was even
possible. Fussing was putting coasters on tables or clipping the
edges of lawns, not fighting for your child's life.

   She wondered how many hours she had spent over the years
sitting in rooms like this, looking at the clock, making up stories about the couples holding hands and the frail, wispy-haired
children sitting on laps. There had been times when this wait-
ing-room community had felt like her family. She thought of
the small kindnesses that had been extended towards her and
that she, in turn, had given; the sympathetic smiles, the con-
spiratorial roll of eyes, the fleeting hands on her shoulder, the
drinks brought for her when it seemed that she couldn't move
from Scott's side even to quench the rapacious thirst caused by
spent tears and the hot, secret hospital air. She had spent four
hours one night holding the hand of a dying woman who had

thought that Josie was her daughter. Josie had wondered where the real daughter was, whether she was even still alive, the tug of the woman's fingers making her feel, in her role of a proxy, as if she too was not quite there but was hovering between life and death.

Dr Moulton was waist-coated behind his desk. He gave her a cautious smile as if he was anticipating difficulty. She thought he looked tired.

'Good morning, Ms Hudson,' he said, and she gritted her teeth. She disliked the title because it felt like an assumption that she cared about her status.

'Would you prefer it if I called you Josie?' he asked, and she felt immediately wrong-footed.

'Yes, that's probably easier,' she said, knowing she sounded petulant.

'Only if you call me Robert,' the doctor said smiling, and she wondered for a fleeting minute whether he was flirting with her. She thought it would be extremely unprofessional if he was, but decided that it was probably what he did with all the mothers to try and put them at ease.

'How's Scott?' the doctor asked.

'He's been better over the last few days,' she said. 'Less tired.'

'That's good. I expect you are here to ask me what our plan is for him.'

'I'm glad to hear you have a plan.' She sat up straighter in her chair.

'The reprieve is likely to be a fairly short one,' the doctor said looking levelly at Josie. 'Once CAV takes hold there is really very little that we can do.'

Josie felt a tremor in her arms and legs. She was familiar with the sensation. It had become an early warning sign that she had to hold on, keep her head up, gird herself for a fight. She wouldn't cry here, with this man, in this sterile little room.

'What about another transplant?' she asked. 'He's young and strong.' She said the words as if she was explaining something.

'He's full of spirit,' the doctor said gently. 'He seems to me to be a very valiant boy.'

Josie felt the tears gathering like an enemy advance. She bit the inside of her mouth until she could taste blood. It was the word valiant that had weakened her. It so accurately described her son's approach to the tricky life he had been given. She wondered, not for the first time, about why he had been chosen for this burden, why she had. The affliction had started out a million miles away. It had hovered over her world and then plummeted like a meteorite, falling, sharp edged and lethal. The damage could have been inflicted anywhere. It could have landed and mortally wounded someone who might have deserved it – a child murderer or a person who took pleasure from inflicting hurt. It could have moved a little to the left or right and chosen someone who was eking out their days in a rattan chair waiting for the light to fade. She remembered her grandmother, a small, fierce woman saying 'You can live too long, you know', and looking at Josie crossly, as if her granddaughter was to blame for her relentless, pain-filled longevity. She thought about the way Scott had always tried to make each day last as long as it could and she felt so angry that she thought she could open her mouth wide like a vengeful harpy and swallow up the hateful room and everything in it.

'Is he on the list?' she asked now and didn't know how she had managed to say the words in a normal voice. Inside her they had felt like a screech.

'As his condition develops, we'll assess his suitability,' the doctor said. 'There's a lot of scar tissue which can sometimes make re-transplantation difficult. I don't think you should give up hope, but perhaps prepare yourself for things not working out.'

She looked at him across the desk.

'Have you got children, Dr Moulton?' she asked.

'No,' he said, looking down at his hands.

'Then you will have no idea how I feel or how the hell one is supposed to "prepare". You make it sound as if such a thing is possible.'

'I've had a lot of patients,' the doctor said. 'Perhaps "prepare" was a clumsy word, but I know it often helps to be aware of the facts.'

'I've been "aware of the facts" for more than ten years.' She got to her feet. She couldn't stay a moment longer.

'I'm sorry,' Dr Moulton said. 'I can't imagine how hard it must be.'

'I'm not giving up,' Josie said. She felt brittle, as if any sudden movement would cause her to crumble to the floor.

'Shall I get you something to drink?' the doctor said, but she was already at the door.

Picasso and Scott went to the harbour in Seahouses for fish and chips. There was enough warmth in the air to allow them to sit outside at a trestle table where they could watch the boats and the groups of visitors wearing shiny new windcheaters. After being in London, surrounded by the bang and grind of the city, Scott felt soothed by the sounds and smells he was so familiar with – the yowl of the gulls, the creak of wet ropes being hitched to cleats, the crack of sails, the throaty drill of an outboard motor firing up, all overlaid with the smell of wet canvas and diesel and the oily brine of the harbour water.

'So what's so special about this Emily person?' said Picasso with his mouth full of chips.

'I don't know really,' said Scott, looking away from his friend, pretending a sudden interest in a family who had come in a noisy rush to sit at the table next to theirs.

'You're clearly smitten,' Picasso announced. 'I know the signs and you have them all.'

'What are the signs, then, you who have so much experience in the ways of women?' Scott asked, thinking of Picasso's constant torments at the hands of Lois, who was more capricious than the weather.

'One,' Picasso said, ignoring Scott's jibe and ticking the points off on his glistening fingers. 'Your face changes when you talk about her. It becomes ridiculously dopey, like a donkey on sedatives. Two, you insert her name randomly into conversations. Three, you barely look at girls, even the very hot one to our left in the green top.'

Scott's eyes swivelled round to the girl in question. She was pretty with her messed-up blonde hair and her long legs in tiny denim shorts, but she lacked Emily's precision and grace. It was like comparing a slab of rock with something intricately carved.

'What happened, anyway?' Picasso asked. 'Did you break up?'

'Something like that,' Scott said.

He remembered the way Emily had pressed her face to his under the shelter of the church portico, as if she had wanted to get as close to him as she possibly could and his chest caught on something hard.

'I'm ill again. That's why I'm back.' It had taken him until now to say the words out loud. He hadn't wanted to spoil the time they had together by telling his friend that there would be an end. The point of being young was that it should all feel endless. Picasso stopped chewing, his cheeks distended with cod.

'Your heart?' he asked when he had swallowed enough to speak.

'Yeah. It's beginning to pack up.'

'So, you get another one, right?' Picasso pushed the hair out of his eyes. He looked earnestly at his friend, wanting to be reassured. For a moment Scott was tempted to placate him. It was what he had always done to those closest to him. It wasn't just that it was easier for them, it was easier for him too. He hated the thought of people trying to reach for the right words when there weren't really any that would fit.

'It's unlikely,' Scott said. 'There aren't many spare hearts knocking around and they usually give them to first timers because they have a better chance of making the most of them. Second transplants tend not to last very long.'

Picasso's face moved in discomfort, as if the mouthful of potato and fish had wedged itself somewhere in his throat.

'But they can patch you up, can't they? Maybe give you one of those metal heart things.'

'I think I may have missed my chance to be a bionic man,' Scott said lightly, wanting to make this as painless as possible.

Picasso leaned forward and took Scott's hand in his greasy one and Scott held on. Neither of them had touched each other before, not in this deliberate, meaningful way. Any previous contact had been of the comradely punch-and-hug variety.

'Oh mate . . . fucking hell . . . what does this mean, exactly?' Picasso asked. Scott felt grateful for the direct question. In return he did his best not to falter and to keep his gaze steady.

'It means that I probably don't have very long.'

Picasso closed his eyes for a moment and when he opened them again, it was as if he wasn't quite sure where he was. He looked at Scott in bewilderment.

'Are you serious?' he asked at last, as if Scott was suggesting something preposterous. He looked even more astonished than he had when Scott had told him what sex was when they were nine years old. When the unimaginable deed had been described to him by Scott who had gleaned most of his information from diagrams of the mating habits of cetaceans, he had fallen about on the grass laughing so hard that he had started hiccupping.

'No one has said the words,' Scott said, 'but I know which way this is likely to go. I'll get worse and worse and then they won't be able to do anything much for me.'

He looked out to sea as he spoke, knowing the truth of what he said, but there was still a part of him that couldn't believe there would come a time when he wasn't part of this booming, cracking world. Picasso was silent for a while and then he released his hand from Scott's and got up and walked round to the other side of the table. He put his arms around Scott and held him in an effortful embrace, as if he was trying to share strength or hold himself together. Scott could feel him shaking and the scratchy push of his ill-shaven face against his own.

'It's all right,' Scott said. 'I've had a long time to get used to it.' He wondered as he said the words out loud whether he would ever be able to relinquish his only partly discovered, incredible life.

Part Three

Summer

Chapter 23

Good morning Scott
    Your mother has inspired me to write a haiku. Here goes:
    Path runs to the gate
    Where silky stone and grass meet
    The raindrops collect.
    M. R. W.

Things with Grant were not moving nearly fast enough for Scott's liking. His mother had gone on another couple of dates with him over the last few weeks, but now things seemed to have stalled.

'What's wrong with him?' he had asked her, trying not to sound irritated. Scott thought that most women would find Grant handsome and on the one occasion Scott had met him when he had come to pick Josie up, he had been friendly to Scott in a non-creepy, straightforward kind of a way. He had brought his mother flowers – a great big bunch that Scott knew would have cost a bit, but Josie hadn't even put them in water but had left them on the kitchen counter, which Scott took to be a worrying sign.

'There's absolutely nothing wrong with him,' his mother had said, which hadn't sounded to Scott like a ringing endorsement. It was clear that he was going to have to take matters into his own hands if the relationship had any chance of moving forward. If Grant didn't turn out to be a keeper, he would be forced to go back to sifting through the messages that were still coming in on a daily basis. There were times when Scott felt that in making the video he had unleashed a monster. He had never imagined there were quite so many desperate people in the world.

Scott was already up when Josie went downstairs, sitting slightly hunched over a bowl of cereal.

'I thought we could go to Holy Island,' he said looking up at her, 'Grant's keen.'

'When did you arrange this?' Josie asked suspiciously. She had a million things to do and she had been a little relieved that she wasn't going to be seeing Grant that day.

'I phoned him,' Scott said calmly. 'He said he couldn't think of anything nicer than going there for a pub lunch and a bit of a wander.'

'Scott!' said Josie looking at him in admonishment.

'What?' Scott answered making an exaggerated shrugging motion.

'You know what. I don't want you getting involved. It's my business.'

'All I'm suggesting is a walk,' Scott said and he turned his head back to his bowl of cereal. 'You don't have to make such a fuss about it.'

'I'll drive,' Scott said when Grant arrived at the house. He saw his mother raise her eyebrows at Grant over the top of the car. She could resist it all she wanted, but Scott was sure there was something between them. Josie got into the passenger seat and Grant sat behind, although Scott had told them he was going to play the part of the chauffeur and that they should both sit on the back seat so that they could chat properly.

'Honestly, Scott!' his mother had hissed at him as she got into the car, but he had pretended not to hear her. He had managed to delay them in a variety of ways – forgetting his headphones and turning the house upside down looking for them when he knew full well they were in his pocket and then, just as they were all finally ready to leave the house, he had pretended he had to take a phone call in his bedroom. His plan would only work if the timings were exactly right. Half an hour one way or the other and the scheme would fall apart.

He opened the car window. He could smell summer. It rose from the hedges and trees in scented bursts and the fields were rich and thick and beginning to shed a dusty haze. In the distance the sea and sky were seamed together in the same, feathered blue.

'I'm starving,' his mother said. 'I'm not sure any of the pubs will still be serving food.'

'Don't worry. I've rung ahead,' Scott said, and Josie gave him another of her *I wish you wouldn't do this* looks.

Scott accelerated as they crossed the narrow causeway that linked Holy Island with the mainland. The road was edged with mud flats that shone like the backs of seals. They had till 2.30 before the tide turned and cut the island off. It was a local sport to spot the fools who neglected to check the timetable and who found themselves facing sudden, fast currents. They had to sit on the roofs of their cars and wait for a helicopter to rescue them or abandon their vehicles altogether and take immediate refuge in a little white shed on stilts situated on the side of the road until the water receded. Ahead of them was the castle, which was not really a proper fortress, more an Edwardian folly, perched on Beblowe Craig, a lump of rock that bulged out of the earth like a goitre. The land on either side was flat, making the castle look like the cobra that swallowed an elephant in the story of *The Little Prince*.

'Slow down, Scott,' Josie said, gripping the sides of her seat as he sped across to the island. 'I'm not THAT hungry.'

On either side of them the waiting tide gathered with a stealthy sheen like a metal door closing. He didn't want his mother taking too good a look at the progress of the water. She was as familiar as he was with the timetable of the sea.

'It will have to be a very quick lunch indeed,' Grant said, looking out of the window as they sped by.

Scott parked in the car park with a screech of his wheels, earning another look from his mother.

He went off to the bar to order the food and get the drinks while Josie sat with Grant. Scott knew they were talking about him; Josie kept sending anxious glances in his direction. She was definitely confiding in Grant, Scott thought. She wouldn't do that if she didn't like him, and they looked good together – both of them dark – what was the word? They complemented each other. He was doing the right thing. He'd order their food and then make some excuse about having to recharge his phone or something. By the time they knew he had gone it would be too late. They barely looked at him as he shouted out that he would be back in a minute and a short while later he was driving back down the causeway, slower this time, watching an arrow of wild geese flying across the shifting sea.

'Scott's been gone for a while,' Josie said, looking around her, and just then the girl behind the bar came over and put their food on the table.

'Where's my son's food?' Josie asked when it was clear that nothing more was forthcoming.

'He told me he wasn't eating,' the girl said slightly defensively.

'He said it was just the two of you having lunch.' Her tone implied that they were bloody lucky to get that. Josie knew she took them for day-trippers. Many of the Holy Islanders resented the modern-day pilgrims to the village – marching about the place, criticising the sandwiches and leaving litter everywhere. The island only really took on its proper character when the sea surrounded it, making it safe. Josie texted Scott, but didn't get an answer. Her attempts to phone him were also met with silence.

'We'd better just eat this and get back to the car,' Grant said, digging into his steak and ale pie, puncturing the pastry with a jab of his knife so that it oozed hotly all over his plate. 'He's probably not hungry and gone for a walk until we are finished.'

'Why would he do that?' Josie said, picking at her baked potato. She had been ravenous only minutes ago, but she seemed to have lost her appetite. A terrible suspicion was beginning to form in her mind.

Half an hour later they were back at the car park and her worst fears were confirmed. The car and Scott had gone. He had set her and Grant up. Grant seemed to find the whole situation funny. He certainly didn't look upset over the prospect of being marooned.

'Try and get a taxi, for heaven's sake,' Josie said.

Grant paced around the car park talking to various people on his phone.

'We're out of luck, I'm afraid,' he said when he returned. 'All available taxis are busy and there won't be one back in time to beat the tide and we certainly haven't the time to walk it.'

'There's no need to look so damn happy,' Josie said, torn between her desire to laugh at Grant's transparent pleasure and her concerns about her son's strange behaviour.

'Let's make an adventure of it,' Grant said, 'book somewhere for the night and then go and have a walk, before retiring to the pub for a pint or three.'

After exploring all the possible places to stay it seemed that there was only one room left in the entire village – a single bed stuck up in the eaves of the pub.

'We don't often offer it for rent,' the man said. 'People find it a little claustrophobic. But if you're desperate, it's all yours for fifty quid and I'll throw in the finest breakfast you'll ever eat.'

'Fifty pounds for what is little more than a cupboard with a camp bed in it,' said Josie, outraged, when they went up to look at it.

'Well, it's either this, or I try and fashion a tepee out of drift-wood on the beach,' Grant said throwing himself down on the bed so that it shook alarmingly.

'Be careful or you'll fall through the floor into the room below,' said Josie laughing.

They walked to the supermarket, which, by some miracle, holy or otherwise, was still open, and they bought toothbrushes and toothpaste and Josie also acquired an extra large T-shirt with a picture of the Lindisfarne Stone on the front of it. There was no way she was going to sleep with Grant in a cupboard just wearing her pants. Afterwards they went onto the beach where a red sky stretched across island and castle in a great fiery blur.

'You've caught the sunset in your hair,' Grant said looking at her, and she pulled a face at him to make light of the seriousness that had entered his voice.

'Now you look like a fearsome Viking who is about to plunge her axe into my head,' Grant said and Josie picked up a bit of wood and pretended to brain him with it, relieved that he had been distracted from what had begun to sound like an avowal of some sort.

In the pub, at her prompting, Grant talked about his mother again.

'When I was small she was always there. She turned up for school things. She made me my favourite things for tea. She, you know . . . seemed to love me. I don't know what happened. It was like she changed overnight. Or at least that's how I remember it.'

'It's hard for children to understand their parents. They don't really think of them as human beings with real feelings. They only notice the changes that affect them directly. Perhaps your mum was going through something you knew nothing about,' Josie said. She was glad he was talking to her so honestly. It made her feel closer to him. Until now he hadn't really divulged much about himself and she had been guarded too.

'I can remember almost to the day when it happened,' Grant said, rubbing at his face. She thought he was a little drunk. He was talking in the exaggeratedly careful way of people who are beginning to fight the slur in their words.

'I came home from school and the house was cold and she wasn't in the kitchen like she normally was. She was lying on the sofa and she smelt funny. It was only afterwards, when I had got used to seeing her like that, that I realised she had been drinking.'

'It's possible she had been drinking for some time and that was the day it finally became too much,' Josie said.

'She was always sad. Sad or asleep. Nothing I ever did made her smile and I capered for her like a fool.'

'You should really try and see her. Take a week off work and go to Paris.'

'There's no point,' Grant said. 'Let's not talk about her anymore. Tell me why you are on your own,' he asked, clearly wanting to change the subject.

'I haven't found anyone good enough.'

'You could do a lot worse than me,' he said, smiling seductively.

'I know I could,' Josie said. 'You're going to make someone a good husband, at least for a year or so until you change your mind.'

'I think my days of rattling around are numbered. It's time I settled down. I've been thinking a lot about what I've got to show for my life.'

He looked so sad that Josie spoke kindly. 'You've got a lot to show for it. You've built up a good business. You've got loads of friends,' she said.

'But what will be left behind when I'm gone?' Grant asked.

'You're drunk.'

'Alcohol always makes me see things very clearly,' Grant said. 'You want someone and I want someone. It's the perfect solution.'

'But I want someone who wants me in particular, rather than just anyone,' Josie said.

'But you're not just anyone. I like you more than anyone else I have ever met.'

'You say that now but you'll be finding reasons to dump me as soon as the novelty wears off,' Josie said. 'In any case, I'm not looking to start a relationship. I have to focus all of my energies on getting Scott better.'

She had told him the last time they had met about Scott's illness. She had thought it might put him off, but he had shown no sign of retreating.

'How bad is he?' Grant asked.

'It's pretty bad, but I'm sure there's something we can do. His doctor is useless. I had the house valued a few days ago and it's worth more than I thought. I'm going to sell it and spend the money on going to America where they are much more proactive about treating heart problems. I've been emailing a doctor in Boston who sounds very positive.'

'Are you sure that's such a good idea?' Grant asked. He seemed suddenly more sober than he had a few moments before.

'I would do anything to save him,' Josie said.

'I know you would,' Grant said. 'Of course you would. It's just maybe . . . maybe it isn't the right thing for Scott, or for you either.'

She didn't answer him but was glad of the way his face had softened. He seemed to really care about her and Scott. She had thought him self-centred but perhaps his sadness about his own mother had given him more empathy than she had imagined.

'I'm just worried about you.'

'I'm fine,' Josie said, although she knew herself not to be. *I'll give Scott my heart*, she thought. *Will they let me do that? What use will it be to me if he's no longer here?* She longed suddenly for something that would take her away from the agitation she felt. She hadn't been sleeping. The night before she had been kept awake by her thoughts and the noise of a circling helicopter. In the dark, with its ominous light and warlike reverberation it had felt threatening. It had seemed to her as it turned and turned again over the house that it was seeking *her* out rather than some errant boy standing flat against a shadowed wall with a computer stuffed down his jacket.

'You are so brave,' Grant said, and even though she knew herself not to be, his words felt like something to hold on to. If Grant thought that of her then perhaps there was a way of getting through the days. Her apparent courage would give her something to hide behind – the way a suit confers authority, or armour bestows the wearer with a look of valour regardless of the doubts and fears that lay in the heart beating beneath the chain mail. When finally he leaned over and kissed her, she kissed him back and was grateful for the way the push of his lips, and his adept fingers on her throat, made her almost forget.

'Let's go upstairs,' she said, when she became aware that they had become the focus of attention in the pub, and they both got unsteadily to their feet.

'Get a room!' some wise ass said as they stumbled by, holding hands.

Josie turned to the lad – a youth with pimples round his hairline and a belligerent look – and fixed him with her hardest stare.

'We have a room, thank you very much, and it's a very nice one indeed,' and Grant pulled her away, laughing.

The narrow bed shuddered and creaked alarmingly under their weight which made them snigger, but then he touched her and the laughter stopped and was replaced by a heat and a craving for something she couldn't even put a name to.

Chapter 24

Scott

I've just watched your video and although I don't cur-
rently seek a girlfriend I am very interested in the Poole
pottery vase I glimpsed in your mother's house. Do you
think she would be interested in selling it?

Avid Poole Collector

Despite the fact that being with Grant had given her a temporary respite, she had woken the next morning with the same
heavy, despairing feeling she had had for weeks. There was
something heedless about the way Scott was behaving that
worried her. She wanted him to be fighting for his life, not setting up elaborate plots to ensure that she spent the night with
Grant. No new love (and a shag on a rickety bed was certainly
not enough to seal the deal) could make the thought of losing
him bearable.

It seemed that every single customer had decided to come
into the shop with the sole purpose of torturing her. It was
only eleven o'clock and already she had dealt with a man who
claimed to be able to hear a squeaking noise in his mattress and
insisted she listen over and over again to the recording he had
made on his phone.

'I'm certain there's a rodent of some sort in there,' he had said, and he'd held firm to his conviction despite her assurances that it couldn't possibly be the case.

'All our mattresses come straight from the warehouse and are still wrapped in the protective plastic sheeting they are covered with at the factory,' she had explained, trying to keep her voice calm and conciliatory. The man clearly had mental health issues and it wouldn't do to inflame him further. He had looked at her as if she was the insane one and had made a jabbing motion with his finger into her face. He had skin the colour of putty and a weave that looked as if an inept child had made it.

'Mice and rats can chew their way through anything,' he had said.

'It really is very unlikely indeed,' she had replied. 'Is there any chance that something might have become caught up in the duvet? Do you, for instance have one of those squeaky toys that you give to pets? It might have lodged itself somewhere. I've got one for my dog.'

She could see the look of dawning realisation on the man's face. He faltered mid-jab and she could tell he was wrestling with himself. He had two choices – he could either admit his error and apologise, or he could carry on the face-saving charade. He chose the latter path and she was treated to another four blustering minutes of complaint, before finally he slunk out, his ratty tail between his legs.

Mouse man was swiftly followed by Mrs Little and Mr Large. The enormous man and his miniature wife tried out every bed in the shop, even insisting that George pull mattresses out of storage for their perusal. Each time they climbed onto a new bed, one of them would find a problem. When he declared a mattress perfect, she would pronounce it too soft and whenever she said they had found the one, he would moan about the springs or the headboard. After a while Josie began to lose patience, particularly since the woman insisted on taking off her shoes and putting them on again each time to walk to the next bed.

'Have you considered twin beds?' she said at last, and they both turned on her and spoke in unison. It seemed that finally they had found something they could agree on.

'We've not spent a night apart in thirty-three years,' they said, looking accusingly at Josie as if they thought she was trying to break up their marriage.

'And we don't intend to start now,' said the titchy wife, drawing herself up to her full height, and then putting her shoes back on before exiting in indignation with her husband lumbering out after her.

'I'm sick of the human race,' said Josie wearily to George, who nodded morosely as if he wondered why it had taken her so long to come round to his way of thinking.

'What, even me!' said Grant, who had come into the shop without her noticing. He threw himself down on one of the beds, almost knocking over a standard lamp in the process.

'A bit lumpy, this one,' he said, wriggling around for a while, trying to get into a comfortable position. Finally, he half sat up and propped his head on his hand and looked at Josie. George gave him a baleful look.

'He's all mustard and mutton chops,' had been his obscure verdict to Josie after Grant had visited the last time and now he made a kind of humphing noise, scratched his bottom ruminatively, went into the office and closed the door.

'Not my biggest fan,' Grant said, grinning. 'I think he has secret designs on you. He wants to lure you back to his unsavoury den and ply you with beer cans.'

'I don't think George has any interest in women, or men for that matter ' said Josie rearranging the carpet, which Grant had rumpled during his exuberant entrance.

'Don't you believe it. No man can live on Greggs's sausage rolls and resentment alone. He'll be into something. Mark my words. Tractors or women with facial hair or men that like to dress up in furry cat costumes.'

'Stop being so mean. He can probably hear you,' said Josie, trying not to laugh.

Grant gave her one of his speculative looks. 'You look dog-tired. Fancy an early night?'

'Thanks,' said Josie, really laughing this time. 'You've managed to make an invitation for sex sound like a mission of mercy.'

He looked handsome lying there on the bed with his hair mussed up and his long legs crossed and Josie felt the pull of him. Sex with him had left her feeling a kind of sensuous delight in her own body. It was as if she had rediscovered her skin which, up till now, had languished, neglected for far too long. She found herself blushing as she remembered the way he had moved his fingers along the soft, inner flesh of her thigh and then placed his hands on either side of her waist, pushing himself up so that he could look at her face and check her reaction. For all his years of practised seduction, he had still seemed tentative, as if this was something new to him. She took a quick look around to check that there were no observers, it wouldn't do, after all, to be caught in a compromising position at work. She didn't want her customers thinking that her goods were shop soiled, and then lay down on the bed next to him.

'So *this* is how you make all those sales!' Grant said, looking into her eyes as they lay side by side. 'Your technique is safe with me.'

She kissed him gently. It was a decorous, middle-of-the-afternoon, we-might-be-seen-at-any-moment kiss, but he pulled her to him. She could feel his mouth opening under her own and the roughness of his skin against hers and at that moment, anyone could have walked in and she wouldn't even have noticed.

'I've got to get up,' she said at last, against his mouth, but still he held her and she felt herself soften into him. From somewhere distant she heard the sound of the doorbell but it took a couple of moments to disentangle herself and get to her feet. Scott was standing there looking at her.

It was pretty embarrassing. It wasn't the sort of thing he had imagined his mother doing – writhing around on a bed in the high street, where anyone at all could have seen them through the shop window. His mother was bright red and looked as if she had been dragged through a hedge backwards. Scott noticed that Grant looked completely unruffled. He hadn't even bothered to get up off the bed, but was lying there with his arms crossed behind his head, grinning. Scott felt a grudging admiration for this display of confidence. Although the man was too old to be pinning his mother down in broad daylight, in public, at least he was carrying the situation off with a certain amount of style. It was clear things had progressed much further than he had dared to hope. They had to be really into each other to risk such a display. He would kiss Emily on a bed if it was slap bang in the middle of Marble Arch, but that was different. He was young. Not that there was any chance of him kissing Emily on a London landmark, or anywhere else, for that matter. He pushed her firmly from his mind.

'Hello, Mum, sorry to barge in on you,' he said.

'I didn't know you were coming in,' said Josie, still looking flustered and smoothing down her creased skirt. She was having trouble looking him in the eye.

'I had no idea your work involved trying out the beds yourself,' he said, attempting but failing, he thought, to sound as if he was taking it all in his stride.

Grant laughed.

'I came in to tell you not to expect me for supper,' he said. 'I'm meeting Picasso at the Red Lion. I'll get something there.'

Grant got up from the bed and suggested they walk together since they were both going in the same direction.

'How are you and Mum getting on?' Scott asked when the two of them had walked a little distance from the shop. He tried to adopt a casual manner. Grant looked sideways at him.

'We're great. We're taking it as it comes,' Grant answered.

They continued walking in silence.

'Do you think you'll stay together?' Scott asked. 'Taking it as it comes' didn't sound nearly as permanent as he wanted, and then he wondered what he had really expected Grant to say. He and his mum had only been together for a short time. He couldn't really expect an avowal of undying love and the promise that he would protect Josie through all of life's sorrows. He realised he would have to ease up on his questions. He didn't want to drive the man away. The thought of going back to trawling through his messages again made him feel very tired. If anything, the proportion of deluded and depraved people responding to the video had risen. It was truly amazing the number of complete head jobs there were in the world, but if Grant didn't follow through, Scott would have no choice. At least there were a couple of good-sounding prospects – the man who flew planes sounded pretty cool and there was another, a lifeguard who looked ripped and would at least be able to save Josie if she ever got into trouble swimming in sub-zero temperatures.

'Are you asking me what my intentions are?' asked Grant smiling.

'No. Not really, well . . .yes,' Scott said.

'Well, it's very early days,' Grant said, which sounded a little more cautious than Scott had hoped. If someone had asked him what he felt about Emily, he would have been much more definite. *I want to be with her forever*, he would have answered, but of course his forever and hers didn't match.

He and Grant parted ways outside the pub and Scott went in and bought himself an orange juice and then sat down at a table outside to wait for his friend. Picasso was often late and he had texted to say that he still had a couple of bed deliveries to do before he could get away. In the course of his project to find someone for his mother to love, Scott had read a number of books called things like *Up Your Dating Rating* and *Your Journey to Love*, and in one of them, the author, an orange-coloured woman who claimed to be a love coach, had written that in every ten people there was one that was a perfect match and that it was just a question of opening your mind and forgetting your preconceptions. Scott thought he would try counting the men who passed him as he sat at the table. It was the end of the working day, so a lot of people were on their way home. He reckoned his vantage point provided optimum conditions to test the theory.

His first tenth man was so bent over that his nose was almost level with the pavement. The second tenth man was singing show tunes under his breath and was wearing a coat done up with string. The third tenth man was holding hands with two children. The fourth looked far too well turned out to be straight. The fifth was . . . Emily dressed in a white linen jacket and trousers. The masculine suit made her look smaller and softer than he remembered. She stopped in front of him and, for a moment, seemed lost for words.

'Your mum said you would be here,' she said. 'I didn't want to phone you in case you told me to go away. Danny gave me her number and I rang her when I got here and she told me where to find you.'

Her hair had grown so that it now touched her shoulders and Scott felt obscurely hurt by this, as if it indicated that there had been other changes since he had seen her last that he hadn't been privy to.

'What are you doing here?' he said at last, immediately thinking it was a stupid thing to ask. It wasn't as if she was wandering through Alnwick on her way to the castle or something and had bumped into him by accident. She had phoned his mother. It was him that she had come to see.

'Are you angry with me?' she asked. 'I've been angry with me for the last few months.'

'Of course I'm not angry with you,' he said. Her appearance had dazzled him. It was as if his longing had conjured her up.

'What can you have thought of me? Leaving you there. Not being in touch.'

'I thought you were sensible.'

'I was terribly cruel,' she said, and her face flushed painfully and her teeth bit into her bottom lip.

'Come and sit down. I'll get you a drink,' Scott said and went into the pub. He leaned against the bar and tried to still his breathing. He ordered the requested pint of Guinness and then had a moment's panic that she would not be there when he got outside again. Seeing her suddenly in his hometown was as improbable and as astonishing as spotting a dolphin in the wild. But when he emerged she was still there, leaning her head on her hand, her feet, in a pair of pale-blue brogues, neatly side by side under the table.

'I like your suit,' he said, sitting down opposite her.

'I made it,' she said. 'I found a pattern from the seventies in a vintage shop.'

He looked at her – she had the same dark brows and full bottom lip, the same economical way of holding herself and yet something in her had changed.

'I've missed you,' he said, wondering if she would think him foolish.

'I'm so sorry,' she said and he saw that her eyes were glistening as if she might be about to cry. 'I wish I had been different . . . better.'

She ducked her head. The hand holding her drink wasn't quite steady. He thought it had cost her a lot to come.

'I don't blame you for the way you reacted,' he said. 'I just sprung it on you out of the blue. I should have told you from the beginning.'

She shook her head and the tiny pearls dangling from her ears moved from side to side. He had an insane impulse to reach over and take one of her earlobes into his mouth. He could feel her soft flesh under his tongue and the cold grit of the pearl. *Get a grip*, he told himself, looking away from her. The last thing she needs is you lunging at her like an idiot.

'How are you?' she asked.

'I've been a bit better but I think I'm getting worse again,' he said, wanting to be truthful to her now.

'What have the doctors said?' she asked, sitting up straight in her chair as if she was trying to show him that she could be told, that she wouldn't run away this time.

'I'm going to carry on getting worse,' he said to her gently and saw the way his words made her tremble.

'I'm not a very good candidate for a new heart, even if they can find me one. At a guess, I think I probably have another few months before my heart fails and anything could happen between now and then.'

'I want to stay with you,' she said. 'I've saved a bit from my work in a bar and my mum's given me some money, and I'll rent somewhere in Alnwick for the summer. At least until term starts again.'

'You don't need to do that.' He didn't know if her announcement made him feel happy or sad. He wasn't sure he wanted her around to witness his inevitable degeneration.

'I know I don't *need* to,' she said with something of her old asperity. 'I *want* to.'

'Won't your mother and grandmother want you to be there over the summer?'

'It was my mother's suggestion that I come. She may have a problem curbing her shopping habit, but she has this uncanny ability to know what the right thing to do is.'

'I'm not sure it *is* right, Emily' he said. 'I think—' he stopped talking as Picasso finally bounced up in front of him.

'Hello, Dolphin Boy. Who's this?' Picasso asked, raking the hair off his face to get a clearer look.

'Emily, this is Picasso,' Scott said, feeling the strangeness of two worlds colliding.

'Ah, so *this* is the famous Emily,' Picasso said, grinning at her. 'I've heard quite a lot about you,' he said, which made Scott want to kick him. The last thing he wanted was for Emily to think he was obsessed with her or anything. He wished he hadn't confided quite so much in his friend.

'Sharp suit!' Picasso said, winking at Scott in what his friend considered was a totally inappropriate way. Picasso wasn't exactly the master of subtlety.

Chapter 25

Scott

You must tell your mother immediately that the sea is extremely dangerous at this time of year. You can never be sure of the rip tides.

Joel Patterson

'We're not going out with each other,' Scott had said in a repressive voice. Josie wished she hadn't said anything. Scott was very prickly when it came to his private life.

'Oh . . . sorry . . . I just presumed,' Josie said.

'Yes, well, don't.' Scott had answered, hunkering down on the sofa as if expecting sniper fire. She hadn't persisted with the conversation although she had seen the way he looked at the girl – the slightly dazed, soft glances he cast in her direction when he thought himself unobserved. When they had been walking in the wood the day before, Emily had stumbled over the root of a tree and Scott had reached for her instinctively and just for a moment Emily had allowed herself to be held, her body leaning into his, the connection between them as clear as if they had shouted it aloud.

He looks completely transformed, Josie thought as she watched Emily and Scott through the kitchen window. They were supposed to be hanging out the washing, but they were fooling around – twirling the line and hitting each other with wet sheets. The girl had achieved more in a few days than Josie seemed to have done in the whole time he had been back. *He's actually got some colour in his face*, she thought. That was what a little love did for you. It was only right that she was no longer the most important person in his life. It would be weird and unhealthy if it was any other way, but she couldn't help feeling bereft. She was no longer the first port of call.

She had agreed to let Emily stay at the house while she was in Alnwick. The girl had very sweetly said that she would help out in the shop in return. There was a spare bedroom so it wasn't as if they didn't have the space and she could tell how much Scott wanted Emily to be there, although he tried to play it down. Things had been tricky between Josie and Scott since he had said that he didn't want to go to America for treatment.

'Dr Moulton's at the top of his game,' he had said. 'If they can't do anything for me here, they won't be able to do anything anywhere. And besides, I don't want to spend whatever time I've got left in a strange place, lying in hospital while the sun is shining.'

'But there is more of everything in America,' she had said. 'More expertise, more hearts, more chance for you.'

'I'm not going. I don't want you to spend the money and, in any case, I need to be here while I can be. I'm still not sure Grant is the perfect match.'

She felt he was letting go and she couldn't bear it. She had to do everything she could to change his mind. Maybe having Emily here would give him a reason to fight.

She watched the girl laughing and running away from Scott across the lawn, pretending to be scared. She was so beautiful with those long legs in bright blue tights, her face shining under her sleek fall of hair. Josie thought her sociable and clever but she seemed to be holding herself back as if she wasn't quite as sure of herself as she pretended to be. What did anyone really know when they were that young? Josie herself had been absolutely clueless, although, of course, she hadn't realised it at the time. When she had met Peter it was as though up to that moment she had simply been marking time, waiting for her life to begin. She shouldn't have been so stupid to imagine that a man, any man, had the power to set things in motion for you. You had to propel yourself through all the days and months and years. The only things of value were the things you made for yourself.

Looking at him fooling around in the garden with a pair of boxer shorts on his head, she wondered what she was to him now. Did he remember anything of what she had told him over the years? Not just the things about looking after his heart, but all the other, regular stuff – check twice before you cross the road. Don't eat food that has been hanging around on a hotplate. Never bury yourself in sand if the tide is coming in. Treat people with respect. Scrape out your cereal bowl before it sets hard. Don't leave things to the last minute. Shout loudly if someone is trying to kidnap you. Wear a condom. The compulsion to make sure he was as armed and as protected as he could be went on and on. She knew he saw it as nagging, but it was, in fact, all she had to offer.

In the afternoon they all made their way to Seahouses. Grant said he had a surprise for them and, despite some rigorous probing, he had refused to say what it was.

'Wait and see,' he had said, looking pleased with himself.

Scott was right to think that she wasn't sure about Grant. When they were in bed together it was perfect, and yet at other times they seemed to annoy each other. He didn't appear to understand the depth of her desperation about Scott, or if he did, he didn't seem able to help her. The other night they had had a terrible row, with her accusing him of not feeling anything and him telling her that she wasn't going about things the right way. She had told him to fuck off out of the house and not come back and he had exited, banging the front door behind him furiously.

After a couple of days she had rung him up to apologise for her outburst and he had come round while Scott was out and they had made love on the sofa. She was agitated and scratchy and when Grant kissed her, she had thought at first that she wouldn't be able to forget long enough to make her body function in the way it needed to, but he was patient. He stroked her, covering her with his warm, wide hands, and she had found herself overwhelmed by a feeling that couldn't quite be called desire; it seemed to be closer to fear. She had unbuttoned her shirt with clumsy fingers, pulled at her jeans. There was a moment of gathering – a curious, urgent stillness – and then nothing but the feeling of his mouth on hers and a peeling apart of flesh. She pushed herself against him, trying to rub herself free.

'How can I even have contemplated doing that?' she had said afterwards, as they lay together. She was ashamed at the way she had allowed herself to let go. She couldn't accept even this temporary pleasure for herself. She waited for the anticipated feeling of peace but it seemed her craving had hardly been touched. An unspecific longing still raged in her. She reached for him and stroked him until he was hard again.

'Steady on! I think I might need to wait a while. I'm not as young as I was,' Grant said laughing, but she ignored him, not wanting him to speak. She wanted only to feel the thrust and clench of being alive.

When they got to the harbour at Seahouses, Grant pointed to a small vessel moored there amongst some other fishing boats.

'I borrowed it from a friend,' he said. 'There's a bottle of champagne on ice and I've got special permission to go out to the Farne Islands, even though you normally have to go on a guided tour. It's not who you are, it's who you know,' Grant said, tapping the side of his nose with a comically complacent air. Scott followed Grant down the metal ladder attached to the harbour wall and helped him to hold the boat steady as Emily and Josie embarked.

'Do you know how to drive it?' he said to Grant, looking at the controls.

'My friend has given me a lesson. It's very straightforward. Much easier than driving a car.'

Once they were settled, Grant turned on the engine, which gave a promisingly healthy roar and instructed Scott and Emily on how to pull up the buffer tyres and secure them to the side of the boat. The water became slightly choppy once they were out of the harbour, but the little boat moved smoothly, barely making any spray.

'Do you want a go?' Grant asked Emily and she took the wheel eagerly. Grant laughingly put a captain's hat on her head at a jaunty angle and stood back to admire her.

'What if I crash into something?' she asked fixing her eyes on the horizon as if she was anticipating the appearance of a cruise ship.

'Just keep your eyes peeled and give everything near you a wide berth,' Grant replied, taking a bottle of champagne out of an ice box and producing four glasses. Josie was looking happy – the breeze blowing her hair back, her cheeks pink. Scott smiled at the way she was now trying to wrest the steering wheel away from Emily. Emily wasn't having any of it. She stood astride, both hands on the wheel as if she did this every day. The captain's hat was a little large for her and kept falling over her eyes. Scott's breath caught when he looked at her.

The sea transferred a kind of grace on them all, and they fell into a state of quiet contemplation. The boat left slices of white and turquoise in its wake and its gentle sway felt like a cradling. They had been travelling for about twenty minutes when Scott became aware of a hot, faecal stench, which seemed out of place in the middle of the ocean. Ahead of them, as if they had just emerged suddenly from the sea, were several monumental stacks of rock, dripping with guano, on which birds clustered on slender ledges in a great cacophony. The sea around the rocking boat had become a thick soup of puffins and terns and gulls, dipping and diving and attacking each other and skittering across the surface of the water in a noisome display of bravado. Jellyfish shone like ghosts just below the surface. It felt to Scott as if he had just entered an ancient, secret world.

'Who knew this was all here?' said Emily, looking wonderingly around her.

They skirted the stacks past Grace Darling's cottage, now the home, according to Grant, for the wardens who guarded the wildlife of the islands, and past the seals, lying fulsomely on flat stones. Scotland had always laid claim to the Selkie legend, but Scott had read that it was on these small islands that the stories about handsome young men who came out of the sea to snatch a few precious hours with their loved ones before once more assuming their blubbery disguises, had first been told. The boat made its way to Inner Farne, where it was possible to moor the boat at a small wharf.

'I planned it so that we would arrive between tours. We have the island to ourselves,' Grant said gleefully, helping Josie and Emily off the boat.

Scott stood for a while before disembarking. He felt a kind of fear at the sight of the life that teemed in the air above the land. It was almost too much – the swirl and squawk of the birds, the farmyard smell, the white gleam of the campion flowers – the sheer vigour of it all. He wasn't sure he had the strength to cut his way through the dash and surge of it. He felt his own weakness acutely in the face of the absurd vitality around him. *This isn't the place for me*, he thought. Nature at its most fulsome seemed to be mocking his own diminishing spark.

'Come on!' Emily shouted from the quay, waving at him, and so he moored the boat to the iron girder in the harbour wall and stepped out.

'It's mad!' Emily shouted. 'I'm being dive-bombed by angry birds!'

And indeed, ten steps down the wooden path that had been laid down for visitors, Scott was set upon by a mass of arctic terns, their livid red beaks, which exactly matched the colour of their claws, wide open in warning. At his feet he could see the reason why. Chicks in their first fluff were cowering amongst the undergrowth – unable yet to fly; their parents were defending them against foreign threat. Ducking from the onslaught they took shelter in St Cuthbert's chapel, a shit-smeared stone building in which a lost tern was flying from end to hopeless end.

They ventured out again when the woman who worked in the tiny gift shop saw they were hatless and kindly supplied them with four baseball caps, which, clearly, had already seen plenty of tern action. It took Scott a while to stop recoiling and cowering and resisting the avid rush around him but then, almost as if it was a decision he had made, he abandoned himself to the tack, tack, tacking of the birds. He gave in with an exhalation to the relentless swell. The ground teemed with movement like lice through hair. Puffins emerged out of their burrows, glanced around with bright, inquisitive eyes, and then disappeared again as quickly.

'They are like that game where you hit plastic moles with a hammer and they go back down the holes,' Emily said.

Scott looked at her. She was smiling at him from under the rim of her cap. A tern was balanced angrily on the visor, poised to peck her.

'Isn't it wonderful?' she said and she moved towards him. In the midst of the noise, it seemed as if the volume was suddenly switched off. The tern battered at her in fury but Emily seemed oblivious. She put her arms around Scott's neck and kissed him.

Her lips were soft and tasted of champagne and the sea. Deep in his chest the stroke of his heart matched hers and it was as if he was feeling its true thud for the very first time. He and she were part of the beat of endless life.

'I love you,' she said. 'I can't help it.'

'You shouldn't,' he said, but he couldn't help it either.

He held her for a moment longer feeling victorious. She loved him now, at this moment, in this place. There was nothing else.

'Come on, you love birds!' Grant said. 'I can think of safer spots for a snog.'

Josie followed behind him smiling, although she had her I knew something was going on and do you really think it's such a good idea face, and they ran back to the boat, the terns following after them, making sure they were safely dispatched.

Chapter 26

Dear Scott

I think you must be a really lovely boy to do this for your mother. You don't say why she hasn't got a partner. Did he die? I lost my wife six months ago and I still miss her so much. It feels as if I am filled up with loss. Which sounds strange because loss is meant to leave a gap, but my grief is like a living thing. It waits for me in the morning and wakes me with its terrible clawing. It's as if it is trying to eat me from the inside. Sometimes when I'm out, I imagine it might come out of my mouth and attack someone. I'll never love anyone again, but I wish you luck with your search.

Very best wishes

Ed

Somewhere between the cereal and the pet-food aisle in Morrisons, Josie was engulfed with a terrible panic. It made her heart beat so fast that she thought she was dying. She leaned against one of the shelves and tried to breathe but it was as if the sides of her throat had adhered to each other and blocked her access to the air. Her boy. Her boy. She was overcome with the thought of what was going to be taken from her, but the real pain came from all that he wasn't going to have. *He won't ever get the chance to say 'I'm tired of this, I want to try something else.' He won't return to his hometown and think it small. He won't pass by a mirror and see me in his own face. He won't ever know if his sacrifices were worth it. He won't have his fair share of life.* She put her head in her hands and wept, oblivious to the stares and the tentative steps towards and then away from her. Finally, she allowed herself to be led away to a room by a woman with arms like tree trunks and a rough, kind voice.

'My son is dying,' Josie said. She put her arms out in front of her, under the woman's still gaze, as if she was holding up the loss for her to see. It is this much. It is much, much more than I can describe. I don't have the words. It turned out the woman knew who she was. Knew who Scott was too. Of course, they were ex-colleagues. Scott had worked in the supermarket on Saturdays. Josie had forgotten the most basic facts under the smothering sorrow.

'Not little Scott!' the woman said and her wide face showed her shock. 'I thought he had gone to university!' As if going away would allow him to escape his illness.

Josie drank the mug of tea she was given much too quickly but welcomed the pain of its burn. She knew she had to allow people to be kind, even if it didn't help. Nothing would help.

Now she was sitting wondering how she was going to move out of the car park, let alone through the coming days. It was not possible, surely, to go through the motions of living. How could she persist with every day, unthinking things like brushing her teeth or stirring a teabag round a cup or pulling up weeds in the garden? It would be like gathering sand in a colander. And yet people did such things every day even while their hearts were broken, even while they waited for a reprieve that never came. She had often wondered, in an abstract sort of a way, how these marked-out people managed it. How did the stunned, bereaved father on the television news hold it together for long enough to say what he wanted to say? What gave the young, recently widowed woman who lived five doors down in Josie's row of terraces the strength, or even the desire, to wash her curtains and put them out in the sun to dry, hung tautly between neat pegs?

She turned when she felt a shadow looming over the car. Dr Moulton was staring through the glass at her. She hastily rubbed the tears from her face and reluctantly opened the window.

'Hello, Josie,' he said. 'You look as if you could do with some company.'

She stared at him, still adjusting to the fact that she was seeing him out of context. He looked so different in his T-shirt and jeans that she wouldn't have recognised him if she had passed him in the street. She felt exposed under his scrutiny as if she had revealed something that she would have preferred to remain private. Of all the people in the world she would allow to see her weeping, Dr Moulton would have been her last choice. She felt the same bristle of animosity she had experienced at the hospital. Why would he imagine that she needed his company? She hardly knew the man.

'What are you doing here?' she asked him.

'My mother-in-law lives in Alnwick. I have been stocking her up with a few things,' the doctor said, lifting up the two carrier bags he was holding.

'Well, it's nice to see you,' she said, although she felt the opposite was true. 'I must get on.'

She put the key in the ignition. The doctor didn't seem to pick up on the fact that she was keen to get away from him. He stayed standing exactly where he was.

'How about I put the bags in my car and we go for a walk somewhere?' he said.

She was startled by his suggestion and the surprise of it must have shown in her face because he laughed.

'I've got things I need to do,' she said.

'I'm sure there isn't anything that can't be postponed for an hour,' he said, and then he made off between the rows of cars. *I could just drive away*, Josie thought, but she continued to sit there. She supposed he was trying to be kind and it would be rude to abandon him. He probably thought that it was part of his medical duties to rescue weeping mothers, and what else did she have to do, after all? It was her day off. She didn't want to go back to the house and try for the millionth time to persuade Scott to explore further treatment options. He seemed obdurate and, in any case, Emily would probably be there with him and Josie didn't feel she could say anything important to Scott when she was around. Every time she tried, hoping that her entreaties would encourage Emily to side with her and help her to make Scott see he was making the wrong decision, Scott would look furiously at her and suggest to Emily that they should go up to his bedroom or to the pub.

Dr Moulton returned to her car and opened the passenger door.

'How about you drive us somewhere nice for a walk? I don't know this area as well as you,' he said, doing up his seat belt. She thought he was someone who was used to getting his own way. She wondered what his wife was like. He must have a wife if he had a mother-in-law. Whoever she was, she was probably dazzled into compliance by his confidence and his taste in waistcoats. She took a surreptitious look at his feet and saw with a kind of sour delight that he was wearing baseball boots.

'Where are we going?' Dr Moulton asked, rubbing his hands together as if they were setting off on a pleasurable excursion.

'Craster,' she said. It was the nearest place she could think of. She didn't want to have to spend more time than she absolutely had to with the man. They could have a quick walk along the cliff towards the castle and he could do his out-reach work or whatever it was that he was thinking he was doing, and then she could get home.

She parked and they walked through the village where, as usual, the smell of kippers, trussed in smoking, golden lines suffused the air, and then turned left on to the path that stretched out across the headland. The sea was a merciless blue. *I wonder if I will ever have the heart to swim in it again?* Josie thought. The ragged, melancholy castle was just ahead, beyond a wide, soft sweep of green.

'I've never done this walk before,' Dr Moulton said. 'It's beautiful.'

Josie nodded her head. She wondered when he was going to start talking about why she had been sitting in her car crying. Maybe it was his technique to wait for her to speak of it first.

'How's the dating going?' he asked.

'I've had a lot of bad ones,' she said.

'Scott cares about you a great deal. About your happiness, I mean.'

'How did he imagine that linking me up with a load of misfits was going to protect me from this?' she asked.

'He wants you to be loved and he's nineteen and is just doing what he thinks is best.'

Josie heard what she thought was criticism in his words and felt suddenly angry. For all his authority on matters pertaining to the heart he didn't have a clue what it was like to feel as she did, and yet he had the gall to hold forth about her son.

'I know how old he is,' she said, and felt the doctor turn to scrutinise her face. She kept her head determinedly down and marched on. On the beach below the tide had left a line of the sinewy seaweed Josie disliked. It was tubed and pinkish and resembled umbilicus.

'Is there anything you want to ask me?' he said.

Josie realised it wasn't his tactlessness that was making her angry, it was the fact that he seemed to her to have all the power. He knew exactly what the inside of her son's body looked like. He knew what could and couldn't be done. He had seen the disease in all its creeping, disgusting forms. She knew then that she wasn't angry so much as humiliated. Scott was her son. She had sponged him in all his most intimate places. He had smeared her with meconium and posset. She had held his head while he was vomiting, wiped blood from his limbs, collected his pearl teeth, cut his toenails, dabbed his fiery acne with ointment, changed his semen-stained sheets, aired his stinking trainers. She had worshipped all his lovely horribleness and yet now he had been overtaken by something that she couldn't check or wipe clean.

'I know you are angry with me because I can't put this right,' he said.

She stopped and looked at him, knowing she should be grateful for his compassion and yet she still resented what she perceived as his advantage. He looked older than he probably was. His face, though strong and well defined with heavy brows and a determined mouth, looked weary.

'People think doctors have all the answers. They sometimes even think that we have power over life and death. But we cannot change much at all. We can hold at bay, we can alleviate, sometimes we can even make things go away, but mostly what we have to cope with is uncertainty.'

'There is surely something left to do,' Josie said, feeling her defences crumble. She felt a wail cutting its way through her so she hid her distress by pushing through the gate at the entrance to the castle and the doctor followed behind. Without saying anything more they climbed up the stone steps of the gatehouse as far as they could go. There was a railed viewing platform that looked out across the sea; Craster harbour to the right of them, Embleton to the left and in between were the curves of the coast, hazy in the sunshine. She had been here so often and had always found it a place of beauty and solace, but now it seemed diminished. She saw how little remained of the fabric of the building. It was just a heap of stones really. They leaned on the railing and looked out across the water.

'I think that's a dolphin,' he exclaimed, pointing, and she followed the direction of his arm and saw it executing an arcing rise out of the water. Even at this distance she could see the sleek gleam of him.

'That's Leonardo,' she said. 'The creature is asking for trouble, coming in this close.'

'I wonder why he's by himself,' he said.

'Scott says dolphins start to get very used to human beings and it's dangerous for them because people can be pretty stupid.'

The dolphin performed another couple of jumps and then crossed the bay until he was out of sight. Josie turned round to look inland and the doctor turned with her.

'When Scott was about ten, he got it into his head that he was going to fly a flag from one of the turrets over there,' she said, pointing towards Lilburn Tower. 'He spent ages sticking pieces of coloured paper to an old sheet I had given him and making a mast out of bamboo canes from the garden. I told him that they wouldn't let him put it up there, but he insisted that they would. We walked all the way, Scott carrying the flag carefully folded up in his bag, and, of course, when he arrived, he discovered what I had said was true. The warden told him the place was far too precious and old, not to mention, delicate to stick flags on it.'

'How did he take the news?' Robert said, smiling.

'He kept asking the increasingly irate warden why one *very light* flag would make any difference. He just wouldn't let it rest.'

'He still knows his own mind,' Robert said, looking carefully at her, as if unsure of her reaction. 'You've done a really good job. You must be so proud of him.'

'Don't be kind to me,' Josie said. 'I'll cry if you are kind to me.'

'Cry if you want to,' Robert said. 'I'm more than a little used to tears.'

She thought he might be about to put his arms around her to comfort her so she moved quickly away from him. For a moment the gaping mouth of the sorrow inside her opened up but then she willed it shut again. She thought that if she allowed herself to cry she would never stop. Her tears would fill the ancient moat and rise beyond its grassy slopes until, in the end, the stony land, the crumpled walls and incomplete turrets would all be submerged under the briny wash.

'I think it's time to go home,' she said, starting back down the stairs.

Chapter 27

Scott

    Question: Would your mother be prepared to live with me in a yurt?

    Darius

'I saw Leonardo the other day,' Josie said.

She was sitting in the window seat trying to knit Scott some socks. He thought by the look of the strange, elongated shape that was emerging from her hands that he was unlikely ever to be able to wear them.

'I can't work out how to do the bloody heel!' Josie said in exasperation. The wool was all tangled up in her lap. She had been unusually quiet recently and had stopped talking to him about going to America or fretting about what Dr Moulton was planning. He wasn't sure exactly what this change in her meant. He wanted to ask her how she was feeling but he thought that if he brought it up, then he would just trigger another argument. She scratched at her head with one of the knitting needles and he felt his throat tighten with love for her. He wanted to tell her what she meant to him but he didn't know how to begin. He was waiting for her to start a conversation that would then allow him to say what needed to be said. He wanted to be able to show his love as comfort. It was the only way in he could imagine.

'Love goes downwards,' she had said the other day, out of nowhere, and he had taken that to mean that she felt that he didn't love her.

'Some of the local kids are having what they call "Porpoise Parties",' Scott said in disgust. 'They wait on the beach drinking beer, getting all psyched up and then dare each other to get on his back. They get points if they can hold onto him for a certain length of time, as if he is some sort of bucking bronco. They don't know what they are doing. One of them will hurt him. I've been to Bowick a couple of times and tried to talk them out of it, but they just tell me to piss off. I had a conversation with a man called Simon, whom I knew from when I volunteered at the Conservation Society. He was really concerned and he came down and put a sign up on the beach, but people just ignore it.'

The door went and Emily came into the room. She had worked at the bed shop all day in order to give Josie a rest. Not that his mother ever rested. When she wasn't running around doing God knew what, she was sitting wrestling with balls of wool.

'Hello!' Emily said, taking off her shoes. Josie had said it didn't matter if she wore them in the house since everyone else did, but Emily insisted on this small courtesy. She was always a little unsure of herself and cautious when she was around his mother. Archie made a beeline for her and settled himself on the sofa with his paws on her lap. The dog was a good judge of character. Perhaps he should send him with his mother to scope out her dates.

'How many beds did you sell?' he asked Emily.

'I sold two actually,' she said proudly. 'A super king-size with one of those horsehair-and-fleece mattresses, complete with fancy silk pillows that are supposed to make you wake up without wrinkles, and a set of bunk beds.'

'Well done!' Josie said and Emily beamed. She had taken her role in the shop very seriously, spending hours poring over catalogues and familiarising herself with the mysteries of air-sprung layers and spruce frames. He loved the earnestness with which she had approached the task. He knew she wanted Josie to like her.

'Are you two going out?' Josie asked, peering at them over the top of her wonky spectacles.

'Yes, Picasso is picking us up in half an hour.'

'Where are we going?' Emily asked.

'Picasso's having a party. It's Lois's birthday and she has announced that she would like a barbecue on the beach and so he is rushing around trying to make it happen.'

'What's Lois contributing?' his mother asked.

'She's gracing us with her presence,' Scott said and they all laughed.

'I'll go upstairs and get ready then,' Emily said.

Josie carried on twitching her knitting needles for a while and then spoke as if she had been resisting saying anything, but couldn't quite help herself.

'Do you think you should be going out so much?' she asked.

'It makes me feel better when I'm doing things,' he answered thinking how drained his mother looked. She had bruise-coloured patches under her eyes and she had lost weight.

'You mean you feel better when you're not with me,' his mother said, with uncharacteristic sharpness. He had never known her to say anything remotely self-pitying. She had once ignored a broken collarbone for a week before George had insisted she have it looked at. She was made of stern stuff but it had never made her hard.

'That's not true,' he said, but he could tell by the way she turned away that she didn't believe him.

'I'm all right, you know,' he said gently. 'I mean I want to live forever, who wouldn't? But I've always known, although there have been times I've managed to forget it, that I was going to die sooner than other people.'

His mother turned back to him. Her eyes were wide and scared behind the magnification of her glasses and she wrapped her arms around herself as if she was trying to keep warm. She was shaking as if she might never stop.

'*I'm* not all right. I'll never be all right,' she said. 'I don't want to live in a world without you in it.'

He didn't know what to say. He could struggle on his own behalf to accept what was coming but he couldn't do the same for her. He had tried to create a future happiness – a man, her house still her own, the knowledge that he was going with regret but, looking at her now, he couldn't imagine a time after he had gone when she might look as she had in that artless, long-ago photograph. *I have brought her nothing but sadness*, he thought. *She should have had a different life.*

'Children are not supposed to die before their parents,' she said as if it was some sort of immutable law that he had wilfully broken. *I wish she would make it easier for me*, he thought. *I can't change what is happening to me, though God knows I wish I could, but she could help me.* He thought he might tell her a little of what he felt, but just then the horn on Picasso's VW van sounded outside and he heard Emily's footsteps coming down the stairs.

'I've got to go, Mum,' he said.

The van was full of crates of beer and bags of crisps and burgers and net sacks of firewood. Scott and Emily shoved some of the things onto the floor and got in, sitting with their legs stretched out over the boxes. Picasso was in high spirits, maybe even a little manic. Lois was her usual languid, beautiful self. Her neck was wrapped round with some sort of thin, pale scarf and she looked to Scott like a woodland flower. By contrast Emily seemed to absorb colour. She was dressed in a peacock-blue dress and her skin was full of sun. In this early evening, milky light she seemed to glow with extra vibrancy. Picasso twisted round and handed a joint to Emily, who took a delicate little drag on it and passed it to Scott.

'Keep your hands on the wheel, David,' Lois said, turning to frown at him. She puckered her glossy lips and her cheekbones hallowed out as she had intended them to.

'Where are we going?' Emily asked.

'A little beach I know,' said Picasso grandly. He always spoke in this slightly artificial way when Lois was around as if he was impersonating an older version of himself.

'It's a little tricky to get to but I've discovered a secret route.'

Picasso was fond of a secret route and his version of secret was more often than not illegal.

'Remember what happened last time we took one of your routes,' Lois said darkly.

'I actually thought it was quite interesting to be rescued by a tractor,' Picasso said blithely.

'I ruined my shoes,' Lois said and passed a thin-fingered hand over her already smooth hair.

'Is anyone else coming?' Scott asked.

'I've invited a few people. Don't know who will turn up,' Picasso said.

The narrow road ahead was dappled. The hedgerows were thick with pungent growth. Swifts gathered and dispersed in great, swooping, gulping crowds. Scott could feel the summer in his body. He looked at Emily and she smiled and touched him on his thigh. She had ignored his entreaties to go back to London.

'I don't want you to see me getting ill,' he had said the day before as they were lying together on the sofa. 'I don't want to involve you in all of this.'

'I'm involved already,' she had said. 'It's too late.'

Picasso took a sudden turn off the road through a gap in the hedge and set off up a barely marked track across a field.

'Where are you going?' Lois asked in alarm, looking out of the window in panic as if he had just launched them all into a stretch of water.

'Short cut,' Picasso said, negotiating the dips and bumps with skill, doing ostentatious spinning moves with the steering wheel.

Emily pulled herself up and through the window in the roof of the camper so that she was standing on the seat with her head out and then with another little kick she pulled herself through.

'Come on up,' she said to Scott. He found it harder to haul himself up than she had. His arms were losing their strength and the exertion required to get through the window made him pant a little.

They sat on the roof holding on to the luggage rack as the van continued its bumpy trajectory across the grass. Picasso turned the stereo up and Mac DeMarco's 'The Way You'd Love Her' rose like something sweet spilt out across the air. Scott took Emily's hand in his. *I'll remember this very minute*, he thought, *this unspooling, beautiful day, the clotted feeling in my chest and the softness of her skin. I'll remember the wild, burdensome joy of being young.*

The van stopped with a lurch and Scott and Emily slid forward across the roof. They clambered back down.

'We're here!' Picasso announced. 'There's a little way to walk down that path over there, but it's not far.'

They got out and Picasso started to distribute the contents of the van.

'You can carry the burgers, you lightweight,' Picasso said, handing Scott a plastic bag. 'We might have to make a couple of trips.'

'I've already got something to carry,' Lois said, indicating her tiny handbag.

They made their way down the path onto the beach. Dust rose in little puffs under their feet and the dog roses and saxifrage that lined the route smelt of sweat and cinnamon. The sea was flat and coppery in the sun.

'I didn't know about this place!' Scott said looking around him at the small, secluded bay, which was sheltered at one end by the cliff face and at the other by a great heap of stones, which looked as if they had only recently fallen into the sea.

'That's because it's my beach,' said Picasso, starting back up the path to collect more stuff. Emily went with him while Lois fussily spread out a small towel and settled herself down on it. Scott wandered off to examine the cliff face. It was second nature to him to scout out potential new fossil sites and the rocks here looked very promising. *Perhaps I should have brought Mum*, he thought. He imagined her sitting at home alone, tussling with wool and he felt guilty. He consoled himself with the thought that Grant would probably come round to see her.

Scott began to set the fire close to the bottom of the cliff where it would be sheltered even though the evening was so still that the flames hardly needed any protection. By the time the logs were burning evenly, everything had been carried down from the van and other people were arriving in small groups. Picasso must have sent out very detailed route instructions because the place was not marked on any map that Scott had ever seen.

The light lost its brightness slowly as if the day was reluctant to let go of it. Someone put music on – 'Vampire Weekend' and then 'Swim Deep' and the beer bottles began to gather in unruly piles. Scott sat at the edge of the sea with Emily. The water was like warm oil on their feet and made a gentle sucking noise as the barely visible tide came in.

'I wish today would last forever,' Emily said, pushing her heels into the wet sand.

'Maybe it will,' Scott said and he put his arm around her shoulders.

The light finally capitulated and when it did, the dark fell quickly and the beach took on a new mystery. People danced by the fire, the sparks flying up between their outstretched arms like music made visible.

'Shall we go in?' Emily said. She got to her feet and pulled off her dress. Her body was slender and white and gleamed like the branches of a silver birch tree. He followed her and when they were waist deep, the sea seemed suddenly to lose its wideness and became only what they could feel around them. Emily raised her arm and the water dripped off it in sparkling drops. She did a half-turn and the sea followed her in luminous lines of light. He could see her smiling in the dark as if she had brought the scintillation to life. He stirred his hands through the water and saw the same incandescence. They splashed each other like children and the water fell in sparkling sprays. Before long, everyone else noticed the strange gleam of the sea and stripped off. Scott saw Picasso leading a sylph-like Lois in by the hand. For ten bright minutes the sea became a noisy, teeming mass of shining and shouting.

'My heart only beats properly when I'm with you,' he said to Emily and she laid her hand on his chest.

'Let's get out,' she said, and they walked back to the shore and wrapped themselves in towels.

'Where are we going?' Scott asked when she led him back up the path, but she didn't answer. Her face looked serious and intent.

When they reached the top she walked a little way from the cars, placing her bare feet carefully on the ground, to a spot protected from sight by an outcrop of rocks.

'Don't walk too far in that direction, you'll fall off the edge of the cliff,' Scott said, but she didn't answer. She spread her towel on the ground and lay down and so he lay down with her. She turned her head to kiss him and moved closer. Where their bodies touched it felt to Scott as if traces of luminescence were on them still, heating them, making them glitter.

'I've never done this before,' she said.

'Are you sure?' he asked her, when he thought that maybe if he went further he would no longer be able to resist the curve of her breasts and the silky feel of her under his fingers. He knew what he was asking her was not whether she was sure she wanted him but rather whether or not she was prepared to accept the coming pain.

'I'm sure,' she said a little impatiently, putting her hand on him and then the shining night, the shouts and screams from the beach below and all his numbered days dissolved and became unassailable feeling.

Chapter 28

Dear Scott

I would like to put myself forward as a candidate for a date with your mother. I've been in love with a married woman for the last fifteen years. I thought she was going to choose me, but she married my brother instead. Nobody knows I love her, except me. It wears me out. Your mother looks very much like the woman I love. I'm now fifty-four. I think it may be time to move on.

T. S.

'Grant makes you happy, doesn't he?' Scott said.

'Yes he does,' Josie answered, muffling the sound of what felt like too emphatic a response with the thud of her hammer against the rock. She knew it was what Scott wanted to hear from her, but in truth she didn't really know quite what she felt about Grant. There were times when she was aware of feeling indifferent, as if there was a wide space between them that she didn't have the energy or the inclination to bridge. She put this down to the fact that she was often so distracted, so consumed with thoughts about Scott that everything else seemed superfluous. She felt she had no more love left to hurt herself with.

Scott seemed satisfied by her response to his question and carried on chipping away at a new stretch of limestone they had found on Beadnell Beach. Emily had gone back for a while to see her mother and so the two of them were alone together again. Despite Josie's misgivings about whether it was good for them to become so attached, she had grown very fond of the girl. Emily had a generosity of spirit – an earnest desire to make those around her feel better – and she clearly adored Scott.

'He's the best person I've ever met,' Emily had said to her a few days ago, her face flushed and her eyes wide and Josie had felt a fearful tenderness for her. She was so ardently, skinlessly open that to Josie she seemed terrifyingly ill-equipped for what was to come, like a colt who was attempting to jump a high gate on fragile, untested legs. 'Hold yourself back,' she had felt like saying. 'Keep part of your heart protected so that the pain, when it comes, will not kill you.' She wondered how they were able to approach what was happening between them as a risk worth taking.

'What makes you like Emily so much?' she asked now, stopping hammering and standing up to look at Scott. It was hot and he was wearing a pair of purple shorts and a scarf tied round his head to keep his hair out of his eyes. His skin was tanned from his days spent on the beach, guarding Leonardo from the curiosity of strangers and, despite his thinness and the way he had to stop from time to time to fight a shortness of breath, a visibly painful struggle that made her own heart clench, you wouldn't know he was as ill as he was. He looked at life in the old unswerving way. The world was still black and white to him. Right and wrong. Great and terrible. Worth consideration and beneath consideration. He was still fearlessly intact in the admirable, infuriating way of the young. He'll be like that forever, she thought.

'She's kind and she makes me laugh. She makes me feel lucky,' he said, looking a little embarrassed but not so much that his pleasure and pride didn't shine out of him.

'She's lovely,' Josie said.

'I'm glad you like her,' he said, bending down again and resuming his efforts.

The beach was empty bar a few families who had made it their temporary home with towels and umbrellas and coolboxes. The impulse to own the space they had found for themselves was evident in the way they had left measured gaps between each other and hung up clothes and placed shoes, staking their claim on each portion of sand like land prospectors.

'Do you think we will ever find it?' Scott asked as they lifted another layer of rock to reveal only the usual collection of corals and plant fossils.

'The elusive, perfect sea lily?' she answered. 'The chances are slim.'

'It's a bit like trying to find someone to love,' he said and she wondered if he was really as convinced as he had seemed to be by her assertion that Grant made her happy.

'You know that even if I was with Hugh Jackman I would still be sad?' she asked.

'He would take the edge off it, though, wouldn't he?' Scott said. 'Everyone thinks he's fit.'

'You don't even know what he's like. He might be a complete loser despite his muscles,' she replied.

'I think that's unlikely,' Scott said. 'He looks like the sort of man who can get himself out of pretty much any awkward situation.'

'You do know that Hugh Jackman himself doesn't actually have self-healing powers, don't you, Scott?' Josie said teasingly.

'Even Wolverine can die by drowning,' Scott answered.

They carried on working for a while, the sound of metal on rock a soothing background. Above them the gulls circled, hoping the work going on beneath them would unearth a meal. After a while, Scott sat down. His breath was laboured and his face was pale.

'How are you feeling?' she asked.

'I'm slowing down,' he said, looking at her with his steady blue gaze.

'What can I do for you?' she asked, on the edge of tears.

'You can be here,' he said and smiled at her and she went over to him and touched his hair. She had a fleeting memory of stroking him in this way when his hair was as soft as thistledown and blew around his face.

'I want to do something,' she said. 'Won't you reconsider the American trip?'

'Will it make you happy if I do?' he asked her.

'It will,' she said, sitting down beside him and holding him as close as she was able.

It was clear she wasn't ever going to give up and he felt her will like a burden. He didn't want to die. There was Emily to live for. Emily with her soft, secret skin and the way she made him feel as if he could accomplish anything at all. He imagined them getting married, although he knew it was bloody silly to think of it – she would be beautiful in white with that vivid face framed by flowers, wearing the perfect shoes her mother would find for her beneath the pile in the bedroom. Underneath her dress there would be complicated lace things that he would be able to take off slowly when everyone was gone and he had her to himself. He hadn't accepted the curtailing of this or any of the other things he had hoped for but he had tried, despite the vertiginous terror that rose in him when he was alone and the incredulity he felt when he allowed himself actually to contemplate what it would be like to leave everything he loved behind, to hold himself fast to the moment; to make himself believe that what he could see and touch was what he would always have.

'You don't know what it feels like when you have a child,' his mother had said once. 'You would do anything, anything at all, to save them,' and she had been so fierce that he had almost been afraid of her, or afraid for her, he wasn't sure which. He looked at her now, pulling apart the loosened rock, peering beneath at the remnants of creatures and plants that had populated this coast when the land around them would have been tropical and the sea would have boiled with life. Her hair was tied back. She was wearing a blue shirt that exactly matched her eyes. She was as indomitable as a whale or the sea or the rocks that defied their search for perfect fossils. He loved her regardless of what she had said about love going downwards. It seemed to him love spread all over the place like bearings in a pinball machine but he yearned for something she didn't seem able to give him. He couldn't quite articulate what it was that he needed from her, but it was something to do with giving him permission. His mother's mobile phone rang and she dusted off her hands and took it out of the pocket of her rucksack. She listened for a moment and then went very still. He could see her back stiffen. Without saying a word, she bent down and put the phone back in her bag. The face she turned towards him was as white as the water left by a breaching dolphin.

'What's wrong?' he asked. She looked so strange that he got up and held on to her arm to steady her.

'Who was that on the phone?'

'It was George,' she said and she sounded bewildered. 'He says that your father is at the shop. He's come back.'

Chapter 29

Scott!

You don't say in your film whether your mother is into dogging. If the answer is in the affirmative, I'd be more than interested! I attach a picture of me in our local woods.

Dog235

Her first thought was that Peter hadn't changed at all. She would have known him anywhere. He still had the restless, loose-limbed look of someone who hadn't quite decided whether he was going to stay or go but was only biding his time before he made a decision. His hair was a little thinner, his features, softer, more mobile, but he had retained his good looks. George was standing guarding him with a determinedly virtuous face, as if he suspected that at any minute the man was going to make off with a double orthopaedic. George knew the story of Peter and had been outraged by his abandonment of Josie.

'I know his type,' he had said when Josie had confided in him. 'He's the sort that sows his seed and then makes off before the reaping.' George often used phrases that were vaguely biblical particularly when customers annoyed him or the weather was bad or when Greggs ran out of sausage rolls.

For a moment, Josie hesitated before going in. Peter hadn't seen them yet and they could just carry on walking. She knew George would never disclose where they lived, but just as she had almost made up her mind that she couldn't bear to go in, Scott went ahead and opened the door. The sound of the bell made Peter look up and he stared intently at his son as if he was making sure of something. Josie followed Scott into the shop and for a moment nobody spoke.

'Do you want me to stay, or, you know ... give you some privacy?' George said with surprising delicacy.

'It's OK, you can go,' she said to him, trying to smile and show that she was in control.

'I'll be in the office,' George said. 'Just say the word and I'll be out in a flash. The devil comes in sheep's clothing,' he muttered darkly as he went, making his hand into a threatening fist and showing it to Josie as if it was important to him to demonstrate his allegiance.

'I expect this is a bit of a shock,' Peter said. Josie stared at him. For a moment she felt again the passage of his finger under the neck of her jumper, that instinctive tremor, but then he smiled at her and the feeling passed and she felt nothing but a kind of bewildered coldness, as if she had woken up in the night and found the bedroom window had been left open.

'It must be a little like seeing a ghost,' he said, smiling again, and she wondered what was wrong with him. *Perhaps he always did this and I never noticed*, she thought. Perhaps he always smiled to cover his tracks.

'Where have you been?' Scott asked, and she wished he wasn't there. His voice was puzzled. She didn't want him to be hurt more than he already was.

'Why don't you go on home?' she said, but Scott wasn't going anywhere. He had the look he always had when he was trying to get to the bottom of something. Despite herself and even as she knew it as a kind of vanity, she hoped that Peter would see Scott's calibre – the way he stood so straight and looked at his father without faltering. *This is the gold you turned down*, she thought.

'I know it must be strange for you,' Peter said. 'It's strange for me. You are taller than I thought you'd be. You've not changed at all, Josie,' he said turning to her.

'I've changed completely,' she said, speaking to him at last, hoping her voice held firm.

'So you really just left,' Scott said. 'There wasn't a kidnapping or a suicide or any of the other versions of your life I've imagined.'

'It was complicated,' Peter said and Josie saw, for the first time, the weakness of his mouth. Had it been like that then? And the way his eyes slid away.

Just then the door opened and a man and woman walked in and started assessing the beds, doing what people always did, sitting on the edge of the mattresses, giving little experimental bounces as if they were testing for potential lift-off.

'Why don't we go somewhere more private?' Peter asked.

'Why have you come back, Peter?' she asked. 'Just tell me and then you can fuck off back to wherever you have come from.'

'I've come to make amends,' Peter said.

Josie stared at him dumbstruck.

'You've come back after 19 years to say you're sorry?' Scott said, his voice high and incredulous. Josie could tell by the way he was leaning against the wall that he wasn't feeling very well.

'I think you should go home,' she said again desperate to protect him.

'I want to know what he has to say. I want to know what makes someone walk out one night and disappear off the face of the earth.'

'I was a different person then,' Peter said and she wanted to hit him. It wasn't his disappearance that galled her now; it was the fact that he had come back. If she had had a gun she would have shot him between the eyes.

'I wasn't ready for fatherhood,' he said. 'It came as a shock. I was going to come back. I really was. I thought I'd just go away for a few days and think about it, get used to the idea, you know.' His slightly plaintive, almost aggrieved voice made her grit her teeth.

'I'm not interested,' she said. 'Come on, Scott, let's go home.' She took his arm.

'George, we are leaving,' she called out and George appeared instantly as if he had been listening at the door.

'I don't want anything to do with him,' she said, looking meaningfully at her colleague.

'Right you are. Sling your hook, mate,' George said to Peter and he ushered him to the door. Peter didn't stand a chance against George's pastry-filled bulk.

'I'm staying in town,' Peter said as he was bundled out of the door. 'I'm not giving up. I want to get to know my son.'

He was smaller than Scott had thought he would be. The photograph had given an impression of a taller, broader man. He could see his mother shaking as they walked home and he took her arm.

'I'm sorry, Scott,' she said.

'What have you got to be sorry about?' he said, stopping in the middle of the pavement and putting his arms around her. Her shoulders were newly fragile under her shirt. He could almost feel her bones. For the first time in his life he saw his mother as being separate from him – a person with feelings and sorrows that were similar to his own. It felt like a revelation.

'He's not my father. He never was,' he said, and stroked her hair. When had he grown taller than her? It had happened without him noticing. He remembered the way she always used to measure him against the kitchen wall on each of his birthdays, making a careful line along the ruler she placed against his head. She always insisted on doing it before he got his presents. He couldn't remember when she had stopped. When he was a teenager, perhaps, and less eager for the gifts, or at least less eager to get up early to receive them. The sketchy ladder was still there on the wall representing the ghost of his fifteen-year-old self.

'Why has he come back?' she asked him.

'I don't know, Mum,' he said. 'Don't even think about him anymore. I'm not going to.' He took her arm again and walked on. Despite the fact that the man was clearly a loser – he had been wearing a U2 T-shirt for a start and stacked-heel cowboy boots, probably to make himself look taller; Scott would never have chosen him if he had applied for a date with his mum – he found that he wanted to know the answer to the question. *Half of who I am is from him*, he thought.

Chapter 30

Scott

I found your film deeply disturbing. As a psychothera-pist of many years standing I recognise you as a victim of a narcissistic mother, one who is manipulating you to endlessly serve her own needs. If you don't disengage from this noxious relationship you will be unable to fulfil your own potential. Please come and see me and we can work together to help you grieve for the mother you should have had.

Yours in therapy

Sylvia Van Mooning

'What do you think about my mother's plan to take me to America?' Scott asked Dr Moulton.

He had come into the hospital for another round of tests and examinations. He felt sore and out of sorts after the prodding he had endured.

'She's actually put the house on the market now and has started packing boxes.'

The doctor looked at him carefully. Scott liked the way he always thought before he spoke. There was something reassur-ing about the way he measured things up. He was cautious, but truthful, Scott thought. Not a bullshitter, which was Scott's very least favourite type of person.

'Well, there's some incredible work going on there in cardiology,' he said.

'Will it save me? Is there a chance it will save me?' he asked.

'They might be able to prolong your life,' the doctor said and his eyes were kind.

'I don't want to go there and have more stuff done to me and die anyway and my mother won't have a house and I will be thousands of miles away from where I want to be.'

'I can't tell you what to do and I certainly can't tell your mother what to do,' Dr Moulton said, smiling wryly.

'I want her to accept it,' he said.

'You are asking a lot of her,' the doctor replied. 'She's angry and frantic and why wouldn't she be?'

'I think she's going to continue to be angry until it's too late.'

'That might be all she can do,' Dr Moulton said.

'I'm worried my mission to find her someone has failed. I'm really not sure about her and Grant. She doesn't seem all that keen.' Scott had watched them together and he hadn't detected in his mother any of the things that he felt when he was with Emily.

'Doesn't she?' said Dr Moulton, looking down at his hands in the way that Scott had come to recognise as something he did when he felt he was disclosing too much.

'And to top it all, my father, my biological father, has turned up out of the blue, and it has upset her.'

'He's come back after all this time?' Dr Moulton said looking astonished.

'His timing is pretty fucking terrible, isn't it?' said Scott. 'It was seeing my video that brought him back. I'm not sure he ever would have otherwise. That's one outcome from Project Boyfriend I never expected.' He tried to laugh but he felt too miserable to pull it off. Despite Josie's best attempts to get rid of him, Peter had hung around in Alnwick and Scott had met up with him a few times without telling her.

'I didn't need him then and I certainly don't need him now,' his mother had said with a set face and narrow lips when Scott had mentioned Peter, testing the water to see how she would react.

He had agreed to see his father the first time simply because he had been curious to hear his version of what had happened. He had thought that he might be able to strike a blow for his mother – make Peter pay for abandoning them by rejecting him now. He had been savagely glad to tell his father about his illness. In his explanation he had spared him no details of what had been and what was yet to come.

'You've left it too late, mate,' he had said, attempting a kind of defiant nonchalance which he thought would impress this man who shared his blood but knew nothing about him. The useful thing about strangers was that you could be whoever you wanted to be. He had been sure that the revelation would send him out of the town as suddenly as he had arrived, but Peter's eyes had filled with tears. Right there in the pub he had wept as if it actually meant something to him.

'I'm going to do everything I can,' Peter had said. 'I want to make up for all the years I've missed.' And although he felt disloyal, Scott had found himself relaxing into Peter's words as a kind of relief. Despite the tears he knew that his father's grief was too newly acquired to have any real meaning but his readiness to express emotion in what seemed an uncomplicated way was curiously comforting. He thought maybe it was some sort of throwback to childhood when he had imagined that if his father had been there he would have been able to prevent Scott's illness. He liked the way the man rallied with a stiff Scotch and a comradely arm across Scott's shoulders as if they were in something together. It was in such stark contrast to his mother's painful love that it felt like something shallow and warm that he could bask in. Emily had been suspicious of him right from the start.

'It's easy to find the right words when you don't really care,' she had said in her most imperious tone of voice, her shoulders hoiked up almost to her ears. 'He's trying to buy you,' she had added for good measure, looking disdainfully at the new phone and leather jacket Peter had bought Scott.

'He's worked very hard,' Scott had protested. 'He was homeless for a while and then he got a little money together and built up his business. He's very successful.' He was secretly a little ashamed of how impressed he had been by the way his father had slapped his credit card down on the shop counter and told Scott he could have anything he wanted.

'I've got nineteen birthdays and nineteen Christmases to make up for,' he had said and caught the shop girl's eye and she had become suddenly skittish, touching her ear and laughing.

'I expect you've got some other crap-hearted people to see,' Scott said now, aware that he had been with the doctor for a long time.

'It's fine,' the doctor said. 'I'm not seeing anyone else till after lunch.'

'Do you like being a doctor?' Scott asked.

'Some of the time,' he answered.

'Which are the good parts?'

'When I manage to make something better.'

'I suppose I'm a bad bit, then,' Scott said.

'It has been a privilege to have you as my patient,' the doctor said with odd formality and he smiled at Scott as if he was telling him a secret.

'Have you got a girlfriend?' Scott asked, feeling that the question might be allowed, now that they were talking so personally.

'I haven't,' the doctor said.

'Is that because you are still sad about your wife?' Scott asked and saw the way the other man shifted in his seat and looked away.

'You don't have to answer, if you don't want,' Scott said hastily, fearful that he had overstepped the mark.

'I can't expect you to tell me your stuff if I won't tell you my stuff,' the doctor said and so Scott waited while he gathered himself, thought of the words that he should say.

'When my wife died she was pregnant with our first child. We had just been to the twenty-week scan. She was looking at the picture of the baby on her phone. We were so happy. We were going for a weekend away. A van pulled out of nowhere. I didn't even see it. It hit the side of the car where my wife was sitting. She died almost straightaway.'

'Bloody hell,' Scott said. As the doctor had spoken he had been able to imagine it in his mind – the woman's bent head looking at the sketchy outline of her baby, trying to see her husband in the half-formed profile and clenched fists, their bags packed in the boot of the car, the road stretching ahead.

'The last thing I remember her saying was, "We'll call him Jack after your father", and then there was this almighty crash and then silence. The radio carried on playing. It was *PopMaster* and a man had just got all his questions right. She was so terribly white and her head . . . I knew . . . although I tried . . . and then I held her until they came.'

Scott didn't say anything. He thought he might have been nodding like an imbecile.

'Since then, well, it just doesn't seem possible to be with anyone else.'

'I can see why,' Scott said. 'But maybe sometime in the future . . .?' He trailed off, Dr Moulton's face looked so very sad.

'I'm not sure I'll ever be as lucky again,' Dr Moulton said.

Scott had arranged to meet his father after his hospital appointment and Peter was waiting in the lobby for him when he came downstairs.

'How did it go?' he asked as they walked to the restaurant.

'The usual,' Scott said lightly. 'I'm thinking Dr Moulton isn't that impressed with Mum's plan to take me to America.'

'I'm going to talk to her. I've done some research and I've identified the best man. I want to pay for it all,' Peter said. 'And then when it's over and you've got a shining new ticker, what do you say we go on a trip to the Maldives and you get some R and R watching the whales? I gather there are twenty-three different species to see.'

'I don't know,' said Scott. For a wild moment he thought that what his father was suggesting might be possible. He had a vision of himself sitting by a wooden building just after the sun had set, the pulse of his new heart pushing the blood smoothly through his body, the moths, attracted by the light above the porch, spinning in burning, doomed spirals to the sand, the smell of the herby, dry scrubland behind the beach and the sound of the rhyming song of the whales coming from far out in the dark sea. It felt like something he had seen and felt. *Perhaps I have dreamt it*, he thought. He had never travelled much – just a scary trip to Prague when a taxi driver had cheerfully relieved him and his fellow travellers of half their spending money on the journey from the airport and a member of the group had been sick all the way down the hotel carpet. The only holidays he had taken with his mother had been to local campsites and a week on a barge that had felt a little like being asleep, with intermittent periods of wakefulness when they navigated the locks.

'Well, think about it anyway,' his father said and they sat at a table with heavy napkins and roses in glass vases.

Scott nodded. Part of him knew it wasn't real, the Maldives and this man with whom he shared nothing but the same long fingers and fast-walking pace, but it made him briefly calm to think that matters might be taken out of his hands.

'She doesn't want to talk to you,' he said.

'She will when I make her understand that this will be the best thing for you,' Peter said. 'She may be as stubborn as hell, but she'll see the sense in it.'

*

271

In the afternoon, Picasso arrived to take Scott out to his secret beach. Although Scott seldom had much of an appetite these days, he always tried to eat some of what his friend brought – meat pies and iced buns – food for people whose arteries were flowing free, although they probably wouldn't for long on that diet. He knew it made Picasso feel as if he was doing something constructive. He had found that what most people wanted when faced by his illness was to feel they were doing something. They avoided the subject of what was to happen in the future by trying to provide diversions. It's terrible, but it's OK. *It's OK that it's terrible*, he wanted to say. His illness made most people uneasy and embarrassed. They weren't even sure about where to look, let alone what to say, and they hovered around him as if they were waiting for a reprieve – a bell to summon them from the room, a fire to extinguish. That's what he liked about his father – he didn't shy away from it. He seemed able to face it head on.

The van bumped over the field and he thought about the night he had last been there when they had all danced in the shining sea. *I had that,* he thought, *and now I have this stretch of green and the lurch of the van and Picasso doing his best, despite his fear.* The sky was full of clouds, which blew aside every few minutes to reveal the sun. It was hard to get a handle on the afternoon because it shifted continually between shadow and light as if a finger was scrolling across a screen adjusting and readjusting the brightness of the display. Through the window he could see a mass of starlings, shape shifting in a great cloud; now a thick, undulating ribbon and then, swollen by another banner of birds, becoming a slowly heaving monster, a dragon, a seal, some strange sea creature moving softly through the sky.

Picasso helped Scott down the path and onto the beach. He laid out blankets and food.

'Where did you get those?' Scott said laughing, pointing at the paper plates which had My Little Ponies around the edges.

'That's all they had at the shop,' Picasso said. 'I just bought them without looking.'

'I like them,' Scott said. 'There're very . . . decorative.'

'I'm hopeless,' Picasso said. 'I can't even get the plates right.'

'You're a sad arse wipe,' Scott said. 'You're a bearded vomit licker.'

'You're a twitting shit shark barnacle,' said Picasso.

'You're an earwax jacker.'

'You're a throbbing minge chomper.'

'You're a tossing dick whistle spunk bubble.'

'You're a leg-humping bung-holed bastard.'

'You're a wrinkled old fawning fart-faced cluster fucking constipated piss flap,' said Scott, sensing victory in this game they always played. He knew he had the upper hand. It was hard to swear at a dying person.

'You're a fart waffle,' said Picasso desperately.

'A fart waffle!' Scott said derisively. 'I already said fart. I win!' And he launched himself at Picasso, pinned him down and sat on him, then started coughing so hard he thought he might throw up. Picasso wriggled himself free and handed him a cup of coke and waited until Scott recovered his breath.

'I love you,' Picasso said. 'I feel so sad. All the time. Every day.' He looked up at the sky and then over at the cliff and then down at his feet as if he didn't quite know where to put himself.

'I love you too,' Scott said.

'I don't know what to do,' Picasso said, and his tousled head almost disappeared into his hunched shoulders.

'You're doing great,' Scott said. 'No one could have had a better friend.'

Picasso made a shooing-away motion with his hand, as if he didn't believe it, and rubbed his face with his sleeve. They didn't dwell on it anymore, just talked of regular, everyday things and sat eating iced buns off My Little Pony plates and watched the sea and another perfect day draw slowly out.

Chapter 31

Hey Scott

Does your mum have tattoos? I have 56 of them, including all the members of Queen and my three, now dead, dogs. Your mum looks like the kind of bird who might have a sneaky rose on her breast or a Celtic cross on her inner thigh. It's not a deal breaker, just a preference.

Jack

'It feels like the beginning of the end of summer,' Emily said and Scott smiled at her.

'It's been a great summer, though, hasn't it?' he asked and she nodded her head. Picasso had twisted dried seaweed through her hair in a crown and she was wearing a white shirt over her long brown legs. He thought she looked like some sort of sea goddess. For the last couple of weeks they had hardy been at home.

'We don't have to do something every day,' Emily had protested as he planned yet another excursion. 'You need to save your strength.'

But he wanted to spend the last of his strength on her. He wanted to show her everything that had ever mattered to him. So they had peered through the railings of his old school and he had pointed out the place beyond the pile of painted rubber tyres where he had had his first kiss with a yellow-haired girl called Julie.

'All first kisses are with girls called Julie and they all have yellow hair,' Emily had said scornfully. 'I bet she's the size of a bus now and makes chutney in jars with gingham hats and her yellow hair has faded to a dingy brown,' and he had been pleased that she had been jealous even of this.

He had shown her a spot in the woods on the edge of town in which there were still the vestiges of the den he and his friends had made. At Cragside, the first house to be powered by electricity, and the site of a memorable school trip when Miss Berilode had had a sartorial mishap and flashed her bra at the whole of Year Ten, they had played in the room in which there were still some old devices for summoning the spark and they had kissed so hard that they had made their own static. In Chillingham Castle, a place that had exerted a curious fascination for him as a child since it was said to be haunted, he had told her the story of the Blue Boy, an unfortunate individual who was accused of treachery and walled up alive and whose remains were found in the twenties alongside the scraps of blue material which were all that remained of his clothes. He knew she was pretending to be more frightened than she was so that she could hold him close as they were led on a ghost trail which featured ghoulish whispers and growls and the creak of doors and the sound of cups rattling and a room with a foul smell. He had shown her views through gaps in trees onto yellow fields which he claimed no one else had ever noticed and they had swum in a secret, green river and afterwards had lain entwined on the bank drinking wine and listening to his playlists, their skin smelling of mud and the sun. He had even persuaded her to eat kippers, a delicacy she had approached with much trepidation.

'They taste like old wood,' she had said, wrinkling up her face, and he had kissed the lines between her eyes.

There had been times when he had been frustrated by his diminishing strength – he hated the fact that he had to stop and rest halfway up a hill and he once fell asleep and missed a whole afternoon of something he had planned, but she had made accommodation for his growing weakness without drawing attention to it. Her kindness gave him the stamina to carry on. Occasionally, he saw the sadness she tried so hard to hide and sometimes they reached for each other in a wordless need for comfort, but for whole, unblemished, golden days they managed to forget.

Now, Emily, Picasso and Scott had scrambled over some fallen limestone at the end of Picasso's beach and were sitting next to each other in a shallow cave in the side of the cliff, sharing a joint. Scott had barely inhaled, the habit of caution still holding sway, but even so the view had taken on a dreamlike, blurred quality. Beneath them the sea moved slowly, insinuating itself into narrow, barnacle-thickened channels, filling and then emptying the rock pools in which tethered weed the colour of dry blood, stretched and then retracted. Scott felt the weakening sun on his arms and legs as something being pulled away.

'Lois has gone with the bloke from the flat below ours to Calais as a witness to the breaking up of the Jungle camp,' Picasso said. He had picked up his ever-present sketchbook and was drawing the three of them on their rocky outcrop – Emily in sea-surf white, swinging her legs, Scott in a straw trilby looking out to sea and Picasso himself with his shock of blond hair, bent over his drawing pad.

'What's she going to do there?' Emily asked.

'I haven't a clue. She said something about taking pictures.'

'Well, that should ensure everything runs smoothly,' Emily said, her shoulders up in combative mode. Emily liked almost everyone, but had developed an aversion to Picasso's girl-friend.

'I'm not sure when she's coming back,' Picasso said. 'I didn't even realise she knew the man.'

'Are you worried?' Scott asked, aware of the carefully casual way his friend was speaking.

'I'm not sure,' Picasso said, shaking the hair from his eyes. 'The bloke in question is French.'

'An hour in Calais trying to find organic kale for her should fuck him right off,' Emily said, grinning and looking almost witch-like, and Picasso laughed ruefully.

Just then the distinctive, ragged crest of Leonardo's fin appeared out of the water. The dolphin was moving fast, performing rapid, low jumps and then disappearing with a smooth, rolling motion. Behind him a small boat with an out-board motor was in pursuit. Scott could see a clutch of young men standing up, holding on to each other to keep from fall-ing. Even from this distance he could hear their excited shouts, louder than the sound of the engine. He wondered for a moment what they were doing and then saw the man at the helm throw-ing out a length of lassoed rope. The boat was gaining on the dolphin, which seemed to be slowing down, perhaps because he was tired or had decided to face-out his tormentors. Scott moved instinctively, shuffling himself forward from the ledge and slithering down to the rocks below.

'What are you doing?' Emily asked, her voice anxious. He didn't reply, but carried on his reckless scramble to the beach. He felt the burn of a rock grazing his leg and then the warm trickle of blood. As he reached the sand, he was aware of his uneven breathing and of a clutching heaviness in his chest. He could hear Emily and Picasso following behind.

'Leave it!' Picasso shouted, but Scott couldn't. There was a red mist in front of his eyes and dancing specks partially obscured his vision. He ran to the edge of the sea waving his arms.

'Hey!' he shouted, trying to catch the attention of the men, but they seemed not to see him. The boat was now alongside the dolphin which was beating his tail flukes up and down. The water churned and the boat swayed alarmingly from side to side.

'Stop! Stop!' he shouted, but he was too far away and his voice made no impact on either the men or the dolphin, which was now moving in tight spirals beside the boat. The man at the helm was crouched, leaning forward, the circled end of the rope stretched out between his hands, like an executioner. Scott kicked off his shoes and began wading into the sea until he was up to his waist in the water. He felt his own weakness. The sea was sucking at his body. The smooth pebbles under his feet shifted so that it seemed that he couldn't get proper purchase. The rope flew out across the water and then it was pulled back and thrown again, scattering glittering drops. There was a brief, intent silence and then a collective cheer rose from the boat and the man, his face gleaming pinkly, was leaning back taking the strain of the newly tautened rope. Scott saw to his horror that he had managed to fasten it around the dolphin's tail.

The creature tossed and rolled. Scott took a deep breath and began to swim towards them. He felt as though his lungs might burst. The water around him rocked with the motion of the flailing creature. The engine started up again and Scott could see that the straining rope was pulling the dolphin along. Emily was calling out to him and, glancing back, he saw that she and Picasso were now in the water too.

Scott gathered all his strength, ignoring the heavy feeling in his chest and the clutch of the freezing water. He swam as fast as he was able using the front crawl drilled into him by his mother. He felt as if he wasn't moving forward at all, but when he took his head out of the water he saw with surprise that he was within a yard of the boat. He reached out his hand and briefly felt the smooth, melon shape of the dolphin's head before the boat jerked forward with a sudden, sickening motion. The water surged around him and he made one final, desperate push and caught hold of the gunwale on the dipping side of the boat and hauled himself up. He could see faces bent towards him and the engine suddenly cut out. He jerked at the rope with one hand, using his unexpected appearance to take the man unawares and felt it come away. He let go of the boat, pulling the rope behind him, and fell back into the sea. The dolphin was so close that he felt its sleek shiver against his skin. The water foamed and he could hear Leonardo making a clicking sound of distress. Then there was a sudden stillness and he knew that the creature had shaken himself free. The pink-faced man shouted something at Scott that he couldn't quite hear and someone threw an empty beer bottle into the sea, narrowly missing his head. The boat started up again with an oily shudder.

Propelled as he had been just minutes before by a surge of energy, now Scott couldn't move. Picasso, who wasn't a strong swimmer, was still a little way away, treading water and splashing his arms, appearing and disappearing behind the furrows left in the boat's wake. The sea buffeted Scott and he felt himself slip beneath the water. He was tired. He rose briefly and then sank again; his eyes were open and he could see the navy abyss beneath his feet. He couldn't breathe. Bubbles like stars rose around him, making for the surface. *This might be as good a way as any to go*, he thought. He felt a surprising calm. There was no need to fight any longer. The sea was carrying him down gently. He thought he heard Emily's voice. He wished for the blessing of his mother.

He was drifting lower. He could feel the sea claiming him, but then there was a sudden, urgent tumult and the sound of creaking and whistling. He felt the brush of sleek skin and he saw the dolphin's eye – its benevolent creases, the centre marble-black rimmed with a crescent of white and the curve of his smiling mouth. He heard the hissing spit of the dolphin's outward blow – sounding like moisture hitting hot stone – and then the water rippled gently and Scott was aware of a sudden absence. There was the drag of hard shingle beneath him and human arms around him, pulling him clear, and then he felt nothing at all.

Chapter 32

Hello Scott

I've just seen the video about your mother. I have been married four times, but none of my marriages have worked out. I'm not sure why. My last wife said it was because I could never love anyone else as much as I love myself, but she is mad and an alcoholic and suffers from low self-esteem. I'm eager and willing to meet the lovely Josie at a place of your choosing. I see that you have requested a picture, so I attach a fairly recent one of myself at a car rally. I'm the one in the metallic-blue Capri.

Rick

Josie sat at the side of the bed and watched her son. He had always looked so perfectly intact in sleep and even now, when it seemed all colour had been leeched from him, his face obscured by a mask, linked by wires and tubes to machines and hanging bags which dripped their contents into him in measured portions, he looked peaceful. She had been told that time wears away memory. That it scraped even the most loved sights away, but she thought what they said couldn't be true. She would bury him deep inside her so that he would never crumble, never lose his perfect outline and she would be able to find him whenever she wanted by digging inward, below the lose rock to where he would always remain intact.

It was the middle of the night and the hospital had a familiar, pulsing hush. Dr Moulton came into the room.

'Don't you ever stop working?' she whispered, surprised to see him so late.

'I'm on duty tonight,' he said. 'I'm glad I was here when he came in.'

He pulled up a chair and sat down next to her.

'I gather the boy was swimming with dolphins,' he said, smiling.

'Yes,' she said, smoothing the sheet over Scott proprietorially, as if to prove that it hadn't happened on her watch. She had endured the call from the local hospital, her heart stopping and then starting up again sluggishly as she heard that it was not death. Not now. Not yet. She had ridden with him in the ambulance to Newcastle, stroking his arm as he lay oblivious. 'I'm here. I'm here,' she had kept saying to him, bending over so that she could speak into his ear, as if she thought he could hear her. An infection, a bad one, and more thickening, more dead-ends, but not dead. Not now. Not yet. There might still be time to make the journey to America. There was still time for a reprieve.

'Will he be well enough to travel next week?' she asked now and she felt the doctor move his hand over her own and leave it there. She knew it as an attempt to soften what was coming and yet she didn't move, willing herself to be comforted, even as she braced herself.

'I think it inadvisable,' he said quietly and she thought she heard his breath catch. 'I've been in touch with the doctor in Boston and we've discussed Scott's state of health. I'm afraid he's of the same mind as me.'

Josie thought of the telephone conversation that must have taken place. The careful listing of symptoms, the polite, mutually agreed decision, the professional courtesies at the end and all the while her son, her *son* – the subject of their words, was lying here waiting for her to save him.

'He isn't a good candidate for another heart transplant,' Dr Moulton said.

'He isn't a *candidate*,' she hissed, getting up, wincing as the legs of her chair scraped noisily against the floor although she felt angry enough to hurl tables and tip beds. She thought she might rage through the hushed hospital shouting at the top of her voice. *I've become a mad woman*, she thought. *My grief has consumed me.* She wasn't sure where to be. Not here, nor at home with the walls emptied of their pictures. There was nowhere to escape to. She would walk, she thought. She would walk through the night, on and on, never stopping.

'Where are you going?' he asked, and she looked at him, bewildered.

'I don't know,' she said.

'Let's go out for a few moments and get some air.' He led her into a lift and out through the huge, glass trap of a front door.

They sat on a low wall and Josie, who was dressed in a thin shirt and jeans, shivered in the new, end of summer chill.

'Have my jacket,' he said, and took it off and placed it around her shoulders. She felt a brief, borrowed warmth.

'What's next?' she asked wearily.

'We'll get him through this patch, attempt some more stenting, but then, I'm very sorry, the disease will take its course and eventually all we'll be able to do is make him as comfortable as possible.'

She didn't want to ask how long. She didn't want to be able to count down the days. The sky above the meagre trees was lilac-coloured and mottled with cloud.

'Tell me how to survive,' she said.

'Little by little,' he said.

An ambulance drew up outside the entrance, making the glass wall shine with sudden, urgent light. The back door was swung open and a woman emerged, sitting upright in her chair, a blanket wrapped to her neck. She looked around her curiously as if trying to work out where this ride had taken her. As she was wheeled past, her eyes met Josie's and she smiled, wide and sweet and unperturbed.

'What can I do for him?' Josie asked as they watched the glass door open and claim the woman.

'You can tell him you'll be all right,' Dr Moulton said.

'But how can I be?' she asked, hearing the evening cry of blackbirds and the city's relentless reverberation.

'Tell him you will be all right, because you will. Not straight-away, but in time.'

He looked at her. His face was pale, his eyes dark. *He doesn't get out enough*, she thought. What can it be like to witness this again and again? Were there days when he felt the futile grind of it? Or was it enough for him to be able to patch up the dam, to buy a little time? What did he know of loss other than the multiple versions he had observed, which must, by now, seem all the same?

'I'm trying to be all right myself,' he said. 'I'm trying to believe that death gives life its meaning. It's difficult . . .'

He trailed off and she wondered what it was that he had been about to say.

'He's the best of me,' she said and she felt the tears come. They felt almost kind, the way they eased the tightness in her chest. They fell silently on her hands.

'He'll always be that,' the doctor said. 'That'll never be taken away.' He touched her on her shoulder and so she turned and found his face close to her own and somehow, without thinking, perhaps because the darkness was gathering and he was there, or perhaps because she wanted to feel the truth in his words that her broken heart would keep on beating, she put her mouth to his.

He froze for a moment. She could feel his still lips against her own, but then he kissed her back, tentatively at first but then with greater force, so that for, one swooping moment, he was all she could feel. It was as if the world had disappeared and there was only the two of them left, joined together by trembling skin and sensation. She thought maybe she had made a noise because he pulled her closer. Another ambulance arrived, sirens at full pitch, bathing them in its blue light, and she was startled awake. She pulled away. He was breathing deeply. In the half-light his eyes looked dazed.

'I'm sorry,' she said getting to her feet. 'I don't know why I did that.'

She felt embarrassed. She wondered how many other grieving mothers had launched themselves at him. It must be an occupational hazard.

'It's OK,' he said, but she was too mortified to reply and turned to go back into the hospital. She could feel him watching her as she went. It wasn't until she got back into Scott's room that she remembered she was still wearing his jacket.

*

Scott woke to see the dark shape of Emily beside him. She was curled up in the chair, fast asleep, with her legs tucked under her. He moved his arms and she was instantly awake. In the dim light her eyes were shining like a night fox. He indicated the mask over his mouth and she pulled it aside so that he could speak.

'How long have you been here?' he asked as she bent over him.

'A couple of hours,' she said and kissed him. Her mouth felt as warm as life and he thought of the dark sea beneath his legs and felt again the nudge of the dolphin's beak against his body.

'How long have I been here?' he asked, and she lay down beside him so that he could touch her hair and pull at her soft ear lobe bisected by a hoop of gold.

'Three days,' she said. 'Your mum's finally gone home to get some proper sleep.'

He felt a passing sense of loss for the days he had missed. Three summer days that he would not have known the lack of if the sea had taken him. *When it ends there will be nothing for me to regret*, he thought, the supple slide of Emily's cheek under his fingers, her breath even and sweet.

'I'll get the nurse,' she said, but he held her back.

'Wait a moment,' he said and so they lay side by side in silence, watching the light through the half-drawn curtains gain strength so that in a while it touched them and he could see clearly – her dark head against the white sheets, the plump curve of her mouth, her fingers with chipped, blue polish resting on his heart. Around them the hospital creaked into life as if it too had been waiting for the light.

Part Four
Autumn

Chapter 33

Hello Scott

I'm homeless although I hope you won't hold that against me. My mother died and I kind of lost it and ended up drinking too much and got the sack and my wife chucked me out because I was scaring the kids. I've been sleeping rough for six months now, which is hard. Someone pissed on me the other night and I'm always getting moved on. People don't see me, they just see the shape of me in my sleeping bag and they think I'm different from them. But I'm not. It's easy to lose everything. A friend who has a phone showed me your video and I thought your mum looked kind. I'll wait until I get myself out of the shit situation I'm in. I know I am nobody's idea of a good boyfriend, but please put me on your list because I hope one day I'll be worth considering.

(P.S. I used to be somebody)

It was the most beautiful autumn Josie had ever seen. She walked slowly with Scott through the thin wood, edged on two sides by fields grooved with recent plough marks into a crumbling softness. The trees with their leaves in every colour from the palest, primrose-yellow to a deep damson seemed lit from within. The bright spindle bushes were heavy with winged fruit and the hawthorn and rosehip berries had a jewelled gleam. Even the sloes had cast off their dull bloom and were as shiny as wet stones. Scott stopped from time to time to rest. Walking was difficult for him now and although he made light of his symptoms, she had seen the way he clutched at the bannister as he dragged himself up the stairs and heard his struggles for breath in the night. Some days he couldn't get up at all and lay in bed sleeping fitfully.

'I've been seeing Peter,' Scott said, stopping and leaning against the trunk of a rowan tree, his feet buried in the twisted, burning leaves that ringed it. She was astonished. She thought Peter had left Alnwick. When he had come to the shop for the third time asking if he could see Scott, she had told him to go away.

'He's not yours,' she had said. 'You've missed your chance.' She had thought her words had been hard enough to reach him at last because he had turned away without protest. She had taken him for the shiftless boy he had been. It was clear she had misjudged him. It seemed he liked to fight for things he had been told he couldn't have.

'Have you?' she said, trying to keep her voice neutral, although she must have conveyed her surprise because Scott sounded defensive.

'I enjoy spending time with him. He's good company,' Scott said and the admiration in his voice made her heart clench.

'I want him to be able to come to the house and see me when I can't make it out anymore,' he said.

'If that's what you want,' she said and began walking again so that he wouldn't see her face. She had never consciously felt resentful for what she had sacrificed but she felt bitter that it was Peter he wanted now that his days were running out. *I've known you from the very beginning*, she thought and she felt a sudden fury that was as incandescent as the blazing trees. Picasso, Emily, Peter; everyone else was more important to him than she was. Had she not earned the right to his regard? She walked quickly so that Scott was left behind. She wanted to put distance between them. Her stride through the mounded leaves reminded her of childhood and of a lost lightness. In the trees above her, rooks were making the cracking, wheezing sounds that made her think of the wind of a key in the side of an old plaything. The anger slipped away and was replaced by contrition. She had thought she was better at love than this. She turned and walked back to him.

'Of course you must see whoever you want to,' she said smiling.

When the car drew up at the house they saw Grant sitting on the doorstep. Josie hadn't been expecting him. She parked and got out and was surprised to see that he looked uncharacteristically dishevelled – his hair was greasy and plastered to his head and the bottom of his shirt was unbuttoned so that she could see his stomach. He got to his feet with difficulty as they approached and held on to the doorframe.

'What's up?' she said, seeing from the rigid way he was standing that he was very drunk.

'My mother's died,' he said and she unlocked the front door and ushered him in. He threw himself down on the sofa. She made a discreet shooing motion with her hands and Scott went upstairs after giving Grant's shoulder a clumsy pat.

'I'm sorry,' Josie said.

'She lay on the floor in her apartment for three months before anyone found her,' he said.

'Oh God, how terrible!' Josie said, moving towards the bottle of brandy on the sideboard and then changing her mind. Grant had already had enough to drink.

'The concierge finally unlocked the door after he realised that she hadn't been seen for quite a long time.'

'She was the world's worst mother, but no one should have to end up like that, should they?' Grant said. As he looked at Josie his eyes filled slowly with tears, and she sat down on the sofa and put her arms around him. She made soothing noises and stroked his back. His large frame seemed to have shrunk.

'During the last conversation we had two years ago, she told me I was an unfeeling bastard because I refused to give her any more money. I didn't want to finance the bar bills of the latest waiter or struggling actor she had hooked up with. She never had any sense. She was always looking for her great love. She once met a man on holiday in Morocco. He was the driver of their tour bus and she told me she knew as soon as he looked at her that they were meant to be together. She kept going on about his poetic eyes and the way he pulled chairs out in restaurants and opened doors for her. She paid for him to come to Paris and within a month he had cleaned out her bank account.'

Josie continued to hold Grant and allowed him to talk.

'I always thought that one day we would . . . I don't know . . . if not love each other, at least come to some sort of understanding. I always thought there was time . . .'

*

Scott wasn't sure how long he had been asleep. It took him longer these days to climb out of dreams that were so vivid that when he woke he could still feel them in the room. It was as if his waking life and the time he spent sleeping were becoming less distinct, the way that the sky and sea merged when you saw them from a distance.

He remembered that Emily was due to come back for a visit that evening and he got out of bed and pulled his clothes on. Term had started and he hadn't seen her for a month. They had talked most days but both of them were aware that they were editing their conversations – she skipped over the parties and the evenings in pubs she knew would hurt him to hear about and he avoided telling her that he thought all the time about what she was doing and who she was with and what she was learning. He wanted her to be free to take hold of the life she was still going to have to live.

He drew the curtain and looked out of the window. He saw to his surprise that Emily had already arrived. She was sitting on the bench in a dress he hadn't seen before – it was full skirted and lemon-coloured. Grant was sitting beside her with his arm along the back of the bench. He couldn't see his mother anywhere. Through the window he could vaguely hear the sound of their voices – Grant's loud and a little mocking – Scott thought he might still be drunk, and Emily's lighter, silvery tones. She put her head back and laughed at something Grant said and Scott could see the white gleam of her throat. He thought she looked beautiful. He wanted her to come upstairs and curl her body against his.

The evening was gathering in and the light was lilac coloured, like a dream, and so, at first, Scott couldn't quite understand what he was seeing. The pair below fell suddenly silent and then Scott saw Grant leaning towards Emily. Scott thought it was that way round – that Grant had moved towards her, although it was hard to tell from where he was standing. It was as if he was watching a scene in slow motion, the way movement becomes slack in the moments before an accident. Grant hesitated for a moment then held Emily's chin and kissed her. They sat locked together. It felt like a long time to Scott before finally she disentangled herself and stood up. He couldn't see her face. She had her back to him. He felt sick and desperate. It was as if someone had stuck a knife in his stomach.

He lay back down on the bed. He didn't have the strength to stand up anymore. He heard hasty footsteps in the hallway and the sound of the front door opening and closing and then Emily's softer tread on the stairs. He wouldn't say what he had seen and maybe if he dreamt again and woke again it would be as if it had never happened.

'Scott, wake up. I'm here,' she said. He didn't want to look at her. She switched on the light and he saw her dark eyes and the way she was holding her arms tightly by her sides.

'I saw you from the window,' he said. 'I saw you kiss him.' He felt so angry that he thought what was left of his heart would tear its way through his chest.

'I was just sitting there and *he* kissed *me*,' she said her face as pale as a sheet, and he didn't know whether he believed her or not. He ran the scene back in his mind. Who had leaned towards the other? Had it been her or him who had made the first move? He couldn't quite remember. Had she said something that Grant might have taken as an encouragement? Had she traced her finger along the top of her lip?

'I didn't see you put up much of a fight,' he said, hearing the mean tone in his own voice.

'He took me by surprise,' she said. 'I was shocked. It was the last thing I was expecting. I think he'd been drinking before I got here.'

'Where's my mother?' he asked.

'She went out to get some things for supper,' Emily said. She sounded to him as if she was pleading.

'So you waited for her to be out of the house before you pounced,' he said.

'Scott! What are you talking about? It wasn't like that. I promise it wasn't like that.'

'What *was* it like, then?' he asked, knowing he was hurting both of them but unable to stop.

'I can't believe you would even think that I would do it. Here in your mum's house. It makes me sick that you think so little of me.'

'So you would have been happy enough to do it somewhere else, then?' he asked, fastening on her words and twisting them. He could feel her fury. Her hands were tight fists. He thought maybe she wanted to hit him.

'How come you didn't come straight up and see me?' he asked. 'How come you were lingering in the garden with him?'

'He said you were sleeping, that I should let you rest for a while,' she said. She made a move towards him and he put up his arm.

'Go back to London. I don't want you here,' he said and she stepped back as if he had tried to hit her.

'This is an easy out for you, isn't it?' she said and he saw her draw herself up. She was fierce and beautiful and he hated her.

'If you think me capable of this, then I don't know why I am bothering with you,' she said. She looked like a queen. 'You can fuck right off.'

She turned and left the room. He listened for a while to the sound of her gathering her things and then her footsteps in the hall and the click of the front door closing after her. He wanted to tell her to come back. But the anger was still poisoning his sluggish blood and he couldn't move. Later, hearing his mother come in and knowing he would have to explain Grant and Emily's absence, he understood that what he had really wanted to say to Emily was, *I know you didn't kiss him. Of course you didn't kiss him. It's just that I am scared that when I'm gone, you'll kiss other people and forget I was ever here.*

Chapter 34

Dear Scott

I watched the film and your mother was talking directly to me. I recognised her straightaway. She made a kind of beckoning gesture with her hand and I am convinced it was a sign that we are meant to be together.

Dorian

'Why did you do it?' Josie asked Grant. Until now she had ignored his messages but this morning he had turned up at the bed shop and so she had been forced to go with him to the café round the corner. It was either that or have the conversation in front of George and a woman she knew vaguely from an exercise class she had taken years ago who had come in to order twin princess beds for her unpleasantly matching daughters. Josie usually loved children, she found even the boisterous ones funny and touching, but these two girls with their air of entitlement and discontented mouths made her shudder.

'I was drunk,' he said. 'You know how drunk I was.'

His eyes were bloodshot and his face was grey and she almost felt compassion for the way his hand was shaking when he picked up his cup, but then she thought of Scott's face when he had told her. He had looked ashamed somehow, as if he thought it might have been his fault.

'It turns out he isn't a keeper after all,' he had said and tried to laugh, but his eyes had been blank.

'When I'm drunk, I tend not to lunge at teenagers,' she said, not wanting to be there with him. She didn't want to talk about it. What did it matter after all?

'I'd just found out my mother had died,' he said, his tone of voice becoming a little indignant as if he thought she wasn't making enough of an effort to understand. 'I wasn't myself.'

'Scott saw you. He stood at the window and watched you kiss his girlfriend. How could you do that to him?'

'Even now what matters to Scott is more important to you than anything else,' he said and he pushed his cup roughly across the table so that it spilled half its contents into the saucer. 'You're not bothered at all about what this means for us.'

'What this means for us,' Josie said, 'is that there will be no us. It was a mistake.'

'You have no feelings for me at all, do you? You never did. You are just using this as an excuse to get rid of me.'

'I don't think it was ever really going to last,' she said. 'We diverted each other for a while.' She was surprised by the look of hurt on his face.

'Come on,' she said more gently, 'you know you'd have moved on pretty soon anyway. It's what you've always done.'

'I thought it was more than that.' She had a sense that he was fighting with himself. He was like a serpent with its own tail in its mouth. 'I think I could have loved you,' he said and lowered his head, as if he too was tired of talking.

'I think you wanted to love me, but you couldn't, not really. I'm not sure you even know what love is.'

He put his head up and looked directly at her and she could see the anger move in him, fast and unforgiving, like the flash of a tongue or the whip of a tail.

'Do *you* know what love is? You deserve to be on your own,' he said, his voice low and distinct, as if he didn't want her to miss a word. 'When Scott dies, you will have nobody.'

She didn't answer. She knew saying anything now would only make him angrier. He needed to burn himself out.

'You think you know everything, but you don't even know that Scott made a film of you and put it on social media so that any old bloke with an itch to scratch could apply for a date with you. He touted you around like a bit of meat.'

He had a bit of spit on his chin and Josie couldn't take her eyes from it. It seemed to be all she could see.

'I've got through to you at last, haven't I?' he said and she could hear his triumph. He could smell her blood. He looked blunt and savage. She wondered that she had ever thought him handsome.

'Thousands of men have seen you wandering around your house, twitching your arse in your wetsuit, talking bloody nonsense about fossils.'

'I'm going now,' she said and she stood up. The ground seemed to slope away from her feet and the sun on the glass-topped table glittered so that everything around her had a sickening sheen. She wanted to be somewhere she couldn't be seen.

*

When she got back to the house she found Scott sitting in the garden. His eyes were closed and for a terrible moment she thought he had gone, but he heard her approach and turned his head.

'How come you're back?' he said.

'I've been talking to Grant,' she said. 'He told me about the video you made of me.' She saw him flinch.

'He's a complete bastard,' he said.

'Why did you do it?' she asked. 'Why would you do such a thing?'

'I wanted to find you someone.' She thought he sounded impatient, as if she was asking him something she should already know. 'It was the best way to do it.'

'Everyone has seen it,' she said. 'They were probably all laughing at me.'

'Nobody was laughing at you. I promise they weren't. Thousands of people wanted a date with you. They wouldn't have applied for one if they thought you were someone to laugh at.'

'Everyone knew but me.'

'If I'd asked you, you'd just have said no.'

She looked at him for a moment – at his dear, child's face. She wanted to weep.

'It's just a game to you, isn't it?' she said. 'You don't care what I feel at all.'

She didn't wait for him to answer. In her bedroom she drew the curtains and lay on the bed. *This is what happened*, she told herself, fighting tears and the pain of feeling that her love had been insufficient. *In the end they left without even looking back.*

Chapter 35

Dear Scott

I hope you don't mind me sending you this message, but I can hardly broach the subject at the hospital. I really shouldn't be broaching it now, but since Josie isn't actually a patient, I think it is (kind of) all right. I wonder (deep breath) if I could have a date with your mother. She is beautiful, of course, although as her son you might not quite see that, but she is also brave and funny and determined and loving, although she does her very best not to show me these things about her. You don't have to agree to a date just because I'm your doctor. You might very well feel I'm not a good match for her. Despite my fancy waistcoats (that I know you admire greatly), which I hope give me the look of someone bold and decisive, I have struggled over the last three years to believe in anything much at all. I'm still floundering and still scared, but I think if I don't at least try to start again, and by that I mean take the risk of getting close to someone new, I will be stuck this way. I loved Marie with all of my heart and as I tried, rather ineptly to tell your mother, love doesn't get taken away. It remains with you forever. I just want to find out if I can add another layer to it. Don't reply if you think it's a terrible idea. I won't hold it against you (you will still be the finest patient I have ever had). So . . . for what it's worth, I, Robert Midgely (I know!) Moulton, officially apply to be considered by the wisest and most open-hearted of sons for a date with Josie Hudson. My three favourite things are bacon sandwiches with brown sauce, early morning skies and lying in bed with someone I love. I await your reply with as much hope as I can muster.

R. M. M.

Scott didn't know what to do about Dr Moulton's request for a date with his mother. He hadn't had even the smallest inkling that the man was interested in her. He hadn't seen any lingering glances and nor had the doctor asked him any leading questions about the kinds of things his mother liked or how she was getting on with Grant (the utter, shit-wanking arsehole). He had been completely poker faced about it which Scott couldn't help feeling slightly put out about, considering he had thought that the man had confided quite a bit in him about his dead wife and everything.

Dr Moulton was a decent bloke, but there was no way his mother was going to fall for him. With his floppy hair and his habit of laughing uproariously at his own, not particularly funny jokes, he was about as far away from his mother's type as it was possible to be. He didn't look particularly active and Scott thought that if the doctor ever found himself in a tricky situation he would probably just sit there polishing his glasses and thinking it all over. Josie had never done anything but criticize him – his waistcoats, his shoes, his decisions about Scott's care, the way he drank his tea and, recently, she hadn't even seemed to want to speak to him. It hadn't gone unnoticed by Scott that she tried to duck out of the room every time he appeared. She had called him a slime-ball the other day, just out of nowhere, for no particular reason, as if she had remembered something he had said or done in the past that had really annoyed her.

In any case, he thought there was no point in telling her since she was still clearly furious with him about the video. She would probably kill him (which, thinking about it, might be a good solution for all concerned) if he brought up the subject of her seeing anyone else. Since her discovery of the film she no longer fussed around him as much as she used to do, and when they were together she didn't keep up her usual endless chatter. Her face was set and tired and she moved her body as if she had become suddenly old. He found he missed her fidgety, impossible ministrations, her offers to read *Moby Dick* (as if he was actually still ten years old), the way she used to touch him as if he was precious. *I've fucked it all up*, he thought.

In the night he now often had to use the oxygen tank that was ready by his bed because his breath got caught up in him. Sometimes it felt as though his heart had finally stopped. Each time this happened he clenched himself in readiness. *Maybe it will be now*, he would think, trying to stay calm. I'll think of her face. I want that to be the last thing I see, but, after a few moments, he would feel his heart under his fingers – that little persistent pulse that kept him tethered to life. He wondered what it was going to feel like to be taken into darkness. Dr Moulton had said that Scott would almost certainly not recognise the exact moment he was going to die.

'When it comes to it you won't be scared,' the doctor had said. 'It won't be a sudden realisation, more like a slow slipping away,' and then he had told one of his terrible jokes, which had been kind of him, although neither of them had really laughed. What made Scott more scared even than the thought of what dying would be like was the fear that when he was gone he would be wiped away; covered over like a beach at full tide. When the wave drew back there would be nothing of him left.

He tried not to think about Emily because each time he did he was full of regret. He thought he had been unkind to her. Although, all things considered, it was probably best that she had gone. What, after all, could he offer her now? *At least I got to use my dysfunctional heart*, he thought and remembered their shining night on the beach. At least I was given that chance. And he fell asleep, grateful for the sudden, snatching oblivion.

'Get up,' she said. 'This room smells of old socks and armpit.' She drew the curtains and opened the window and Scott flinched awake in the sudden onslaught of light. To his dazzled eyes everything in the room was indistinct like a Polaroid picture in the moments before it drew forth what had been there.

'I've got a surprise for you.'

Emily was standing in his room with her hands on her hips as if she meant business. She was dressed in a pair of oversized overalls looking like she was about to paint a room or bust a ghost. He felt the ardent happiness the sight of her always brought him. *I will never stop feeling this way*, he thought. This blaze will endure because it will never dim.

'Where are we going?' he asked, smiling at her.

'Not far,' she said.

Emily drove to Embleton and by the time they got there, a mist had fallen and gathered itself over the sea. As they walked hand in hand through the damp grass she looked around her in a worried fashion.

'Where's the sun gone?' she asked.

The cows grazing at the foot of the castle breathed heavily through shell-coloured, dripping nostrils so that their warm vapour became part of the mist too. It was the sort of a day when you could readily imagine dragons curling their tails round rocks and hear the sound of lethal swords clashing. It was the Northumberland of folklore and a hundred jigsaw puzzles. He remembered a sad story his mother used to read to him about a mermaid who fell in love with a king who lived in a castle, but he never saw her and so she was doomed to swim round and round, waiting for him until she grew old and fell to the bottom of the sea and became a stone.

'This is the place,' Emily said when they reached the giant's arm. She ordered him to sit down, although the rocks were sticky from the mist and the larger waves were coming perilously close, sending a fine, spitting spray up into the air.

There had been times recently when Scott felt that he was absenting himself from wherever he was. He had taken to imagining the place he found himself in but with himself rubbed out. He had no illusions that when he died he would go somewhere else and be able to watch the people he loved from above, and yet, regardless, on some future day, Emily might be here again, looking just as she did now and the mist would be the same too and the cows with their faintly steaming flanks would churn up the same grass on the same slope. He looked at Emily who had wandered a little way away and was talking into her mobile. He hoped she would love someone else after him.

Two things happened at once. It was a kind of magic. The mist disappeared, as if the submerged giant had taken a huge indrawn breath and sucked the air clean and a flag appeared at the turret of Dunstanburgh Castle. It looked for a minute as if it was simply going to hang there but then it caught the breeze and unfurled itself and spread out, red with a white sun in the middle and gold all around that glinted in the sudden brightness. Emily danced around him, smiling and delighted.

'I arranged it for you,' Emily said. 'To make up for the flag you couldn't put up when you were a little boy.'

He found he was crying at the impossible, foolish beauty of it all – the flag and the sun and her smiling face.

On the way home Emily suddenly pulled over when they came to a gap in the hedge and parked the car a little way along a track where they were hidden from the road. They pushed the passenger seat back and Emily pulled up her skirt, guiding his hands to her. They kept breaking off to laugh and Scott could not help wondering what a passer-by would make of his naked bum shining through the windscreen, but he felt a solemnity and a gratitude he had never even imagined when he had thought about sex. He had learned the mechanics of it all, had done his share of looking at the lurid stretch of opened flesh that the Internet provided, but he hadn't expected this tearful tenderness or the way his own dazed gladness was reflected in her face.

'I love you,' he said afterwards. 'I have done for ages. I hate that I've wasted so much of our limited time together – I should have told you sooner.'

They sat looking out across the shorn field. The golden drums of wheat were waiting to be rolled away and stored against the slender months when nothing would be growing. He got out of the car and she followed him. They walked for a while along the edge of the field and then lay down. He could feel the sharp, shorn spikes and the shifting earth, settling itself down to sleep.

'Thank you,' he said, looking up at the sky, which was a faint, flecked blue.

'What for?' she asked, turning her head to look at him, her face still soft.

'For taking me with you,' he said. 'For allowing me to live afterwards.'

She looked at him steadily, her hair dark against its tawny background, and she put her hands to her mouth as if to keep her words in. Her tears didn't spill over, but were held, shining, as if it was all she would allow.

Part Five

Winter

Chapter 36

To Scott

It has come to a pretty pass when we have to tout for love online. Where will it end? Perhaps your mum would contemplate having sex with her chosen candidate in a follow-up film, quite a long one, which you could post on her behalf. I, for one, will not be watching.

Morris

It was hard to choose the right tree, especially since Scott wasn't there. Every year until this one he had come with her to the farm shop and patiently pulled tree after tree from the rack, spinning them around on their sharpened trunks so that she could inspect them from all sides. He had always found it funny the way she obsessed about finding the perfect one.

'What about this one?' he would ask, indicating a perfectly acceptable specimen, but she would walk around it dismissing its girth or the gaps between the branches or the quality of the needles or the suitability of the top spike to accommodate the tatty Christmas angel she brought out of the box every year.

'I'm looking for a really shapely one,' she would say and he would laugh and keep going – pulling and spinning – so that in the end she could no longer distinguish one tree from another and would settle for one chosen almost at random.

'Christmas can now begin,' he would announce solemnly when at last the tree was shoved through its metal tunnel into netting and squeezed into the car. It was almost always too tall, taller than they had thought when it was amongst others, so that they would have to drive with the window open. She could smell the car now if she closed her eyes – the dusty blast of the heater turned to full capacity, the slightly sour boy odour of him and the captured pine lying across the back seat, smelling of resin and promise.

She had always stuck to a cycle of traditions – she had placed snowdrops in the small glass vase on the windowsill, made pancakes that had stuck inevitably to the pan that had been eaten regardless of their scrambled state, hidden eggs in the hollows of trees long after his childish thirst for chocolate had abated, made the first fire of the season on the beach, taken the first swim, gathered blackberries with which she made one crumble before leaving the rest in the freezer in a fat, triangular bag, scooped pumpkins so that he could carve them with lopsided leers, made a ritual of unearthing the Christmas decorations and then another of their careful packing away, which always provoked the melancholy sense in her of not knowing what might happen between their dispatch into the darkness of the under-stairs cupboard and their next resurrection. He had mocked this too.

'I expect this will be the last time we see these,' he had said last Christmas, looking sideways at her as they had wrapped each piece carefully in tissue paper, a smile curling around his mouth. She had done it all for him. She had tried to make the outline of his life clear and safe. It had all been an illusion.

However hard she had tried to anchor him, he had eluded her careful tethering.

There had been several hospital stays since the day of the flag, which had marked the real beginning of his decline, and now he was at home. He had been clear he wanted no further medical interventions including the implantation of a defibrillator.

'I don't want to be shocked back to life over and over again,' he had said firmly and she had had to accept this too even though, given the choice, she would have made a different decision on his behalf. She wanted him to have every intervention possible. She would have grabbed at anything that would have given her more time. A specialist nurse came every day to move and bathe him and check and refill his syringe driver that pumped the medicines he needed in regular doses. Dr Moulton visited as often as he could, sitting with Scott and talking quietly. She often heard laughter from the room when they were together and she had a sense of being excluded. The doctor was very polite, almost formal with her now and she thought probably he was behaving like this because he felt ashamed of the way he had kissed her. He was married and she was almost a patient, it had been all sorts of wrong. In between the visits from Scott's friends who came with stricken young faces carrying chocolates or flowers, as if trying out what they understood as the etiquette of illness and who left looking bewildered, Scott slept or read as assiduously as ever.

'There's so much I still don't know,' he said to her and she felt herself wince as if she had been cut. Peter came all the time with ludicrous, expensive things – a machine that made swirling light shapes all over Scott's bedroom ceiling, an enormous cashmere pillow to prop Scott up, a fan Scott could adjust with a remote control, a cream containing crushed urchin shells and pollen that was said to soothe dry skin. He would play video games with Scott and feed him wine through a straw, even though Josie had told him several times it would make Scott sick.

Emily made the trip from London as regularly as possible. She moved quietly around the house, helping out, trying to remain cheerful although Josie could see what it was costing her in the strain around her mouth and the way her shine only came out when she was with Scott. Josie had seen them through the half-open bedroom door, lying together, sharing a set of headphones, she with her arm around him, he with his fingers in her hair. Scott always banished Emily when it was time to wash him or deal with his catheter.

'I don't want you to think of me like that,' she had heard him tell Emily and she'd seen the girl retreat obediently outside in even the bitterest of weather and sit on the wood store in the garden, her hands in her lap, looking blankly in front of her. Josie thought it was as if she was trying to gather herself so that when she came back into the house she would be able to be what he needed her to be. Josie thought her heartbreakingly brave.

'This must be so hard for you,' she had said to Emily, when they were standing in the kitchen waiting for the nurse to finish upstairs.

'I want to be here,' the girl had said, looking at Josie as if she thought she was going to be banished.

'But still,' Josie had said, 'it must be terrible,' and she had touched the girl on the arm in consolation.

'I didn't know it would be so . . . brutal,' Emily said, 'the way a body shuts down – the smell and the sight of it, the swelling and the soreness, the pain. There's a constant feeling of dread that never goes, even when you try your best to fight it.' She moved restlessly, picking up a tea towel and then putting it down, running her hands over the wooden counter top as if trying to find the words to explain what she felt in its cracks and blemishes.

'He's so alive,' she said. 'He makes living look easy, even now, with his legs propped up and his mouth red and torn and his skin bursting and his shame that he has to be helped to piss and crap. I know it hurts him more than he ever says but he has . . . it's something that's hard to put into words . . . a kind of certainty,' and she had turned to Josie with a look that was halfway between sorrow and astonishment.

'I think he wants to talk to you,' she had said then, looking at Josie cautiously.

'I'm the last person he needs,' Josie had said, trying not to sound bitter. 'I think I make things more difficult for him.'

'He thinks you are angry with him.'

'I'm not angry,' she had said, although she knew she was. Her anger was sharp-toothed inside her. It was eating her alive. It allowed her no rest.

'You need to say everything while you can,' Emily had said, her voice almost stern, and Josie had had a glimpse of the woman Emily would become and her heart caught on what Scott would never know.

'I'll talk to him,' she had promised, although she still didn't know what to say. There were so many words. She didn't know which to choose.

Josie tugged the first tree in the row from its stand and hauled it over to the man who was taking payment and then began dragging it across the car park by its netted end. It was heavy and the needles bit into her hand.

'Can I help you with that?' Dr Moulton said appearing in front of her so suddenly that she jumped, startled out of her reverie. He was carrying a tiny tree on a stand and had a wreath over his arm, but he put both things down on the ground so that he could take the weight of her tree. She should have bought something smaller. She didn't really have time to decorate a tree this big. What had she been thinking of? Now he would have to help her to wrestle it into the back seat of the car and she would feel awkward.

'I'm fine,' she said, trying to take the tree from him and to continue by herself, but he ignored her.

'Shopping for your mother-in-law again?' she asked when he had finished cramming the tree into the car by flattening the passenger seat so that it rested against the windscreen. He was certainly a very dutiful son-in-law. How come his wife never seemed to be with him when he made these trips?

'Yes. Christmas is a difficult time of year for her,' the doctor said. 'I try and do what I can.'

'That's very kind of you,' Josie said.

'How's Scott today?' he asked, looking at her.

'He's a little worse, I think,' she said trying to keep her voice steady. 'The nurse is looking after him very well.'

She wanted to tell him that it seemed to her that everyone else was coping much better than she was, that when she was with Scott she felt a terrible panic so that she could barely stay in the room, that she felt that he no longer loved her and perhaps never had, that she couldn't bear the thought of him leaving her when things between them were so strained and strange, but she didn't say anything at all.

'I'd better get these to their destination,' he said, indicating the tree and wreath on the ground, but he didn't move and she had the sense that he wanted to say something and wasn't sure whether he should.

'Have a lovely Christmas,' she said to fill the silence that had fallen between them.

'I don't actually like Christmas very much,' he said.

'Why?' she asked. 'It can be frantic and people argue and drink too much and all the things you have thought about and planned seem to be over in minutes, but I still love it. At least . . . I always have. This year, not so much.' She plucked at the front of her coat where some needles had lodged themselves.

'If it wasn't for Christmas we would all be starved of light for months.'

'My wife died on Christmas Eve,' he said, looking away from her.

'Oh,' she said, surprised. 'I thought you said you go and see your mother-in-law . . . I assumed . . .'

'She's never quite recovered,' he said. 'It makes her feel better to see me. I'm her last connection with her daughter. I thought Scott would have told you.'

'He didn't,' she said, and again she had the feeling that he was weighing up his words, feeling his way towards something, but he fell silent again.

'I'm so sorry about your wife. How long ago did she die?'

'Three years ago,' he said.

'That's still very recent,' she said, looking at him differently now, seeing sadness in the slant of his eyes and in the weariness she had assumed was due to the rigours of his job – all those failing hearts he had to keep pumping. He wore those ridiculous waistcoats to keep it all from him, she thought, the way I'll probably take to wearing mad hats or dye my hair red after Scott dies. What she had read as vanity, was, in fact, defiance.

'Anyway, I must go,' he said, and he went as suddenly as he had appeared, before she had the chance to say anything else.

Josie had decided to put the tree up in his bedroom and now it stood in the corner, lopsided and with its top hacked off. It had proved to be a good metre too tall for the room and his mother had cut the end off with a kitchen knife, wrestling with the tree as if she was fighting a monster. Shapely it most certainly wasn't. He thought she must have picked it out with her eyes closed. He had directed the adorning of it from his bed, advising her that she should put the bulk of the hanging decorations on the lowest branches, knowing it would make her laugh. He didn't ask her what it felt like to unwrap each familiar thing – the pipe-cleaner Santa he had made at school, the ice-skating girl, the pearly snowman, the tiny red shoes on red ribbon, the faded elf with its dented ping-pong-ball body that had belonged to her mother – the things he had watched her put away last year with her usual end-of-season gloom. Maybe this time she would fear the dismantling less, because she would have less to dread. Or perhaps it didn't work like that.

His whole body hurt although the pain lessened when the medicine really kicked in. He had come to rely on the soft whirr of his syringe driver. He tried to let himself have things done for him without complaint, although he felt ashamed that someone he barely knew washed him and flushed his waste away and smeared his body with cream and moved him up against the fancy cushion Peter had bought him. He tried to take it because he knew he had to, but he hated his helplessness and the rank smell of his own body. Dying was a disgusting, bitter thing that made him feel like a child again. He hated his struggle to breathe and the stuff that came out of his swollen legs and the things they shoved up him to make him shit. When people came to visit, they often wearied him. He didn't have the strength anymore to make them feel better. He liked to lie with Emily because she was so peaceful and seemed not to need him to be anything other than he was. I think she's a keeper, he thought, loving the way she smiled for him, even though he knew her heart was breaking. There were times when he longed for his mother and her old battling spirit, which he missed as something familiar and comforting, but he couldn't reach her. Although she still did all the things for him she had always done, he felt that she had somehow removed herself from him and he didn't know why nor how he could bridge the gap between them. *I want her to let me go*, he thought, watching as she moved slowly around his room moving things from place to place as if she was trying to put something right.

It snowed in the night and although it would have made her happy on any other year to have a white Christmas, now it felt to her like something wasted. As if the perfect conditions had presented themselves but were no longer wanted. It was Scott's twentieth birthday and this morning Peter and Emily and she had clustered around his bed and blown out the candles on a brownie cake he had pretended to eat and then they had sung 'Happy Birthday' at his request, although her throat had closed up at the memory of all the birthdays there had been and the ones that would not now come.

When she went into his room, she saw that Scott had disentangled himself from his drip and morphine feed and had got up, drawn the curtains, and was standing by the window looking out.

'You must get back into bed,' she said. 'You'll get cold.' But he held the window ledge tightly, as if he didn't want to be parted from it.

'I love the snow,' he said. 'It makes me feel peaceful. I wish I could go out in it now.'

She stood with him and gazed at the garden and the field beyond it. The sky was bruised and spent. It had emptied its democratic load so that the table and water butt and trees had all taken on the same plush texture. The snow covered the bumpy roof of the shed in a great pillowy slice. It had wiped out the half-finished path and the broken struts of the fence. The sound of traffic and of voices had been blotted out in the overwhelming, implacable mass of it.

'There's a deer over there!' Scott exclaimed and pointed, and she saw the animal, its outline dark and defined – the alertness of its back and ears clear in the wiped-out field, standing knee deep in snow so that it seemed fixed there. *I wish the snow would fill the house*, she thought, *and bury all of this under its disguise so that we won't feel anything but its bright coldness and we too will be softened and hidden*. Perhaps when they were shovelled free, there would be something different underneath and they would grow into a new shape.

She persuaded him to get back under the covers. Even this small walk across the room had weakened him. In the hard, white light cast through the window his face was paler than the snow and he breathed in little wheezing gasps. She had a terrified sense of time running out and of things being unresolved. She reached for the right words, but just then Emily came in, bringing the icy air with her. She was dressed in a coat and hat and her gloved hands were cupped around a snowball.

'I've brought you a birthday present!' she said, sitting by him on the bed and showing it to him as if she had found something unique and rare, and he smiled at her and his face was open and tender, as if the sight of it was truly exceptional.

'There isn't another anywhere. Not exactly like it,' Emily said.

She gave him the snowball and he held it out on his palm and then his hand circled round it with an old reflex, as if he was thinking he might throw it. Josie thought of his plump, flushed face as he had crouched behind the fence when he was eight or nine, she wasn't sure, it was hard now to separate the winters out, thinking himself unseen, his ammunition gathered ready at his feet, waiting to ambush her and how she had walked so willingly into the trap, her hands held up in subjugation, welcoming the coming sting.

'My last snow!' he said now, his eyes wide and bright, and she knew she would cry, so she left them lying on the bed. She thought of the snowball dripping onto the sheets, getting smaller and smaller until it was no longer there, but only felt in the prickle of his fingers and in the memory.

She brought the snow in to him. She passed it from her hand to his and he held it tightly, hearing it creak as it contracted between his fingers. He brought it close to his face and could taste its icy crunch on his tongue and smell its clean, metallic tang. He saw its uneven finish – greasy and slick on one side and powdery on the other.

'Have my gloves,' she said, but he wanted to hold the gift against his skin and feel its frigid burn. He thought of her gathering snow from the lawn, taking only the fresh, top layer so that it was as perfect as she could make it, and of the deer, half buried in the field looking for the shelter of familiar trees and of the wide, white stretch of the world that lay beyond.

'Let me take it now,' she said as it softened, but he still held on and so she put a towel under his hands to catch the water as it dripped from between his fingers.

'I love you,' he said and he felt his heart's true beat as he saw the side of her face, still pinked from the snowy air, and the resolute line of her mouth as she concentrated on the task of keeping his sheets dry.

'I want you to make a million snowballs,' he said. 'Tell me you will,' and she nodded and smiled as if she could imagine them stacked up as high as the sky, each one new, each one a wonder.

Scott heard a fox. He thought it was perhaps a vixen making her eerie mating calls although it was still early in the season. He knew that foxes could make thirty different sounds and found food by feeling the magnetic pull of the earth. It didn't matter, after all, that there was so much he still didn't know. It would all be there regardless, adapting, learning new tricks to survive, and whether he was there or not the screaming fox would find her mate and in the spring there would be cubs, maybe a whole leash of them, and they would climb trees and learn to hunt, even through the snow, by feeling the tug of the earth.

He slept and woke and slept again. There was pain – a terrible grinding and stretching that consumed his whole body. He couldn't breathe. He felt himself being moved, rolled over, gentle hands on his skin. He felt things in his mouth and nose. He was sore. His legs were swollen and his stomach was tight. He could smell pus and blood and shit. There was the puff of shaken sheets. There was the whirr of the syringe driver and a brief, blissful easing. There were dreams of light and colour and some that made him shake and cry. There were people. He tried to smile but thought maybe his face wasn't doing what he wanted it to. Emily came and he heard music 'The Way You'd Love Her' – and he saw Picasso with his face wet, trying to tell him something. Through the window the snow still fell. He thought of Leonardo in tropical waters, rolling through the sea.

*

It's easier than I expected. It's harder than I expected. He was alone and scared. He thought perhaps he had shouted out because suddenly his mother was there. Her hand was holding his, pulling him back from where he had been going. He felt a sudden urgency. He wasn't ready after all. He kicked upwards through the water.

'I'm sorry,' he said.

'For what, my darling?' she asked. Her eyes were as blue as all the skies he had ever seen.

'For thinking you were not enough. Just you, as you are. That stupid film.'

'At least I got to meet a man who picked his teeth with a golf tee,' she said, trying to laugh.

'Are you angry with me?' he asked.

'I'm not angry,' she said and found that her words were true. 'I've been so very fortunate.' She touched the little scar by his ear which he'd got when he'd fallen on some rocks.

'I'll do my best to live,' she said. 'My very best.'

'I couldn't have had a better mother, even if I'd made you up,' he said, using the last of his energy to form the words as clearly as he could. She remembered his five-year-old voice saying the same thing. How could she have thought that he had forgotten all they had been together?

'I couldn't have had a more perfect son,' she said, and he heard the permission that he had been waiting for in her voice.

'It hurts,' he said.

'It's OK, my love,' she said, and her voice was as light as air. 'Everything is all right. I'll always have you.'

He held on. He held on for her. He could see the dim outline of her face. He thought she was smiling.

'Let go,' she said. 'It's fine to let go,' and so he obeyed her. His hold loosened. He stopped kicking and felt himself drift downwards. He could breathe again, great, clean, blessed air. His chest inflated. His skin felt silky. His heart took on a miraculously even beat. His blood flowed. The bubbles rose, glittering like gold. He turned his head to tell her.

Part Six
Spring

Chapter 37

SHE HAD TO FORCE HERSELF OUT INTO THE GARDEN. THEY had been a long time coming, but there they were – just emerging over the stone edge of the flowerbed, looking like the smallest offering at the smallest grave. He would expect it of her and so she knelt on the wet lawn and picked the tallest flowers and took them inside and placed them in the snowdrop vase on the windowsill.

It had been two months since he had died and she still listened for him and each morning when she woke, she felt the shock of his loss as if it was something new. He had gone early on Christmas Day. She had thought at first that she wouldn't know what to do and had almost called for the nurse who was sitting waiting downstairs, but instinct had taken over. The single thing she had hoped for was that he would see that she was smiling. She had let him go. It was her last, most difficult task. He had turned his head. She thought perhaps he had looked at her and that he had something still to say, but then he had emptied out. She had felt his passing as a breath over her skin. She had stood in the snow afterwards, feeling the first stirrings of the town. Sleepless children were gathering in shadowy rooms expecting magic. If they were amongst the fortunate ones, parents were girding themselves up to provide it, forgetting as they struggled, complainingly awake that the opportunity to conjure magic was a blessing.

Since then she had lived dimly through the days wondering where he was. There had been a funeral, which had been attended by so many people that she hadn't been able to talk to them all. Many of them had been young – his old school friends and Danny, his housemate at college, who had taken hold of her hand and said: 'He was so much more special than he knew. He taught me to be brave,' and Simon, who had tried to help him with Leonardo, and lots of other people she didn't know. Grant had brought flowers and kissed her carefully on both cheeks. George had sat hunched and silent. Even Freya had made it out in a squashed felt hat. Emily had worn red and cried quietly, her head up, the tears pouring down her face, and Picasso had stuck a picture on the coffin of himself, Emily and Scott sitting on a ledge somewhere. Peter had been by Josie's side and he had cried hard, wrenching sobs that made his shoulders shake. Dr Moulton in one of his most lurid waistcoats had done a reading and said some words about how it had been a privilege to look after him and then Picasso had got up and talked about how Scott was his brother. He had tried to start a story about something the two of them had done when they were both small, but had been overcome with tears and had to be led away. She hadn't cried at all. All the feeling was stuck solid in her. It couldn't get past her chest and throat. She seemed only to be able to watch it happening around her as if it was someone else's story.

The house was empty now. The visitors had stopped coming. There was, it seemed, a time for everything and now it had been judged that it was time for her to heal alone, although how she was to do that she couldn't imagine. Emily had gone back to college after the funeral. She had held Josie in a fierce embrace.

'I won't ever, ever forget him,' she had said, her face older, her neat movements less quick.

Peter seemed devastated by Scott's death and although she knew that his sadness was largely born of regret for things he hadn't done, she felt a certain comfort in having him alongside her. He had lost part of himself too.

'I knew him for such a short time,' he said and she had felt no rancour, only grief for what they no longer had.

'There isn't anything for me here now,' he had said before he left. He waited, looking down at the floor as if he thought she might give him a last-minute reprieve.

'Scott was glad to get to know you,' she had said. 'He always wondered what you were like.'

'Do you think I was a disappointment to him?'

'Scott never saw what he didn't have, only the portion that he had been given,' she had said. 'I think he saw the best of you.'

She had watched him from the window getting into the car and then, once he had strapped himself in and turned on the ignition, sitting for a while without moving and staring ahead as if he wasn't sure where he was going. When finally the car pulled away, she had found herself hoping that in the end he would find the place where he was supposed to be.

She had been given as much time off Sweet Dreams as she wanted since Picasso and George had said that between them they could manage without her. She felt as if there was nothing for her to latch on to. *What should I do next, Scott? What shape should this day be? I'll walk*, she thought. *I'll make myself walk and when I come back, perhaps I will dare to go into your room and start to pack up some of your things.* Until now she had avoided going in. The nurse had taken away all the medicines and tubes and rolled up the soiled sheets and put them in the washing machine. It had been a kindness that these things had been done for her but it had meant that she hadn't had to face his absence. There were times when she had found herself treading softly on the hallway floor half pretending, half hoping that he was still in his bed asleep.

She put on her coat and boots and went out. She passed a chestnut tree which was just opening into bud, and some impulse of longing made her reach up and touch one of the cones of overlapping leaves. It was as downy and yielding as a baby's earlobe. The wind was raw and the cars moved slowly down the roads. Her body ached with the cold and with lack of use. It seemed as if she had spent a lifetime crouched, holding herself tight. In the window of a coffee shop she saw her neighbour, the young woman who had lost her husband the year before, leaning towards a blond-haired man, their hands entwined on the table. Josie thought about the way the woman had pegged out her sheets and swept her steps and changed the flowers in the pot by the front door as soon as they wilted as if the only thing that made any sense to her was to carry on. She passed St Michael's Pant, the drinking fountain topped with a knight and a vanquished dragon. In warm weather Scott used to dip his flip-flopped feet into the shallow basin of water, and now she took off her glove and put her hand in, feeling the icy clutch that travelled from her fingers to her heart.

The house that had felt cold before seemed warm on her return. She hung her coat on the empty rack and went upstairs. As she opened the door to his room the airplane mobile moved gently. There wasn't anything there. He had taken himself away. She picked up some unworn clothes and put them in the chest of drawers and returned the books to the shelf. His computer was on the floor and without thinking she opened it up. She switched it on and the screen lit up with a request for a password. It seemed as if this was the only thing left of him in the empty room and so she typed in his name, not really expecting it would be so easy, but the computer allowed her access. She would just look at what he did the very last time, she thought. She didn't want to delve into his privacy, but in the absence of anything else she was desperate for a remnant – something he had seen and reacted to that she could share.

There were three hundred and twenty emails waiting in his inbox. Messages he would never read. She scrolled down and saw they were all from people who were asking for dates with her. She had had no idea that responses to his video were still coming in. The last one was only from the day before. There was a request from a man who lived in Berlin to paint her, a taxi driver who worked the night shift and was too tired in the day to meet someone new, some lines from the Bible, a woman who had written saying she thought Josie was her sister, a man with throat cancer asking for money, a man looking for someone to share road trips with, someone extolling the virtues of spanking paddles and a man offering to fix her fence. The messages went on forever and she sat there reading them all, imagining Scott trawling through this outpouring, looking for someone for her to love.

She clicked on his sent box and saw that he had replied to several hundred of them. She couldn't believe that he had taken the time and trouble to do so. His messages varied from the come on, mate, get real variety, to sympathetic responses to people who were in despair.

Hello Tony

I am so sorry to hear about the death of your wife, (he had written to one man whose wife had died of breast cancer), *I can't give you much advice because I have never experienced what you have. You are hurting because you loved her and I'm thinking she knew that and if she did, then you have done everything you possibly could. I don't think you are ready yet to meet my mum, but I hope one day you will meet someone new to love. When you have done it once, I don't think you ever forget how to.*

Hello Gavin

You don't say exactly what it is that has caused you to lose your confidence with women but if I was you, I wouldn't give up. I can't say I am an expert, but in my limited experience women are just as rubbish as men at confidence. I find it helps to pretend you are more confident than you are and then it works out. Wilson's bird-of-paradise, which comes from Indonesia, is a case in point. Although he is just about as colourful as it is possible to be, he is kind of solitary and shy. He hangs around for ages looking for a mate. He waits until the light is just right, he clears a space on the jungle floor so that he will get noticed, but in the end, if he waits long enough and the conditions are just right, a female bird will come and then when he sees his chance he goes for it. He puffs out incredible green neck feathers and he shines and she is hooked, just like that. My mother isn't that confident either, although I haven't a clue why, so I don't think you are very well matched. I hope you find your bird.

Hello M. N.

I think you should see a doctor. I know it is embarrassing but you can't carry on wearing baggy clothes and hoping for the best. Doctors have seen everything there is to see, believe me. They won't be shocked. It makes doctors happy to be able to put things right. I am sorry to turn down your request to meet my mum, but I really think you should get yourself sorted before you think about dating. Good luck!

Hello RAM23

I think my mother would want someone with more human attributes. I'm guessing here but I think it unlikely that she would enjoy having sex with your robot, although I have to say I'm pretty impressed with your skills.

Dear Paddy

I'm really looking for someone of about my mum's age or perhaps a bit older, so you are just a little too mature. You sound very lonely and I'm sorry about that. Have you *thought about getting a dog? I have a dog called Archie who is old but great to have around because he just loves you regardless of how long you have been away or the fact you are always chucking him out of your room. He just seems to exist to gnaw the sofa and eat and love. There is plenty of evidence to show that stroking animals makes people feel much better about things. Also it will mean you get to meet other people with dogs and you will get talking. I recommend a Cavalier King Charles spaniel since they are gentle, adaptable and good for first-time dog owners.*

She sat reading until it was dark. His letters made her weep and laugh and they made her miss him and feel regret for all the incredible things he might have done in the future, but mostly they filled her with pride. It was when she was just about to finally switch off the computer that she noticed a message from Dr Moulton and clicked on it, imagining it was something about an up-coming appointment. It was so astonishing that she had to read it twice to make sure she had understood it correctly the first time.

Chapter 38

PICASSO ARRIVED PUNCTUALLY ON MONDAY MORNING IN HIS van. He had rung the day before asking if she was free. He had sounded so formal and with all the messages on Scott's computer still in her mind, she had thought for one wild moment he was asking her out on a date.

'There's something I think you'd like to see,' he had said, but she hadn't been able to get any more information out of him than that.

'It's a surprise,' was all he would say.

She was waiting for him when he honked his horn and she came out straightaway so that he wouldn't block the street.

'How've you been?' he asked her when she got in. The van was strewn with clothes and bits of paper and empty beer cans and had a strange, mouldy smell as if something half eaten had been left under one of the seats.

'It's been hard,' she said. 'It's still hard,' and he nodded seriously.

'It's the mornings I hate the most,' he said. 'I keep forgetting he's not here.'

'I know exactly what you mean,' she said and gave his arm a squeeze.

'He was the best.'

'He was,' she said and clutched the sides of her seat as Picasso hurtled through the town showing scant regard for the speed restrictions. She wondered how the beds ever got to their destinations intact.

'Where are we going, Picasso?' she asked.

'You'll see,' he said. He wasn't a boy who showed much in his face and in any case it was hard to see his features clearly under his mound of hair, but she thought he might have been smiling.

She sat back and let herself be taken wherever it was he wanted her to go.

'I gather you've broken up with Lois,' she said as he swerved to miss a car that was pulling out of a side road. He made some sort of energetic movement with his hand at the startled driver.

'Yes. She decided the bloke downstairs was more her type,' he said ruefully. 'She told me I didn't have a proper social consciousness.'

'I don't want to speak out of turn,' Josie said, 'but I don't think she was anywhere near good enough for you. I always thought she was a bit self-centred.'

He laughed. 'Do you know she used to sleep in gloves,' he said. 'She would put cream on and then the gloves. It was kind of creepy.'

'Bet she had soft hands, though,' Josie said and he turned his head towards her making her worry that he would crash into the truck in front of them.

'Soft hands, hard heart,' he said and put the stereo on and the van filled with music she didn't recognise.

'Scott loved this,' Picasso said.

Beyond the town, the fields were touched with green and the hedgerows had started to thicken. She could sense the push of spring although the weather was still chilly.

Picasso turned sharply off the road, causing her to exclaim in alarm.

'Don't worry, it's all under control,' Picasso said as he drove across a muddy track in a field.

'Are we actually supposed to be here?' she said, feeling the wheels of the van slipping around.

'There's no sign saying we can't be,' he said.

They stopped eventually, just about at the point when she thought he had plans to keep on driving over the edge of the cliff, and they got out.

'Mind your step,' he said as they half walked, half skidded down the path to the beach.

'I didn't even know this was here,' she said, looking around her at the hidden cove.

'Only a select few do,' he said. 'It was my secret beach before but I've renamed it Scott's Bay.'

He led her over to a pile of rocks at the end of the beach and indicated that she should follow him and so she scrambled after him trying to copy his agile jumps over the slippery stones.

'Can you get up there?' he said, indicating a cave in the side of the cliff.

'I'll have a go,' she said and climbed behind him. When he reached the ledge he turned to pull her up by the arm. The cave smelt of wet earth and weed. Down below the sea churned and sucked at the rocks.

'Close your eyes,' he said, and so she did. Behind her there was the sound of stones being shifted and then the click of a cigarette lighter.

'You can turn round now,' he said and his voice was solemn and excited all at once.

At first she didn't quite know what she was looking at, but when her eyes adjusted to the pink light cast by the candle lantern, she saw an immaculate fossil of a sea lily stretching across the floor of the cave.

'We found it by accident,' Picasso said, his eyes gleaming. 'Scott was mucking around in here one day and he dislodged part of the rock and saw it. We spent days chipping it free.'

She knelt down and traced her fingers over the fossil's flower-like shape, feeling its bulb which was made up of star-shaped nodules and then the ridged spread of its stem and branches, each one ending in a series of thinner tributaries, lying like feathers in the stone. Its perfect, ancient, new bones shone in the dim light.

'He told me to bring you here,' Picasso said. 'I hope you like it.'

'I do. I do,' she said and put her arms around him. 'Thank you.'

'He said to tell you that anything was possible, even finding a perfect sea lily.'

They stayed for a while sitting on the ledge, looking at the sea and then they replaced the stones and blew out the candle.

'I don't think anyone else will come across it,' he said, 'and if they do, they'll know not to spoil it. Even a real twat would know not to.'

'I'm going to come and take pictures of it,' she said.

On her way back across the rocks and beach and even while she was sitting in the van being driven home, her body and legs felt shaky as if she had run a long way. She thought she could still feel the sinuous spread of the sea lily's tendrils under her fingers.

Dr Moulton rang that afternoon, while she was in the midst of cleaning the long-neglected kitchen. She pulled off her rubber gloves to answer the phone.

'I was just wondering how you are,' he said, 'and whether perhaps you might like some company.'

He said it in a rush as if he had to speak before someone stopped him.

'I'm cleaning the kitchen,' she said.

'Ah,' he said and then there was a pause, which she was not quite sure how to fill. Presumably he didn't know that she had read his message to Scott, which made her feel a bit awkward, as if she had seen something he had never intended her to. She wasn't sure why Scott hadn't shared the doctor's request with her. Maybe it had been because he had felt she and the doctor would not make a good match. Reading Scott's messages she had been amused to see how strictly he had adhered to his slightly mysterious set of criteria when he accepted or declined her suitors. He had turned down a very nice-looking man with a string of hotels because he didn't approve of the hat he had been wearing in his photograph. Scott had compiled notes on all the candidates in a lengthy Word document. He had been too polite to actually draw attention to the man's headgear which had been of the leather variety and looked a bit Crocodile Dundee. Instead, he had said that he thought the man had too

343

many commitments that would keep him out of the country. *She needs someone who will be there all the time for her*, he had written. But, on the other hand, Scott had once paired her with a wood elf, so perhaps he hadn't been quite as discerning as he had thought himself to be. He had carried on insisting that each of the men should state their three favourite things and some of their selections had made her smile. One man's top three were feet, cracking his toes in the morning, and new socks. Another cited the smell of plastic, the smell of tarmac and the smell of hot light bulbs. A third had just typed: 'Pussy, Pussy, Pussy.' She was glad she hadn't had to meet that one.

'Well, if you're busy . . .' he said. 'It's just that I'm in town and thought you might like to meet up for a drink.'

'All right, that would be lovely,' she found herself saying, although she wasn't sure why. The evening lay ahead and she didn't have anything else to do once she had scrubbed months of grease from the walls around the cooker and sorted out the pan drawer.

'Great!' he said, sounding ridiculously pleased.

When finally she had finished cleaning the kitchen, she barely had enough time to wash her hands and face and apply a little make-up before she had to leave. As she walked briskly into the centre of town she thought there was still a strong whiff of bleach about her person and her jeans had dark patches from when she had kneeled on the slate floor, trying to reach under the cooker. She supposed she really ought to start calling Dr Moulton Robert now that they were going out for a drink, although it was such a habit to refer to him by his professional name that she wondered if she would be able to manage it.

He was already there when she arrived. She might have guessed that he would be punctual. His face lit up at the sight of her.

'I thought maybe you had changed your mind,' he said.

There were the usual little awkwardnesses about drinks and where to put her coat which reminded her of some of the early dates that Scott had set up on her behalf. *This is not a date*, she told herself. This is just a meeting with my son's doctor, although when she thought about it, being with Robert without her son's health to discuss felt strange, almost as if they were doing something behind his back.

'And is your kitchen now clean?' he asked her.

'It's gleaming,' she said. 'You could cook an egg on the floor.'

'I've always thought that was an odd expression; why would anyone want to do that?' he said smiling and she saw that his slightly combative tone was intended to be bantering, but that he was too nervous to quite pull it off. *It isn't fair*, she thought, *that I know about the message and he doesn't know I know.*

'I wasn't snooping, exactly,' she said, 'but I came across some of the emails on Scott's computer from people who were asking to meet up with me.'

'Oh yes,' he said with a wary look.

'I saw the one from you,' she said, and he stared at his hands.

'It was written in a moment of madness.'

'I thought it was a lovely message,' she said. 'I was flattered.'

'Did he not tell you about it?' Robert asked.

She shook her head.

'When he didn't mention it, I just assumed he didn't think I was the kind of man you would fall for,' he said. 'I never brought it up. I didn't want him to feel bad on my behalf.'

'Well, you would certainly have been a better choice than some of the men he set me up with. There were many times when Scott's plan to get me a boyfriend exasperated me, not least the night I found myself having to endure the company of a bloke who kept feeding himself from my plate and then afterwards sat back and farted.'

He laughed and she thought he looked much more approachable when he was relaxed.

'It's difficult, finding someone,' he said and his face, which had briefly lit up, shadowed again.

'It must be particularly hard when you have lost someone you loved,' she said and her own grief, which was never in abeyance for long, clamoured again. She had thought sorrow was a quiet thing, but it screeched through her like the grind of metal on metal.

'Yes. It makes you wonder if your chance has been and gone,' he said and for a moment she envied the woman who had provoked such desolation in his face. *Three years on and he still loves her*, she thought. His strange-shaped eyes were dark with it.

'How are you coping?' he asked as if he couldn't or didn't want to talk about himself.

'I know he's gone, but I still can't believe it,' she said. 'It's like I'm two people – the one that talks quite calmly on the phone to friends and relatives about how I am feeling and who cleans the kitchen in rubber gloves, and another who is like some sort of savage, bewildered animal scrabbling around in the dark, trying to find a place of safety.'

'I think what happens after a time is that those two parts of you join up,' he said. 'The part of you that is coping finds a place for the lost creature.'

'Is that what you tell all the relatives of dying children?' she asked, feeling the old antagonism.

'I'm sorry. I don't want to seem glib. The fact is it's shit. It'll always be shit, you just get used to it.' He moved restlessly and looked around him as if he thought perhaps he shouldn't have come after all.

She felt contrite. She hadn't meant to be rude to him. He had always been so kind to Scott, to both of them, and she wanted him to think that they had deserved that care.

'I'm sorry. I would put it down to grief, but I've always been this way, so it's no excuse.'

'What way?' he asked, looking at her intently.

'I don't know how to describe it ... watchful, defensive; prone to saying things I don't really mean and not saying things I do.'

'You've had to cope with a lot on your own,' he said gently, and suddenly she felt overcome with emotion. There was something about the way he was weighing up what she said as if it was of interest to him that made her want to weep. She thought perhaps he saw her as she was or maybe as she wanted to be. Scott had said he was someone who made you want to do your best, and although she had scoffed at the time, she knew now what he meant.

'I'm a mess,' she said. 'Truly I am.'

'We all are,' he said. He looked at her for what seemed like a long time. It was she who broke eye contact and looked away.

'Scott always thought that I would be able to cope with losing him if I found someone to love. He was so clever about so many things, but perhaps not this.'

347

'Don't you want that?' he asked. 'Someone to love?' He looked at her again, scanning her face, his gaze resting for a moment on her mouth. She felt a pulse of attraction; a kind of fluttering akin to those first surprising moments when the child inside you begins his tentative, small turns. He was an ardent man, she thought, someone who didn't give up easily. That was why he had hung on so long to his lost love.

'I'm not sure what I feel just now. I'm mainly just sad,' she said.

'I don't think even Scott thought that finding someone for you was going to stop you being sad when he died. I think it was more that he wanted to think of a future life for you when you might be happy, despite everything.'

'Maybe I'm just not as optimistic as he was.'

'I think Scott didn't want his death to be an ending for you.'

'I always wanted him to think me capable and brave rather than needy,' she said.

'You are brave and capable and he thought so too,' he said. 'Forgive me if I'm being presumptuous, but I think that you've forgotten how to imagine life for yourself. You've spent so long hoping for his. He was barely out of his teens and some of his ideas about what was best for you might have been ill-conceived, but he was a remarkably generous person. I think the thing that he fretted about the most was the idea that he had ruined your life. We talked about it quite a lot.'

She was crying in earnest now even though she knew she was attracting the attention of some of the customers. It was a quiet drink-after-work kind of a pub for regulars who were not accustomed to sobbing women in their midst. A couple of them looked positively disgusted, as if she had purposely ruined their sanctuary from misery when they had their own tears to face on their return home.

'Can I get you a tissue, or something? A glass of water?' Robert said and without waiting for an answer, he darted to the bar and brought her back a handful of paper napkins.

'Some habits die hard,' she said trying to laugh.

'Yes, we doctors panic at the first sight of tears. We are trained in identifying symptoms, but not how to cope with the effects of them. Our impulse is always to try and bung up sorrow.'

'What do doctors do about their own sadness?' she asked, sniffing and dabbing at her face with a napkin, wondering if she should allude so directly to his own loss.

'We work a bit harder,' he said. 'Well, that was what I did anyway.'

'And did that help?' she asked.

'It tired me out so I was able to sleep a little, if that's what you mean by helping,' he said.

'Did your wife take all of your love?' she asked.

'I thought so until recently,' he said and he looked at her again and his face moved as if he was about to say something more. Josie felt a sense of panic and so she turned the conversation to safer ground – her thought that she might sell her house after all, even though she no longer needed the money for Scott; Archie's recent visit to the vet; the fossil that Picasso and Scott had unearthed in the cave. He talked about his mother-in-law, a Caribbean holiday that he had taken when he was younger, a research project he was beginning work on and the collective madness that seemed to have gripped the world.

'I must go home,' she said at last. 'Thank you so much for taking me out and distracting me.'

As they were parting he kissed her on the cheek and she had a memory of their embrace outside the hospital.

'You know where I am,' he said.

When she glanced back, she saw he was standing looking after her.

Part Seven

Summer

Chapter 39

FREYA WAS MINUS HER TROUSERS WHEN JOSIE KNOCKED ON the door on Saturday morning. She was wearing a lilac-coloured jumper and her sneakers and there was nothing in between but her thin, white legs.

'Hello, you,' she said, a cigarette hanging out of the corner of her mouth.

Josie hustled her inside and began looking amongst the pile of clothes in the centre of the sticky carpet for a pair of trousers, which, when found, she handed to Freya who put them on without comment and sat down on her chair.

'That dolphin's back,' Freya said. She was poring over the paper with her monocle held over one eye. The new spectacles that Josie had been with her to the opticians to collect were lying neglected and dusty on the sideboard. Freya said they hurt her nose and made her look old in the mirror which meant that she hadn't liked the lines in her face which seemed to her, short-sighted as she was until she had the new glasses, to have appeared overnight.

'I'm not sure where all the time has gone,' Freya had said looking around her as if she thought she might have mislaid a portion of it under one of the piles of things on her floor.

'It says here that someone has started a business charging tourists five pounds a pop to swim with it,' she said now, her finger tracing the line of text.

Josie leaned over Freya's shoulder to have a look. In the photograph accompanying the article a sharp-faced youngster was holding a fan of home-made tickets aloft.

'He's the apprentice from hell,' she said.

'I sell lemonade out the front when the weather's hot,' Freya said.

'Leonardo's going to end up dead,' Josie said, thinking of Scott standing on Bowick Beach in the pouring rain giving out leaflets.

'It's a nice little earner,' Freya said.

Josie got up to take the Cumberland pie out of the oven. It wasn't really the weather for pie. It was blisteringly hot, but Freya wouldn't countenance eating anything else. On the TV a man with a squint had just unearthed a seventeenth-century picture frame from the back of a storage unit.

'Funny eyes, one's at home and one's playing away,' Freya remarked glancing at the screen and then pushing the pie to one side and tapping a cigarette out of the packet.

'I've got to go,' Josie said sighing. 'Try and eat something. I don't want to see that pie sitting there when I come next time.'

'I'm going out later with a young man,' Freya said grinning. 'I need to keep an appetite.'

Josie gathered up her bag and phone and turned to go. 'I'll see you tomorrow,' she said.

'Not if I see you first,' Freya said, flicking her cigarette ash onto the floor, completely ignoring the side plate Josie had put next to her on the table for the purpose. She was just about to go out of the front door when she heard Freya shout after her so she went back and put her head into the room.

'Did you say something?' she asked.

'Scott wants you to try and move Leonardo on,' Freya said. 'I think you should do it. Do it. Yup.' As if the task was as easy as pushing aside a pie or extinguishing a cigarette.

Back at the house Josie made herself a cool drink and then settled down on the sofa to read. She had applied to do a degree in Earth Sciences at the Open University and was reading some of the texts in advance of the start of term. It had been so long since she had done any formal learning that she knew she had to ease herself back in gently. She had gone down to working three days at the bed shop to allow her the time to study and had been thinking about getting a lodger to stay in Scott's room to make up the lost income. She could hear Scott's voice exhorting her to get on with it, but it would be hard to allow his space to be taken over by someone else. There were still days when she needed the comfort of sitting on his bed, trying to conjure up his smell, imagining that he was hidden behind the curtain, standing looking out of the window, as he had so often done as a child. As she sat trying to concentrate on her reading, Freya's words about the dolphin kept coming back and distracting her. Was it even possible to move a dolphin on? How might it be managed? Maybe it could be caught in a net and taken a long way out to sea. But even if she could somehow arrange for that to happen, what would stop Leonardo from simply returning to his old haunt? She didn't know the answer to her questions, but she thought she knew someone who did.

Simon seemed pleased to hear from her and once the inevitable conversation about how she was getting on was over, she asked him about the dolphin.

'You don't want to do anything that will frighten it,' he said. 'You can do a lot of damage trying to get hold of a dolphin. Even experts with exactly the right equipment have to be very careful.'

'Is there another way of doing it other than catching it?' she asked.

'I've heard of cases where dolphins have allowed themselves to be guided out of a particular bay. You get some tasty bait – they love fresh squid – and dangle it from a boat and with a bit of luck they'll follow you.'

'But wouldn't Leonardo just swim right back once he has eaten all he wants to?' she asked.

'There was an over-friendly dolphin in Cornwall who was successfully persuaded away by a group of people standing in the shallows. There were quite a few of them and they formed a kind of human wall. Dolphins are pretty clever creatures. This one seemed to take the hint and stayed away.'

'But it should just be one boat that does the leading-out bit?' she asked.

'Yes. You don't want hundreds of people milling around. Dolphins might be smart but they rely on sound to establish their location. People yelling and splashing and lots of boats would be likely to disorientate him and he could end up stranded on the beach.'

'Would you come on the boat?' she asked him. 'I'd feel happier if there was someone with me who actually knew what they were doing.'

'I'd be glad to. It's definitely worth a shot,' Simon said, 'as long as you can find enough people to help form the barricade. I can muster a few, but you'll need a lot of bodies.'

'I'll put my mind to it,' she said. 'Thanks so much for saying you'll help.'

'You know it might not work, don't you, Josie?' Simon said.

'I want to try at least,' she said.

In the middle of the night, Josie thought of a solution to the problem of where she was going to get enough volunteers to participate in Leonardo's liberation. She would contact the people who had responded to Scott's film, tell them the end of the story and ask for their help. She would be careful to exclude the more bizarre respondents and the ones who were based abroad, but maybe some of the people who lived locally would come. It meant she would risk seeing the golf tee man and the wood elf again but this potential awkwardness would be worth enduring if the dolphin could be saved. *It's a wild thing with its own name*, Scott had said. *If I could save just one thing, then my life will have mattered.* When finally she went to sleep she dreamt he was running down the beach, his white curls blowing in the wind while she watched him from the cliff top.

Chapter 40

'THERE'S SOMETHING YOU SHOULD SEE,' ROBERT SAID ON THE phone.

It was early in the morning and Josie was barely awake and the sound of his voice gave her a little shock. She had found herself thinking about phoning him on more than one occasion over the last few weeks, but something had always prevented her. Grief still held her in its grip and she found that the only way to get through the days was to be still and not resist its hold. A loud noise, a sudden gust of the hot, dust-laden wind that they had been having recently or an unexpected knock at the door disturbed her out of all proportion. She wanted nothing that would make her too aware of the life around her. She was still skinless and sore and wanted only to be bathed in the emollient of peace and space.

'What is it?' she said.

'I've just found an email that I put into one of my work folders by accident without reading it,' Robert said.

Still befuddled with sleep, she couldn't work out what he was saying to her or why he was ringing at six thirty in the morning to talk about emails. There was a time when such an early call would have snapped her instantly from sleep but there was nothing now in the world that warranted such vigilance.

'It's a message from Scott,' he said and her heart missed a beat.

'What does it say?' she asked.

'He sent me a link,' Robert answered.

'A link to what?' Josie asked.

'It says in his email that I was to send it to you, after . . . you know . . . after.' He ground to a halt. It seemed to Josie that his voice held tears in it.

She felt a sharp covetousness for this scrap, this little piece of something new that would bring Scott back to her, if only for a moment. She had thought there was nothing more of him to discover and that she would have to make do with what she already had – the memories she pored over and ran continuously through her mind. She was as avaricious with what remained as a miser with a hoard of gold who counts his coins knowing he would acquire no more.

'I think I should perhaps be there when you get it,' Robert said tentatively.

'I would like to see whatever it is on my own,' she said, but she said it gently so that he would know that she had recognised his kindness.

'Of course. Of course,' he said hastily. 'Of course you would want that. I'm sure Scott intended that. I'll just send it to you.'

'Thank you,' she said and rang off. She pushed aside the thin sheet that was all she seemed to be able to bear against her skin, and put on her dressing gown and went downstairs to the kitchen where her computer was. She sat at the table and pulled Archie against her legs for comfort. He seemed to know what was required of him, because he stayed close to her.

She clicked on the link as soon as it appeared in her inbox. It took her to a video. She saw an image of Scott in his mustard-coloured shirt, his hair in a topknot. With her heart in her mouth, her hand shaking, she clicked on the arrow that partly obscured his face. He was there. Intact and beautiful, sitting close to where she was now; she recognised the vase of flowers in the background: chrysanthemums. It must have been November or December. He seemed just for a moment to be at a loss; as if he was struggling to order what it was he wanted to say. His hands with their long fingers were restless on the table but then he gathered himself and she heard his loved, lost voice.

'I've spent a lot of time trying to find my mother someone to love,' he said. 'I've asked so many men their three favourite things in an attempt to choose between them but it was all such a waste of time. I should have known she didn't need anyone else. She has always been able to look after herself and me.' He rubbed his forehead the way he did when he was thinking and Josie felt the wonder of what was still there and yet gone. That gesture would remain with her forever although she would not see it in life again. He sat straighter in his chair.

'Now I want to tell you my three favourite things about *her*,' he said. For all his hesitation at the beginning, his voice was calm and certain.

'One,' he said, holding up a finger. 'When she's doing something, she is *really* doing it. That's not to say everything she does is perfect. She's no potter or knitter or baker and her singing voice gives me a headache, but she commits completely to the task in hand. She has a kind of optimism that things will work out. She's a finisher, my mum.

'Two,' he continued, ignoring Archie who had his paws on the table and was trying to get his attention. 'She's fierce. I've railed against her will over the years, but it has sustained me. I've always known she would fight for me whether I wanted her to or not. She is the strongest person I know. It's what a boy with an ailing heart needs. I know she will use that same strength to carry on when I'm not here.'

Josie felt her eyes fill and she rubbed her face with the sleeve of her dressing gown. She needed to be able to see every second as clearly as possible.

'Three,' he said. 'She's full of love. It comes out of her in ways you might not expect, but it is always there, burning away, unstoppable. You can feel it right across a room. It's a maddening, wonderful, precious thing. It has taught me all I ever needed to know.'

He stopped for a moment and she thought that he had said everything he wanted to say. He stroked Archie's eager head. He shifted in his seat. Behind him, through the window, the sky was a sweet blue. He took a breath.

'Thank you for my life,' he said and looked at her, his eyes steady and full of love.

'It has been a great thing,' and he smiled one of his wide, guileless smiles, and then he was gone.

Chapter 41

IT TOOK SOME TIME TO SETTLE ON THE DAY OF LEONARDO'S release. After she had established when Simon was free, Josie wrote to the people listed in Scott's computer. She sent the same message to them all, telling them about Scott's death and the reason why her son had embarked on his search to find her a partner. *He didn't want me to be alone after he had gone,* she wrote. *He was a great believer in the power of love. This is an invitation to quite another sort of date. It won't end in romance, but I think Scott would still approve of what I'm trying to do.* She furnished them with the details of the task, the location and the time and asked them not to reply since she wasn't going to be able to get back to everyone. *I'm not nearly as organised as Scott was,* she wrote, *nor do I have his almost photographic memory. I often wonder how I could have produced such a boy.*

The day turned out to be a beautiful one. The sticky weeks of August were over and the morning had a freshness that felt like a new beginning. The years slipped by so fast, Josie thought, as she got dressed. You didn't have time to get the measure of them. All you could do was snatch whatever you could reach from on board the giddy turn. Simon was bringing the boat to the beach and of course the friends she had asked would come, but she wondered if any of Scott's suitors would think it worth their while to travel to Bowick Beach. She had hesitated before ringing Robert Moulton to tell him about her plan. The fact that Scott had sent him the link to the video made her think that he had wanted to keep the connection between her and his doctor alive. Why else had he sent it to him rather than to her? He would have known that Robert would see it first and be there for her if she needed him. It was typical of Scott's thoughtfulness to try and make things as easy for her as possible. At the very least she was certain Scott would have wanted Robert to be part of Leonardo's release and as soon as she heard his voice on the phone, she had found that she wanted the same thing. There was something almost courtly, a kind of restrained thirst, in the way he spoke that made her heart race. She thought of the way he had brushed the hair from her face when she had cried in the pub. It had been a surprisingly confident gesture despite its gentleness. It had felt like a touch message that he could take it all – her snot-smeared cheeks, her sorrow and her resistance and anything else she was willing to share with him.

When she arrived at Bowick Bay with Freya, Simon was already there making the boat ready and stowing buckets of squid on board. There were also several of her friends who had brought other people with them. George was perspiring in a pair of enormous waders and Picasso bowled up in the van with a noisy group. There were about fifty people but Josie thought they needed more. It would take at least two hundred to stretch the entire length of the beach. Simon got everyone together and spoke about the importance of not making too much noise.

'We don't want him to die of fright,' he said to one of Picasso's friends who had brought a loudspeaker with him.

'Is Leonardo here today?' Josie asked Simon.

'He's already made several passes,' Simon replied. 'He'll almost certainly be back again soon.'

Josie spotted Emily coming across the beach towards them and went to meet her.

'Picasso told me this was happening,' she said, smiling. 'I had to come.'

Josie hugged her. 'How are you?' she asked, scrutinising the girl's face.

'I'm better than I was,' she said. 'I carry him with me,' and she put her hand over her heart.

'I hope it's not too great a burden,' Josie said.

'I've been surprised by how comforting it actually is,' said Emily.

'I'm trying to do all the things I told him I would do. I did OK in my exams despite crying for two hours straight before my first one.' She gave Josie a rueful look.

'It's doing the things that he would have wanted to do that hurts the most, isn't it?' Josie asked and Emily nodded, her lovely face sad.

'Oh yes, I wanted to tell you something,' she said in a brighter voice. 'I did a donor card drive at uni and got three hundred and fifteen people to sign up. I've also written a piece about it for the university magazine. My very first published article!' She grinned at Picasso who had also come over to greet her.

'Hello, you,' Picasso said and Josie noted the alert look in his usually muffled gaze. She thought he had also had a haircut.

She walked back to Simon.

'I suppose we should get on with it,' she said. 'I don't think anyone else is going to come.'

'I wouldn't be so sure of that,' Simon said, indicating over her shoulder, and she turned round to see a line of people snaking its way across the beach. Robert was leading the advance party.

'I found a whole group of them wandering around, completely lost,' he said.

The first group was soon joined by another and then another. Josie couldn't believe her eyes. Some of them had come alone, but others were walking arm in arm or hand in hand with partners. A few of them appeared to have brought children and elderly relations. One man was trying to push a woman in a wheelchair across the beach, but gave up after a while and scooped her into his arms.

'I came because of Scott,' a man with sparse facial hair said to her. 'I didn't get a date with you, but I've really been working on my confidence. I'm trying to channel Wilson's bird-of-paradise.'

There were men who had been touched by Scott's story and others who had come in response to Scott's kindness.

'I'm so sad he has died,' one beautiful young man with green eyes said to her. 'I would really have liked to have met him. He wrote an entire page to me about the importance of finding something to believe in.'

'I got the exact dog he advised me to get,' said an elderly gentleman with thick brows trying to rein in a bounding spaniel and Josie recognised him as the lonely man who never went out.

'Can't move for dog-walking companions now,' he said in a grumbling voice.

'He told me never to give up,' a shy-looking man with a stutter said, 'and then I found her.' He pushed forward an equally reticent-looking woman with a dark fringe. 'He said there would be someone right under my nose and it turned out she was at the desk next to mine at the call centre.'

Simon was marshalling the crowd into some semblance of order, spreading them out across the beach, advising the older ones to stay on dry ground and the others to wade into the sea as far as their knees. Freya wandered amongst them handing out Kit Kats from a plastic bag. People were discarding shoes and socks and rolling up trousers and pulling off tights. *I wish Scott could see this*, Josie thought, her eyes filling up with tears. She moved through the crowd, shaking hands, thanking people for coming.

'I'm sorry for your loss. He was ace,' a boy with mad curls and a guitar said and she recognised Scott's friend Travis, the boy who had written poems on hands.

'He loved you very much,' a man with watery blue eyes said and stroked her clumsily on the shoulder.

Simon walked down the line of people, telling them his plan.

'When I put up my hand on the boat, I want those of you in the sea to make a gentle splashing motion,' he said. 'You on the shore make a humming sound, not too loud, imagine you're a bee.'

There was a fair amount of jostling for position and a few people who lost their footing and ended up fully dressed in the sea, but on the whole the gathered company seemed to be taking the task in hand very seriously indeed.

'Exactly what sort of a bee do you mean?' a man in an unnecessary sou'wester asked. 'There are over two hundred and fifty species in the UK. The honey bee sounds quite different from the leaf-cutter bee.'

Josie thought he and Scott would probably have had a lot in common.

'I can see him,' Simon suddenly shouted, pointing out to sea, and Josie saw Leonardo's ragged fin and his white blow.

'We should get into the boat,' he said and so she took off her jeans and swam out with him. He pulled himself aboard first and helped her in. He started the engine and steered the boat out carefully. Leonardo breeched high, turning the sea to foam, and Josie heard the responding murmur from the crowd. Soon, they were alongside him. He swam quite close to the boat, surfacing from time to time, the hiss of his breath loud.

'Do you think he can smell the squid?' Josie asked.

'Dolphins don't actually have a sense of smell,' Simon said.

Josie leaned over the boat at the very moment when the dolphin rose in a curving jump. She had never really understood Scott's passion for the creatures but at that moment she saw the dolphin's perfection and felt his power. Simon dangled a squid over the side and dropped it and Leonardo inhaled it immediately.

'I think he's hungry,' Simon said. 'We'll keep going straight and you keep dropping squid.'

He lifted his arm and Josie could hear the obedient splashing and humming from the people on the beach. It sounded like an old song. It seemed to Josie that the dolphin stilled a moment, as if he was listening. The boat moved forward. After about ten minutes the noise from the beach faded. Leonardo swam doggedly alongside.

'How far out are we now?' Josie asked. She had lost track of time and it felt as if they would carry on out to sea, the dolphin spooned beside them forever.

'Only a couple of miles, we need to go a little further.'

She could no longer see the beach. The seagulls had found them and followed the white slash of their wake in twos and threes. Josie could see right into their opened mouths. The boat rolled as the waves grew bigger and Leonardo rolled with them.

'We are almost out of squid,' she said after some indeterminate period of time.

'Space them out a little more,' Simon replied and they carried on and the sun lost its heat and the sea darkened so that it seemed that they had entered another, wilder world. Josie hung over the boat with the last squid in her hand. Leonardo rose to receive it and for just a moment Josie could see his eye, dark and familiar, beast not fish, and therefore kindred, and then the curve of his mouth.

'Goodbye,' she said touching him briefly on the bulb of his head. She thought his skin felt as silky as a child's. After a second or two he ducked back down under the water.

Simon cut the engine and the sudden silence felt strange. The boat rocked gently. Josie looked around her but Leonardo was nowhere to be seen. Maybe he was under the boat? Josie found she was holding her breath.

'There he is!' Simon said after a moment or two and Josie stood up and saw his white spume. He was already some distance from them, moving at speed. *Swim, swim, swim*, Josie said in her head. She felt the same instinct when she was driving under the path of an airplane that was taking off from a runway – *Up, up, up*, as if its flight was dependent on her will.

'I think he's gone,' Simon said a little later when even the distant speck of him was free.

Something has been saved, Scott, she thought. *One small, significant link in the intricate chain has been held fast in your memory. You have been here and you have made your difference.* She looked down and thought of the navy depths he had described and of their solace. It was a choice worth consideration. The boat rocked violently, caught on a sudden swell. It seemed, after all, despite the brief lure of the water, that her instinct was to crouch down and hold hard until the wave passed and the boat righted itself again. She felt the slide of the wood under her fingers. The boards beneath her feet were swollen and pungent. The sea had stilled again to a perfect, beaten gold. Her breathing body was held fast, floating between the sky and the smeared, waiting land. She would go back. She would take all that was offered and love it for as long as she was able. She would do it for him and for herself. Her heart turned as she felt the great, empty, fullness of the world.

Chapter 42

S HE DIDN'T KNOW WHETHER TO GO OR NOT. *I'LL JUST HAVE this cup of tea and then decide*, she thought, leaning on the kitchen counter and looking out of the window. The flowers in the garden were hanging on – the last roses curling softly at the edges and the hydrangea drying from milky white to crimson. When she reached for her cup she found the tea had cooled. She had fifteen minutes before she should leave.

It was just a meeting, she told herself as she wandered around the house, doing things that didn't really need to be done, but she remembered how he had looked when he had asked her and she knew there would be no going back. 'Make the most of the day,' Scott had always said so firmly, as if he thought he could actually catch the hours and command them. 'Time plays tricks on you. It stretches the days and shrinks the years,' she had said in response and he had shaken his head. 'So make the most of the stretch,' he had said, as if it was obvious and, of course, it was, if only you could school yourself to remember in time. She touched the photograph of the sea lily that she had taken and framed and put up above the fireplace.

'I'll be waiting at Dunstanburgh Castle in a week's time. Twelve o'clock. At the turret,' Robert had said.

There had been a few stragglers who had decided to stay on the beach, but most of Scott's suitors had gone by the time she had returned after Leonardo's release. Some had left flowers and Josie had detected the hand of Emily and Picasso in a huge sand-castle with a Kit Kat wrapper flag. Robert had been sitting by himself watching for the boat and he had helped her ashore.

'If you don't come I'll know you've made up your mind,' he had said, and he had looked into her eyes and traced her face with his fingers and she had felt herself leaning into him as if moving towards the source of something warm. Seeing the tender shape of his mouth she had wanted to kiss him then, but he had turned away quickly as if he felt there was an obstacle between them still. Something she needed to surmount before anything more could be expressed. She knew he wanted her to show that she had actively chosen him, not simply been carried along by the curve of their bodies. She thought of him now making the journey to the castle, not knowing whether she would be there or not. She might hurt him. They might hurt each other. His eyes still had his wife in them. It was easier not to hope and yet he had touched her face as if she might be someone worth having. She could make it if she left the house now. Did she need a jumper? The weather was turning colder. She would go without and take the risk. There was no time left to waste.

She had forgotten that there was a festival happening in town. The high street was lined with market stalls and the traffic was at a standstill. She couldn't turn back to go another way because there were cars in front of her and behind her. She would be late. How long would he wait? She reached for her bag and tipped its contents onto the passenger seat. Her phone was not there.

She had an image of it on the arm of the sofa in the living room. It was all right. If she missed him at the castle she would ring later to explain. Traffic happened. He would understand. And yet, despite what she was telling herself, she wasn't comforted. Getting there on time felt like a last chance. She thought of him waiting for her, checking his watch every now and again and then finally giving up. He would walk back down the stairs thinking that she couldn't love him.

The car in front of her moved forward and then stopped again. She craned her head out of the window. The sixth car in the line had broken down and a crowd had gathered to push it out of the way. She looked at her watch. He would probably have arrived already. Even if the traffic started moving now it would take her at least twenty-five minutes to get there. She inched along the road and then all of a sudden, the car in front gathered pace and they were released.

'Wait for me,' she said. She drove fast, overtaking where she could, muttering in exasperation at a tractor that pulled out in front of her. It was her fault. Why hadn't she left the house earlier? She parked her car at an angle and ran up the sloping road that led to the castle and arrived at the shop where they sold the tickets for admission. She tried not to dance from foot to foot as a man took a ridiculously long time to decide on which sword he was going to buy for his son. Ticket finally in hand, she started running along the path that crossed the castle grounds. He was still there. She could see him. He was standing looking out to sea. He didn't know yet that she was there. She climbed the stairs.

'I'm here,' she said. 'I'm sorry. I'm here.'

He turned to her. He was smiling. 'I knew you'd come,' he said. 'I waited because I knew you'd come.'

She went to him at once. She lifted her face up to his and he pulled her close. His hands were in her hair and his mouth moved against hers. As she kissed him she felt the day stretch out.

Dear Mr and Mrs Kohli

I know that when it comes to meeting you today I will not find the right words and so I am writing this letter. I have never been very good at saying what I feel. At the moment of your most profound loss you were able to reach beyond and that seems miraculous to me. I am not sure I would have had the strength to think about a stranger in the midst of my own grief. You have given me the chance to see my boy grow up. There are no words for that, written or spoken. I hope in some small way you will feel the comfort of what your son has passed on to mine. I know my boy will make the very most of the weeks and months and years. I don't know how long he will have. I pray it will be long enough for them to discover something new that will save him again. In the meantime, I will try my best to celebrate the time we have. It seems we cannot have joy without sorrow, nor can we live without the prospect of death, even though we fight against it. It gives our lives shape and grace. I thank you from the bottom of my heart.

Josie

Acknowledgements

I would like to thank my dear agent Luigi Bonomi and also Alison Bonomi who copes with my queries with patience and humour.

Before We Say Goodbye has come about through the efforts of many people and I thank Joel Richardson for his early interventions (and because his mother won't read the book otherwise), Eleanor Dryden, Sarah Bauer and all at Bonnier who have played their part with such commitment.

I owe a debt to Tricia Dendle and Martin Kitching from MARINElife for suggesting the story of the over-friendly dolphin. Dr David Thaler and his colleagues at Tufts Medical Center in Boston thought up the boy with the ailing heart. All the mistakes I have made about both dolphins and hearts are my own.

Much gratitude also to Simon Youl for all he does to try and organise my affairs, even though I do my best to thwart him.

My wonderful sisters, Tania and Thomasina and my mother Valerie are always and unfailingly alongside as is my husband

David who still manages to smile when I read passages of the work in progress aloud to him. Without him I would not be able to do anything at all.

Lastly, I would like to thank my precious boys and their friends who have, in bits and pieces provided the inspiration for Scott and the depiction in the book of the joys and pains of motherhood.

Want to read
NEW BOOKS
before anyone else?

Like getting
FREE BOOKS?

Enjoy sharing your
OPINIONS?

Discover
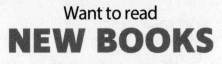
READERS FIRST
Read. Love. Share.

Sign up today to win your first free book:
readersfirst.co.uk